D1499711

French Short Stories

FRENCH

Short Stories

Introduced by Brian Masters
Illustrated by Véronique Bour

The Folio Society

LONDON 1998

This selection and author biographies
© The Folio Society Ltd 1998

Introduction © Brian Masters 1998

Illustrations © Véronique Bour 1998

The Folio Society would like to thank Nicholas White
for his help and advice on the French translations.

Set in Ehrhardt with Friz Quadrata display
Printed at St Edmundsbury Press, Bury
St Edmunds on Ibis White Wove paper
and bound at Hunter & Foulis, Edinburgh
in full cloth using a design
by Malcolm Harvey Young

Contents

Illustrations

Introduction

In the course of a heavily-public literary squabble with François Mauriac, Jean-Paul Sartre delivered the splendidly impertinent rebuke that God did not make a very good novelist (*'Dieu n'est pas un bon romancier'*). His argument was that Mauriac interfered too much with the development of his characters, controlled their destinies, pushed them in a direction of his choosing towards a conclusion designed to prove a point, whereas they should be given their freedom to grow and act according to the complex unpredictable deviations of human character. Sartre may well be right, but if he is, then God would make a very good writer of short stories.

Whereas the novel deals on an ambitious scale with events which occurred or might occur, the short story in the French tradition is a confection of simplicity, obviously contrived, and with a clear, urgent purpose. The author must therefore retain total control of the direction his story will take and keep the people within it, who are essentially ciphers, as simple as possible. He is like a puppeteer, manipulating his creatures with a concentrated focus on the message he wishes to convey. In novels, as in life, people do not always reveal their motive. In the short story or *conte* they have to, for they exist only in order to give it expression.

Moreover, the subject of a *conte* is usually a particular moment, or a crisis, something exceptional in the vast flow of life, isolated and spotlighted by the author with singular compression. If the novelist's function is to describe the mighty flood of a great river, that of the *conteur* is to pick up and examine one of the pebbles it deposits in the estuary.

Given these common characteristics, however, there is much variety in the form and subject-matter of the French short story, which has a robustly heterogeneous past. Neither the fairy story which survived by oral tradition and came mostly from Italy, nor the verse-story which flourished in the Middle Ages, is here represented. But one of the earliest prose short stories is: 'The Boy Who Bedded His Mother and His

Sister' from the *Heptaméron* by Marguerite de Navarre, with its nicely symmetrical structure and archly titillating theme of mistaken sexual partners. As one would expect from a writer of the emerging Renaissance, it is also slyly iconoclastic, mocking some habits that churchmen had adopted to test their chastity.

A great burgeoning of prose short stories came towards the end of the sixteenth century, with Madame d'Aulnoy, Mademoiselle Lhéritier and the most famous, Charles Perrault, who was in fact a distinguished man of letters and a lawyer, though he is nowadays only remembered for his book of short stories which included 'The Sleeping Beauty' and 'Bluebeard'. In the next century, the short story was dominated by exotic and absurd tales with a pseudo-oriental flavour, which even Montesquieu acknowledges in the title of his *Lettres Persanes* (1721). The pendulum then swung against such extravagance in the Age of Enlightenment, when the French passion for categories and definitions sought to pin down the short story as it had other literary forms. Diderot, in *Les Deux Amis de Bourbonne* (1770), divided the genre into three types: the *conte merveilleux*, which was all fantasy, but a little stab at perfection of style; the *conte plaisant*, which was imaginative and inventive, seductive, entertaining, and pointless; and the *conte historique*, admirable, lively, but not always true. In the present collection, Théophile Gautier's 'The Mummy's Foot' might be said to exemplify the first kind, Alphonse Daudet's 'The Stars' would fit the second, and Stendhal's 'The Duchess of Palliano' could answer for the third, although all three writers, of course, post-date Diderot.

Voltaire, however, was a contemporary of Diderot's and, like him, a dedicated theorist. He sought to banish imagination and fanciful idealism from the short story and replace them with a classical adherence to psychological truth. This is a difficult feat to achieve in a restricted space, where the writer is denied the leisured pace and opportunity for scattered allusion afforded by the novel. Voltaire said that the short story should not be trivial but should 'permit a subtle truth to be revealed beneath the veil of fable', and his key word for the means to accomplish this was the rule of *la vraisemblance*. It is an important word, for it underlies the technique of a good number of the writers included here, and therefore demands to be understood. Normally translated as 'probability', in terms of literary theory it should more accurately be termed 'plausibility' or 'inherent conviction', and is based on the notion that what is plausible is a surer guide to truth than what is strictly true. Guy de Maupassant wrote that '*le vrai peut quelquefois n'être pas vraisemblable*' ('truth is occasionally implausible'). The short-story writer therefore must be selective and manipulative in the handling of his material, must dominate it and shape it in order to bring out the hidden moral (must 'play God', in a way). Such a method may be seen not only in Voltaire's own story, which is so mathematically ordered one might imagine him using a ruler to dissect it into three movements and a coda, but also in those by Balzac, Hugo, Mérimée, Zola, Charles de Bernard, Flaubert and Anatole France. They are all driven by an ineluctable chain of circumstances.

The moral lessons of these stories are various. Stendhal's is the instability of human affairs, Dumas' that honour is rare, though honours be common, Hugo's that imprisonment is a brutalising, not a civilising influence, Balzac's that poverty empties the soul. They point to prejudices, absurdities, vanities, errors, with a view to instruct as well as entertain. There are others which eschew all moral purpose. Théophile Gautier has no lesson to impart, save that to write beautifully is to write enough. Jules Verne's fantasy is interesting in so far as we can identify the twentieth-century inventions he uncannily predicted, and Charles Nodier's 'Dead Man's Combe' has no pretensions to be anything more than a good yarn. But they all nevertheless share that stylistic discipline which is essential to the genre, and which uses several literary devices and features not often found elsewhere.

Whether their stories are didactic or escapist, the authors generally absent themselves from their pages. Maupassant is utterly invisible, and one could never intuit from any of his superbly crafted stories that he was to die in a madhouse. Flaubert made it a strict rule to drain any image of himself from his writing and strove only to be a mirror. He saw his function as to '*faire et se taire*' ('do it and shut up'), and he never intrudes on his own stage. Rather grandly, he told George Sand in a letter that the artist should no more appear in his work than God does in Nature. De Musset and Proust are not even shadows behind their words, and Gautier aspires to be an anonymous craftsman. And if Zola and Hugo are present in the wings, it is because they have been summoned there by the uncontainable strength of their social consciences.

Secondly, the central figure in each story appears to have only one trait of personality, because all others, for the sake of concision, have been excluded. The doctor in Charles de Bernard's story is greedy and deceptive; we do not know what else he might be. De Musset's Mimi

Pinson is charitable; Haraucourt's main character is vengeful, Proust's hypocritical, Mérimée's jealous.

Thirdly, the style is spare and succinct, with no wasted or redundant words, no elaborations. Flaubert was notoriously meticulous in his self-editing, convinced that only one word or phrase would do to convey any given idea and that the writer must pray and struggle to achieve it. The simplicity of his story in this collection, 'A Simple Heart', does not betray the labour spent upon its creation; Flaubert was known to work up to sixteen hours a day in his study, honing and polishing, reducing, searching to improve, hunting the fugitive word. Mérimée, too, strove to ensure that his work was terse, clear, vivid and concise, shorn of verbosity. He was a master at shining light on a significant detail which might have gone unnoticed, but which was pregnant with the meaning he sought to illuminate, and one suspects the detail was the grain from which the story grew. He admitted to being an anecdotalist (*'Je n'aime dans l'histoire que les anecdotes'*), and it is strange to think of his working at 'Carmen', for instance, during time off from his official duties as Inspector of Ancient Monuments (it is to Prosper Mérimée that we owe the survival of the Roman arenas at Arles and Orange).

Maupassant's style is also severely restrained, with not an adjective out of place, and Gautier's lovely story 'The Mummy's Foot' is pure style, a jewel of gorgeous words and images precisely put together with a miniaturist energy which is unique in French literature. The phrases he gives to the Egyptian princess as she addresses her severed foot might have come from one of his jewel-like poems – 'I smoothed your heel with pumice-stone mixed with palm oil; your nails were cut with golden scissors and polished with a hippopotamus tooth'– and, incidentally, the fact that his story is without use or purpose beyond its beauty well befits the man who coined the expression *l'art pour l'art* and was revered as the leader of the Parnassian movement. Charles Nodier likewise delights in a story which is not socially useful, but dark and mysterious. In his day, he was the foremost populariser of fantastic tales inspired by the Scottish Highlands and the Balkan peninsula and led a group of young writers called Le Premier Cénacle. On the other hand, he was not with Gautier or Flaubert in subordinating himself to technique; he stated that art should be free of technique altogether, though it is difficult to square this aim with the evidence of a short story which is cunningly constructed within a small space and leading to a gruesome conclusion.

Which brings us to the fourth attribute shared by most of these stories: the deft use of a laconic closing line, usually ironic, always surprising, and so satisfying to the intellect that the entire preceding story seems in retrospect to be a preparation for it. (This is one of the reasons why a *conte* can be successfully read aloud, while a novel sounds a bit cumbersome.) The significant closing line is here in Jean-Paul Sartre, in de l'Isle-Adam, in Anatole France, in Maupassant, and, especially perhaps, in Émile Zola. Once read, the two words at the end of his 'The Attack on the Mill' are unlikely ever to be forgotten – 'Victory! Victory!' Coming after a tale of escalating sacrifice, fear and dull unhappiness visited upon unfortunate peasants who are powerless to avoid them, innocent victims of the greater event of war which swallows them up and spits them out with contemptuous indifference, the final words can hurt with actual pain, like a vicious slap. This is a fine use of sardonic irony, a device which Zola employs several times in the body of his massive novels, but never to better effect than in this short story.

Some in this collection are written on an intentionally modest scale, with no attempt at revolutionary impact. We have already seen that Flaubert's 'A Simple Heart' is but superficially plain (indeed, it reads deceptively as though anyone could have written it). The artful depiction of an ingenuous and uneducated mind through the various stages of bereavement in life, as each one of Félicité's potential objects of love is removed from her, is just as potent as Zola's more clamorous style, and just as carefully structured towards its pitiful conclusion. Daudet's naïve portrait of country affection is even less eventful. Both of these, in effect, illustrate the notion mentioned above: that the short story can more resemble the pebble on the shore than the great wave that placed it there, and they are in direct opposition to the other precept that the proper subject of a *conte* is a moment of crisis or challenge. The French short story, then, can cover the large, brash canvas of a Victor Hugo or an Émile Zola, or the quiet, gentle water-colour of an Alphonse Daudet. They both want to tell the truth in as arresting a manner as possible.

Constantly underlying all these propositions of intent and style is this problem of how truth is to be revealed. Flaubert was enigmatic on the subject, saying that he wrote 'A Simple Heart' in order to evoke feeling in the reader, to make him weep (*'je veux apitoyer, faire pleurer les âmes sensibles, en étant une moi-même'*), suggesting thereby that he had no higher purpose than the naïve Daudet. He certainly claimed to deviate from the Realist fashion which surrounded him, and with which, to his consternation, he was frequently identified (though he did want to be 'realistic' sufficiently to have a live parrot on his desk as he was writing the final pages). Art should not aspire to performing a socially useful act, he said, and yet the 'message' of his story is undoubtedly a truthful social comment, albeit muted. The later Naturalists were much more forthright. Their high priest, Zola, wrote in *Le Roman expérimental* that Idealists were fraudulent in maintaining that one had to alter the truth in order to extract from it the requisite moral lesson, whereas the Naturalists asserted that it was impossible to be moral unless the truth were stated in all its intolerable nakedness. Yet even Zola fashions the truth by dramatic licence, as do both Sartre and Camus, who securely belong to the Naturalist tradition in so far as they squarely face the world as it is and have no truck with make-believe or fantasy. Honoré de Balzac and Victor Hugo are also demonstrably moved by a desire to evoke indignation in the reader, and thereby achieve a 'socially useful act'.

Charles Nodier attains his truths in quite a different manner. He said that the writer was best able to discern the moral essence by returning to the superstitions of childhood, since the fantastic creations of the imagination threw a larger and deeper light upon what was ultimately real than any slavish observation of reality could hope to do. The stories of Jules Verne and Alexandre Dumas are similarly inspired by apparently unsophisticated insights. Indeed, the truths illumined by Dumas' story (why urchins have wit and doctors sell ill-health) are strongly reminiscent of the gentle ironies discovered by Saint-Exupéry's Little Prince.

What all these writers have in common is the ability to devote concentrated vision upon one aspect of life and cast all else, for half an hour or so, out of the frame. Of course, it is *their* vision, but the challenge of their art is to impose it upon the reader and cause him to ponder. As Guy de Maupassant wrote in his preface to *Pierre et Jean* (1887), *'les grands artistes sont ceux qui imposent à l'humanité leur illusion particulière.'* Nowhere is this more evident than in the short story, where the writer's task is not to engage and enlarge the reader's imagination, but to overwhelm it with his own. It might be said that the reader contributes to the experience of a novel by reaching out in an act of collaboration, whereas he is entirely passive before the *conteur*; he must accept what he is given. By that standard, here is a collection of individual perceptions which exact from the reader a measure of delightful recognition.

BRIAN MASTERS

French Short Stories

Marguerite de Navarre

Marguerite de Navarre (1492–1549), also known as Marguerite d'Angoulême or d'Alençon, was born in Angoulême and received a humanist education like her brother, the future King François I. After the death of her first husband, she married, in 1527, the King of Navarre. Under the influence of the Archbishop of Meaux and other members of L'Évangélisme she took a keen interest in Luther and Calvin, and protected leading Reformers. The most memorable aspect of her prolific legacy is the *Heptaméron*, a cycle of seventy-two tales inspired by Boccaccio's *Decameron*. First published in Boaistuau's edition of 1558, under the title *Histoire des amants fortunés*, they focus on relations between the sexes and the insoluble conflict – apparent below the surface of courtly life – between rampant male desire and a female ideal of marital fidelity.

The Boy Who Bedded His Mother and His Sister

A young gentleman, of from fourteen to fifteen years of age, thought to lie with one of his mother's maids, but lay with his mother herself; and she, in consequence thereof, was, nine months afterwards, brought to bed of a daughter, who, twelve or thirteen years later, was wedded by the son; he being ignorant that she was his daughter and sister, and she, that he was her father and brother.

IN THE TIME OF KING LOUIS THE TWELFTH, THE LEGATE AT Avignon being then a scion of the house of Amboise, nephew to George, Legate of France, there lived in the land of Languedoc a lady who had an income of more than four thousand ducats a year, and whose name I shall not mention for the love I bear her kinsfolk.

While still very young, she was left a widow with one son; and, both by reason of her regret for her husband and her love for her child, she determined never to marry again. To avoid all opportunity of doing so, she had fellowship only with the devout, for she imagined that opportunity makes the sin, not knowing that sin will devise the opportunity.

This young widow, then, gave herself up wholly to the service of God, and shunned all worldly assemblies so completely that she scrupled to be present at a wedding, or even to listen to the organs playing in a church. When her son was come to the age of seven years, she chose for his schoolmaster a man of holy life, so that he might be trained up in all piety and devotion.

When the son was reaching the age of fourteen or fifteen, Nature, who is a very secret schoolmaster, finding him in good condition and very idle, taught him a different lesson to any he had learned from his tutor. He began to look at and desire such things as he deemed beautiful, and among others a maiden who slept in his mother's room. No one had any suspicion of this, for he was looked upon as a mere child, and, moreover, in that household nothing save godly talk was ever heard.

This young gallant, however, began secretly soliciting the girl, who complained of it to her mistress. The latter had so much love for her son and so high an opinion of him, that she thought the girl spoke as she did in order to make her hate him; but, being strongly urged by the other, she at last said:

'I shall find out whether it is true, and will punish him if it be as you say. But if, on the other hand, you are bringing an untruthful accusation against him, you shall suffer for it.'

Then, in order to test the matter, she bade the girl make an appointment with her son that he might come and lie with her at midnight, in the bed in which she slept alone, beside the door of his mother's room.

The maid obeyed her mistress, who, when night came, took the girl's place, resolved, if the story were true, to punish her son so severely that he would never again lie with a woman without remembering it.

While she was thinking thus wrathfully, her son came and got into the bed, but although she beheld him do so, she could not yet believe that he meditated any unworthy deed. She therefore refrained from speaking to him until he had given her some token of his evil intent, for no trifling matters could persuade her that his desire was actually a criminal one. Her patience, however, was tried so long, and her nature proved so frail that, forgetting her motherhood, her anger became transformed into an abominable delight. And just as water that has been restrained by force rushes onward with the greater vehemence when it is released, so was it with this unhappy lady who had so prided herself on the constraint she had put upon her body. After taking the first step downwards to dishonour, she suddenly found herself at the bottom, and thus that night she became pregnant by him whom she had thought to restrain from acting in similar fashion towards another.

No sooner was the sin accomplished than such remorse of conscience began to torment her as filled the whole of her after-life with repentance. And so keen was it at the first, that she rose from beside her son – who still thought that she was the maid – and entered a closet, where, dwelling upon the goodness of her intention and the wickedness of its execution, she spent the whole night alone in tears and lamentation.

But instead of humbling herself, and recognising the powerlessness of our flesh, without God's assistance, to work anything but sin, she sought by her own tears and efforts to atone for the past, and by her own prudence to avoid mischief in the future, always ascribing her sin to circumstances and not to wickedness, for which there is no remedy save the grace of God. Accordingly she sought to act so as never again to fall into such wrongdoing; and as though there were but one sin that brought damnation in its train, she put forth all her strength to shun that sin alone.

But the roots of pride, which acts of sin ought rather to destroy, grew stronger and stronger within her, so that in avoiding one evil she wrought many others. Early on the morrow, as soon as it was light, she sent for her son's preceptor, and said:

'My son is beginning to grow up, it is time to send him from home. I have a kinsman, Captain Monteson, who is beyond the mountains with my lord the Grand Master of Chaumont, and he will be very glad to admit him into his company. Take him, therefore, without delay, and to spare me the pain of parting do not let him come to bid me farewell.'

So saying, she gave him money for the journey, and that very morning sent the young man away, he being glad of this, for, after enjoying his sweetheart, he asked nothing better than to set off to the wars.

The lady continued for a great while in deep sadness and melancholy, and, but for the fear of God, had many a time longed that the unhappy fruit of her womb might perish. She feigned sickness, in order that she might wear a cloak and so conceal her condition; and having a bastard brother, in whom she had more trust than in anyone else, and upon whom she had conferred many benefits, she sent for him when the time of her confinement was drawing nigh, told him her condition (but without mentioning her son's part in it), and besought him to help her save her honour. This he did, and, a few days before the time when she expected to be delivered, he begged her to try a change of air and remove to his house, where she would recover her health more quickly than at home. She went, with only a very small following, and found there a midwife who had been summoned as for her brother's wife, and who one night, without recognising her, delivered her of a fine little girl. The gentleman gave the child to a nurse, and caused it to be cared for as his own.

After continuing there for a month, the lady returned in sound health to her own house, where she lived more austerely than ever in fasts and disciplines. But when her son was grown up, he sent to beg his mother's permission to return home, as there was at that time no war in Italy. She, fearing lest she should fall again into the same misfortune, would not at first allow him, but he urged her so earnestly that at last she could find no reason for refusing him. However, she instructed him that he was not to appear before her until he was married to a woman whom he dearly loved; but to whose fortune he need give no heed, for it would suffice if she were of gentle birth.

Meanwhile her bastard brother, finding that the daughter left in his charge had grown to be a tall maiden of perfect beauty, resolved to place her in some distant household where she would not be known, and by the mother's advice she was given to Catherine, Queen of Navarre. The maiden thus came to the age of twelve or thirteen years, and was so beautiful and virtuous that the Queen of Navarre had great friendship for her, and much desired to marry her to one of wealth and station. Being poor, however, she found no husband, though she had admirers enough and to spare.

Now it happened one day that the gentleman who was her unknown father came to the house of the Queen of Navarre on his way back from beyond the mountains, and as soon as he had set eyes on his daughter he fell in love with her, and having licence from his mother to marry any woman that might please him, he only enquired whether she was of gentle birth, and, hearing that she was, asked her of the Queen in marriage. The Queen willingly consented, for she knew that the gentleman was not only rich and handsome, but worshipful to boot.

When the marriage had been consummated, the gentleman again wrote to his mother, saying that she could no longer close her doors against him, since he was bringing with him as fair a daughter-in-law as she could desire. The lady enquired to whom he had allied himself, and found that it was to none other than their own daughter. Thereupon she fell into such exceeding sorrow that she nearly came by a sudden death, seeing that the more she had striven to hinder her misfortune, the greater had it thereby become.

Not knowing what else to do, she went to the Legate of Avignon, to whom she confessed the enormity of her sin, at the same time asking his counsel as to how she ought to act. The Legate, to satisfy his conscience, sent for several doctors of theology, and laid the matter before them, without, however, mentioning any names; and their advice was that the lady should say nothing to her children, for they, being in ignorance, had committed no sin, but that she herself should continue doing penance all her life without allowing it to become known.

Accordingly, the unhappy lady returned home, where not long afterwards her son and daughter-in-law arrived. And they loved each other so much that never were there husband and wife more loving, nor yet more resembling each other; for she was his daughter, his sister and his wife, while he was her father, her brother and her husband. And this exceeding love between them continued always; and the unhappy and deeply penitent lady could never see them in dalliance together without withdrawing to weep.

'You see, ladies, what befalls those who think that by their own strength and virtue they may subdue Love and Nature and all the faculties that God has given them. It would be better to recognise their own weakness, and instead of running a-tilt against such an adversary, to betake themselves to Him who is their true Friend, saying to Him in the words of the Psalmist, "Lord, I am afflicted very much; answer Thou for me."'

'It would be impossible', said Oisille, 'to hear a stranger story than this. Methinks every man and woman should bend low in the fear of God, seeing that in spite of a good intention so much mischief came to pass.'

'You may be sure', said Parlamente, 'that the first step a man takes in self-reliance removes him so far from reliance upon God.'

'A man is wise', said Geburon, 'when he knows himself to be his greatest enemy, and holds his own wishes and counsels in suspicion.'

'Albeit the motive might seem to be a good and holy one,' said Longarine, 'there were surely none, howsoever worthy in appearance, that should induce a woman to lie beside a man, whatever the kinship between them, for fire and tow may not safely come together.'

'Without question,' said Ennasuite, 'she must have been some self-sufficient fool, who, in her friar-like dreaming, deemed herself so saintly as to be incapable of sin, just as many of the friars would have us believe that we can become, merely by our own efforts, which is an exceeding great error.'

'Is it possible, Longarine,' asked Oisille, 'that there are people foolish enough to hold such an opinion?'

'They go further than that,' replied Longarine. 'They say that we ought to accustom ourselves to the virtue of chastity; and in order to try their strength they speak with the prettiest women they can find and whom they like best, and by kissing and touching them essay whether their fleshly nature be wholly dead. When they find themselves stirred by such pleasure, they desist, and have recourse to fasts and grievous discipline. Then, when they have so far mortified their flesh that neither speech nor kiss has power to move them, they make trial of the supreme temptation, that, namely, of lying together and embracing without any lustfulness. But for one who has escaped, so many have come to mischief that the Archbishop of Milan, where this religious practice used to be carried on, was obliged to separate them and place the women in convents and the men in monasteries.'

'Truly,' said Geburon, 'it would be the extremity of folly to seek to become sinless by one's own efforts, and at the same time to seek out opportunities for sin.'

'There are some', said Saffredent, 'who do the very opposite, and flee opportunities for sin as carefully as they are able; nevertheless, concupiscence pursues them. Thus the good Saint Jerome, after scourging and hiding himself in the desert, confessed that he could not escape from the fire that consumed his marrow. We ought, therefore, to recommend ourselves to God, for unless He uphold us by His power, we are greatly prone to fall.'

'You do not notice what I do,' said Hircan. 'While we were telling our stories, the monks behind the hedge here heard nothing of the vesper bell; whereas, now that we have begun to speak about God, they have taken themselves off, and are at this moment ringing the second bell.'

'We shall do well to follow them,' said Oisille, 'and praise God for enabling us to spend this day in the happiest manner imaginable.'

At this they rose and went to the church, where they piously heard vespers; after which they went to supper, discussing the discourses they had heard, and calling to mind various adventures that had come to pass in their own day, in order to determine which of them were worthy to be recounted. And after spending the whole evening in gladness, they betook themselves to their gentle rest, hoping on the morrow to continue this pastime which was so agreeable to them.

And so was the Third Day brought to an end.

Voltaire

Voltaire, the pseudonym of François-Marie Arouet (1694–1778), was one of the most witty and elegant voices of eighteenth-century thought. Driven by a vision of religious tolerance in a modern secular society, he championed the establishment of *mores* and principles based on the Enlightenment virtue of reason. His encyclopaedic intellectual interests were reflected in the diversity of his writing, ranging from *Oedipe* (1718), a tragic drama in the mould of Corneille and Racine, to his later works which marked him as a *philosophe* who addressed the major moral, social and political questions of his time. He wrote passionately in defence of victims of contemporary injustice such as Calas, and his controversial views led to several periods of imprisonment. In 1726 he was forced to flee to England where he met Walpole, Pope and Swift, among many other political and literary figures. His *Lettres philosophiques* (1733–4) which extolled the qualities of 'republican' England have been described as 'the first bomb thrown at the *Ancien Régime*'. He also turned his hand to shorter fiction, notably the philosophical tale *Zadig* (1748), *Micromégas* (1752) and his satirical masterpiece *Candide* (1759).

Cosi-Sancta: A Little Ill for a Great Good

'T IS A MAXIM FALSELY ESTABLISHED THAT WE MUST NOT commit a little ill if a great good will result. Saint Augustine was entirely of this opinion, as may easily be seen by the account of a little adventure which happened in his diocese, during the proconsulate of Septimus Acindynus, and related in the Book of the City of God.

At Hippo there lived an old parish priest, a great inventor of confraternities, confessor to all the girls in the quarter, with the reputation of being a man inspired by God, because he dabbled in fortune-telling, an occupation in which he had some success.

One day they brought him a girl named Cosi-Sancta, the most beautiful in the whole province. Her father and mother were Jansenists, who had brought her up in the principles of the most rigid virtue; and not one of all her admirers had ever been able to cause her one moment's lack of attention during her prayers. She had been betrothed for some days to a little, dried-up, old man named Capito, a prominent lawyer of Hippo. He was a peevish, surly, little man, not without wit but affected in his conversation, sneering and rather sharp-tongued in his jests. He was as jealous as a Venetian and nothing in the world would have induced him to endure the position of being friendly to his wife's admirers. The poor young creature was doing all she could to love him, because he was to be her husband; she was trying as hard as she could but without the least success.

She came to consult her parish priest to know whether her marriage would be happy. The old fellow said to her in prophetic tones: 'Daughter, your virtue will cause many misfortunes but you will one day be made a Saint through having been three times unfaithful to your husband.'

This oracle astounded and cruelly embarrassed this fair and innocent girl. She wept and asked for an explanation, thinking that these words hid some mystic sense; but all the explanation she could obtain was that the three times must not be taken to mean three rendezvous with the same lover, but three different adventures.

Cosi-Sancta then protested violently; she even insulted the parish priest and vowed she should never be made a Saint. But she was, as you will see.

Soon after, she was married. The wedding feast was extremely gallant; she endured quite well all the unpleasant talk she had to undergo, all the insipid equivocations, all the ill-concealed grossness with which the modesty of young brides is usually embarrassed. She danced very gracefully with several extremely handsome and well-built young men in whom her husband detected a very graceless air.

She got into bed with little Capito with some repugnance. She spent most of the night in sleep and woke up much preoccupied. Her husband was however less the subject of her reflections than a young man named Ribaldos, who had occupied her mind without her knowing it. This young man seemed to have been formed by the hands of Cupid; he had Cupid's graces, boldness and trickery; he was rather indiscreet but only with those who wished him well; he was the darling of Hippo. He had set all the women of the town at loggerheads and was in the same position himself with all the husbands and mothers. He usually fell in love from heedlessness and a little from vanity; but he was really in love with Cosi-Sancta and loved her the more madly because it was more difficult to conquer her.

Like a man of wit he first tried to make himself agreeable to the husband. He made him a thousand advances, praised his good looks, his easy and gallant wit. He lost money to him at play and made some unimportant confidence to him every day. Cosi-Sancta thought him a most charming young man. She was already more in love with him than she realised; she did not guess it, but her husband guessed it for her. Although he was as conceited as a little man can be, he had no doubt that Ribaldos's visits were not made to him alone. He found some pretext to quarrel with him and forbade him to enter the house again.

Cosi-Sancta was very sorry for this but dared not say so; and Ribaldos, rendered still more amorous by these difficulties, spent his whole time waiting for moments when he could see her. He disguised himself as a monk, as a woman pedlar, as a Punch and Judy showman; but he did not do enough to triumph over his mistress and did too much not to be recognised by the husband. If Cosi-Sancta had been in league with her lover they would have arranged their measures so well that the husband would never have suspected anything; but as she was struggling against her inclination and had nothing to reproach herself with, she saved everything except appearances, and her husband thought her most guilty.

The little old man, who was very irascible and thought his honour depended upon his wife's fidelity, insulted her cruelly and punished her because someone had thought her beautiful. She found herself in the most horrible situation in which a woman can be, accused unjustly, maltreated by a husband to whom she was faithful and torn by a violent passion she was trying to overcome.

She thought that if her lover ceased to pursue her, her husband might cease his injustice and that she would be fortunate enough to recover from a passion which was no longer fed. With this idea she plucked up courage to write the following letter to Ribaldos:

'If you have any virtuous feeling, forbear to render me unhappy; you love me and your love exposes me to the suspicions and violence of a master I have taken for the remainder of my life. Would to Heaven this were the only risk I may have to run! Pity me and cease your pursuit. I beg you by that very love which renders you unhappy and me also, and which can never make you happy.'

Poor Cosi-Sancta had not foreseen that a letter so tender, though so virtuous, would have an effect exactly contrary to that she hoped for. It inflamed her lover's heart more than ever and he resolved to risk his life in order to see his mistress.

Capito, who was fool enough to want to know everything, and who had good spies, was warned that Ribaldos had disguised himself as a begging friar to ask his wife's charity. He thought he was lost; he imagined that a friar's gown was more dangerous than any other to the honour of a husband. He posted servants to beat brother Ribaldos and was but too well served. When the young man entered the house he was received by these gentry; in spite of his cries that he was an honest friar and that poor monks are not to be treated in this way, he was beaten and died a fortnight later from a blow on the head. All the women in the town mourned him. Cosi-Sancta was inconsolable; even Capito was sorry, but for another reason, for he found he had involved himself in a very unpleasant affair.

Ribaldos was a relative of the proconsul Acindynus. The Roman wished to inflict an exemplary punishment for this assassination; and, since he had formerly quarrelled more than once with the lawcourts of Hippo, he was not sorry to be able to hang one of their members, and he was very glad that the lot had fallen on Capito, who was the vainest and most intolerable pettifogger in the whole country.

So Cosi-Sancta had seen her lover murdered and was near to seeing her husband hanged; and all because she had been virtuous, for, as I have already said, if she had granted her favours to Ribaldos, the husband would have been much more skilfully deceived.

Thus the first half of the priest's prediction was accomplished. Cosi-Sancta then remembered the oracle and began to fear she might carry out the rest of it; but, having reflected that no one can overcome his destiny, she abandoned herself to Providence, which led her to the goal by the most honest means imaginable.

The proconsul Acindynus was a man more debauched than voluptuous, taking very little interest in preliminaries, brutal and familiar, a mere garrison hero, greatly dreaded in the province, with whom all the women in Hippo had had an affair solely to avoid quarrelling with him.

He sent for Madame Cosi-Sancta, who arrived in tears; but they made her only the more charming.

'Your husband, madame,' said he, 'is about to be hanged and only you can save him.'

'I would give my life for his,' said the lady.

'That is not what I ask,' replied the proconsul.

'And what must I do?' said she.

'I only want one of your nights,' replied the proconsul.

'But they do not belong to me,' said Cosi-Sancta, 'they belong to my husband. I would give my blood to save him, but I cannot give my honour.'

'But suppose your husband consents?' said the proconsul.

'He is the master,' replied the lady, 'and everyone does as he pleases with his own property. But I know my husband; he will never consent; he is a little man who would rather allow himself to be hanged than let anybody else touch me with the end of his finger.'

'That's what we shall see,' said the judge in a rage.

He had the criminal brought before him at once and gave him the choice of being hanged or a cuckold. There was no room for hesitation. The little man, however, was reluctant. At last he did what anyone else would have done in his place. His wife charitably saved his life; and this was the first of the three times.

The same day her son fell ill of a very extraordinary illness unknown to all the doctors of Hippo. There was only one doctor who knew how to cure this illness; and he lived at Aquila, several leagues from Hippo. At that time it was forbidden for a doctor established at one town to exercise his profession in another. Cosi-Sancta herself was obliged to go to him at Aquila with her brother, whom she loved tenderly. On the way they were captured by brigands. The chief of these gentlemen thought her very charming; and, as they were about to kill her brother, he went up to her and told her that if she would be a little kind to him, her brother should not be killed and that it would cost her nothing. The matter was urgent. She had just saved the life of a husband she did not love; she was about to lose a brother she loved very much; moreover the dangerous state of her child alarmed her. There was not a moment to lose. She commended herself to God, did all that was required; and this was the second of the three times.

She reached Aquila the same day and went to the doctor's house. He was one of those fashionable doctors who are sent for by women when they have the vapours or when there is nothing wrong with them at all. He was the confidential friend of some and the lover of others, a polite, obliging man, rather out of favour with the Medical Association which he had often made the subject of jokes.

Cosi-Sancta explained her child's illness and offered him a sestertium. (Notice that a sestertium was worth more than a thousand crowns in modern French money.)

'Madame,' said the gallant doctor, 'that is not the money I require in payment. I would myself offer you all my property, if it were to your taste to be paid for the cures you are able to make; only cure me of the malady you cause me and I will restore your child to health.'

The lady thought this proposition extravagant; but Fate had rendered her accustomed to strange things. The doctor was an obstinate man who would take no other price for his services. Cosi-Sancta's husband was not there for her to consult; and how could she allow the child she adored to die for lack of the trivial help she could give him? She was as good a mother as sister. She purchased the remedy at the price demanded; and this was the last of the three times.

She returned to Hippo with her brother, who kept thanking her all the way for the courage with which she had saved his life.

Thus, Cosi-Sancta through being too virtuous caused her lover to be murdered and her husband to be condemned to death; and, by being obliging, she saved the lives of her brother, her son and her husband. Such a woman was considered to be very useful to her family. After her death she was made a Saint because by mortifying herself she had done so much good to her relatives, and they carved on her tombstone:

'A little ill for a great good.'

Marquis de Sade

Perhaps the most telling legacy of Donatien-Alphonse-François, Marquis de Sade (1740–1814), is the term 'sadism' to which he gave his name. Born into an impoverished aristocratic family, Sade married for money and was never exactly a 'good husband'. Horrified by his behaviour (which included sexual assaults and attempted murder), his wife's family pursued him through the courts and finally took advantage of the new legislation born of the Revolution to enforce a separation. Sade attempted to accommodate himself within the new regime, even obtaining his *carte de citoyen actif*, but he was never far from scandal. The publication of *Justine ou les malheurs de la vertu* in 1791 sent shock waves through the literary public, with its tale of rapes and perverse cruelties visited upon an innocent orphan. Imprisoned as a result of Napoleon's moral campaign, Sade spent his final years in the mental asylum at Charenton where he continued to write prolifically. Banned for many years, his works have recently undergone a critical reappraisal and now sit amongst the canonical volumes of the scholarly Pléiade editions. The avant-garde, particularly Roland Barthes, Maurice Blanchot and Georges Bataille, have replied to Simone de Beauvoir's question, 'Should we burn Sade?' with a resounding 'No'.

The Self-Made Cuckold, or the Unexpected Reconciliation

ONE OF THE GREATEST FAILINGS OF ILL-MANNERED PEOPLE is that they are forever making indiscreet remarks, slanderous comments, and libellous statements at the expense of anyone and anything that lives and breathes. They will even do this in the hearing of people they do not know. Who can tell how much unpleasantness, duels even, have resulted from such loose talk? Indeed, is there any self-respecting man who can stand by and hear ill spoken of those he cares for and not rebuke the blockhead who spoke it? Educators do not give the principle of decent self-restraint enough importance in the training of the young who are not adequately taught to know society – the names, titles, and connections of the people with whom their station in life requires them to associate. Instead, their heads are filled with endless silly notions which are fit only to be trampled underfoot once they arrive at the age of reason. One is left with the impression that they are brought up like Capuchin monks: bigotry, mummery, and useless knowledge at every turn, and not a useful moral maxim in sight. Go further into the matter and question any young man about his proper duties to society: ask him to say what he owes to himself and what he owes to others and how he should behave if he intends to be happy. He will tell you that he was brought up to go to Mass and say the litanies but that he does not rightly understand what you mean; that he was taught how to dance and sing but not how to get on with other men. The particular incident which resulted from the failing we speak of was not serious: that is, no blood was spilt. But the outcome was in point of fact rather amusing, and it is to recount it that we shall trespass for a few moments on the patience of our readers.

Monsieur de Raneville, then aged about fifty, was one of those phlegmatic characters you can never come across in a social gathering without finding the experience entertaining. He did not laugh much himself but he made other people laugh a great deal, not simply with scathing, witty comments but also with the deadpan way he had of delivering them. Just by saying nothing at all or by giving his normally inexpressive face a comic twist, he found he could keep the gatherings to which he was invited much better amused than those ponderous, boring gossip-mongers who always have a story that they must tell you which has had them in stitches for an hour already but which never comes anywhere near to wiping the scowl off the faces of their listeners. He was something in taxes, something rather important in fact. To console himself for a rather bad marriage which he had made some while previously at Orléans, where he had abandoned his unfaithful wife, he now lived in Paris, quietly getting through 20,000 or 25,000 livres a year with the pretty woman he kept and with a small circle of friends all as congenial as himself.

Monsieur de Raneville's mistress was not exactly a courtesan but a married woman, which of course made her all the more desirable. For it cannot be denied that a small pinch of adultery often adds a great deal of spice to an affair. She was very pretty, thirty years of age, and had the most marvellous figure imaginable. Separated from her dull, boring husband, she had come to Paris from the country to seek her fortune and had not been long in finding it. Raneville, a libertine by nature, constantly on the watch for juicy morsels, made sure this one did not drop off his fork. For the last three years, by means of his highly considerate treatment of her, a great deal of wit and a considerable outlay of money, he had succeeded in blotting from the young woman's mind all the sorrows which it had pleased the god of marriage to strew on the conjugal path she had trod. Both having experienced the same fate, they consoled each other and became more convinced than ever of a great truth which, however, never changes anyone for the better: the reason why there are so many bad marriages and consequently so much unhappiness in the world is that parents, because they are miserly or just plain stupid, prefer to arrange matches between two piles of money rather than between two people. 'For', as Raneville would often remark to his mistress, 'it is quite clear that had Fate united the two of us instead of giving you to a ridiculous tyrant of a husband and me to a rutting whore of a wife, then roses would have sprung up beneath our feet instead of the briars with which we had so long to contend.'

A passing circumstance, which we need not go into, led Monsieur de

Raneville one day to that miry, unwholesome village known as Versailles where kings, who are surely meant to be revered in their capitals, give every appearance of taking refuge from their subjects, who would much prefer to have them within reach; where day in, day out, ambition, avarice, revenge, and pride drive a herd of hapless wretches who, riding on wings of boredom, pay homage to each passing fashion; where the élite of the French aristocracy, who could render useful service by staying at home on their estates, are instead only too keen to loiter in the humiliating antechambers of the great, pay base court to door-keepers, and on bended knee beg a dinner (never as good as the one they could get at home) as a favour from one or other of those persons whom Fortune raises briefly from the mists of obscurity only to send them back whence they came a moment later.

His business done, Monsieur de Raneville got into one of those court carriages known as a *pot-de-chambre*, where he found himself quite by chance thrown into the company of a Monsieur Dutour, a very talkative, very fat, and very dull-witted, supercilious man who, like Monsieur de Raneville, was also something in tax, though he was based at his birthplace, Orléans, which, as we have said, was also Monsieur de Raneville's home town. They began to talk and soon Raneville, as laconic as ever and giving nothing away about himself, was acquainted with the Christian name, surname, origins, and business of his travelling companion long before he had even opened his mouth. Having conveyed these details, Monsieur Dutour then enlarged upon society matters.

'So you have been to Orléans, sir,' said Dutour. 'I believe you said you had.'

'I lived there for some months a long time ago.'

'And did you, pray, ever meet a Madame de Raneville, one of the most consummate harlots ever to live in Orléans?'

'Madame de Raneville? A rather pretty woman?'

'The very same.'

'Yes, I did run across her in society.'

'Well, I can tell you in confidence that I had her. It lasted three days. The usual thing. If ever husband was a cuckold, it was surely poor old Raneville.'

'Do you know him?'

'Only in this connection. They say he is a thoroughly bad lot who is ruining himself in Paris with whores and other rakes like himself.'

'I can't tell you anything about him. I never met him. But I do feel sympathy for cuckolded husbands. I don't suppose you are one by any chance, sir?'

'Which of the two do you mean, husband or cuckold?'

'Why, both. These days the two are so closely linked that it really is very difficult to see daylight between them.'

'I am a married man, sir, and was unfortunate enough to hit on a wife who never learned to put up with me. Mark you, I myself never much cared for her character either and we agreed to an amicable separation. She wanted to go to Paris and retire from the world with a relative of hers who is a nun at the Convent of Sainte-Aure. She has gone to live there. She writes to me now and again, but I don't see anything of her.'

'Is she very devout?'

'No. Perhaps I'd rather she were.'

'Ah, I see. So, although your current business obliges you to remain in Paris for some time, you have not been sufficiently curious about her to enquire how she is?'

'No. To tell the truth, I don't care for convents. I'm a man who likes a spree and a good time. I was meant for the pleasures of life and I am very much in demand. I have no intention of rushing off to some convent parlour and run the risk of having to put up with my lady's vapours for the next six months.'

'But a woman . . .'

'. . . is someone who has a claim on our attentions for only as long as she serves her purpose. But you must be firm and send her packing the minute you have good cause for parting with her.'

'What you say is rather callous.'

'Not at all. It's philosophical, it's the modern way, it's the language of reason. You have to go along with it, otherwise people will think you're a fool.'

'But that assumes that your wife is in some way guilty. What do you mean exactly? A defect of nature, some failure to please, something to be desired in her behaviour?'

'A little of all that, sir, elements of all those things. But pray let us drop the subject and return to dear Madame de Raneville. By God, I cannot believe that you were in Orléans and never had some sport with the trollop. Everybody had her.'

'Not everybody, for as you see I never did. I do not care for married women.'

'I have no wish to pry, but pray tell me, sir, with whom do you spend your time?'

'Business acquaintances in the main, but there is also a rather pretty creature with whom I have supper now and then.'

'You are not married, sir?'

'I am.'

'And your wife?'

'Is in the country. I leave her there just as you allow yours to stay at Sainte-Aure.'

'Married, sir? You are married? And would you be a member of the Antler Club by any chance? I'd be obliged to know.'

'Did I not say that husband and cuckold are synonyms? The moral depravity of modern manners, the taste for luxury, so many stumbling-blocks to make a woman trip and fall.'

'That, sir, is true, very true indeed.'

'You speak like a man well versed in these matters.'

'Not I, sir. But I take it then that it is a very pretty woman who consoles you for the absence of a neglected wife?'

'You are quite right. A very pretty woman. I should like you to meet her.'

'Sir, you do me too much honour.'

'Oh, come now, let us not stand on ceremony. But here we are. I shall not insist this evening because you have business to attend to. But tomorrow without fail I shall expect you for supper at this address. Let me write it down for you.'

Raneville was careful to supply a false identity to which he immediately alerted his servants so that anyone who called asking for him under the name he had given would be able to locate him without difficulty.

The next day, Monsieur Dutour duly appeared at the appointed time and, arrangements having been made for him to find Raneville at home, in spite of the assumed name, he was admitted at once. When the initial civilities were over, Dutour appeared uneasy at not yet catching a glimpse of the divine creature he had reckoned on meeting.

'Such impatience!' said Raneville. 'But I see what you are after. You were promised a pretty woman and are anxious to make a start on her. You are used to deceiving the husbands of Orléans, and I sense you have a mind to hand out much the same treatment to the lovers of Paris. I wager you would be highly delighted if you could put me on the same footing as the unfortunate Raneville you told me about so entertainingly yesterday!'

To this, Dutour replied like an irresistible womaniser and accomplished fop, which is to say foolishly, and the conversation brightened for a moment. Then, taking his friend by the hand, Raneville said:

'Come, you heart-breaker, prepare to enter the temple where the divine creature awaits you.'

And so saying, he ushered Dutour into a sensuously decorated boudoir where Raneville's mistress, primed for the jest and fully in the picture, was reclining minimally but fetchingly clad on a plush-covered Ottoman. She wore a veil. There was nothing to hide the grace and lushness of her body: only her face remained concealed.

'Zounds! what a beautiful creature!' exclaimed Dutour. 'But why deny me the pleasure of admiring her face? We have not strayed into the harem of the Great Turk by any chance, have we?'

'No. But keep your voice down. There's her modesty to consider.'

'Modesty?'

'Absolutely. You don't think that all I have in mind is to let you see my mistress's figure and the way she dresses? My triumph would not be complete if I did not demonstrate how fortunate I must be to have full rights over such grace and beauty, and for this I shall need to remove her veils. But she is an unusually modest young woman and what I propose would be highly embarrassing to her. She has agreed to it but on the express condition that her face remains hidden. You know what modesty and niceness of manners mean to women, Monsieur Dutour. A man of taste and fashion like yourself would never allow himself to be put off by such things.'

'No, really, are you going to show me . . . ?'

'Everything. I told you. There is not a man alive who has less jealousy in him than me. I always think one-sided happiness is a poor thing. For me, I can only take delight in love that is requited.'

And to convince him of the truth of this notion, Raneville began by removing a film of gauze, thereby revealing the most beautiful bosom imaginable. Dutour licked his lips.

'Well?' said Raneville. 'What do you think?'

'Why, these are the orbs of Venus herself!'

'Believe me, breasts so snowy and so firm were made to inflame a man's passion. But touch them, feel for yourself, my dear fellow. Sometimes our eyes deceive us. In matters of pleasure, my view is that we must allow all the senses to be brought into play.'

Dutour held out a trembling hand and rapturously squeezed the most beautiful bosom in the world, quite unable to understand how his friend could be so unbelievably accommodating.

'Let us fix our sights lower,' said Raneville, lifting the filmy chiffon petticoat above her waist, 'and let there be no limit to the foray. Well, what do you say to such thighs? Tell me, did ever the temple of love stand on such fair columns?'

And good Monsieur Dutour ran probing hands over the features which Raneville proceeded to enumerate.

'I can read your thoughts, you rogue,' continued the complaisant friend. 'This comely temple decked with fine-spun moss by the Graces themselves . . . you burn to open these portals, do you not? And yearn to plant a kiss there, I wager?'

The dazzled, stammering Dutour's only answer was in the violence of his sensations which were stimulated by all he saw. He was encouraged to go further. His libertine fingers caressed the portico of the temple which was unlocked by sensuality in response to his desires. Then the divine kiss which he was allowed was duly planted and savoured for a full hour.

'Friend,' said he, 'I can bear no more. Either turn me out or allow me to go further.'

'What do you mean, further? Where the devil do you want to go, pray?'

'You do not take my meaning. Alas, I am mad with love and can contain myself no longer!'

'But what if the woman turns out to be ugly?'

'No woman who possesses such divine attributes could possibly be ugly.'

'But if she were?'

'Let her be whatever she likes! My dear sir, I tell you I can control myself no longer!'

'Then, my fiery friend, so be it. Since you must be gratified, go to it. But at least say you are grateful for my complaisance.'

'I do. Wholeheartedly.'

Gently, with one hand, Dutour began pushing his friend away, intimating that he should be left alone with the woman.

'Leave you? I couldn't possibly do that,' said Raneville. 'Surely you aren't so particular that you would find satisfaction in my presence impossible? Between grown men, scruples like these are hardly the thing. Besides, those are my conditions: either it is done with me here or it is not done at all.'

'I wouldn't care if I did it in front of the Devil himself,' said Dutour, unable to contain himself any longer and making a rush for the sanctuary where his incense was to be burned. 'If you insist, I agree!'

'But', said Raneville phlegmatically, 'are you sure you have not been misled by appearances? Are the sweet pleasures promised by so many charms real or illusory? Still, I never saw a more seductive sight in my life.'

'But this damned veil, sir, this perfidious muslin; am I not to be allowed to remove it?'

'Why of course, but at the last moment, at that truly delicious instant when, with all our senses beguiled by the rapture of the gods, a woman makes us as blest as they, and indeed often more so. The surprise will heighten the bliss: to the charm of possessing Venus herself you will add the inexpressible delight of gazing upon the face of Flora, and with every sensation combining to swell your joy, you will plunge all the more ecstatically into that ocean of delight in which a man finds such sweet consolation for his existence. But you'll have to say when.'

'Oh, you may count on it,' said Dutour. 'I shall work myself up to that instant.'

'So I see. You have hot blood, sir.'

'None hotter! Ah! dear friend! the celestial moment approaches! Strip away, tear back the veil that I may look upon heaven itself!'

'And so you shall,' said Raneville, whipping away the muslin, 'but have a care lest there be but a step between this paradise and Hell itself!'

'Good God!' exclaimed Dutour, recognising his wife. 'Upon my soul! *You*, madame? Sir, what bizarre joke is this? You deserve to be . . . This harridan . . .'

'Hold hard a moment, O man of hot blood. It is you who thoroughly deserve everything you've got. Mark me, my dear fellow, and learn: a man needs to be a little more circumspect with people he doesn't know, and a great deal more so than you were with me yesterday. The unfortunate Raneville whom you treated so abominably in Orléans – I am that man, sir. You observe that I hereby return the compliment in Paris. You will further note that you have succeeded far better than you ever imagined. You thought that you were making a cuckold out of me, whereas you have just cuckolded yourself!'

Dutour swallowed his medicine. He held out his hand to his friend and agreed that he had got everything that was coming to him.

'But as to this perfidious creature . . .'

'But has she not simply followed your example? What barbaric law is it that binds her sex with inhuman chains while granting us men total freedom? Is such a law equitable? And by what natural right do you lock up your wife at Sainte-Aure while you cuckold husbands in Paris and Orléans? My friend, it is simply not just. This charming woman whose worth you never appreciated came in search of other conquests. She was right to do so. She found me. I have made her happy: you may do as much for Madame de Raneville; you have my permission to try. Let all four of us live happily, and let not those whom Fate has brought low also turn out to be the victims of men.'

Dutour saw that his friend was in the right, but by an impenetrable twist of fate he now fell madly in love again with his wife. Though Raneville was an extremely caustic man, his heart was too noble to deny Dutour's pleading that she be returned to him. The young woman consented and the whole episode, which is probably unique, furnishes a most singular example of the workings of destiny and the waywardness of love.

Charles Nodier

Charles Nodier (1780–1844) was the son of an active Jacobin, and his childhood in Besançon was marked deeply by the Terror which followed the Revolution. Romantics such as Vigny and Lamartine met at his literary salon, and although his role as 'pilot' of Romanticism was later eclipsed by the emergence of Victor Hugo, he exhibited a conspicuous interest in the supernatural, dream-states, madness and folklore, which now intrigue critics of a psychoanalytical persuasion. In addition to amorous fictions such as *Le Peintre de Salzbourg* (1803) and *Thérèse Aubert* (1819), he is well known for his fantastic tales, many of which, despite their darkness, display witty, almost whimsical qualities.

Dead Man's Combe

I N THE YEAR 1561 THE ROAD FROM BERGERAC TO PÉRIGUEUX was far from being in as good condition as it is today. The great forest of chestnut trees through which it still passes was much more extensive, and the way much narrower; and, at the place where it runs along the edge of a deep gorge, then called the Hermit's Combe, the mountain slope dropping down to the valley was so steep and dangerous that the most fearless travellers hardly dared to venture there even by daylight. On the first of November, which is All Saints' Day, in that year, it might have been considered quite impracticable at eight o'clock in the evening, so much had its natural dangers been increased by the early onset of winter. The sky, which had been darkened all day by a bitter, hissing blizzard, a mixture of snow and hail, could not be distinguished from the blackest horizon since the sun had set; and, as its blackness mingled with the blackness of the earth, so did the sounds of the earth mingle with its sounds in a horrible tumult that made the traveller's hair stand on end. The hurricane, growing in violence every minute, gave long-drawn-out wails like a crying child, or an old man mortally wounded and calling for help; and it was impossible to tell whence most of these awful lamentations came, from the clouds above, or the echoing precipice below, for with them were mingled the moaning of the forests, the lowing of cattle in the byres, the shrill whistling of the dry leaves driven in whirls before the blustering wind, and the falling of dead trees, shattered by the gale; it was horrible to hear.

The deep, dark combe I mentioned offered a striking contrast to all this in one place, where a fixed yet bright, flaring light blazed from below like the mouth of a volcano; and from the wide-open door through which it came rose shouts of laughter, gay enough to kill despair. It was the forge of Toussaint Oudard, the blacksmith, who had reached the age of forty without making a single enemy, and was celebrating the anniversary of his fête-day with great rejoicings by the light of his furnaces in the company of his workmen, dazed with merry-making and wine.

Not that Toussaint had ever desecrated the sanctity of Saints' days by shoeing a horse or mending a wheel, unless he had been obliged by unforeseen accidents befalling travellers on the road, and then he took no payment for his labour; but his forge never ceased blazing at any time, on even the most scrupulously observed Saints' days, for it served as a beacon to the poor lost wanderers, who always received a welcome; and when the peasants living in the Combe spoke of the house of Toussaint Oudard, son of Tiphaine, they usually called it the Tavern of Charity.

Suddenly Toussaint went into the large kitchen adjoining the forge, where several pieces of game and butcher's meat were roasting in front of a bright, well-fed fire that might have roused the envy of the forge, blazing in the fireplace of one of those chimneys that wealth seemed to have invented for the exercise of hospitality.

'All goes well!' he cried gaily to an old woman sitting on a stool in the chimney-corner, an old woman whose sweet, grave face shone in the bright glow from a copper cresset with three beaks that stood on a moulded-plaster bracket black with smoke and age. 'It seems all the children are in bed, and the pretty bevy of girls from the Combe are keeping you as good company as usual for this evening's vigil. God for-bid I should allow it to be disturbed by my rowdy boys, whose ears are so used to the noise of the anvil that they cannot hear each other speak unless they howl like wolves. I have just sent them off to my bedroom, whence their shouts will no longer disturb you, and where, my dear mother, you will please have the rest of these chitterlings brought up to us by one of your servants, the oldest and most sour-faced if possible, and for good reason. Yet keep a good portion for the poor fellows who may be driven here by the storm; and as for your fair girlfriends, see that they make a good feast of chestnuts roasted in the embers, sprinkling copiously over them the sweet white wine, fresh-drawn from the vat, sparkling to a nicety. When all is gone there will still be more . . . I would not trouble you thus, my beloved mother,' continued Toussaint, wiping away a tear and kissing the old woman, 'if my dear Scolastique was still alive; but it was God's will you should be my children's only mother and their father's special providence!'

'All shall be done as you wish, my good Toussaint,' said the kindly Huberte, as much moved as her son by the memory his last words evoked. 'Make merry in what remains of your fête, for the hours pass quickly. When the church bell begins to toll for the prayers for the dead, it will be time to think of them. So be happy, and do not trouble yourself about your guests. Here are two already, praised be God, whom we will try to welcome and who will be indulgent enough to overlook the smallness of our means, if we cannot receive them as well as we should wish.'

'The Lord be with them,' continued Toussaint, greeting the strangers, whose presence he had not noticed till then. 'And may they feel as much at home here as in the bosom of their own families! Tell them pleasant stories to while away the time, and do not stint the fare, for the workman's house provides him with his daily bread.'

Then he kissed his mother again, and went away.

The two men whom the aged Huberte had mentioned, had risen an instant from their seats as if to respond to Toussaint's courtesy, and then they had seated themselves again, and remained motionless and silent on the other side of the fireplace.

The first looked like a man of good birth; he wore a doublet with points, above which projected a broad white ruff with large goffers, well starched and plaited; a good pair of leather gaiters were buckled round his legs and reached up above his knees to the bottom of his cloth cloak, and his slouch hat was overshadowed by a flowing plume that fell over his eyes. His pointed grey beard indicated a healthy old age, and his grave reserved demeanour made him look like a doctor.

The other, judging from his stunted form, was probably a child of the people; but his extraordinary attire had at once attracted the attention of Huberte and the girls from the Combe, who were sorry they could not catch a glimpse of his features under the enormous tufts of red hair that covered nearly the whole of his face; he wore very tight doublet and hose, and the top of his head was concealed beneath a woollen skullcap of the same colour, while his bright red frizzly hair, which gave him so strange an appearance, bristled out all round it. This cap was fastened under his chin by a strong strap, like the muzzle of a snappish cur.

'You will excuse us all the more readily for not acquitting ourselves well of our duty, master,' continued Huberte, resuming her chatter and addressing the elder of the strangers, 'because this desolate, out-of-the-way spot rarely has the honour of welcoming travellers such as you. Some unexpected chance must have brought you here.'

'Chance or the Devil,' answered the dark man in a hoarse voice, so rasping that the sound of it made the girls shudder.

'That has been known to happen,' interpolated the dwarf, throwing himself backwards with a deafening burst of laughter, but taking care to show none of his face, except an enormous mouth full of teeth as sharp as needles and white as ivory.

After which he gave his stool a jerk nearer the red-hot andirons, and held his two long bony hands out to the blaze, which glowed through them and made them look as if they were made of horn.

The dark man paid little attention to this coarse mockery at the moment.

'My accursed horse,' he continued, 'scared by the gale or driven by some demon, took me astray for three whole hours, from forest to forest, ravine to ravine, until he decided to throw me over a precipice, where I left him, dead, I believe. I reckon I have travelled quite thirty leagues, and I only found my way in this strange place thanks to the light of your forge and the mercy of God.'

'His holy will be done in all things,' said old Huberte, crossing herself.

'The mercy of God could do no less', said the mischievous little man, intervening again, 'for the most renowned and reverend gentleman, Pancrace Chouquet, formerly a founder of the Convent of the nuns of Sainte-Colombe, Minister of the Gospel, Rector of the University of Heidelberg, and Doctor of Four Faculties.'

And this sally was followed by shouts of laughter more obstreperous than before.

'What right has an ill-bred upstart like you to dare to interrupt me and attribute to me names and titles that, for all you know, I may not possess?' cried the Doctor, gnashing his teeth. 'Where did you meet me?'

'Pardon, pardon, dear master! do not be annoyed,' answered the young fellow, patting the cloak and the sleeves of the aged Doctor with his huge hand. 'I saw you in Cologne when I was travelling round Europe in search of knowledge, in accordance with the earliest wishes of my father, and I was present at one of your lectures where you were translating Plutarch into most excellent Latin, when you suddenly stopped short at the Treatise, "De sera Numinis vindicta", as paralysed as if Satan held you by the throat. It is a fine and learned subject. You had your own affairs to see to that day, it is true, for they were beginning to warm a bed for you behind the tomb of the three Kings, hotter than the hearth of Dame Huberte. It is a comic enough story, and I'll tell it gladly, if it so please our charming and merry company.'

'If you mention that subject again,' whispered the Doctor, 'I will drive it back down your throat with my dagger. It is amazing', he added gruffly, 'that such a knave should be received in a respectable household.'

'I thought he was your servant,' answered Dame Huberte, 'and, for my part, I know not who he may be.'

'Nor I! Nor I!' cried the girls, flocking together like little birds caught in their nest.

'Nor *I* either,' said Cyprienne, hiding her head in the trembling lap of Maguelonne.

'Oh, how crafty they are!' cried the traveller in the red cap, from the hearth where he was crouching to snatch the roasting chestnuts with his fingers. 'I should not be surprised if they were sly enough not to recognise me in my Sunday clothes! Yet, just look, Dame Huberte, and see if there is any change in your little groom, Colas Papelin, formerly a student, and now a stable-boy at your service. Master Toussaint has not shod one of our mares without my first washing her, rubbing her down, currying and brushing her, cleaning and polishing her hoofs, making her coat as smooth as a mirror, and not one whose mane I have not combed with my fingers at all hours of the night, if not of the day. That is why I am always welcome at the forge, for the groom and the blacksmith are hand and glove together, as the saying goes.'

As he spoke he pushed back the thick curls of his flaming red hair, so as to reveal his face, and, roaring with laughter to shake the walls of the house, he showed them a fairly hideous countenance, livid and yellow as the wax of an old torch, furrowed with queer wrinkles, with two little red eyes in his forehead, brighter than coals sparkling under the breath of the bellows. Everyone made a gesture of terror.

Dame Huberte knew full well she had never seen him before; but she had a feeling that warned her it was not wise to say so.

'If ever I've seen this phantom before,' growled Pancrace, 'it must have been in Hell!'

'Quite possible,' retorted Colas Papelin, still laughing, 'and I have as good reason as you to be surprised at the chance that brings us here together. Who would have thought of seeking Master Pancrace Chouquet at the Hermit's Combe?'

'The Hermit's Combe!' shrieked Pancrace . . . 'Oh!' he added, biting his fist.

'Oh!' echoed Colas Papelin, with a burst of derisive laughter; 'but do you not agree with me, Doctor, that it would be interesting for us men of learning, who combine love of knowledge with love of gold and pleasure, to try and find out why this unhappy valley was given this name? The story must be a curious one, and I am of the opinion that Dame Huberte, who knows all the stories in the world, will willingly tell us this one between two pitchers of sweet wine.'

'I care not for stories, my good fellow,' retorted Pancrace, making as if to rise.

'If not that tale, you shall hear mine,' cried Colas Papelin, holding him in his seat with his powerful arm, which clasped him like a vice. 'Oh, what a pleasure for us, Dame Huberte, to listen to you telling it!'

'I had promised the girls to tell it,' answered the old woman, 'and the telling is not long. First you must know that this country was wilder and bleaker even than it is now, when a holy man came here, more than a hundred years ago, and built a little hermitage for himself on one of the rocks overhanging the precipice. People say he was a wealthy young lord who had turned his back on the Court, lest he should not be able to save his soul there; but he was known only by the name of Odilon, in which name our Holy Father beatified him, until such time as he may be canonised.'

'Heyday!' cried Colas Papelin.

'Indeed, no one could doubt', continued Huberte, 'that he had brought a great deal of money with him, for the whole aspect of the Combe changed in less than no time. He had the arable land cultivated, mills built on the streams, a small hospital, a presbytery, a monastery erected, and his liberality brought to the Combe men of all the trades useful to travellers, and their families still live quite comfortably off, never ceasing to bless the name of the blessed Saint, who made them his heirs. That is why this valley is called the Hermit's Combe, because he never came out of his hermitage, and, like God, he bestowed his benefits on mankind without being seen by them. May the Lord keep his soul before Him, as it says in the Church Calendar.'

'Your story is very edifying,' said Doctor Pancrace, 'and I am ready to give it credence this time, although I have heard its like in all the monastery districts I know; but the weather seems to be clearing; the wind has ceased blowing, nor does the rain beat against the window-panes.'

'It will be a real pleasure to be travelling soon,' Papelin remarked gaily, holding the Doctor in his seat; 'but it would not be quite seemly to abandon Dame Huberte at the beginning of such an interesting and instructive tale.'

'The story is told,' answered the Doctor impatiently, 'and it tells us clearly all we wanted to know, namely, the origin and etymology of the name of this valley; not a word is missing.'

'Oh, but a peripeteia is missing,' retorted Colas, 'a denouement and a moral which you would not have suffered us to overlook on the benches when you took the trouble to explain to us the Rhetoric of Guillaume Fichet peripatetically; and to prove I am right, Dame Huberte is ready to go on with her story now she has had time to get her breath.'

She did in truth continue her story: 'The blessed Odilon had lived thus in retreat and prayer for nearly three-quarters of a century, when a young man, who for some months had attracted attention by his piety and assiduity at the Sacraments, went to him and offered to assist him in his sacred duties. As he was as well read as a priest, eloquent as a preacher, apparently as pious as a saint, for never had a penitent been known to mortify himself with greater austerity, the doors of the hermitage were easily opened to him. I cannot for a moment call his name to mind, although I fancy I heard it not long ago.'

'The name of the person is not essential to your story,' murmured the Doctor, biting his fingertips again.

'Master Pancrace Chouquet', repeated Colas Papelin in a loud, shrill voice, 'thinks the name of this person is not essential to your story, my worthy hostess! Do you hear', he added, shouting even louder, 'that your story can be told without the name of this honest fellow, who looks to me like some infernal hypocrite. Such is the opinion of Messire Pancrace, of Messire Chouquet, of Messire Pancrace Chouquet! Do you not remember now, Dame Huberte?'

'The scoundrel means to be the death of me,' thought the Doctor, with a furtive glance at the door.

'Not yet,' said little Colas Papelin, answering his unspoken words and spluttering with laughter close to his ears.

'For many years we had feared lest the treasure of the Saint should tempt thieves,' continued the good widow of Tiphaine, who had hardly noticed these interruptions. 'We now knew that, after distributing a large part in pious works, he had divided the rest between the presbytery and the monastery, for the education of the children, the relief of travellers, and the solace of those afflicted by the scourges of nature. So when the young priest arrived the whole of the Combe was enjoying a calm and happy well-being, sent by Providence in its mercy to bless the hermit's old age. "Now, to be sure," we said as we chatted in the evenings, "the holy man will have someone with him to close his eyes and ask the benediction of Heaven over him with the Last Sacrament."'

'Oh, what a noble thought, good woman!' exclaimed Colas Papelin, sobbing. 'I would have blessed the good old man myself, I promise you, if such had been the will of God! . . . What says my master, Messire Pancrace Chouquet?'

Pancrace pulled at his beard, moved uneasily on his stool, glanced at the door again, and did not answer.

'Those are worthy sentiments,' the old woman went on. 'One night, Tiphaine rose suddenly from my side with a start: it was exactly thirty years ago, gentlemen, on this same All Saints' Day, a little before the service in honour of the dead.'

'What?' said Colas Papelin. 'Do you think, my good Dame, that it will indeed be exactly thirty years since that day, thirty years to the very hour, neither more nor less, when the bells ring for Matins?'

'It must indeed be so, honest master Papelin,' answered Huberte, 'since it was in 1531. I asked Tiphaine what made him get up so early, thinking he might be ailing. "Do not be anxious," he answered, "and have no fear, dear love: it is a bad dream that filled me with anguish, and I must see if there is any meaning in it before I can close my eyes again; for dreams are sometimes warnings from Heaven. I dreamed the aged Saint Odilon was being murdered, and, since I got up, I am haunted by a mysterious sound of wailing and moaning; I hope to reassure you in a few minutes." So saying, he hastened to the hermitage with some of his workmen, who were disturbed by the same fear, and they learned that sleep had warned them of what was only too true! . . .'

'The poor hermit was dead!' added Colas. 'Master, do you hear?'

'He was dying when Tiphaine arrived; but, although his murderer had taken him for dead when he had fallen, he had found strength enough to drag himself out of his cell a moment afterwards, while the rascal was making a useless search for the supposed treasure, which he had just lost his soul to pay for!'

'And his murderer was the crafty, hateful monster who had stolen his affection and prayers under the mask of piety! Master, do you hear?'

Pancrace answered only by a sort of stifled groan, like the howl of a wild beast.

'Yes, that is true!' cried Huberte. 'Meantime, the door of the cell had fallen-to behind the Saint, by means of a spring invented by Tiphaine, a secret spring the murderer did not know of.'

'So he was caught!' cried Colas Papelin, with his horrible burst of laughter; 'a few minutes more, and the righteous shall be avenged! Master, do you hear?'

'No, it was not so,' continued Huberte, shaking her head. 'Tiphaine and his men found no one in the cave; and as it was suddenly filled with a smell of bitumen and sulphur, everyone believed the stranger had made a pact with the Devil in order to escape from the danger that threatened him, which proved to be true, for it came to be known later on that he had studied at Metz or at Strasbourg under the wicked sorcerer Cornelius of whom you may have heard! . . .'

'Oh, his bargain was not a good one, for all that!' interrupted Colas Papelin, with renewed outbursts of joy. 'Master, do you hear? . . .'

'I hear, I hear,' retorted Pancrace Chouquet, with affected calm. 'I hear the language of the foolish superstitions with which Papistry feeds these ignorant people. May the light of truth descend upon them!'

And he made a sudden movement to get away from his neighbour's side. Colas Papelin did not follow him; he gazed at him with scorn and derision.

'One thing is certain,' added the old woman, a trifle annoyed, 'and that is there remained in the cave the fragment of a document, stained with blood, and marked with five great black fingernails, like a royal seal, promising the murderer thirty years' respite, as was shown by the translation made by the Grand Penitentiary; for it was written in the language of the Devil.'

'Either I have a ringing in my ears', murmured Colas Papelin, 'or there are the bells chiming for Matins. Master, do you hear? . . .'

'Anyway,' concluded Huberte, 'the murderer was never found, although he left a clue in the hermit's hand, a thick tuft of hair with some bleeding skin, which never grew again, no doubt.'

'Honour to Saint Odilon!' cried Colas Papelin, rising and sending the Doctor's plumed hat flying with a back-stroke of his arm.

One side of Master Pancrace Chouquet's head was as bald and smooth as if it had been burnt.

He glared threateningly at Colas, picked up his hat, and made for the door, glancing behind him to see if the stable-boy was following; but the little man was busy striking the red-hot andirons with an iron poker, and making the sparks fly up the great open chimney.

The door closed behind him. The group of women remained silent and motionless, overawed by a strange fear, as if they were petrified. Colas Papelin noticed this, and with a peal of laughter louder than ever, he made them a bow, pushing back his tousled hair with the elegant gesture of a man of the world, nurtured in good learning and gentility.

'Fare you well, Dame Huberte, and you too, fair maidens,' he said, taking leave of them. 'I thank you for the hospitality we have received; but it enjoins other duties still: I will follow this fine gentleman, lest he go astray.'

An instant after, they heard the door swing on its hinges, and the strong bolts and chains clang.

'Has the Devil gone too?' cried the fair-haired Julienne, raising her trembling little fingers towards Heaven.

'The Devil! Oh!' exclaimed Anastasie, clasping her hands as if in prayer. 'Do you think he looks like that?'

'It appears he does,' observed Dame Huberte, gravely; for some time past she had never ceased telling her beads.

'But did he not tell us his name?' resumed Julienne, a little reassured. 'Can Colas Papelin and the Devil be the same person?'

'The two names are perfectly synonymous,' added Ursula, sedately; she was the niece and godchild of a priest.

'I recognised him all of a sudden,' said Cyprienne. 'I have so often seen him poking the fire like that, when I was falling asleep at my spindle!'

'And I have seen him mischievously tangling the hair of our goats, when I was keeping watch in our stable!' said Maguelonne.

'And it must be he who leads our asses astray with his whistling in the woods!' suddenly observed little Annette, the daughter of Robert the miller.

'He has tried to lead us astray too,' answered her sister Catherine in a whisper, 'and the Evil One in the red doublet has played more than one of his pranks on the brink of the stream in the Combe.'

'*Libera nos, Domine!*' cried old Huberte, falling on her knees.

The girls naturally followed her example, and when the bell rang for Matins they did not separate until they had purified Dame Huberte's kitchen by saying prayers and burning consecrated boxwood and sprinkling holy water.

On the morning of the next day, as the people of the hamlet were wending their way to the service at the monastery, separated from it by

only a few thickets, Toussaint Oudard suddenly let go his mother's arm and stood still in front of his little group, warning them by a gesture and a shout not to advance any further, for he wished to spare them the sight of the hideous thing on which his eyes had just fallen.

It was a horribly mangled body, so deformed by the death agony, so shrunken and shrivelled by a celestial or infernal fire that it no longer bore the semblance of a man; only, lying close by, were the shreds of a black cloak and of a hat with a flowing plume.

And ever since then, the Hermit's Combe has been known as the Dead Man's Combe.

Stendhal

Born Henri Beyle, Stendhal (1783–1842) grew up in Grenoble with a disdain for provincial life. The account in his unfinished autobiography, *Vie de Henri Brulard*, of the young Henri sitting on the knee of the old woman on whom the Marquise de Merteuil of *Les Liaisons dangereuses* was supposedly based, is indicative of the tension he felt between nostalgia for the order of the Ancien Régime and his taste for Republicanism and Romanticism. He moved to Paris in 1799, but it was in Milan, after he had crossed the Alps with Napoleon's armies in May 1800, that he found his spiritual home. He spent the rest of his life torn between these two cities, a division which clearly marks his greatest novels, *Le Rouge et le Noir* (1830) and *La Chartreuse de Parme* (1839). For him, Italy came to represent beauty, passion and joy (as it also did for Byron, whom he met in Milan); his native France only heartless reason. That Italy offered Stendhal access to a life of the emotions is clear from his amorous endeavours; his stormy affair with the Milanese Angela Pietragrua was followed by an unconsummated passion for Matilde Dembrowski, which is echoed in his study *De l'amour* (1822). In the words he penned for his own epitaph: *Errico Beyle, Milanese: visse, scrisse, amò* (Henri Beyle, Milanese: he lived, wrote, loved).

The Duchess of Palliano

Palermo, 22 July 1838

I AM NOTHING OF A NATURALIST; I HAVE ONLY A VERY MODERATE acquaintance with the Greek language; my chief object in coming to visit Sicily has not been to observe the phenomena of Etna, nor to throw light, for my own or for other people's benefit, on all that the old Greek writers have said about Sicily. I sought first of all the pleasure of the eyes, which is considerable in this strange land. It resembles Africa, or so people say; but what to my mind is quite certain is that it resembles Italy only in its devouring passions. The Sicilians are a race of whom one might well say that the word *impossible* does not exist for them once they are inflamed by love or by hatred, and hatred, in this fair land, never arises from any pecuniary interest.

I observe that in England, and above all in France, one often hears people speak of *Italian passion*, of the frenzied passion which was to be found in Italy in the sixteenth and seventeenth centuries. In our time, that noble passion is dead, quite dead, among the classes that have become infected with the desire to imitate French ways, and the modes of behaviour in fashion in Paris or in London.

I am well aware that I may be reminded that, from the time of Charles V (1530), Naples, Florence and even Rome were inclined to imitate Spanish ways; but were not these noble social customs based upon the boundless respect which every man worthy of the name ought to have for the motions of his own heart? Far from excluding emphasis, they exaggerated it, whereas the first maxim of the *fats* who imitated the Duc de Richelieu, round about 1760, was to appear *moved by nothing*. The maxim of the English dandies, whom they now copy at Naples in preference to the French *fats*, is it not to appear bored by everything, superior to everything?

Thus *Italian passion* has ceased to exist, for a century past, among the good society of that country.

In order to form some idea of this *Italian passion*, of which our novelists speak with such assurance, I have been obliged to turn to history;
and even then the major histories, written by men of talent, and often
too pompous, give us practically no details. They do not condescend to
take note of the foolish actions except when these are committed by
kings or princes. I have had recourse to the local history of each city; but
I am appalled by the abundance of material. Every little town proudly
offers you its history in three or four quarto volumes of print, and seven
or eight volumes in manuscript; the latter almost undecipherable, teem-
ing with abbreviations, giving unusual shapes to the letters, and, at the
most interesting moments, crammed with forms of speech in use in the
district but unintelligible twenty leagues away. For, in the whole of this
fair land of Italy, whose surface love has sown with so many tragedies,
three cities only, Florence, Siena and Rome, speak more or less as they
write; everywhere else the written language is a hundred leagues apart
from the spoken.

What is known as *Italian passion*, that is to say the passion that seeks
its own satisfaction, and not to give one's neighbour an enhanced idea of
oneself, begins with the revival of society, in the twelfth century, and
dies out, among people of refinement at least, about the year 1734. At
this date the Bourbons ascend the throne of Naples in the person of Don
Carlos, son of a Farnese heiress married as his second wife to Philip V,
that melancholy grandson of Louis XIV, so intrepid amid shot and shell,
so listless, and so passionately fond of music. We know that for twenty-
four years the sublime eunuch Farinelli sang to him every day three
favourite airs, which never varied.

A philosophic mind may find something curious in the details of a
passion as felt in Rome or Naples, but I must say that nothing seems to
me more absurd than those novels that give Italian names to their characters. Are we not all agreed that passions alter whenever we move a
hundred leagues farther north? Is love the same thing at Marseilles as in
Paris? At most, we may say that countries which have long been subjected to the same form of government show a sort of outward similarity
in their social customs.

Scenery, like passions and music, changes also whenever we move
three or four degrees farther north. A Neapolitan landscape would seem
absurd in Venetia, were there not a convention, even in Italy, to admire
the fine works of nature round Naples. In Paris, we go one better, we
imagine that the appearance of the forests and tilled plains is absolutely

the same round Naples as round Venice, and would like Canaletto, for instance, to use absolutely the same colours as Salvator Rosa.

But the crowning absurdity, surely, is an English lady endowed with all the perfections of her Island, but considered not to be in a position to portray *hatred* and *love*, even in that Island: Mrs Anne Radcliffe giving Italian names and grand passions to the characters of her celebrated novel: *The Italian, or the Confessional of the Black Penitents.*

I shall make no attempt to adorn the simplicity, the occasionally startling bluntness of the all too true narrative which I submit to the reader's indulgence; for instance, I translate literally the reply of the Duchess of Palliano to the declaration of love made by her cousin Marcello Capecce. This family monograph occurs, for some reason, at the end of the second volume of a manuscript history of Palermo, of which I can furnish no details.

This narrative, which I have shortened considerably, much to my regret (I omit a mass of characteristic features), consists of the ultimate adventures of the ill-fated house of Carafa, rather than of the interesting history of a single passion. Literary vanity suggests to me that perhaps it might not have been impossible for me to enhance the interest of several situations by developing them farther, that is to say, by guessing and relating to the reader, with details, what the characters felt. But can I, a young Frenchman, born north of Paris, be quite sure of my power to guess what was felt by these Italian hearts in the year 1559? At the very most, I can hope to be able to guess what may appear elegant and thrilling to French readers in 1838.

This passionate manner of feeling which prevailed in Italy about the year 1559 required deeds, not words. And so the reader will find very little conversation in the following narrative. This is a handicap to my translation, accustomed as we are to the long conversations of the characters in our fiction; for them a conversation is a duel. The story for which I claim all the reader's indulgence shows a singular element introduced by the Spaniards into Italian manners. I have nowhere departed from the office of a translator. The faithful reproduction of the mental attitudes of the sixteenth century, and even of the narrative style of the chronicler who, apparently, was a gentleman attached to the household of the unfortunate Duchess of Palliano, constitutes, to my mind, the chief merit of this tragic tale, if there be any merit in it.

The strictest Spanish etiquette prevailed at the *court* of the Duke of Palliano. Bear in mind that each Cardinal, each Roman Prince had a similar court, and you will be able to form some idea of the spectacle furnished, in 1559, by the civilisation of the city of Rome. Do not forget that this was the period in which Philip II, requiring for one of his intrigues the support of two Cardinals, bestowed upon each of them a revenue of two hundred thousand lire in ecclesiastical benefices. Rome, although lacking an effective army, was the capital of the world. Paris, in 1559, was a city of barbarians not without charm.

LITERAL TRANSLATION OF AN OLD NARRATIVE WRITTEN ABOUT THE YEAR 1566

Gian Pietro Carafa, although sprung from one of the noblest families of the Kingdom of Naples, behaved in a harsh, rude, violent manner more befitting a keeper of flocks or herds. He assumed the *long coat* (the cassock) and left at an early age for Rome, where he benefited by the favour of his cousin, Olivero Carafa, Cardinal and Archbishop of Naples. Alexander VI, that mighty man, who knew everything and could do anything, made him his *camérière* (roughly what we should call nowadays groom of the chambers). Julius II nominated him Archbishop of Chieti; Pope Paul created him Cardinal, and finally, after endless intriguing and disputes among the Cardinals enclosed in Conclave, he was elected Pope, taking the name of Paul IV; he was then seventy-eight years old. The very Cardinals who had just called him to the throne of Saint Peter soon shuddered when they thought of the firmness and fierce, inexorable piety of the master whom they had set over themselves.

The news of this unexpected election caused a revolution at Naples and Palermo. Before many days had passed, Rome saw arrive within her gates innumerable members of the illustrious house of Carafa. All of them found places; but, as was only natural, the Pope showed particular favour to his three nephews, sons of the Conte di Montorio, his brother.

Don Giovanni, the eldest, who was already married, was made Duke of Palliano. This duchy, taken from Marcantonio Colonna, to whom it belonged, included a large number of villages and small towns. Don Carlo, the second of His Holiness's nephews, was a Knight of Malta and had seen active service; he was created Cardinal, Legate of Bologna and First Minister. He was a man of great determination; loyal to the traditions of his family, he made bold to hate the most powerful monarch in the world (Philip II, King of Spain and of the Indies), and furnished him with proofs of his hatred. As for the new Pope's third nephew, Don Antonio Carafa, since he was married, the Pope made him Marchese di Montebello. Finally he proposed to give in marriage to Francis, Dauphin of France and son of King Henry II, a daughter whom his brother had got by a second marriage; Paul IV was to settle upon her as her dowry the Kingdom of Naples, which would first be taken from Philip II, King of Spain. The Carafa family hated this mighty king, who, with the help of the said family's own weaknesses, succeeded in wiping it out, as you shall see.

After he had ascended the throne of Saint Peter, the mightiest in the world, and one which, at that time, eclipsed even that of the illustrious Spanish monarch, Paul IV, as we have seen occur with most of his successors, set an example of all the virtues. He was a great Pope and a great Saint; he set to work to reform abuses within the Church, and by so doing to avoid the General Council for which all parties at the Roman court were clamouring, but which a wise policy refused to grant.

In accordance with the custom of that age, which our age has let fall into oblivion, the custom which forbade a Sovereign to repose his confidence in men who might have interests other than his own, the States of His Holiness were governed despotically by his three nephews. The Cardinal was First Minister and carried out his uncle's wishes; the Duke of Palliano had been created General of the forces of the Holy Church; and the Marchese di Montebello, Captain of the Palace Guard, allowed only such persons as it suited him to admit to cross its threshold. Soon these young men were committing the wildest excesses; they began by appropriating for their own use the possessions of the families opposed to their rule. The people did not know where to turn to obtain justice. Not only had they cause to be afraid for their possessions, but, horrible to relate in the land of the chaste Lucrece, the honour of their wives and daughters was not safe. The Duke of Palliano and his brothers carried off the most beautiful women; it was enough to have been so unfortunate as to take their fancy. People were amazed to see them show no respect for exalted birth; worse still, they were in no way restrained by the sanctity of the cloister. The people, in despair, knew of no one to whom they might complain, so great was the terror which the three brothers had inspired in everyone who approached the Pope's presence; they were insolent to the Ambassadors, even.

The Duke had married, before his uncle's rise to greatness, Violante di Cardone, of a family of Spanish origin which, at Naples, belonged to the highest aristocracy.

It was numbered in the *Seggio di Nido*.

Violante, famed for her rare beauty and for the charm which she knew how to assume when she sought to attract, was famed even more for her overweening pride. But, to do her justice, it would have been difficult to have a more exalted mind, as she showed to all the world by admitting nothing, in the hour of her death, to the Capuchin friar who came to shrive her. She knew by heart and used to repeat with infinite charm the admirable *Orlando* of Messer Ariosto, most of the *Sonnets* of the divine Petrarch, the *Tales* of Pecorone, etc. But she was even more entrancing when she deigned to entertain her company with the odd ideas that suggested themselves to her mind.

She had a son who was styled Duca di Cavi. Her brother, Don Ferrante, Conte d'Aliffe, came to Rome, attracted by the prosperous state of his brothers-in-law.

The Duke of Palliano maintained a splendid court; the scions of the first families of Naples fought for the honour of belonging to it. Among those whom he most cherished, Rome marked out, by its admiration, Marcello Capecce (of the *Seggio di Nido*), a young gentleman celebrated at Naples for his intelligence, no less than for the godlike beauty which Heaven had bestowed upon him.

The Duchess had as favourite Diana Brancaccio, then thirty years of age, closely related to the Marchesa di Montebello, her sister-in-law. It was rumoured in Rome that, with this favourite, she threw off her pride; that she confided to her all her secrets. But these secrets related only to politics; the Duchess aroused passions in others, but reciprocated none.

On the advice of Cardinal Carafa, the Pope declared war against the King of Spain, and the King of France sent to the Pope's assistance an army commanded by the Duc de Guise.

But we must confine ourselves to events at home, inside the court of the Duke of Palliano.

Capecce had long appeared more or less mad; he was seen to perform the strangest actions; the fact was that the poor young man had fallen passionately in love with the Duchess, his *mistress*, but dared not reveal his condition to her. At the same time, he did not absolutely despair of attaining his end, for he saw the Duchess intensely annoyed by a husband who neglected her. The Duke of Palliano was all-powerful in Rome, and the Duchess knew, without any shadow of doubt, that almost every day the most famous beauties among the ladies of Rome came to visit her husband in her own *palazzo*, and this was an insult to which she could not grow reconciled.

Among the chaplains to His Holiness Pope Paul IV was a respectable cleric with whom he used to repeat his breviary. This gentleman, at the risk of his own downfall, and perhaps at the instigation of the Spanish Ambassador, made bold one day to reveal to the Pope all his nephews' misdeeds. The holy pontiff was ill with grief; he tried not to believe the report; but overwhelming evidence came in from every side. It was on the first day of the year 1559 that the event occurred which confirmed all the Pope's suspicions, and perhaps brought him to a decision. It was therefore, on the actual Feast of the Circumcision of Our Lord, a coincidence which greatly aggravated the offence in the eyes of so pious a Sovereign, that Andrea Lanfranchi, secretary to the Duke of Palliano, gave a magnificent supper to Cardinal Carafa, and wishing to add to the excitement of the palate that of the flesh, invited to this supper Martuccia, one of the most beautiful, most notorious and wealthiest courtesans of the noble city of Rome. Fate so willed it that Capecce, the Duke's favourite, the same who was secretly in love with the Duchess, and was reckoned the handsomest man in the capital of the world, had for some time past been attached to Martuccia. On the evening in question he searched for her in all the places where he had any hope of finding her. Not seeing her anywhere, and having heard that there was a supper party at Lanfranchi's house, he had a suspicion of what was happening, and towards midnight appeared at Lanfranchi's door, accompanied by a numerous body of armed men.

The door was opened to him; he was invited to sit down and partake of the feast; but, after a few words had been exchanged with a certain constraint, he made a signal to Martuccia to rise and leave the house with him. While she was hesitating, greatly confused and with an inkling of what was going to happen, Capecce rose from the chair on which he was sitting, and, going up to the girl, took her by the hand, and attempted to carry her off with him. The Cardinal, in whose honour she had come to the party, strongly opposed her departure; Capecce persisted, endeavouring to drag her from the room.

The Cardinal First Minister, who, that evening, had assumed a garb very different from that which indicated his high rank, took his sword in hand, and endeavoured, with the vigour and courage which all Rome knew him to possess, to prevent the girl from leaving. Marcello, blind with rage, summoned his men; but they were mostly Neapolitans, and, when they recognised first of all the Duke's secretary and then the Cardinal, whom the unusual clothes which he was wearing had at first disguised from them, they sheathed their swords again, declined to fight, and intervened to settle the dispute.

During this uproar, Martuccia, who was surrounded by the rest, while Marcello Capecce kept hold of her left hand, was clever enough to escape. As soon as Marcello noticed her absence he hastened after her, and his men all followed him.

But the darkness of the night gave rise to the strangest reports, and on the morning of 2 January the capital was filled with accounts of the perilous encounter which had occurred, it was said, between the Cardinal's nephew and Marcello Capecce. The Duke of Palliano, Commander-in-Chief of the forces of the Church, understood the affair to be more serious than it actually was, and, as he was not on the best of terms with his brother the Minister, had Lanfranchi arrested that same night, while early on the following morning Marcello himself was put in prison. Then it was discovered that no life had been lost, and that these imprisonments served only to increase the scandal, the whole of which fell upon the Cardinal's shoulders. The prisoners were quickly set at liberty, and the three brothers combined their enormous influence to hush up the affair. They expected at first to be successful; but, on the third day, the whole story came to the ears of the Pope. He sent for his two nephews and spoke to them as a Prince might speak who was so pious and so profoundly shocked.

On the fifth day of January, which saw a great number of Cardinals assembled in the congregation of the Holy Office, the Pope was the first to speak of this horrible affair; he asked the Cardinals present how they had dared refrain from bringing it to his knowledge:

'You keep silence! And yet the scandal affects the sublime dignity with which you are invested! Cardinal Carafa has had the audacity to appear in the public streets in lay attire and with a drawn sword in his hand. And with what object? To take forcible possession of a shameless harlot!'

One may imagine the deathly silence that prevailed among all his courtiers during this outburst against the First Minister. Here was an old man of eighty inveighing against a beloved nephew, the master until then of his will. In his indignation, the Pope spoke of taking the hat from his nephew.

The Pope's anger was fanned by the Ambassador of the Grand Duke of Tuscany, who came to complain to him of a recent insult on the part of the Cardinal First Minister. This Cardinal, so powerful until then, presented himself before His Holiness in the course of his duty. The Pope kept him for four whole hours in the ante-room, waiting where everyone could see him, then sent him away without admitting him to an audience. One may imagine the blow to the Minister's unbounded pride. The Cardinal was annoyed, but not disposed to yield; he felt that an old man bowed down with years, dominated all his life long by the love he bore his family, and moreover little accustomed to the handling of temporal matters, would be obliged to have recourse to his activity. The saintly Pope's virtue won the day; he summoned the Cardinals together, and after gazing at them for a long time without speaking, finally burst into tears and had no hesitation in making what apology he could.

'The feebleness of age', he said to them, 'and the attention that I pay to matters of religion, in which, as you know, I am trying to destroy all the abuses, have led me to entrust my temporal authority to my three nephews; they have abused that authority, and I banish them now for ever.'

A brief was then read by which the nephews were deprived of all their dignities and confined to miserable villages. The Cardinal Prime Minister was banished to Città Lavinia, the Duke of Palliano to Soriano, and the Marchese to Montebello; by this brief, the Duke was deprived of his fixed revenue, which amounted to seventy-two thousand piastres (more than a million in 1838).

There could be no question of disobeying these stern orders: the Carafa had as enemies and watchers the entire population of Rome, who detested them.

The Duke of Palliano, escorted by the Conte d'Aliffe, his brother-in-law, and by Leonardo del Cardine, established his quarters in the little village of Soriano, while the Duchess and her mother-in-law came to live at Gallese, a wretched hamlet within two leagues of Soriano.

The neighbourhood is charming, but they were in exile; and they were banished from Rome, where but a little while since they had held an insolent sway.

Marcello Capecce had followed his mistress, with the rest of the courtiers, to the wretched village to which she had been banished. Instead of the devotion of all Rome this woman, so powerful a few days earlier, who had exulted in her position with all the arrogance of her pride, now found herself surrounded only by simple peasants, whose very amazement kept her in mind of her downfall. She had no consolation; her uncle was so old that probably death would overtake him before he had recalled his nephews, and, to complete their misfortune, the three brothers hated one another. It was even said that the Duke and the Marchese, who were not liable to the fiery passions of the Cardinal, alarmed by his excesses, had gone to the length of denouncing them to the Pope their uncle.

Amidst the horror and shame of this abject disgrace, something occurred which, unfortunately for the Duchess and for Capecce himself, showed plainly that, in Rome, it had not been a genuine passion that had drawn him in the wake of Martuccia.

One day when the Duchess had sent for him to give him an order, he found himself alone with her, a thing which did not happen more than once, perhaps, in a whole year. When he saw that there was no one else in the room in which the Duchess received him, Capecce stopped short and remained silent. He went to the door to see whether there was anyone that could hear them in the next room, then found courage to speak as follows:

'Signora, do not vex yourself, do not take offence at the strange words which I am about to have the temerity to utter. For a long time past I have loved you more than life itself. If, in a rash moment, I have ventured to gaze as a lover upon your heavenly beauty, you must impute the fault not to me, but to the supernatural force which urges and distracts me. I am in torment, I burn; I ask for nothing to quench the flame that is consuming me, but simply that your generosity may take pity upon a servant filled with misgivings and humility.'

The Duchess appeared surprised, and, what was more, annoyed.

'Why, Marcello, what have you ever seen in me', she said to him, 'to encourage you to speak to me of love? Does my life, does my conversation so far depart from the rules of decent behaviour as to afford you any justification for such insolence? How could you have the audacity to suppose that I could give myself to you or to any other man, except my lord and master? I forgive you for what you have said to me, because I consider that you are in a frenzied state; but take care not to make the same mistake again, or I swear I will have you punished for both pieces of impertinence at once.'

The Duchess left him in a towering passion, and indeed Capecce had failed to observe the laws of prudence: he should have let his love be guessed and not have spoken. He stood there speechless, greatly alarmed lest the Duchess should tell her husband of what had happened.

But the sequel proved to be very different from his apprehensions. In the solitude of this village, the proud Duchess of Palliano could not help taking into her confidence and revealing what had been said to her to her favourite lady-in-waiting, Diana Brancaccio. This was a woman of thirty, devoured by burning passions. She had red hair (the chronicler harps again and again upon this peculiarity, which to him seems to account for all Diana Brancaccio's mad actions). She was hotly in love with Domiziano Fornari, a gentleman attached to the household of the Marchese di Montebello. She wished to take him as her husband; but would the Marchese and his wife, with whom she had the honour to be connected by ties of blood, ever consent to her marriage to a man actually in their service? This obstacle was insurmountable, or seemed so at least.

There was but one chance of success: she would have to obtain some practical support from the Duke of Palliano, the Marchese's elder brother, and Diana was not without some hope in this direction. The Duke treated her as one of his family rather than as a servant. He was a man with an element of simplicity and goodness in his nature, and attached infinitely less importance than his brothers to questions of pure etiquette. Although, as a young man would, the Duke made full use of all the advantages of his exalted position, and was anything but faithful to his wife, he loved her dearly, and, so far as one might judge, could not refuse her any favour were she to ask it with a certain amount of persistence.

The confession which Capecce had ventured to make to the Duchess seemed to the dark mind of Diana an unlooked-for piece of good fortune. Her mistress had been until then maddeningly prudent; should she prove capable of feeling passion, were she to commit a sin, at every moment she would need Diana, who in turn might look for anything in the world from a woman whose secrets she would know.

So far from giving any hint to the Duchess first of all of what she owed to herself, and then of the terrible danger to which she would be exposing herself amid so sharp-sighted a court, Diana, carried away by the heat of her passion, spoke of Marcello Capecce to her mistress as she was in the habit of speaking to herself of Domiziano Fornari. In the long conversations with which they beguiled their solitude, she found some pretext daily for recalling to the Duchess's memory the charm and beauty of that poor Marcello who seemed so unhappy; he belonged, like the Duchess, to one of the first families in Naples, his manners were as noble as his blood, and he lacked only those worldly possessions which a caprice of fortune might at any time bestow upon him, in order to become in every respect the equal of the woman whom he ventured to love.

Diana was delighted to observe that the first effect of these speeches was to increase the confidence which the Duchess placed in her.

She did not forget to give a report of what was happening to Marcello Capecce. During the burning heat of that summer the Duchess often strolled in the woods which surround Gallese. At the close of day she would await the turn of the sea breeze on the charming hills which rise in the midst of those woods, hills from the summit of which the sea is visible at a distance of less than two leagues.

Without infringing the strict laws of etiquette, Marcello also might stroll in these woods: he would conceal himself there, it was said, and took care only to catch the Duchess's eye when she had been led to think kindly of him by the speeches of Diana Brancaccio. The latter would then give Marcello a signal.

Diana, seeing her mistress on the point of yielding to the fatal passion the seeds of which she herself had sown in the other's heart, herself gave way to the violent love which Domiziano Fornari had inspired in her. Now at last she was certain of being able to marry him. But Domiziano was a sober-minded young man, cold and reserved by nature; the extravagances of his fiery mistress, so far from attaching him to her, soon became distasteful to him. Diana Brancaccio was closely related to the Carafa; he might be certain of being stabbed, should the faintest rumour of his amours come to the ears of the terrible Cardinal Carafa who, albeit younger than the Duke of Palliano, was, as a matter of fact, the real head of the family.

The Duchess had yielded, some time since, to Capecce's passion, when one fine day Domiziano Fornari was not to be found in the village to which the court of the Marchese di Montebello had been banished. He had disappeared: it was learned later on that he had taken ship in the little port of Nettuno; doubtless he had changed his name, and nothing more was ever heard of him.

How is one to describe Diana's feelings? After listening good-humouredly for some time to her inveighings against Fate, one day the Duchess of Palliano let her see that this topic of conversation seemed to her to be exhausted. Diana saw herself scorned by her lover; her heart was a prey to the most cruel forces; she drew the strangest conclusion

from the momentary irritation which the Duchess had felt on hearing a repetition of her complaints. Diana persuaded herself that it was the Duchess who had compelled Domiziano Fornari to leave her for ever, and who, moreover, had furnished him with the means of travelling. This fantastic idea had no basis apart from certain remonstrances which the Duchess had once addressed to her. Her suspicion was swiftly followed by revenge. She sought an audience of the Duke and told him all that had occurred between his wife and Marcello. The Duke refused to believe her.

'Bear in mind', he told her, 'that during the last fifteen years I have not had the least fault to find with the Duchess; she has withstood the temptations of the court and the pitfalls of the brilliant position we enjoyed in Rome; the most attractive Princes, the Duc de Guise himself even, the General of the French Army, found it a waste of time, and you would have her yield to a mere Esquire!'

As ill-luck would have it, the Duke finding time hanging on his hands at Soriano, the village to which he had been banished, and which was but a couple of leagues from that in which his wife was living, Diana managed to secure frequent audiences from him, without their coming to the Duchess's knowledge. Diana had an amazing faculty of invention; her passion made her eloquent. She furnished the Duke with a mass of details; revenge had become her sole pleasure. She repeated that, almost every night, Capecce made his way into the Duchess's room about eleven o'clock, and did not leave until two or three in the morning. These reports made so little impression, at first, on the Duke's mind, that he refused to take the trouble to ride a couple of leagues at midnight in order to go to Gallese and pay a surprise visit to his wife's room.

But one evening when he happened to be at Gallese, the sun had set, and yet it was still light; Diana, quite dishevelled, made her way into the room in which the Duke was. Everyone else withdrew. She informed him that Marcello Capecce had just entered the Duchess's bedroom. The Duke, who doubtless was in an ill-humour at the moment, took up his dagger and ran to his wife's room, which he entered by a secret door. There he found Marcello Capecce. The lovers did, indeed, change colour when they saw him come in; but, as a matter of fact, there was nothing reprehensible in their attitude. The Duchess was in bed, engaged in making a note of a small sum which she had just paid; a maid was in the room; Marcello was on his feet, at a distance of three yards from the bed.

The Duke in his fury seized Marcello by the throat, and dragged him into an adjoining closet, where he ordered him to fling away the dirk and dagger with which he was armed. After which the Duke summoned the men of his guard, by whom Marcello was at once led away to the prisons of Soriano.

The Duchess was left in her own house, but under close guard.

The Duke was by no means a cruel man; it appears that he did think of concealing the scandal of the affair, so as not to be obliged to have recourse to the extreme measures which honour required of him. He wished it to be thought that Marcello was being kept in prison for a wholly different reason, and taking as a pretext a number of huge toads which Marcello had bought at a high price two or three months previously, he gave out that the young man had attempted to poison him. But the true nature of the crime was too well known, and the Cardinal, his brother, sent to ask him when he was going to think of washing out in the blood of the guilty the insult that had been offered to their family.

The Duke called to his assistance the Conte d'Aliffe, his wife's brother, and Antonio Torando, a friend of the family. The three of them, forming a sort of tribunal, passed judgement upon Marcello Capecce, accused of adultery with the Duchess.

The instability of human affairs brought it to pass that Pope Pius IV, who succeeded Paul IV, belonged to the Spanish faction. He could refuse nothing to King Philip II, who demanded of him the lives of the Cardinal and of the Duke of Palliano. The brothers were brought before the local tribunal, and from the minutes of the trial which they had to undergo we learn all the circumstances of the death of Marcello Capecce.

One of the many witnesses who were called gave evidence as follows:

'We were at Soriano; the Duke, my master, held a long conversation with the Conte d'Aliffe . . . Late at night we went down into one of the cellars, where the Duke had made ready the cords required for putting the accused to the question. There were present the Duke, the Conte d'Aliffe, Don Antonio Torando and myself.

'The first witness to be called was Captain Camillo Griffone, the intimate friend and confidant of Capecce. The Duke addressed him thus:

' "Tell the truth, my friend. What do you know of Marcello's doings in the Duchess's room?"

' "I know nothing: for the last three weeks and more I have not spoken to Marcello."

'As he refused obstinately to say anything further, the Lord Duke called in some of his guards from outside. Griffone was tied to the cord by the Podestà of Soriano. The guards pulled the cords, and in this way raised the witness four fingers'-breadth from the ground. After the Captain had been suspended thus for fully a quarter of an hour, he said:

' "Let me down and I will tell you all I know."

'When they had set him down on the ground, the guards withdrew, and we remained alone in the cellar with him.

' "It is true that on several occasions I have gone with Marcello to the Duchess's room," said the Captain, "but I know nothing more than that, because I used to wait for him in a courtyard near at hand until one o'clock in the morning."

'The guards were at once re-called, and, on an order from the Duke, drew him up again, so that his feet were clear of the ground. Presently the Captain cried out:

' "Let me down, I will speak the truth. It is true", he went on, "that, for many months past, I have observed that Marcello was making love to the Duchess, and I meant to inform Your Excellency or Don Leonardo. The Duchess used to send every morning to enquire for Marcello; she kept making him little presents, among other things, preserves of fruit prepared with great care and very costly; I have seen Marcello wearing little golden chains of marvellous workmanship which he had obviously had from the Duchess."

'After making this statement, the Captain was taken back to prison. The Duchess's porter was brought in, but said that he knew nothing; he was bound to the cord and raised in the air. After half an hour he said:

' "Let me down and I will tell you all I know."

'Once on the ground again, he pretended to know nothing; he was raised once more. After half an hour he was let down; he explained that he had been only a short time in the Duchess's personal service. As it was possible that the man did really know nothing, he was sent back to prison. All this had taken a long time on account of the guards, who were made to leave the room each time. They were intended to suppose that the trial was one of an attempt at poisoning, with the venom extracted from the toads.

'The night was already far advanced when the Duke ordered in Marcello Capecce. The guards having left the room, and the door being duly locked:

' "What business have you", he asked him, "in the Duchess's room, that you stay there until one, two, and sometimes four o'clock in the morning?"

'Marcello denied everything; the guards were called, and he was strung up; the cord dislocated his arms; unable to endure the pain, he asked to be let down; he was set upon a chair; but after that became confused in his speech and did not seem himself to know what he was saying. The guards were called and strung him up once more; after a long spell, he asked to be let down.

' "It is true", he said, "that I have entered the Duchess's apartment at these improper hours; but I was making love to Signora Diana Brancaccio, one of Her Excellency's ladies, to whom I had given a promise of marriage, and who has granted me all, save such things as honour forbids."

'Marcello was led back to prison, where he was confronted with the Captain; also with Diana, who denied everything.

'After this Marcello was brought back to the cellar; when we were near the door:

' "My Lord Duke," he said, "Your Excellency will recall that he has promised me my life if I tell the whole truth. It is not necessary to give me the cord again; I am going to tell you everything."

'He then went up to the Duke, and, in a tremulous and barely articulate voice, told him that it was true that he had won the favour of the Duchess. At these words, the Duke flung himself upon Marcello and bit him in the cheek; he then drew his dagger, and I saw that he was on the point of stabbing the culprit. At this point I suggested that it would be as well for Marcello to write down in his own hand what he had just confessed, and that such a document would serve as a justification of His Excellency's action. We went into the cellar where there were writing materials; but the cord had so injured Marcello's arm and hand, that he was able to write only these few words: "Yes, I have betrayed my lord; yes, I have stolen his honour."

'The Duke read the words as Marcello wrote them. At this point, he flung himself upon Marcello and struck him three blows with his dagger, from which he expired. Diana Brancaccio was present, within an arm's-length, more dead than alive, and, no doubt, repenting a thousand times over what she had done.

' "Woman unworthy to be of noble birth," cried the Duke, "and sole cause of my dishonour, for which you have laboured to serve your own infamous pleasures, I must now give you the reward of all your treacheries."

'So saying he seized her by the hair and sawed through her throat with a knife. The wretched woman shed a torrent of blood, and at length fell down dead.

'The Duke had the two bodies flung into a sewer that ran by the prison.'

The young Cardinal Alfonso Carafa, son of the Marchese di Montebello, the one member of the family that Paul IV had kept in his court, felt it his duty to tell him of these events. The Pope's only answer was:

'And the Duchess, what have they done with her?'

It was generally thought, in Rome, that these words were tantamount to the unfortunate woman's death warrant. But the Duke could not steel himself to that great sacrifice, either because she was pregnant or because of the intense affection he had felt for her in the past.

Three months after the great act of virtue which the saintly Pope Paul IV had performed in parting from the whole of his family, he fell ill, and, after three months of illness, expired on 18 August, 1559.

The Cardinal wrote letter after letter to the Duke of Palliano, incessantly reiterating that their honour demanded the death of the Duchess. Seeing their uncle dead and not knowing what the next Pope's attitude might be, he was anxious to have the whole affair finished as quickly as possible.

The Duke, a simple man, good-natured and far less scrupulous than the Cardinal over mere points of honour, could not bring himself to the terrible extremes demanded of him. He reminded himself that he had frequently been unfaithful to the Duchess, without taking the slightest pains to conceal his infidelities from her, and that they might have led so proud a woman to take her revenge. At the very moment of entering the Conclave, after hearing Mass and receiving the Holy Communion, the Cardinal wrote to him again that he was being tormented by these continual delays, and vowed that, if the Duke did not finally make up his mind to do what the honour of their house required of him, he would take no further interest in his affairs, and would make no attempt to be of use to him either in the Conclave or with the new Pope. A reason quite unconnected with the point of honour helped to determine the Duke's action. Although the Duchess was closely guarded, she contrived (it is said) to send word to Marcantonio Colonna, the Duke's mortal enemy, on account of his Duchy of Palliano which Carafa had secured for himself, that if Marcantonio were to succeed in saving her life and delivering her from captivity, she, for her part, would put him in possession of the fortress of Palliano, the commandant of which was her devoted servant.

On 28 of August, 1559, the Duke sent to Gallese two companies of soldiers. On the 30th, Don Leonardo del Cardine, the Duke's kinsman, and Don Ferrante, Conte d'Aliffe, the Duchess's brother, arrived at Gallese, and entered the Duchess's apartments to take her life. They told her that she was to die; she received the news without the slightest change of countenance. She wished first to make her confession and to hear the Holy Mass. Then, on these two gentlemen's approaching her, she observed that they were not acting in concert. She asked whether there were an order from the Duke, her husband, authorising her death.

'Yes, Signora,' replied Don Leonardo.

The Duchess asked to see it; Don Ferrante showed it to her.

(I find in the report of the Duke's trial the deposition of the friars who were present on this terrible occasion. These depositions are greatly superior to those of the other witnesses, this being due, I should say, to the fact that these monks had no fear when speaking before a court of justice, whereas all the other witnesses had been more or less the accomplices of their master.)

Fra Antonio di Pavia, a Capuchin, gave evidence as follows:

'After Mass, at which she devoutly received the Holy Communion, and while we were giving her comfort, the Conte d'Aliffe, brother of the Lady Duchess, entered the room with a cord and a hazel rod of the thickness of my thumb, and about half an ell in length. He bandaged the Duchess's eyes with a handkerchief, which she, with great coolness, pulled lower down over her eyes, so that she should not see. The Conte put the cord round her throat; but, as it did not run well, removed it and drew back a few feet; the Duchess hearing his step pulled the handkerchief from her eyes, and said:

' "Well, what is happening now?"

'The Conte answered:

' "The cord was not running well, I am going to fetch another, so that you shall not suffer."

'So saying, he left the room; shortly afterwards he returned with another cord, arranged the handkerchief once more over her eyes, placed the cord round her throat, and, passing the rod through the loop, twisted it and so strangled her. The whole affair, on the Duchess's part, was conducted in the tone of an ordinary conversation.'

Fra Antonio di Salazar, another Capuchin, concludes his evidence with these words:

'I wished to retire from the pavilion, from a scruple of conscience, so as not to see her die, but the Duchess said to me:

' "Do not go away from here, for the love of God." '

(Here the friar relates the incidents of her death, exactly as we have reported them.) He adds:

'She died like a good Christian, frequently repeating: "*Credo, credo.*" '

The two friars, who apparently had obtained the necessary authority from their superiors, repeat in their depositions that the Duchess always insisted upon her complete innocence, in all her conversations with them, in all her confessions, and particularly in that preceding the Mass at which she received the Holy Communion. If she was guilty, by this act of vanity she cast herself into Hell.

When Fra Antonio di Pavia, the Capuchin, was brought face to face with Don Leonardo del Cardine, the friar said:

'My companion said to the Count that it would be as well to wait until the Duchess had been confined; "she is in the sixth month," he went on, "we must not destroy the soul of the poor little creature she is carrying in her womb; he must have an opportunity of baptism."

'To which the Conte d'Aliffe replied:

' "You know that I have to go to Rome, and I do not wish to appear there with this mask on my face" ' (meaning, 'with this insult unavenged').

Immediately the Duchess was dead, the two Capuchins insisted that her body be opened without delay, so that the rite of baptism might be administered to the child; but the Conte and Don Leonardo would not listen to their entreaties.

Next day, the Duchess was buried in the local church, with ceremony of a kind (I have read the account of it). This event, the news of which at once spread abroad, made but little impression; it had long been expected; her death had several times already been reported at Gallese and in Rome, and in any event an assassination outside the city and during a vacancy of the Holy See was nothing out of the common. The Conclave that followed the death of Paul IV was very stormy, and lasted for no less than four months.

On 26 December, 1559, the unfortunate Cardinal Carafa was obliged to concur in the election of a Cardinal supported by Spain, and unable, consequently, to decline to take any of the harsh measures which Philip II would invoke against Cardinal Carafa. The new Pope took the name of Pius IV.

Had the Cardinal not been in banishment at the moment of his uncle's death, he would have had control of the election, or at least would have been in a position to prevent the nomination of an enemy.

Soon after this, both the Cardinal and the Duke were arrested. King Philip's order was evidently that they should be put to death. They had to reply to fourteen separate charges. Everyone who could throw any light upon these charges was examined. The report, which is extremely well drafted, consists of two folio volumes, which I have read with great interest, because one finds on every page of them details of custom which the historians have not thought worthy of the solemn garb of history. I observed among others certain extremely picturesque details of an attempt at assassination aimed by the Spanish party against Cardinal Carafa, then the all-powerful Minister.

Anyhow, he and his brother were condemned for crimes which would not have been crimes in anyone else, that for instance of having put to death the lover of an unfaithful wife and the wife herself. A few years later, Prince Orsini married the sister of the Grand Duke of Tuscany; he suspected her of infidelity and had her poisoned in Tuscany itself, with the consent of the Grand Duke her brother, and yet this was never imputed to him as a crime. Several Princesses of the House of Medici died in this way.

When the trial of the two Carafa was ended, a long summary of it was prepared, and this, on several occasions, was examined by congregations of Cardinals. It is obvious that once it had been decided to punish with death a murder committed to avenge an act of adultery, a sort of crime to which justice never paid any attention, the Cardinal was guilty of having persecuted the Duke until the crime was committed, as the Duke was guilty of having ordered its execution.

On 3 March, 1564, Pope Pius IV held a Consistory which lasted for eight hours, and at the end of which he pronounced sentence on the Carafa in the following words: '*Prout in schedula.*'

On the night of the 4th, the Fiscal sent the Bargello to the Castel Sant' Angelo, to carry out the sentence of death passed upon the two brothers, Carlo, Cardinal Carafa, and Giovanni, Duke of Palliano, which he did. They dealt first with the Duke. He was transferred from the Castel Sant' Angelo to the prisons of Tordinone, where everything was in readiness; it was there that the Duke, the Conte d'Aliffe and Don Leonardo del Cardine had their heads cut off.

The Duke bore that dread moment not merely like a gentleman of exalted birth, but like a Christian ready to endure all for the love of God. He addressed a few noble words to his two companions, encouraging them in the hour of death; then wrote to his son.

The Bargello returned to the Castel Sant' Angelo, with an announcement of death to Cardinal Carafa, giving him no more than an hour to prepare himself. The Cardinal showed a greater strength of character than his brother, all the more as he said less; speech is always a strength which one seeks outside oneself. He was heard only to mutter these words in a low tone, on receiving the grim tidings:

'I to die! O Pope Pius! O King Philip!'

He made his confession; repeated the seven Penitential Psalms, then sat down on a chair and said to the executioner:

'Proceed.'

The executioner strangled him with a silken cord, which broke; he was obliged to make a second and a third attempt. The Cardinal looked at him without deigning to utter a word.

(*Note added*)

Not many years later, the sainted Pope Pius V ordered a revision of the proceedings, which were annulled; the Cardinal and his brother had all their honours restored to them, and the Procurator General, who had done most to cause their death, was hanged. Pius V ordered the suppression of the report; all the copies existing in the libraries were burned; people were forbidden to preserve one on pain of excommunication: but the Pope forgot that he had a copy of the report in his own library, and it was from this copy that all those were made which we see today.

Honoré de Balzac

Honoré de Balzac (1799–1850) gave up a legal apprenticeship to try his hand at writing, but found artistic and financial success initially elusive. However, by the time of his funeral, at which Victor Hugo delivered a eulogistic oration, Balzac was recognised as one of the fathers of modern literary realism, with a place in the Académie Française. Remembered primarily for perfecting French prose – the matter of his writing was always less important than its form – he is also renowned for his vast enterprise *La Comédie humaine*, a secular response to Dante's *Divine Comedy*, which returns persistently (not least through the technique of recurring characters) to the aim of writing the 'secret history' of post-revolutionary French society. Balzac claimed that the project was based on 'two eternal truths: monarchy and religion', and barely managed to conceal a reactionary political disposition, yet Karl Marx praised the economic awareness and almost sociological thoroughness apparent in his categorisation of his novels and stories. These categories include *Scènes de la vie parisienne*, *Scènes de la vie de campagne*, *Scènes de la vie militaire*, and *Scènes de la vie politique*, from which 'An Episode of the Reign of Terror' (1830) is drawn. To maintain this colossal effort Balzac would work through the night, attired in monk's robes and firing his epic imagination with coffee made of unroasted beans.

An Episode of the Reign of Terror

ABOUT EIGHT O'CLOCK IN THE EVENING OF 22 JANUARY, 1793, an old woman walked down the Faubourg Saint-Martin towards the church of Saint-Laurent in Paris. Her footsteps could scarcely be heard, for the snow had fallen heavily during the day. The streets were deserted and the natural fear inspired by such stillness was increased by the terror with which the whole of France was then stricken. The old woman had met no one. Her failing eyesight prevented her from seeing the few other pedestrians, thinly scattered shadows, on the broad thoroughfare.

She walked resolutely through the deserted streets as though her age might prove a talisman against all dangers; but on leaving the Rue des Morts she thought she could hear the firm and heavy tread of a man behind her. She felt that unconsciously she had been aware of this sound for some time. Terrified at the thought of being followed, she attempted to walk faster, towards a brightly lit shop window in the hope of allaying her fears. Then, in the shadow beyond the rays of light cast across the pavement, she turned abruptly and caught sight of a figure looming through the freezing fog. That vague glimpse was enough. For an instant she reeled with terror, certain now that this stranger had tracked her, step by step, from her house. However, the hope of escape lent her strength and she hurried towards a confectioner's shop, entered it and collapsed into a chair that stood in front of the counter. A young woman, busy with her embroidery, looked up on hearing the creaking latch and, recognising through the glass door the old lady's old-fashioned mantle of purple silk, went at once to a drawer as if in search of something put aside for the visitor. Both the action and manner of the young woman suggested that she was anxious to be rid of her strange and unwelcome visitor. Finding the drawer empty, she gave an exclamation of anger. Without looking at the old lady she turned from the counter and, going to the back of the shop, called her husband, who appeared at once.

'Wherever have you put—?' she began mysteriously, glancing at the customer by way of finishing the sentence.

The confectioner could only see the old lady's huge black silk bonnet, trimmed with purple ribbons, but he looked at his wife as if to say: 'Do you think I would leave *that* lying about in your drawer?'

The old lady remained so still and silent that the shopkeeper's wife was surprised. She turned to her again and was seized with a sudden feeling of compassion and curiosity. Although the woman's colouring was naturally pale, and suggested that she was used to frugal living, it was easy to see that some recent alarm had given her face an added pallor. Her head-dress was so arranged as almost to conceal hair that was white, no doubt with age, for there was not a trace of powder on the collar of her dress. Its extreme plainness, and her grave and noble manner, gave her an air of religious severity. In former days, the manners and habits of people of quality were so different from those of other classes that it was easy to distinguish people of noble birth. The shopkeeper's wife was sure that her customer was an ex-aristocrat and that she had once belonged to the court.

'Madame?' she said with automatic respect, forgetting that the use of such a title was now forbidden.

The old lady made no answer. She kept her eyes fixed on the window of the shop as though some fearful object were painted on it.

'What is the matter, *citoyenne*?' asked the shopkeeper, who had returned at that moment. He drew the attention of his visitor to a small, blue cardboard box which he held out to her.

'It is nothing, my friends, nothing,' she answered in a gentle voice, looking up at the man as if to thank him with a glance. Then, seeing the red cap on his head, a cry escaped her: 'Ah! you have betrayed me!'

The indignant response of the young woman and her husband brought colour to the old lady's face; perhaps she felt relief, perhaps she blushed for her suspicions.

'Forgive me,' she said with a childlike gentleness. Then, taking a gold coin from her pocket, she gave it to the confectioner, saying, 'Here is the sum we agreed upon.'

There is a poverty which poor people instinctively recognise. The shopkeeper and his wife looked at each other, with a glance at the old lady which expressed the same thought. The coin was doubtless her last. The lady's hands trembled as she offered the money, looking at it sadly but ungrudgingly as if aware of the full extent of her sacrifice. The undoubted traces of hunger and misery were as easy to read on her face as were the signs of asceticism and fear. Her clothing, of well-worn silk, hinted at former grandeur; the mantle, though faded, was clean; the lace trimming carefully mended. The shopkeeper and his wife, torn between pity and self-interest, began by easing their consciences with words:

'*Citoyenne*, you seem to be very weak—'

'Perhaps Madame would like to take something?' said the wife, cutting her husband short.

'We have some good soup,' he added.

'It is so cold tonight. Perhaps you have caught a chill, Madame. Why not rest here and warm yourself?'

'We are not as bad as we look,' cried the husband.

These kind words won the heart of the old lady. She told them that a stranger had been following her and she was afraid to go home alone.

'Is that all?' replied the man in the red cap. 'Wait for me, *citoyenne*.'

He handed the gold coin to his wife and went to put on his National Guard's uniform as if wishing to make some adequate return for the old lady's money; an idea which sometimes strikes a tradesman when he has received an exorbitant price for an article of little value. He took up his cap, belted on his sword, and reappeared in full dress. But his wife had had time for thought and, as is often the case, reflection had closed the open hand of benevolence. Fearful of seeing her husband mixed up in something unpleasant, she pulled at the tail of his coat in an attempt to stop him. The worthy man, however, obeying his own charitable feelings, repeated his offer to see the old lady home before his wife could stop him.

'It seems that the man who has frightened her is still prowling around the shop,' said his wife nervously.

'I am afraid so,' the old lady replied innocently.

'Suppose he is a spy. It may be a conspiracy. Don't go. Take the box away from her.' These words whispered in the shopkeeper's ear froze the sudden courage that had inspired him.

'Well, I will just say a word or two to the fellow and get rid of him,' he said as he opened the door and hurried out.

Passive as a child and almost paralysed with fear, the old lady sat down again. But the confectioner returned almost immediately. His naturally ruddy face, reddened further by the bakehouse fire, had suddenly turned pale; such terror overcame him that his legs trembled and his eyes rolled like those of a drunken man.

'Wretched aristocrat!' he shouted in fury. 'Do you want to get our heads cut off? Go away from here. Take to your heels and don't you dare to come back. Don't come to me for material for your plots.'

So saying, the confectioner tried to regain possession of the little box which the old lady had slipped into one of her pockets. But at the touch of his hands on her clothes she seemed to regain all the agility of youth, preferring to face the dangers of the street, with no other protector but God, to losing what she had purchased. She rushed to the door, flung it open, and disappeared, leaving the husband and wife trembling with amazement.

Finding herself alone on the street she walked away rapidly; but her strength deserted her when she once again heard the sound of the snow crunching under the heavy footsteps of her pursuer. She stopped in her tracks; the man did likewise. She would have spoken to him but she dared not, either on account of her terror or because she could not think what to say. Then she went on again, but at a slower pace. The man slackened his pace, too, always keeping the same distance behind her, moving as her shadow. The clock struck nine as the silent couple retraced their steps past the church of Saint-Laurent.

It is in the nature of even the weakest of minds that calm must follow any violent agitation, for if feeling is infinite, our capacity to feel is limited. So the old lady, deciding that her persecutor meant her no harm, began to imagine him as an unknown friend, anxious to protect her. She cast her mind back over the numerous other appearances of the mysterious stranger, trying to find some plausible basis for this comforting theory, and felt inclined to credit him with good intentions rather than bad. Forgetting the fright he had given the confectioner, she walked on with a firmer tread towards the upper end of the Faubourg Saint-Martin.

After walking for about half an hour she came to a house at the corner where the road to the Pantin barrier branches off from the main thoroughfare – even today one of the loneliest streets in Paris. The north wind blew from the Buttes Chaumont and whistled through the houses, or rather cottages, scattered over this sparsely inhabited little valley where the fences are heaps of earth and bones. This desolate place seemed to be the natural refuge of poverty and despair. The sight of it seemed to make an impression on the man, still intent on following the poor creature who was bold enough to walk alone at night through the silent streets. He paused, as if deep in thought, and in the flickering light of a street lamp seemed to hesitate. Terror sharpened the woman's vision, and she fancied she saw something sinister in the features of this unknown man. Her old terrors revived, but taking advantage of his seeming hesitation, she slipped like a shadow to the door of the solitary dwelling, touched a spring, and vanished.

Still without moving, the man stood gazing at the house, which was typical of the miserable buildings in this suburb of Paris: a tumbledown hovel, built of rough stone, its yellowish stucco so full of cracks that it looked ready to blow down in the next gust of wind. The roof, covered with brown, moss-grown tiles, had given way in several places and looked as though it might collapse altogether under the weight of the accumulated snow. There were three windows in each storey, their frames rotten with damp and warped by the sun and evidently no barrier to the cold. This lonely dwelling stood like an ancient tower that Time had forgotten to destroy. A faint light shone from the attic windows, irregularly placed in the roof; the rest of the house was in darkness. With difficulty the old lady climbed the clumsy stairway, keeping a fast hold on the rope handrail. She knocked lightly on the door of a lodging under the roof before opening it and sank on to a chair which an old man offered her as she entered.

'Hide! hide!' she cried. 'Though we so seldom go out, everything that we do is known, every step watched—'

'What has happened?' asked another old woman, sitting near the small fire.

'The man who has been hanging about the house followed me again tonight.'

At this news the occupants of the place looked at each other in terror. The old man seemed the least concerned of the trio, probably because he was in the greatest danger. When weighed down by misfortune and threatened with persecution, a courageous man begins, as it were, to prepare for the sacrifice of himself; he looks upon each day as a victory snatched from Fate. The eyes of the two women, fixed as they were upon the old man, showed plainly that he alone was the object of their extreme anxiety.

'Why distrust God, my sisters?' he said in a hollow but impressive voice. 'Did we not sing His praises amidst the shrieks of assassins and the cries of their victims in the convent? Surely if it so pleased Him to save me from that slaughter, it must be because I have been reserved for some fate which I shall accept without a murmur. God protects His own, He disposes of them according to His will. It is of yourselves that we must think – not of me.'

'No,' said the first woman; 'what are our lives compared with that of a priest?'

'I have considered myself as dead ever since the day that I found myself outside the Abbaye des Chelles,' said the nun seated near the fire.

'Here,' said the one who had just come in, holding out the little blue box to the priest. 'Here are the holy wafers— Listen!' she cried, interrupting herself. 'I hear someone on the stairs.'

All three listened intently. The noise ceased.

'Do not be alarmed if somebody tries to come in,' said the abbé. 'A person on whom we can depend has made the necessary arrangements for you to cross the frontier; he will shortly call here for the letters I have written to the Duc de Langeais and the Marquis de Beauséant, asking them what can be done to get you out of this dreadful country, and away from the death or the misery that await you here.'

'Can you not come with us?' said the two nuns, in soft, despairing tones.

'My place is near the victims,' said the priest, simply.

The nuns were silent, gazing at him with rapt admiration.

'Sister Martha,' he said, speaking to the nun who had fetched the wafers, 'the messenger must answer "*Fiat voluntas*" to the word "Hosanna".'

'There is someone on the stairs,' cried the other sister, hastily uncovering a hiding-place built into the roof.

This time it was easy to hear, in the deep silence, a man's footsteps mounting the rough, mud-covered stairs. With some difficulty, the priest slid into the narrow space and the nuns hastily covered him with clothes.

'You can shut me in, Sister Agatha,' he said, in a muffled voice.

He was scarcely hidden when three knocks upon the door made the nuns tremble with apprehension. They exchanged looks of enquiry without daring to utter a word. They had lived out of the world for forty years and grown so accustomed to the life of the convent that they could scarcely imagine any other. Like hothouse plants, to them a change of air meant death. And so when, one morning, the bars and gratings of the convent were torn down they shuddered to find themselves free. It is easy to imagine the state of nervous weakness which the events of the Revolution had produced in these simple souls. They were quite incapable of bringing the ideas of the convent into harmony with ordinary

life; they could not even understand the situation in which they found themselves; like children suddenly deprived of a mother's care, they had taken refuge in prayer as children take to tears. Now, in the face of imminent danger, they were silent and passive, with no other defence but Christian resignation.

The intruder, taking their silence for consent, presently opened the door and entered the room. The two nuns trembled as they recognised the person who had been watching the house for several days and making enquiries about them. They stood stock-still, looking at him with frightened curiosity, much as children will stare at a stranger. The newcomer was tall and stout. There was nothing in his manner or appearance to suggest that he was a bad man. Like the nuns, he kept quite still, his eyes roving slowly around the room.

Two bundles of straw placed on planks served as the nuns' beds. In the centre of the room was a table, upon it a copper candlestick, a few dishes, three knives, and a round loaf of bread. The fire in the grate was low, and the few bits of wood piled in a corner of the room were further evidence of the poverty of the occupants. The roof was clearly in a bad state, for the walls, once painted, were badly stained where the rain had leaked through, and the ceiling was a network of brown stains. A sacred relic, rescued, no doubt, from the looting of the Abbaye des Chelles, adorned the chimney-piece. Three chairs, two chests, and a broken chest of drawers completed the furniture. A door near the fireplace suggested that there was a second room beyond.

The intruder had soon taken mental note of the contents of the little room. An expression of pity crossed his face and he threw a kindly glance at the two startled women, appearing as much embarrassed as they were. The strange silence in which all three stood looking at one another lasted but a moment, though it seemed longer, for the stranger appeared to guess at the weakness and inexperience of the two women. Trying to speak gently, he said:

'I have not come as an enemy, *citoyennes.*' He paused, then went on: 'Sisters, if anything should happen to you, be sure that I shall not have been the cause of it. I have come to beg a favour of you.'

Still they remained silent.

'If I ask too much – if I am annoying you – I will leave at once; believe me, I am heartily devoted to you, and if there is anything I can do for you, you have only to tell me. I, and I alone, perhaps, am above the law, now that there is no longer a king.'

There was such a ring of sincerity in these words that Sister Agatha, who belonged to the ducal house of Langeais and whose manner showed that she had at one time moved in aristocratic circles, pointed gravely to a chair as if asking their guest to be seated. The stranger seemed half pleased, half distressed by her invitation. He waited until the sisters were seated before sitting down himself.

'You are giving shelter to a venerable abbé who has refused to take the oath of allegiance to the Republic and miraculously escaped the massacre at the Carmelite convent,' he said.

'Hosanna,' said Sister Agatha, interrupting the stranger and looking at him with anxious curiosity.

'That is not his name, I believe,' he replied.

'But, monsieur, there is no priest here,' said Sister Martha quickly, 'and—'

'Then you should be more careful,' said the visitor gently, reaching out to the table and taking up a breviary. 'I do not think you understand Latin and—'

He stopped short, for the extreme distress on the faces of the poor nuns warned him that he had gone too far; they were trembling and their eyes had filled with tears.

'Do not fear,' he said, 'I know your names and the name of your guest. For the past three days I have been aware of your position and your brave devotion to the venerable Abbé de—'

'Hush!' said Sister Agatha, ingenuously placing a finger on her lips.

'You see, sisters, that if I had had the horrible idea of betraying you, I could easily have done so, time and again.'

As he uttered these words the priest emerged from his hiding-place and appeared in the centre of the room.

'I cannot think, monsieur,' he said courteously, 'that you can be one of my persecutors. I trust you. What do you want with me?'

The saintly confidence of the old man and the nobility of mind which showed on his face might well have disarmed a murderer. The mysterious stranger who had brought an element of excitement into lives of misery and resignation stood contemplating the group before him; then he turned to the priest and said in a trusting voice:

'Father, I came to ask you to celebrate a Mass for the repose of the soul – of – of a sacred being whose body can never be laid to rest in consecrated ground.'

The abbé gave an involuntary shudder. The nuns, who did not yet understand to whom the stranger referred, had turned their faces towards the speaker, in an attitude of eager curiosity. The priest looked searchingly at the stranger; there was no mistaking the anxiety in the man's face, the look of earnest entreaty in his eyes.

'Very well,' said the priest at length. 'Come back at midnight and I shall then be ready to celebrate the only Requiem Mass that we are able to offer in expiation of the crime of which you speak.'

A shiver ran through the stranger, and then a sweet and solemn joy seemed to prevail over some great and secret grief. He took his leave respectfully, and the abbé and the two sisters were left in no doubt of his unspoken gratitude.

Two hours later the stranger returned, knocked cautiously at the garret door, and was admitted by Mademoiselle de Langeais, who showed him into the second room of their humble lodging where everything had been made ready for the ceremony. The sisters had moved the old chest of drawers between the two chimney-breasts, and covered it with a magnificent altar-cloth of green moiré. A large crucifix of ebony and ivory, hanging on the discoloured wall, immediately caught the eye because it stood out in sharp relief from the surrounding bareness. Four small candles, which the sisters had managed to fix to the altar with sealing-wax, cast a dim glimmer almost absorbed by the dingy walls. The rest of the room was in semi-darkness. But the faint light illuminating the sacred objects seemed like a ray from Heaven shining down upon the unadorned altar.

The floor was damp. An icy wind swept in through the cracks in the attic roof which sloped sharply on each side of the room. Though far from stately, nothing could have been more solemn than this midnight service. A silence so profound that one could have heard the faintest sound from outside lent a kind of sombre majesty to the scene; while the grandeur of the ceremony was in such marked contrast to the poor surroundings as to generate a feeling of reverent awe. The nuns knelt on either side of the altar as if unaware of the damp floor; while they prayed aloud, the priest robed in his pontifical vestments placed a golden chalice, encrusted with gems, upon the altar – a consecrated vessel rescued, no doubt, from the pillage of the Abbaye des Chelles. Near this chalice, which had been a royal gift, the wafers and wine of the eucharist stood ready in two drinking glasses hardly fit to grace the tables of the poorest tavern. For want of a missal the priest had laid his breviary on a corner of the makeshift altar. An earthenware dish of water had been placed ready for the washing of hands that were pure and undefiled with blood. It was at once majestic and mean, poor yet noble, sacred and profane in one.

As the stranger knelt devoutly between the sisters he suddenly noticed that, having no other means of marking the Mass as a funeral service, the priest had tied a knot of black crape around the crucifix and the chalice – it was almost as if the abbé had put God Himself in mourning. The sight appeared to call up some overwhelming memory for the mysterious visitor, for beads of perspiration gathered on his forehead. The four actors in this awful drama looked at each other in silent sympathy; their souls, acting one upon another, communicated to each the thoughts of all, uniting them in a feeling of awe and pity. It seemed as if their minds had evoked the presence of the royal martyr whose remains had been consumed by quick-lime, but whose ghost now stood before them in all the majesty of a King.

They were celebrating a Requiem Mass without the presence of the deceased. In these humble surroundings four Christians were conducting a funeral service without a coffin, and offering prayers to God for the soul of a King of France. No thoughts of self sullied this purest of all devotions, this act of marvellous loyalty. Maybe, in the eyes of God, it was like the gift of the cup of cold water which ranks with the highest of virtues. The prayers of the priest and the two women represented the whole Monarchy, and perhaps also the Revolution in the person of the mysterious visitor, for the remorse on his face clearly showed that he was fulfilling a duty inspired by deep repentance.

When the priest came to the Latin words, '*Introibo ad altare Dei*,' the abbé, with an almost divine intuition, looked down upon his congregation of three, who represented Christian France, and said instead, as though to blot out the poverty of the garret: 'We are about to enter the sanctuary of God.'

These words, uttered with deep devotion, struck awe into the hearts of the participants. God had never revealed Himself in greater majesty, even beneath the great dome of St Peter's in Rome, than to the Christians gathered under these rough rafters, so true is it that no mediation is needed between God and man, for His greatness comes from Himself alone. The stranger's devoutness was evidently sincere – the same feelings united the prayers of these four servants of God and the King. The sacred words rang through the silence like heavenly music. At one moment the stranger broke down and wept; this was during the *Pater noster*, to which the abbé added a prayer in Latin and which no doubt the visitor understood: *Et remitte scelus regicidis sicut Ludovicus eis remisit semetipse* ('Forgive the Regicides as Louis XVI himself forgave them'). At this point the sisters saw the tears pouring down the cheeks of their visitor.

Then the office for the dead was intoned. The *Domine salvum fac regem*, chanted in low tones, profoundly moved these faithful Royalists as their thoughts turned to the infant King, for whom the prayer was offered, and who even then was a captive in the hands of his enemies. Perhaps fearing that a new crime might be committed, in which he must needs play an unwilling part, the stranger shuddered. When the service was over, the priest made a sign to the two nuns who retired to the outer room. As soon as he was alone with the visitor, the old man approached him with a gentle sadness and said, in a fatherly tone:

'My son, if your hands are stained with the blood of the martyred King, make your confession to me now. There is no sin in the eyes of God which may not be washed away by a repentance as deep and sincere as yours seems to be.'

An involuntary gasp of terror escaped the stranger at these words, but he soon recovered his composure.

'Father,' he said, in a voice that nevertheless trembled, 'no one is more innocent than I of the blood shed—'

'I am bound to believe you,' said the priest.

He paused and looked closely at the stranger; then, certain that the man before him was one of those timorous members of the Assembly who had sacrificed a sacred and inviolable head to save their own, he went on gravely:

'Remember, my son, that something more than not having taken part in that great crime is necessary to absolve from guilt. Those who left their swords in their scabbards when they should have drawn them to defend their King will have a heavy account to render to the King of Kings. Yes,' said the priest, shaking his head, 'yes, heavy indeed! For, by standing idle, they became accomplices in a terrible transgression.'

'Is it your belief', said the stranger in a surprised tone, 'that even indirect participation will be punished? The soldier under orders to fall into line – was he guilty?'

The abbé hesitated.

The stranger was glad of the dilemma in which he had placed this Royalist – forcing him to choose between the dogma of passive obedi-

ence on the one hand (for the upholders of the Monarchy maintained
that obedience was the first principle of military law) and the equally
important dogma which consecrates the person of the King. In the
priest's hesitancy, he was eager to exonerate himself from the doubts
that troubled him. Then, as if to allow the priest no further time for
reflection, he said quickly:

'I would be ashamed to offer you any fee for the Requiem Mass you
have just celebrated for the repose of the soul of the King and for the
relief of my conscience. We can only pay for things of inestimable value
by offerings that are also beyond price. Be pleased to accept, monsieur,
the gift of a holy relic. The time may come when you will realise its
value.'

With these words the stranger gave the priest a small box of light
weight. The priest automatically held out his hand and took it, so astonished was he by the solemn tone of the man's words and the reverence
with which he held out the box. Then they returned to the outer room
where the two nuns were waiting for them.

'You are living', said the stranger, 'in a house owned by Mucius
Scaevola, the plasterer on the first floor, who is well known in this
arrondissement for his patriotism. All the same, he is an adherent of the
Bourbons. He used to be Monseigneur le Prince de Conti's huntsman
and he owes everything to him. So long as you are able to stay here, you
are safer than you would be in any other part of France. Do not leave this
house. Certain pious souls will supply your needs and will watch over
and protect you while you wait without fear for better times. A year
hence, on this same twenty-first of January' (he gave an involuntary
shudder as he uttered these words), 'I shall come again to celebrate the
Mass of expiation—'

He could not finish the sentence but bowed to his silent audience
and, casting a last, lingering look upon the evidence of their poverty,
disappeared.

This event had all the interest of romance to the two innocent
women. When the priest had told them of his mysterious gift, and the
solemn manner in which it had been offered, the box was placed upon
the table and, in the dim light of the tallow candle, the three anxious
faces betrayed an indescribable curiosity.

Mademoiselle de Langeais opened the little box and took from it an
exquisite handkerchief made of very fine lawn, stained with perspiration. When she unfolded it, some darker stains appeared.

'That is blood!' exclaimed the abbé.

'It is marked with the royal crown!' cried the other nun.

With gestures of horror, the sisters let this precious relic fall to the floor. The mystery that surrounded the stranger was inexplicable to these simple souls, and as for the abbé, from that day on he did not even attempt to solve it.

Before long the three fugitives noticed that, in spite of the Terror, a powerful arm was stretched out to protect them. First they received firewood and provisions; then the sisters guessed that some woman must be associated with their protector, for they were sent linen and clothes which would make it possible for them to go out without attracting attention by the aristocratic style of the clothing they had been forced to wear until then. After a while, Mucius Scaevola provided them with certificates of citizenship. Then they started receiving information vital to the priest's safety from the most unexpected places. These friendly warnings always proved so singularly opportune that they could only have been sent by someone in possession of the secrets of the State. Famine was widespread in Paris at this time, yet rations of white bread were left regularly at the door of the garret, always put there by invisible hands. Although at first the two sisters suspected that Mucius Scaevola had a hand in this beneficence, which was always as ingenious as it was well directed, they became increasingly convinced that their secret protector was none other than the mysterious stranger with whom they had celebrated Mass on 22 January, 1793. A special prayer for him was added to their daily supplications; morning and night, these pious souls prayed for his happiness, prosperity, and redemption. God was entreated to remove any temptations from his path, to deliver him from his enemies, and to grant him a happy, long, and peaceful life.

Their gratitude, renewed daily, as it were, was imbued with a curiosity which grew more intense with each day. The circumstances surrounding the stranger's appearance were an endless source of conjecture, and there was the added benefit that he served to distract their minds from other thoughts. The sisters were determined that on his next visit, to commemorate the anniversary of the death of Louis XVI, the stranger should not be allowed to escape their friendship.

That night, so impatiently awaited, arrived at last. At midnight the wooden staircase echoed with the stranger's heavy footfalls. The room was ready to receive him, the altar prepared for the sacrament. This time the sisters opened the door and hurried to show a light at the entrance. Mademoiselle de Langeais even descended a few stairs so that she might get a first glimpse of their benefactor.

'Come!' said she, her voice trembling with emotion. 'Come in, we are expecting you.'

The man raised his head, looked gloomily at the nun, and made no answer. She felt as though a mantle of ice had fallen over her, and she said no more. At the sight of him, the gratitude and curiosity died in the sisters' hearts. Perhaps he was less cold, less taciturn, less stern than he seemed to these simple creatures, whose own emotions had led them to expect a responsive echo of their flow of friendship, but it was clear to them that this mysterious visitor wished to remain a stranger so they acquiesced with resignation. The abbé, though, fancied he detected a smile, quickly repressed, on the visitor's lips, as he noted the preparations made to receive him. He listened to the Mass, prayed with them, and disappeared immediately afterwards, politely declining the invitation of Mademoiselle de Langeais to remain and partake of the humble fare they had prepared for him.

After the 9th Thermidor (the fall of Robespierre), the sisters and the Abbé de Marolles could go about Paris without fear. The old priest's first excursion was to a perfumer's shop at the sign of the Queen of Roses, kept by Citizen Ragon and his wife, formerly the court perfumers. The Ragons had remained faithful to the Royalist cause and provided the Vendéens with a channel of communication with the exiled princes and the Royalist committees in Paris. The abbé, in the ordinary dress of the time, was just about to leave the shop – which was situated between the church of Saint-Roch and the Rue des Fondeurs – when a mob of people crowding down the Rue Saint-Honoré prevented his departure.

'What is happening?' he said to Madame Ragon.

'Nothing much!' she replied. 'Just the tumbrel and the executioner going to the Place Louis XV. Oh, we saw more than enough of that last year! But now, only four days after the anniversary of the twenty-first of January, one can watch that ghastly procession with equanimity.'

'Why?' enquired the abbé. 'What you are saying is unchristian.'

'But, Monsieur l'Abbé, this is the execution of Robespierre's accomplices. They saved themselves as long as they could but now it is their turn to go where they sent so many innocent people.'

The crowd which choked the Rue Saint-Honoré surged on like a wave. The Abbé de Marolles, yielding to an irresistible impulse, raised his eyes above the sea of heads and saw, standing erect in the cart, the stranger who but three days ago had joined in the second celebration of the Mass of commemoration.

'Who is that?' he said, 'that one standing—'

'The executioner,' answered Monsieur Ragon, giving him the name he had had under the monarchy.

'Help! help!' cried Madame Ragon. 'Monsieur l'Abbé has fainted.'

She quickly took out a flask of toilet vinegar and he was soon restored to consciousness.

'He must have given me the handkerchief that the King used to wipe his brow as he was led to his martyrdom,' said the old priest. 'Poor man! . . . There was a heart in that steel blade when all France was without one . . .'

The perfumers thought that the poor abbé was raving.

Alexandre Dumas

Alexandre Dumas (1802–70), dubbed 'the King of Romance', swiftly became famous for novels which remain popular today – not least through the numerous films and serialisations based on *Le Comte de Monte-Cristo* (1844–5) and *Les Trois Mousquetaires* (1844). His glamorous historical play, *Henri III et sa cour* (1829), the sensational *Antony* (1831) and the medieval tragedy *La Tour de Nesle* (1832) assured his place in the Romantic revolution in drama. As well as his vastly successful historical novels, such as *Vingt ans après* (1845) and *La Reine Margot* (1845), and popular fiction, travel writing, biography and autobiography, he wrote the volume of short tales, *Nouvelles contemporaines* (1826), from which this story comes. His complete works fill 103 volumes in the Calmann-Lévy edition and his output, his exuberance, his popularity, the fortune he made and the ease with which he spent it, ensured his reputation as one of the prodigies of the nineteenth century. His son (Alexandre Dumas *fils*) followed in his father's footsteps, writing *La Dame aux camélias* on which Verdi's *La Traviata* was based.

The Adventures of Seven Stars on Earth

THERE WAS ONCE A KING WHO LIKED TO THINK OF HIMSELF as a poet. But, as one cannot do two things at once, this king, crowned as he was with a golden diamond-studded circlet, was such a dreadful poet that whenever there was a riot in his kingdom (and that happened often enough and happened, indeed, once too often when he was forced to give the crown to his son) and the crowd had been called to order three times according to custom, the mayor would step on to a platform which was rolled behind him for exactly this purpose, and would read some of the royal verse to the rather ill-tempered crowd. Should the riot be a comparatively mild one he would need to read only a couple of verses; if it was stormy, then more verses were needed. But it was rarely more than a third of a lengthy poem before the mob, no matter how large, would melt away as if by magic.

Now, it so happened that I was travelling through the royal poet's kingdom and was visiting many of the most interesting places in the country. For although the monarch was not a man of much imagination himself he was, curiously, quite a patron of the arts. After I had looked at all the statues and wandered through the various museums and palaces, there was nothing left for me to visit but the prisons. I was not particularly keen to do this for I have no fondness for studying that type of art, if such it may be called. But I had a guide given to me, one of those guides whose hearts are made of stone, so I meekly followed him into one of those gloomy buildings.

The prison in the capital of the king-poet's country was very much like all such similar prisons, and would have been nothing out of the ordinary if it were not for the fact that it held no prisoners. In fact, it had had one not so long before who was to have been in residence there for some three weeks but had stayed for only three days. He was a journalist from Vienna, and finding himself in the king-poet's capital had made use of the chance to do something by poking fun at the royal poetry. The chief of police, finding out who was the author, took upon himself to arrest the rather naughty author and to secretly put him in gaol. Not only this, but he ordered him to write a letter to the city's only newspaper publicly begging the king's pardon.

Luckily the king somehow learned what had happened. He immediately called for the state coach and to the great amazement of the coachman when he closed the door behind him ordered:

'To the prison!'

In about five minutes the prisoner was told that he had a visitor who was none other than his majesty the king. The prisoner had only just the time to slip into a table drawer a story that he had just finished, and which also made fun of a king, when the royal personage came into his cell.

This time, however, the writer instead of attacking an earthly king poked fun at the ruler of Olympus, in the hope that Jupiter would be rather less touchy than his unexpected visitor.

But, after all, the king was not as thin-skinned as the writer imagined. He walked in, hat in hand, as any author should in the presence of his critic or, indeed, as an accused before his judge, beseeched the prisoner to forgive the rudeness of the police, and come and have dinner with him at the palace.

It naturally followed that it was impossible for the unfortunate man to get his story out of the drawer and take it away with him. So there it lay until its author had left the country, when it was found by the gaoler whose job it was to clean out the cell. In due course the king was told of the discovery. The Viennese had by now returned to Austria.

The king commanded that the story be sent back to its author by a reliable messenger. 'And above all,' he said, 'be sure that it doesn't fall into the hands of the chief of police.'

But up to the day I visited the prison no reliable messenger had been found.

'Are you, by any chance, going to Vienna?' asked the gaoler who was showing me round and who told me all that I have told you.

'I should be there in about three days,' I replied.

'Will you promise to give these papers to the poet and writer who was locked in here?'

'Most certainly, and with the greatest of pleasure.'

'Then please give me a receipt for them.'

I gave him the receipt and at the same time handed him a crown piece. That night I left for Vienna.

A couple of days later I called on the journalist and before we parted I gave him in exchange for his story one of mine. Six years had passed since my story was published in his paper; I had not forgotten his, but thought that I must have lost it. One day when I was turning over some old papers I came across some in a strange hand and at once knew that this could only be the story that had been entrusted to me by the gaoler at the king-poet's prison and given to me in exchange. Here, then, it is.

Very long ago when the heavens were called Olympus, the god who ruled there and was named Zeus, or Jove, or Jupiter (these three words mean very much the same thing) one day had a strange idea.

This was to make the human race happy.

It will be seen how he was cured of this desire and how the other gods who came after him were cured of it too.

Nobody knows how on earth, or rather in the heavens, such a thought came into his head. But it is pretty certain that when Jupiter told of his plan to his favourite advisers, Neptune the god of all the seas, and Pluto the god of Hell, those two worthies thought that the idea was so ridiculous that they cried out in one voice:

'Oh, your majesty, what a comical thought! By Jupiter, or Jove or Zeus, what an odd idea!'

But when a god gets an idea into his head, good or bad, he always sees it through to the end, even if it be the laughable one of trying to make mankind happy.

How was it to be done? Jupiter thought for a time and then, suddenly raising his head, exclaimed: 'I've got it!'

And he summoned the seven stars of the Little Bear to his presence. The stars hurried to obey. The people of the earth stared in amazement at the heavens, for, seeing seven stars shooting through space leaving sparkling tails behind them, they thought that the end of the world was near.

The seven stars cried out together:

'Here we all are, king most splendid and terrible! Why have you called for us?'

'Every one of you will pack your things and set out on a visit to earth,' was the answer, and he went on, 'You will receive five francs a day for your travelling expenses.'

'But what are we to do on earth?'

'I have taken it into my head to make mankind happy,' Jupiter replied. 'But as they may not believe in their good luck if I give it to them for nothing I order you to sell it for what you can get. In other words, you are going to be my commercial travellers.'

'We will obey your command, all-powerful majesty,' the stars said in unison, and in such melodious voices that the people on earth below again looked skywards for they knew that only such sweet sounds could come from Heaven. 'But what will we sell to these people?'

Jupiter then commanded the stars to stand in line and pass before him one by one. The stars did as they were told.

Then Jupiter said to the first: 'You will sell Wit.' To the second: 'You will sell Virtue.' To the third: 'You will sell Health.' To the fourth: 'You will sell Long Life.' To the fifth: 'You will sell Honour.' To the sixth: 'You will sell Pleasure.' And to the last: 'You will sell Riches.'

Jupiter, judging by the prayers mankind offered up to him, thought that when men and women were allowed to have all seven of his commands they would be perfectly happy. And I think that you would have thought so too.

'Now, be off,' he said to the stars, 'and sell as much of your heavenly goods as you possibly can.'

But Neptune and Pluto were no more convinced than they had been before. They began to laugh more heartily than ever, saying once again: 'Oh, what an odd idea, your majesty! By Jupiter, what a comical thought!'

The seven stars packed up their seven kinds of goods in seven different boxes provided for them by the storekeeper of Heaven, and flying down to earth started to do business in the first large town they came to.

'Wit! Wit! Who'll buy Wit?' called out star number one. 'Here it is, all fresh and hot. Wit! Wit! Buy my Wit!'

Laughter greeted the cry.

'Good heavens, does this silly girl take us all for fools?' said the journalists, the story-writers, the playwrights and the producers of pantomimes.

'She's a lovely girl with a pretty figure,' said the fops, staring at the Wit-seller through their eyeglasses, their spectacles, or binoculars, switching as they did so at their boots with canes they held in their yellow-gloved hands. 'What a shame it is that she looks rather like a bluestocking.'

'What is this little minx doing here?' asked the women. 'She would have done much better if she had brought some silks from Lyon, lace from Valenciennes, shawls from Algiers, coral from Naples, pearls from Ceylon, rubies from Visapore, or diamonds from Golconda. But, Wit! We can have that for nothing. It can be found everywhere. She will have to eat her own goods to keep herself alive, and even then she will die of hunger.'

And so the poor little star wandered along one street after another without selling any of her wares, until at last she came to an open door and went in without knowing where she was going. In fact, she had entered the Academy of Authors at the very moment when they were welcoming a new member. He had just finished making his speech of thanks and the secretary of that august assembly had risen to his feet to reply.

'Wit! Wit! Wit for sale!' cried the innocent little star.

Everyone burst into laughter but the secretary who, much put out, sniffed a pinch of snuff that went the wrong way and which made him sneeze for a good half an hour.

The president called to the attendants, and said: 'Put that stupid creature out and tell the door-keeper that she must never be allowed to enter the Academy again.'

The attendants pushed the star out into the street, and the door-keeper heard the president's instructions and obeyed them from then on.

Poor little first star went away feeling very sorry for herself. But as she was a well-meaning little star she wanted to do her duty as she had been told to do. After having walked for a short way along the quay she crossed a bridge and saw that she had reached an island. On the island was a public square on which stood a statue, and on the further side was a large building. Up and down the steps leading into it she saw a crowd of hurrying people, people who looked so very busy and so lacking in Mother Wit that she thought that this was the very place where her wares would be welcome. She could not know that the more stupid people are, the less likely they would be to think that they needed wit.

The star pushed her way through the crowd and entered a great hall where three men were sitting at a table in black robes and wearing square black caps. On either side of them were other men, dressed like themselves in gowns and black caps. Then the star realised that she was in a court of justice, and that the men in black were the judges and lawyers.

A very important case was being heard and the court was crowded. The lawyer for the plaintiff, an ugly unwashed little man with a cheerless face and a flattened nose, had just finished speaking so that there was a pause for the moment as the star entered. She thought that this was a happy chance and called out cheerfully:

'Wit, gentlemen! Who'll buy Wit? Wit for sale cheap!'

Unluckily, however, both the lawyer who had just spoken and the one who was about to speak thought that this was some hidden joke which was being poked at them; they, for once, agreed with one another and blamed the unlucky star. The result was that the little seller of Wit was put into the dock and accused of contempt of court.

Happily, the senior judge was quite a young man with a good deal of wit himself, and so he was quite content to order that the star should be taken out of the courtroom by two policemen. The policemen took hold of the star on either side by a ray and led her out on to the street, saying as they did so:

'You've got off with a fright this time, my dear, but don't you come here again.'

Poor first star went away feeling much puzzled. But as she had made up her mind not to leave the city without making a sale of some sort she walked, and walked, and walked until she came to another big square with another monument in its centre.

'Ah,' she said to herself, 'this looks like a temple that I've seen in Athens, and the Athenians have so much wit that I am sure that these people will be only too glad to buy more of it, too, at any price I ask.'

So she began to call out: 'Buy my Wit, Athenians, buy my Wit.'

Two men passed her, one holding a case crammed with pieces of paper of all kinds, the other with a notebook in which he was scribbling figures as he walked along.

'I think she called us Athenians,' said the man with the case.

'Yes, I imagine I heard her say something of the sort,' answered the man with the notebook.

'What on earth does she mean by "Athenians"?' asked the man with the case.

'It's probably some sort of a new society that they've just started,' the man with the notebook replied.

'Wit! Who'll buy my Wit?' cried the little star, following the two men.

'Ah,' said the man with the case, 'another company gone bankrupt, I suppose.'

And they both entered the Grecian temple which was none other than the Stock Exchange. The star followed them and marched through the noisy crowd, shouting as loudly as she could: 'Wit! Wit! Who'll buy Wit?'

A stockbroker came up to her and asked: 'What on earth are you selling?'

'Wit.'

'Wit? Oh!'

'Do you know what it is?'

'I've heard it spoken of.'

'You should buy some even if it is only a little, and if only to get to know what it's like.'

'Is it quoted on the share list?'

'No.'

'Then what are you doing with it here?' And he turned his back on the star, saying to a friend as he did so, 'She's not licensed to sell her goods; come away.'

They both went away in search of three other brokers, who pointed out the star to a police officer. He asked to see her permit to enter the building, and being told that she had none, called to two of his men who took poor first star to the police station.

The sergeant would have sent her to prison, but seeing that the girl did not seem to know that she had done any wrong and was a stranger (which was easy to see from the sort of goods she was trying to sell) he did no more than order her to leave the city within twenty-four hours.

The star was so utterly tired of all the rudeness shown to her by the people of the first town she had tried that she saved twenty-three-and-a-half hours of that time by leaving straight away.

But at the gates stood a tax collector, and he stopped her.

'What have you in that box?' he asked sharply.

'Wit.'

'What did you say – victuals?'

'No, only Wit.'

'Hah! Smuggling!' the man shouted, for he always said that of any goods of which he had never heard before.

He told his men to seize the star, and she was fined three francs and fifty centimes. Then two of the Customs men took her box from her, smashed the little bottles in it, and poured the contents into the gutter. After that two others grabbed her by her rays and marched her through the gates, telling her never to dare to return on pain of three months in gaol.

Ever since then wit has flowed freely in the gutter, and that is why street urchins who drink of it have so much wit.

Now, while first star was leaving the city by one gate, second star was entering by another, calling out as she did so: 'Virtue! Virtue! Who'll buy Virtue?'

The first people to hear her could not believe their ears. But the star, full of faith in her goods, shouted so loudly and clearly that some of the most unbelieving could not mistake her meaning any longer. Some of them turned up their noses at her, saying to each other:

'It must be some poor mad creature who has escaped from Bedlam.'

The rich ones added: 'They build such small houses these days that ours are already crowded with furniture, so where on earth could we put Virtue?'

The poor muttered: 'What could we poor creatures do with such precious stuff? It's not worth our while trying to save up and buy it, for if we did so no one would believe that we had it.'

The young said: 'Virtue! Why, we already have horses and packs of hounds. If we bought Virtue as well it would serve us right if our parents turned us out of the house for our wastefulness.'

Only one woman went up to the seller of Virtue. She was the widow of a deputy sub-postmaster.

'How much does Virtue cost?' she demanded.

'Nothing.'

'What, nothing?'

'Only the bother of keeping it.'

'It's too dear,' said the widow of the deputy sub-postmaster, and turned her back on the star.

So the star, seeing that the people of this city did not come to her, decided to go to them. So she entered the first door.

'What do you want?' a sharp voice called out. A tall, thin, withered woman was sitting there and her dog, which looked as ill-natured as its owner, began barking at the stranger.

'Excuse me, madam,' the star said humbly, 'but I am a pedlar.'

'I don't want anything.'

'Everyone in the world needs what I am selling.'

'What's that?'

'I sell Virtue.'

'If you sell Virtue, shouldn't you buy it too?'

'Of course, but why do you ask?'

'Because I have some to sell,' the old maid answered.

'Let me see it. Perhaps we can do some business.'

Then the woman brought a piece of Virtue from a cupboard. But it was old and patched, and so full of tears, so stained and moth-eaten, that the star could not tell what it had been like when it was new, all of twenty years ago.

'How much will you give me if I will sell it to you?' asked the woman.

'How much will you give me if I buy it from you?' answered the star.

'You impertinent creature!' the woman shouted, tearing the piece of stuff away from second star.

But the poor stuff was so tattered and easily torn that it fell to pieces as if it had been a spider's web. It was a sorry business, for the old maid threatened to go to law and have the poor star punished for saying that her Virtue was worthless; and the little pedlar ran the risk of being fined or even put in prison. So she offered to give the woman a nice new piece to replace the worn-out one.

The woman made the star turn out her whole boxful of goods. But although it contained all manner of virtues her grumbling customer could find nothing to suit her fancy.

And so second star was forced to offer her money instead, and after long bargaining the sum was fixed at five francs. The star took from her pocket a new ten-franc coin and politely asked her for five francs change. The old woman left the room pretending to go and get the money, but came back with a policeman.

'Here's the young woman who stole into my house to rob me,' she said. 'Arrest her and take her to prison.'

It was in vain that second star pleaded her innocence, and repeated that she was waiting for her change. The constable, who came from the provinces, did not understand very clearly what the old woman had told him, so he told the seller of Virtue that she must come with him to the police station. The star could do nothing else but obey.

As she was marched along the two or three streets leading from the old maid's house to the police station all the little street-boys ran at her heels calling out: 'Thief! Thief!'

When she was taken into the presence of the sergeant the little star told her tale so simply and quietly that that good man who, thanks to a sharp eye, knew many things that nobody else guessed, sent the constable away and when he was left alone with his prisoner asked how she earned her living.

The star opened her box and showed him her wares. The sergeant burst out laughing. 'My dear child,' he said, 'yours is a trade that's no good at all, and if you have no other way of making a living I must ask you to leave the city. It has enough poor already.'

The poor little star hung her head and made her way out of the city leaving her box with the sergeant who, at a dinner given to his men on the following Christmas Day, gave its contents away as presents.

And that is why, ever since then, most policemen have always been so very kind and helpful.

On that same day the third star also entered the very same city. She was the one given the command to sell Health.

'Health! Health for sale!' she cried. 'Who lacks Health?'

'What! You're selling Health?' people on all sides called out when they heard her.

'Yes. Health for sale! Health for sale! Who'll buy?'

In the twinkling of an eye she was surrounded by a large crowd. Everyone wanted Health, everyone clamoured for it, until the stage was reached when the poor star didn't know who to listen to first. But most of those who stretched out eager hands for the magic cure had long ago ruined their own health and had chased it from their bodies. Health, which has its own pride, never particularly cares to return to places where it has been treated with such disdain.

Others asked the star: 'Does it cost much to keep your Health?'

'Oh, good heavens, no,' she replied.

'What does it eat? What does it drink? How must we look after it?'

And the little pedlar answered: 'It eats not too much and not too little. It drinks pure clear water, goes to bed early and gets up with the sun.'

At this the crowd turned up their noses, and said: 'It's perfectly clear that this girl has no idea of how to sell her wares. One might just as well become a hermit to try to keep your Health.'

But there were two kinds of people in the crowd who muttered to themselves:

'If by any bad luck this Health-seller should make a fortune, we are ruined.' These were the doctors and the gravediggers.

I have said 'two kinds of people', but I ought to have said only one, for in this city the doctors and the gravediggers had joined together and started in business as 'Messrs Death and Company'. So they clustered together and talked the matter over, in the end making up their minds to rid the city of this strange pedlar and her wares, cost what it may.

The gravediggers were to see to the wares, while the doctors were to take charge of the pedlar. So, on the sly, one of the gravediggers grabbed the box and ran off with it.

The unfortunate little star ran after him, crying: 'Stop thief! Stop thief! He has stolen my Health!'

A doctor hurried to catch up with her and when he had reached her, said in a soothing voice: 'Come with me, my dear, come with me. Your box will be returned to you.'

Third star looked at him, and seeing that he was well-dressed, although looking rather glum, she took him at his word and followed him. He took her to a hospital.

When the poor star realised where she had been brought she tried to get out as quickly as she could, but the door was closed on her. She saw that she had been caught in a trap.

'Oh, Doctor, Doctor!' she cried, 'have pity on me and let me out. I am quite well.'

'You are wrong,' he answered. 'You are very ill.'

'But I eat well.'

'Bad sign.'

'I drink well.'

'Bad sign.'

'I sleep well.'

'Bad sign.'

'I have clear eyes, an even pulse, a clean pink tongue . . .'

'Bad sign. Bad sign. Bad sign.'

As the star kept on saying that she was quite well and would not go to bed, the learned man left her with two nurses who undressed little third star in spite of herself, and tied her down in bed.

'Aha,' said the doctor when he returned, 'so you'll interfere with us by selling good health when we sell ill-health, will you? Instead of joining us, you want to work against us, do you? You'll see, you'll see, my fine friend.'

And he sent for three other doctors and they held what they called a 'consultation', and what their allies, the gravediggers, called 'a sentence of death'. They decided that she should have what they described as a 'special kind of treatment' which would work quickly.

First, they put her on a special diet. Then they bled her every day. Finally, under the pretext that she slept too much they tickled the soles of her feet every time the star closed her eyes.

Luckily, she was a star, this little seller of Health, and therefore immortal. She did not die, because she couldn't, but she was very, very ill. Luckily, again, the keeper whose duty it was to keep an eye on her fell asleep one night. The tiny patient managed first to free one of her arm-rays and then the other, then one of the leg-rays and then the other. At last she slipped quietly out of bed, opened a window, tied a sheet to the bars, wrapped herself in another, and slid down into the hospital garden.

The garden was enclosed by walls, but all along one side climbing fruit trees were trained and the little creature scrambled up the wall with their help. Once outside that terrifying place the star set off running as fast as she possibly could.

The hospital and the cemetery were next door to each other, so that everyone who passed by thought that she must have come not from the hospital but from the cemetery. Instead of taking her for an escaped invalid they believed that she was a ghost risen from the dead. Indeed, the sheet with which she had covered herself made her look even more like a ghost. So, instead of running after her and stopping her, everybody in the street, even including the sentry who stood at the gates of the city, shrank from her and let her pass.

'Oh,' she said to herself, 'if Jupiter has another boxful of Health to send to the earth, he can find some other messenger.'

Now I, being the recorder of these wonderful adventures, have made enquiries and found out that the gravedigger who stole the box of Health from the star took it to his comrades, telling them what was inside. Then all of them set to work to dig an enormous hole in the form of a ditch in the cemetery, threw all the Health into it, and filled it up again.

So no one but the dead profited by Jupiter's good intentions, for it is ever since then that the dead have been so well.

While the star of Health was being coaxed by trickery into the hospital, where most certainly she would have died if she had not been immortal, someone in another part of the city was calling out her wares, but with no greater success. This was the fourth star who was trying to do good business, and was shouting:

'Who wishes for a Long Life? Who wants to live for ever? Buy as many years as you like! Buy! Buy!'

At the sound of her voice the whole city seemed to be turned topsy-turvy.

A wealthy banker who had houses in Paris, Frankfurt, New York, Vienna and London, ordered his agent to raise as many millions as were needed to buy the box and all its contents for him alone.

The lords of the manor begged that the star should be closely guarded in case the ordinary people should be able to buy any of the precious stuff. The bishops and all the rest of the clergy hurried to meet and consult together about the matter. As a result the archbishop telegraphed to the Pope, who replied:

'Those who buy Long Life should pay tithes, a year for every ten years they buy.'

Parliament ordered that everybody who bought Long Life should pay a special tax.

The banker came along with his millions to buy up the star's whole stock, but there was a riot with shouts of 'Fair shares for all!', and they beat him up and very nearly killed him.

Then the king, who was a good king, forbade the tax that Parliament had ordered and commanded that Long Life should be sold openly and that all, except those condemned to death, should have the right to buy, each according to his means. Immediately everyone crowded round the star, one hand full of gold and the other empty:

'Long Life! Long Life! Here's my money, take my money – oh, *please*, do take my money!' everybody begged her.

'Long Life to *me*, please – to *me*, ME, ME!'

'All in good time, ladies and gentlemen,' the star answered, 'but have you bought the goods which my three sisters were selling?'

'What were they selling?' was asked in chorus, the buyers eager to get the precious wares from the star's box.

'The first was Wit.'

'We haven't bought any.'

'The second sold Virtue.'

'Nor any of that either.'

'The third sold Health.'

'We know nothing about the sale.'

'Then', replied the seller of Long Life, 'I am very sorry, but without Wit, Virtue and Health, Long Life would be of no use to you.' And she closed her box, refusing to sell her wares to those who hadn't had the sense to buy what her three sisters had offered to sell.

But when she had packed up, the star found that she had overlooked one little piece of Long Life – a sample of her goods. It was a scrap that gave three hundred years of life. Close by her a parrot was sitting on its perch.

'Have you had your breakfast, Jacquot?' she asked.

'No, Margot,' the bird replied.

The star laughed. She gave him the piece of Long Life she was holding. The parrot ate it to the last crumb.

And that is why parrots live such a long, long time.

While the seller of Long Life was watching the bird gobbling up its strange meal she heard a great noise in the crowd.

'Honour! Honour! Who'll buy Honour?'

It was, of course, the fifth star who had entered the city.

All the people who had refused to buy Wit, Virtue and Health, and who had been refused Long Life because of that, started an uproar. At the cry of 'Honour! Honour!' they had made up their minds not to buy any of the new wares but to get hold of them, if they could, for nothing and by any means possible. So they rushed at the unlucky fifth star who, finding herself threatened, opened her box and shook it.

A thousand things fell out – titles, crosses of honour, ribbons, gold watches, epaulettes, and so on. Every single person in the crowd fell upon one or the other of these prizes and rushed away, each thinking that he was carrying off Honour when, of course, the clever little star had only shaken out 'honours'. Which is not the same thing at all.

The real, the true, Honour stayed at the bottom of the star's box, just as Hope was left in Pandora's box.

And that is why Honour is so rarely found, and why honours are so common.

While all this was happening the sixth star came on the scene calling: 'Pleasure! Who'll buy Pleasure?'

All who heard the call ran after her. Even those who had got their full share of honours wanted to find out what these new goods were like. So all of them, with crosses on their breasts, titles in their pockets, ribbons about their necks, gold watches on their chains, and epaulettes on their shoulders, hurried with the others to get their turn at Pleasure also.

But all the others cried out angrily that these men wanted too many of the good things of life, and they called them, among other rude things, greedy. Soon there was another riot. Someone tore the box of wares from the star's grasp, then, again, others snatched it away from whoever was holding it.

In the middle of all this hullabaloo the box fell on the pavement and broke into pieces. Pleasures were scattered over the road in every direction, and one and all scrambled madly for them. So that it happened not that each got hold of the pleasure he wanted and which he thought suited him; but, in fact, each got his neighbour's pleasure so, although they all had a share of the goods, it was all very much of a lottery.

That old rogue, Chance, had great delight by mocking the poor wretches with his gifts; to the women he gave the manly pleasure of the chase and hunting, to the men laces and ribbons, to the gouty a love of dancing, to the deaf a liking for listening to music, to the blind a love of painting and sculptures, to the old men calf-love, and to the old women sisterly love.

In short, he gave to no one what he wanted to have, and so no one was happy and everyone cursed the poor little pedlar. The result was that the star took to her heels and hurried out of the town without being paid.

Ever since then the pleasures of life have been so badly shared out among mankind that we look upon a man as a fool if he lives for pleasure alone.

As soon as the unfortunate seller of Pleasure, who had been so shamefully robbed of her wares, had left the city she came across her seventh sister who, you may remember, was to sell Riches lying senseless in a ditch by the side of the road.

The star of Pleasure ran to her and threw herself down by the girl. She took the poor star's head upon her knees and made her sniff some smelling-salts which luckily she had with her. But it was only after some time that the seventh star recovered her senses.

As soon as she was well enough to talk she told her story, and it was this:

'Scarcely had I come within sight of the city, scarcely had I been silly enough to tell the people what I was selling, scarcely had they learned that I was laden with Riches, than they all fell upon me, robbed me, and left me for dead, as you have seen.'

'But who were these dreadful people?' asked the other five stars who had just joined the pair. 'Thieves? Paupers? Starving men?'

'Oh, no! They were millionaires, my dear sisters,' sighed the seventh star.

When the seven stars had flown back to Olympus and told their master of the way they had been treated on earth, Jupiter scowled a terrible scowl.

But Neptune and Pluto burst out laughing. 'What did we tell you, your majesty?' they cried. 'It was such a comical thought!' And they repeated, both together as in a duet: 'Oh, it was such an odd idea!'

In the end Jupiter reluctantly had to agree with them.

And this, word for word, is the story found by the gaoler in the table drawer of the prisoner's cell in the king-poet's capital.

Victor Hugo

Victor Hugo (1802–85), one of the greatest of French writers, was expert in almost every genre and deeply committed to the political and cultural life of the nation. No collection of French short stories would be complete without him. His mother encouraged his precocious literary talent and he began writing classical tragedies at the age of thirteen. However, it was in the defence of Romanticism that Hugo first achieved fame: by 1826 his salon had replaced Nodier's as the fulcrum of Romantic thought; and the uproar surrounding his drama *Hernani* (1830) assured the movement's success. His developing political career in the 1840s was checked by a series of personal and professional catastrophes: his play *Burgraves* (1843) was booed off stage, his daughter Léopoldine drowned, and he himself was caught *in flagrante* with one Léonie d'Aunet. Son of a Napoleonic general, the young Hugo had co-founded the royalist *Le Conservateur littéraire*, but when his opposition to Napoleon III became manifest in his pamphlet *Napoléon le petit* (1852), he fled to the Channel Islands where he remained until the Emperor's abdication in 1870. He returned to France a few years before his death and his own funeral was attended by two million people.

Claude Gueux, King of Thieves

C LAUDE GUEUX WAS A POOR WORKMAN, LIVING IN PARIS
about eight years ago, with his mistress and child. Although his
education had been neglected, and he could not even read, the
man was naturally clever and intelligent, and thought deeply over matters. Winter came with its attendant miseries – want of work, want of
food, want of fuel. The man, the woman, and the child were frozen and
famished. The man turned thief. I know not what he stole. What signi-
fies, as the result, was the same: to the woman and child it gave three
days' bread and warmth; to the man, five years' imprisonment. He was
taken to Clairvaux – the abbey now converted into a prison, its cells into
dungeons, and the altar itself into a pillory. This is called progress.

Claude Gueux the honest workman, who turned thief from force of
circumstances, had a countenance which impressed you – a high forehead somewhat lined with care, dark hair already streaked with grey,
deep-set eyes beaming with kindness, while the lower part clearly indicated firmness mingled with self-respect. He rarely spoke, yet there
was a certain dignity in the man which commanded respect and obedience. A fine character, and we shall see what society made of it.

Over the prison workshop was an inspector, who rarely forgot that he
was a gaoler also to his subordinates, handing them the tools with one
hand, and casting chains upon them with the other. A tyrant, never
using even self-reasoning; with ideas against which there was no appeal;
hard rather than firm, at times he could even be jocular; doubtless a
good father, a good husband; really not vicious, but *bad*. He was one of
those men who never can grasp a fresh idea, who apparently fail to be
moved by any emotion; yet with hatred and rage in their hearts they
look like blocks of wood, heated on the one side but frozen on the other.
This man's chief characteristic was obstinacy; and so proud was he of
this very stubbornness that he compared himself with Napoleon – an optical delusion, like taking the mere flicker of a candle for a star. When

he had made up his mind to a thing, however absurd, he would carry out that absurd idea. How often it happens that, when a catastrophe occurs, if we enquire into the cause we find it originated through the obstinacy of one with little ability, but having full faith in his own powers.

Such was the inspector of the prison workshop at Clairvaux – a man of flint placed by society over others, who hoped to strike sparks out of such material; but a spark from a like source is apt to end in a conflagration.

The inspector soon singled out Claude Gueux, who had been numbered and placed in the workshop, and finding him clever, treated him well. Seeing Claude looking sad (for he was ever thinking of her he termed his wife), and being in a good humour, by way of pastime to console the prisoner he told him the woman had become one of the unfortunate sisterhood, and had been reduced to infamy; of the child nothing was known.

After a time Claude had accustomed himself to prison rule, and by his calmness of manner and a certain amount of resolution, clearly marked in his face, he had acquired a great ascendancy over his companions, who so much admired him that they asked his advice, and tried in all ways to imitate him. The very expression in his eyes clearly indicated the man's character; besides, is not the eye the window to the soul, and what other result could be anticipated than that the intelligent spirit should lead men with few ideas, who yielded to the attraction as the metal does to the lodestone? In less than three months Claude was the virtual head of the workshop, and at times he almost doubted whether he was king or prisoner, being treated sometimes like a captive Pope, surrounded by his cardinals.

Such popularity ever has its attendant hatred; and though beloved by the prisoners, Claude was detested by the gaolers. To him two men's rations would have been scarcely sufficient. The inspector laughed at this, as his own appetite was large; but what would be mirth to a duke, to a prisoner would be a great misfortune. When a free man, Claude Gueux could earn his daily four-pound loaf and enjoy it; but as a prisoner he daily worked, and for his labour received one pound and a half of bread and four ounces of meat; it naturally followed that he was always hungry.

He had just finished his meagre fare, and was about to resume his labours, hoping in work to forget famine, when a weakly-looking young man came towards him, holding a knife and his untasted rations in his hand, but seemingly afraid to address him.

'What do you want?' said Claude, roughly.

'A favour at your hands,' timidly replied the young man.

'What is it?' said Claude.

'Help me with my rations; I have more than I can eat.'

For a moment Claude was taken aback, but without further cere-mony he divided the food in two and at once partook of one-half.

'Thank you,' said the young man; 'allow me to share my rations with you every day.'

'What is your name?' said Claude.

'Albin.'

'Why are you here?' added Claude.

'I robbed.'

'So did I,' said Claude.

The same scene took place daily between this man old before his time (he was only thirty-six) and the boy of twenty, who looked at the most seventeen. The feeling was more like that of father and son than one brother to another; everything created a bond of union between them – the very toil they endured together, the fact of sleeping in the same quarters and taking exercise in the same courtyard. They were happy, for were they not all the world to each other?

The inspector of the workshop was so hated by the prisoners that he often had recourse to Claude Gueux to enforce his authority; and when a tumult was on the point of breaking out, a few words from Claude had more effect than the authority of ten warders. Although the inspector was glad to avail himself of this influence, he was jealous all the same, and hated the superior prisoner with an envious and implacable feeling – an example of might over right, all the more fearful as it was secretly nourished. But Claude cared so much for Albin that he thought little about the inspector.

One morning as the warders were going their rounds one of them summoned Albin, who was working with Claude, to go before the inspector.

'What are you wanted for?' said Claude.

'I do not know,' replied Albin, following the warder.

All day Claude looked in vain for his companion, and at night, finding him still absent, he broke through his ordinary reserve and addressed the turnkey. 'Is Albin ill?' said he.

'No,' replied the man.

'How is it that he has never put in an appearance today?'

'His quarters have been changed,' was the reply.

For a moment Claude trembled, then calmly continued, 'Who gave the order?'

'Monsieur D——.' This was the inspector's name.

On the following night the inspector, Monsieur D——, went on his rounds as usual. Claude, who had perceived him from the distance, rose, and hastened to raise his woollen cap and button his grey woollen vest to the throat – considered a mark of respect to superiors in prison discipline.

'Sir,' said Claude, as the inspector was about to pass him, 'has Albin really been quartered elsewhere?'

'Yes,' replied the inspector.

'Sir, I cannot live without him. You know the rations are insufficient for me, and Albin divided his portion with me. Could you not manage to let him resume his old place near me?'

'Impossible; the order cannot be revoked.'

'By whom was it given?'

'By me.'

'Monsieur D——,' replied Claude, 'on you my life depends.'

'I never cancel an order once given.'

'Sir, what have I ever done to you?'

'Nothing.'

'Why, then,' cried Claude, 'separate me from Albin?'

'Because I do,' replied the inspector, and with that he passed on.

Claude's head sank down, like the poor caged lion deprived of his dog; but the grief, though so deeply felt, in no way changed his appetite – he was famished. Many offered to share their rations with him, but he steadily refused, and continued his usual routine in silence – breaking it only to ask the inspector daily, in tones of anguish mingled with rage, something between a prayer and a threat, these two words: 'And Albin?'

The inspector simply passed on, shrugging his shoulders; but had he only observed Claude he would have seen the evident change – noticeable to all present – and he would have heard these words, spoken respectfully but firmly:

'Sir, listen to me; send my companion to me. It would be wise to do so, I can assure you. Remember my words!'

On Sunday he had sat for hours in the courtyard, with his head bowed in his hands, and when a prisoner called Faillette came up laughing, Claude said: 'I am judging someone.'

On 25 October, 1831, as the inspector went his rounds, Claude, to draw his attention, smashed a watch-glass he had found in the passage. This had the desired effect.

'It was I,' said Claude. 'Sir, restore my comrade to me.'

'Impossible,' was the answer.

Looking the inspector full in the face, Claude firmly added: 'Now, reflect! Today is the twenty-fifth of October; I give you till the fourth of November.'

A warder remarked that Claude was threatening Monsieur D——, and ought at once to be locked up.

'No, it is not a case of the blackhole,' replied the inspector, smiling disdainfully; 'we must be considerate with people of this stamp.'

The following day Claude was again accosted by one of the prisoners, named Pernot, as he was brooding in the courtyard.

'Well, Claude, you are sad indeed; what are you pondering over?'

'I fear some evil threatens that good Monsieur D——,' answered Claude.

Claude daily impressed the fact on the inspector how much Albin's absence affected him, but with no result save four-and-twenty hours' solitary confinement. On 4 November be looked round his cell for the little that remained to remind him of his former life. A pair of scissors, and an old volume of *Émile*, belonging to the woman he had loved so well, the mother of his child – how useless to a man who could neither work nor read!

As Claude walked down the old cloisters, so dishonoured by its new inmates and its fresh whitewashed walls, he noticed how earnestly the convict Ferrari was looking at the heavy iron bars that crossed the window, and he said to him: 'Tonight I will cut through those bars with these scissors', pointing to the pair he still held in his hand.

Ferrari laughed incredulously, and Claude joined in the mirth. During the day he worked with more than ordinary ardour, wishing to finish a straw hat which he had been paid for in advance by a tradesman at Troyes – Monsieur Bressier.

Shortly before noon he made some excuse to go down into the carpenters' quarters, a storey below his own, at the time the warders were absent. Claude received a hearty welcome, as he was equally popular here as elsewhere.

'Can anyone lend me an axe?' he said.

'What for?'

Without exacting any promises of secrecy he at once replied: 'To kill the inspector with tonight.'

Claude was at once offered several; choosing the smallest, he hid it beneath his waistcoat and left. Now, there were twenty-seven prisoners present, and not one of those men betrayed him; they even refrained from talking upon the subject among themselves, waiting for the terrible event which must follow.

As Claude passed on he saw a young convict of sixteen yawning idly there, and he strongly advised him to learn how to read. Just then Faillette asked what he was hiding.

Claude answered unhesitatingly: 'An axe to kill Monsieur D—— tonight; but can you see it?'

'A little,' said Faillette.

At seven o'clock the prisoners were locked in their several workshops. It was then the custom for the warders to leave them, until the inspector had been on his rounds.

In Claude's workshop a most extraordinary scene took place, the only one of the kind on record. Claude rose and addressed his companions, eighty-one in number, in the following words:

'You all know Albin and I were like brothers. I liked him at first for sharing his rations with me, afterwards because he cared for me. Now I never have sufficient, though I spend the pittance I earn on bread. It could make no possible difference to the inspector, Monsieur D——, that we should be together; but he chose to separate us simply from a love of tormenting, for he is a bad man. I asked again and again for Albin to be sent back, without success; and when I gave him a stated time, the fourth of November, I was thrust into a dungeon. During that time I became his judge, and sentenced him to death on November the fourth. In two hours he will be here, and I warn you I intend to kill him. But have you anything to say?'

There was a dead silence. Claude then continued telling his comrades, the eighty-one thieves, his ideas on the subject – that he was reduced to a fearful extremity, and compelled by that very necessity to take the law into his own hands; that he knew full well he could not take the inspector's life without sacrificing his own, but that as the cause was a just one he would bear the consequences, having come to this conclusion after two months' calm reflection; that if they considered resentment alone hurried him on to such a step they were at once to say so, and to state their objections to the sentence being carried out.

One voice alone broke the silence which followed, saying, 'Before killing the inspector, Claude ought to give him a chance of relenting.'

'That is only fair,' said Claude, 'and he shall have the benefit of the doubt.'

Claude then sorted the few things a poor prisoner is allowed, and gave them to the comrades he mostly cared for after Albin, keeping only the pair of scissors. He then embraced them all – some not being able to withhold their tears at such a moment. Claude continued calmly to converse during this last hour, and even gave way to a trick he had as a boy, of extinguishing the candle with a breath from his nose. Seeing him thus, his companions afterwards admitted that they hoped he had abandoned his sinister idea. One young convict looked at him fixedly, trembling for the coming event.

'Take courage, young fellow,' said Claude, gently; 'it will be but the work of a minute.'

The workshop was a long room with a door at both ends, and with windows each side overlooking the benches, thus leaving a pathway up the centre for the inspector to review the work on both sides of him. Claude had now resumed his work – something like Jacques Clement, who did not fail to repeat his prayers.

As the clock sounded a quarter to nine, Claude rose and placed himself near the entrance, apparently calm. Amidst the most profound silence the clock struck nine; the door was thrown open, and the inspector came in as usual alone, looking quite jovial and self-satisfied, passing rapidly along, tossing his head at one, grinding words out to another, little heeding the eyes fixed so fiercely upon him. Just then he heard Claude's step, and turning quickly round said:

'What are you doing here? Why are you not in your place?' just as he would have spoken to a dog.

Claude answered respectfully, 'I wish to speak to you, sir.'

'On what subject?'

'Albin.'

'Again!'

'Always the same,' said Claude.

'So then', replied the inspector, walking along, 'you have not had enough with twenty-four hours in the black hole.'

Claude, following him closely, replied: 'Sir, return my companion to me!'

'Impossible!'

'Sir,' continued Claude, in a voice which would have moved Satan, 'I implore you to send Albin back to me; you will then see how I will work. You are free, and it would matter but little to you; you do not know the feeling of having only one friend. To me it is everything, encircled by the prison walls. You can come and go at your pleasure; I have but Albin. Pray let him come back to me! You know well he shared his food with me. What can it matter to you that a man named Claude Gueux should be in this hall, having another by his side called Albin? You have but to say "Yes", nothing more. Sir, my good sir, I implore you, in the name of Heaven, to grant my prayer!'

Claude, overcome with emotion, waited for the answer.

'Impossible!' replied the inspector, impatiently; 'I will not recall my words. Now go, you annoyance!' And with that he hurried on towards the outer door, amidst the breathless silence maintained by the eighty-one thieves.

Claude, following and touching the inspector, gently asked: 'Let me at least know why I am condemned to death. Why did you separate us?'

'I have already answered you; because I chose,' replied the inspector.

With that he was about to lift the latch, when Claude raised the axe, and without one cry the inspector fell to the ground, with his skull completely cloven from three heavy blows dealt with the rapidity of lightning. A fourth completely disfigured his face, and Claude, in his mad fury, gave another and a useless blow; for the inspector was dead.

Claude, throwing the axe aside, cried out, 'Now for the other!'

The other was himself; and taking the scissors, *his wife's*, he plunged them into his breast. But the blade was short, and the chest was deep, and vainly he strove to give the fatal blow. At last, covered with blood he fell fainting across the dead. Which of the two would be considered the victim?

When Claude recovered consciousness he was in bed, surrounded by every care and covered with bandages. Near him were Sisters of Charity, and a recorder ready to take down his deposition, who with much interest enquired how he was. Claude had lost a great deal of blood; but the scissors had done him a bad turn, inflicting wounds not one of which was dangerous; the only mortal blows he had struck were on the body of Monsieur D——. Then the interrogatory commenced.

'Did you kill the inspector of the prison workshop at Clairvaux?'

'Yes,' was the reply.

'Why did you do so?'

'Because I did.'

Claude's wounds now assumed a more serious aspect, and he was prostrated with a fever which threatened his life. November, December, January, February passed, in nursing and preparations, and Claude in turn was visited by doctor and judge – the one to restore him to health, the other to glean the evidence needful to send him to the scaffold.

On 16 March, 1832, perfectly cured, Claude appeared in court at Troyes, to answer the charge brought against him. His appearance impressed the court favourably; he had been shaved and stood bare-headed, but still clad in prison garb. The court was well guarded by a strong military guard, to keep the witnesses within bounds, as they were all convicts. But an unexpected difficulty occurred; not one of these men would give evidence; neither questions nor threats availed to make them break their silence, until Claude requested them to do so. Then they in turn gave a faithful account of the terrible event; and if one, from forgetfulness or affection for the accused, failed to relate the whole facts, Claude supplied the deficiency. At one time the women's tears fell fast.

The usher now called the convict Albin. He came in trembling with emotion and sobbing painfully, and threw himself into Claude's arms. Turning to the Public Prosecutor, Claude said:

'Here is a convict who gives his food to the hungry,' and stooping, he kissed Albin's hand.

All the witnesses having been examined, the counsel for the prosecution then rose to address the court. 'Gentlemen of the jury, society would be utterly put to confusion if a public prosecution did not condemn great culprits like him, who, etc.'

After a long address by the prosecution, Claude's counsel rose. Then followed the usual pleading for and against, which ever takes place at the criminal court.

Claude in his turn gave evidence, and everyone was astonished at his intelligence; there appeared far more of the orator about this poor work-man than the assassin. In a clear and straightforward way he detailed the facts as they were – standing proudly there, resolved to tell the whole truth. At times the crowd was carried away by his eloquence. This man, who could not read, would grasp the most difficult points of argument, yet treat the judges with all due deference. Once Claude lost his temper, when the counsel for the prosecution stated that he had assassinated the inspector without provocation.

'What!' cried Claude, 'I had no provocation? Indeed! A drunkard strikes me – I kill him; then you would allow there was provocation, and the penalty of death would be changed for that of the galleys. But a man who wounds me in every way during four years, humiliates me for four years, taunts me daily, hourly, for four years, and heaps every insult on my head – what follows? You consider I have had no provocation! I had a wife for whom I robbed – he tortured me about her. I had a child for whom I robbed – he taunted me about this child. I was hungry, a friend shared his bread with me – he took away my friend. I begged him to return my friend to me – he cast me into a dungeon. I told him how much I suffered – he said it wearied him to listen. What then would you have me do? I took his life; and you look upon me as a monster for killing this man, and you decapitate me; then do so.'

Provocation such as this the law fails to acknowledge, because the blows have no marks to show.

The judge then summed up the case in a clear and impartial manner – dwelling on the life Claude had led, living openly with an improper character; then he had robbed, and ended by being a murderer. All this was true. Before the jury retired, the judge asked Claude if he had any questions to ask, or anything to say.

'Very little,' said Claude. 'I am a murderer, I am a thief; but I ask you, gentlemen of the jury, why did I kill? Why did I steal?'

The jury retired for a quarter of an hour, and according to the judgement of these twelve countrymen – *gentlemen of the jury*, as they are styled – Claude Gueux was condemned to death. At the very outset several of them were much impressed with the name of Gueux (vagabond), and that influenced their decision.

When the verdict was pronounced, Claude simply said: 'Very well; but there are two questions these gentlemen have not answered. Why did this man steal? What made him a murderer?'

He made a good supper that night, exclaiming, 'Thirty-six years have now passed me.' He refused to make any appeal until the last minute, but at the instance of one of the sisters who had nursed him he consented to do so. She in her fullness of heart gave him a five-franc piece.

His fellow-prisoners, as we have already noticed, were devoted to him, and placed all the means at their disposal to help him to escape. They threw into his dungeon, through the air-hole, a nail, some wire, the handle of a pail: any one of these would have been enough for a man

like Claude to free himself from his chains. He gave them all up to the warder.

On 8 June, 1832, seven months and four days after the murder, the recorder of the court came, and Claude was told that he had but one hour more to live, for his appeal had been rejected.

'Indeed,' said Claude, coldly; 'I slept well last night, and doubtless I shall pass my next even better.'

First came the priest, then the executioner. He was humble to the priest, and listened to him with great attention, regretting much that he had not had the benefit of religious training, at the same time blaming himself for much in the past.

He was courteous in his manner to the executioner; in fact he gave up all – his soul to the priest, his body to the executioner.

While his hair was being cut, someone mentioned how the cholera was spreading, and Troyes at any moment might become a prey to this fearful scourge. Claude joined in the conversation, saying, with a smile, 'There is one thing to be said – I have no fear of the cholera!' He had broken half of the scissors – what remained he asked the gaoler to give to Albin; the other half lay buried in his chest. He also wished the day's rations to be taken to his friend. The only trifle he retained was the five-franc piece that the sister had given him, which he kept in his right hand after he was bound.

At a quarter to eight, the dismal procession usual in such cases left the prison. Pale, but with a firm tread, Claude Gueux slowly mounted the scaffold, keeping his eyes fixed on the crucifix the priest carried – an emblem of the Saviour's suffering. He wished to embrace the priest and the executioner, thanking the one and pardoning the other; the executioner simply repulsed him. Just before he was bound to the infernal machine, he gave the five-franc piece to the priest, saying, 'For the poor.'

The hour had scarcely struck its eight chimes, when this man, so noble, so intelligent, received the fatal blow which severed his head from his body.

A market-day had been chosen for the time of execution, as there would be more people about, for there are still in France small towns that glory in having an execution. The guillotine that day remained, inflaming the imagination of the mob to such an extent that one of the tax-gatherers was nearly murdered. Such is the admirable effect of public executions!

*

We have given the history of Claude Gueux's life, more to solve a difficult problem than for aught else. In his life there are two questions to be
considered – before his fall, and after his fall. What was his training, and
what was the penalty? This must interest society generally; for this man
was well gifted, his instincts were good. Then what was wanting? On
this revolves the grand problem which would place society on a firm
basis.

What nature has begun in the individual, let society carry out. Look at
Claude Gueux. An intelligent and most noble-hearted man, placed in
the midst of evil surroundings, he turned thief. Society placed him in a
prison where the evil was yet greater, and he ended with becoming a
murderer. Can we really blame him, or ourselves? – questions which
require deep thought, or the result will be that we shall be compelled to
shirk this most important subject. The facts are now before us, and if the
government gives no thought to the matter, what are the rulers about?

The Deputies are yearly much occupied. It is important to shift
sinecures and to unravel the budget; to pass an Act which compels me,
disguised as a soldier, to mount guard at the Count de Lobau's, whom I
do not know, and to whom I wish to remain a stranger, or to go on
parade under the command of my grocer, who has been made an officer.
I wish to cast no reflections on the patrol, who keep order and protect
our homes, but on the absurdity of making such parade and military
hubbub about turning citizens into parodies of soldiers.

Deputies or ministers! it is important that we should sound every
subject, even though it end in nothing; that we should question and
cross-question what we know but little about. Rulers and legislators!
you pass your time in classical comparisons that would make a village
schoolmaster smile. You assert that it is the habits of modern civilisation
that have engendered adultery, incest, parricide, infanticide, and
poisoning – proving that you know little of Jocasta, Phaedra, Oedipus,
Medea, or Rodoguna. The great orators occupy themselves with
lengthy discussions on Corneille and Racine, and get so heated in literary argument as to make the grossest mistakes in the French language.
Very important indeed all this is, but we consider there are subjects of
far greater consequence. In the midst of such useless arguments, what
answer would the Deputies give if one rose and gravely addressed them
in the following words:

'Silence, all those who have been speaking! silence, I say! You consider yourself acquainted with the question? You know nothing about it.

The question is this: In the name of justice, scarcely a year ago, a man at Panners was cut to pieces; at Dijon a woman's head was taken off; in Paris, at St Jacques, executions take place without number. This is the question! Now take your time to consider it, and you who argue over the buttons of the National Guards, whether they should be white or yellow, and if *security* is preferable to *certainty*!

'Gentlemen of the Right, gentlemen of the Left, the great mass of the people suffer! Whether a republic or a monarchy, the fact remains the same – the people suffer! The people are famished, the people are frozen. Such misery leads them on to crime: the galleys take the sons, houses of ill-fame the daughters. You have too many convicts, too many unfortunates.

'What is the meaning of this social gangrene? You are near the patient: treat the malady. You are at fault: now study the matter more deeply.

'When you pass laws, what are they but expedients and palliatives? Half your codes result from routine.

'Branding but cauterises the wound, and it mortifies, and what is the end? You stamp the crime for life on the criminal; you make two friends of them, two companions – inseparables. The convict prison is a blister which spreads far worse matter than ever it extracts; and as for the sentence of death, when carried out it is a barbarous amputation. Therefore branding, penal servitude, and sentence of death are all of one class; you have done away with the branding, banish the rest. Why keep the chain and the chopper now you have put aside the hot iron? Farinace was atrocious, but he was not ridiculous.

'Take down that worn ladder that leads to crime and to suffering. Revise your laws; revise your codes; rebuild your prisons; replace your judges. Make laws suited to the present time.

'You are bent on economy; do not be so lavish in taking off the heads of so many during the year. Suppress the executioner; you could defray the expenses of six hundred schoolmasters with the wages you give your eighty executioners. Think of the multitude; then there would be schools for the children, workshops for the men.

'Do you know that in France there are fewer people who know how to read than in any other country in Europe? Fancy, Switzerland can read, Belgium can read, Denmark can read, Greece can read, Ireland can read – and France cannot read! It is a crying evil.

'Go into your convict prisons, examine each one of these condemned men, and you will observe by the profile, the shape of the head, how many could find their type in the lower animals. Here are the lynx, the cat, the monkey, the vulture, the hyena. Nature was first to blame, no doubt: but the want of training fostered the evil. Then give the people a fair education, and what there is of good in these ill-conditioned minds, let that be developed. People must be judged by their opportunities. Rome and Greece were educated: then brighten the people's intellect.

'When France can read, then give the people encouragement for higher things. Ignorance is preferable to a little ill-directed knowledge; and remember, there is a book of far greater importance than the *Compère Mathieu*, more popular than the *Constitutionnel*, and more worthy of perusal than the charter of 1830 – that is the Bible.

'Whatever you may do for the people, the majority will always remain poor and unhappy. Theirs the work, the heavy burden to carry, to endure; all the miseries for the poor, all the pleasures for the rich.

'As such is life, ought not the State to lean to the weaker and helpless side?

'In the midst of all this wretchedness, if you but throw hope in the balance, let the poor man learn there is a heaven where joy reigns, a paradise that he can share, and you raise him; he feels that he has a part in the rich man's joy. And this was the teaching Jesus gave, and He knew more about it than Voltaire.

'Then give to those people who work and who suffer here the hope of a different world to come, and they will go on patiently; for patience follows in the footsteps of hope.

'Then spread the Gospel in all our villages, let every cottage have its Bible; the seed thus sown will soon circulate. Encourage virtue, and from that will spring so much that now lies fallow.

'The man turned assassin under certain circumstances, if differently influenced would have served his country well.

'Then give the people all encouragement; improve the masses, enlighten them, guard their morals, make them useful, and to such heads as those you will not require to use cold steel.'

Prosper Mérimée

Prosper Mérimée (1803–70) is best remembered as the author of the tale *Carmen* (1847), which Bizet transformed into something rather less acerbic in his opera. Its themes of passion, crime and violence are typical of the work of this writer of Romantic fiction who was a close friend of Stendhal and Turgenev. Mérimée worked as an inspector of historical monuments (doing much for the preservation of Avignon), and much of his literary output has a historical flavour, notably the violent play *La Jacquerie* (1828), his reworking of the Cenci tale, *La Famille de Carvajal* (1828), and his *Chronique du règne de Charles IX* (1829), a novel inspired by Scott which recounts the St Bartholomew's Day Massacre of 1572. The evocation of suspicion, betrayal and death in 'The Etruscan Vase', which appeared in the collection *Mosaïque* (1833), is typical of Mérimée's blend of tragedy and irony.

The Etruscan Vase

AUGUSTE SAINT-CLAIR WAS NOT AT ALL A FAVOURITE IN society, the chief reason being that he only cared to please those who took his own fancy. He avoided the former and sought after the latter. In other respects he was absent-minded and indolent. One evening, on coming out of the Italian Opera, the Marquise A—— asked him his opinion on the singing of Mademoiselle Sontag. 'Yes, Madame,' Saint-Clair replied, smiling pleasantly, and thinking of something totally different. This ridiculous reply could not be set down to shyness, for he talked with great lords and noted men and women and even with Society women with as much ease as though he were their equal. The Marquise put down Saint-Clair as a stupid, impertinent boor.

One Monday he had an invitation to dine with Madame B——. She paid him a good deal of attention, and on leaving her house, he remarked that he had never met a more agreeable woman. Madame B—— spent a month collecting witticisms at other people's houses, which she dispensed in one evening at her own. Saint-Clair called upon her again on the Thursday of the same week. This time he grew a little tired of her. Another visit decided him never to enter her salon again. Madame B—— let it be known that Saint-Clair was an ill-bred young man, and not good form.

He was naturally tender-hearted and affectionate, but at an age when lasting impressions are taken too easily. His too demonstrative nature had drawn upon him the sarcasm of his comrades. He was proud and ambitious, and stuck to his opinion like an obstinate child. Henceforth he made a point of hiding any outward sign of what might seem discreditable weakness. He attained his end, but the victory cost him dear. He learned to hide his softer feelings from others, but the repression only increased their force a hundredfold. In Society he bore the sorry reputation of being heartless and indifferent; and, when alone, his restless imagination conjured up hideous torments – all the worse because unshared.

How difficult it is to find a friend! Difficult! Is it possible to find two men anywhere who have not a secret from each other? That Saint-Clair had little faith in friendship was easily seen. With young Society people his manner was cold and reserved. He asked no questions about their secrets; and most of his actions and all his thoughts were mysteries to them. A Frenchman loves to talk of himself; therefore Saint-Clair was the unwilling recipient of many confidences. His friends – that is to say, those whom he saw about twice a week – complained of his indifference to their confidences. They felt that indiscretion should be reciprocal; for, indeed, he who confides his secret to us unasked generally takes offence at not learning ours in return.

'He keeps his thoughts to himself,' grumbled Alphonse de Thémines one day.

'I could never place the least confidence in that deuced Saint-Clair,' added the smart colonel.

'I think he is half a Jesuit,' replied Jules Lambert. 'Someone swore to me that he had met him twice coming out of Saint-Sulpice. Nobody knows what he thinks about. I must say I never feel at ease with him.'

They separated. Alphonse encountered Saint-Clair in the Boulevard Italien. He was walking with his eyes on the ground, not noticing anyone. Alphonse stopped him, took his arm, and, before they had reached the Rue de la Paix, he had related to him the whole history of his love affair with Madame——, whose husband was so jealous and so violent.

The same evening Jules Lambert lost his money at cards. After that he thought he had better go and dance. While dancing, he accidentally knocked against a man, who had also lost his money and was in a very bad temper. Sharp words followed, and a challenge was given and taken. Jules begged Saint-Clair to act as his second, and, at the same time, borrowed money from him, which he was never likely to return.

After all, Saint-Clair was easy enough to live with. He was no one's enemy but his own; he was obliging, often genial, rarely tiresome; he had travelled much and read much, but never obtruded his knowledge or his experiences unasked. In personal appearance he was tall and well made; he had a dignified and refined expression – almost always too grave, but his smile was pleasing and very attractive.

I am forgetting one important point. Saint-Clair paid attention to all women, and sought their society more than that of men. It was difficult to say whether he was in love; but if this reserved being felt love, the beautiful Countess Mathilde de Coursy was the woman of his choice.

She was a young widow, at whose house he was often seen. To prove their friendship there was the evidence first of the almost exaggerated politeness of Saint-Clair towards the Countess, and vice versa; then his habit of never pronouncing her name in public, or if obliged to speak of her, never with the slightest praise; also, before Saint-Clair was introduced to her, he had been passionately fond of music, and the Countess equally so of painting. Since they had become acquainted their tastes had changed. Lastly, when the Countess visited a health resort the previous year, Saint-Clair followed her in less than a week.

My duty as novelist obliges me to reveal that early one morning in the month of July, a few moments before sunrise, the garden gate of a country house opened, and a man crept out with the stealthiness of a burglar fearing discovery. This country house belonged to Madame de Coursy, and the man was Saint-Clair. A woman, muffled in a cape, came to the gate with him, stood with her head out and watched him as long as she could, until he was far along the path which led by the park wall. Saint-Clair stopped, looked round cautiously, and signed with his hand for the woman to go in. The clearness of a summer dawn enabled him to distinguish her pale face. She stood motionless where he had left her. He went back to her, and took her tenderly in his arms. He meant to compel her to go in; but he had still a hundred things to say to her. Their conversation lasted ten minutes, till at last they heard the voice of a peasant going to his work in the fields. One more kiss passed between them, the gate was shut, and Saint-Clair with a bound reached the end of the footpath. He followed a track evidently well known to him, and ran along, striking the bushes with his stick and almost jumping for joy. Sometimes he stopped, or sauntered slowly, looking at the sky, which was flushed in the east with purple. In fact, anyone meeting him would have taken him for an escaped lunatic. After half an hour's walk he reached the door of a lonely little house which he had rented for the season. He let himself in with a key, and then, throwing himself on the couch, he fell into a daydream, with vacant eyes and a happy smile playing on his lips. His mind was filled with bright reflections. 'How happy I am!' he kept repeating. 'At last I have met a heart that understands mine . . . Yes, I have found my ideal . . . I have gained at the same time a friend and a lover . . . What depth of soul! . . . What character! . . . No, she has never loved anyone before me.' How soon vanity creeps into human affairs! 'She is the loveliest woman in Paris,' he thought, and his imagination conjured up all her charms. 'She has chosen me before all the others. She had the flower of Society at her feet. That colonel of hussars, gallant, good-looking and not too stout; that young author, who paints in water-colours so well, and who is such a capital actor; that Russian, Lovelace, who has been in the Balkan campaign and served under Diébitch; above all, Camille T——, who is brilliantly clever, has good manners and a fine sabre-cut across his forehead . . . She has dismissed them all for me! . . .' Then came the refrain – 'Oh, how happy I am! how happy I am!' – and he got up and opened the window, for he could scarcely breathe. First he walked about; then he tossed on his couch.

A happy lover is almost as tedious as an unhappy one. One of my friends, who is generally in one or other of these conditions, found that the only way of getting any attention was to give me an excellent break-fast, over which he could unburden himself on the subject of his amours. When the coffee was finished he was obliged to choose a totally different topic of conversation.

As I cannot give breakfast to all my readers, I make them a present of Saint-Clair's ecstasies. Besides, it is impossible always to live in cloud-land. Saint-Clair was tired; he yawned, stretched his arms, saw that it was broad day and at last slept. When he awoke he saw by his watch that he had hardly time to dress and rush off to Paris, to attend a luncheon party of several of his young friends.

They had just uncorked another bottle of champagne. I leave my readers to guess how many had preceded it. It is sufficient to know that they had reached that stage which comes quickly enough at a young men's dinner party, when everybody speaks at once, and when the steady heads get anxious for those who cannot carry so much.

'I wish,' said Alphonse de Thémines, who had never missed a chance of talking about England – 'I wish that it was the custom in Paris, as it is in London, for each one to propose a toast to his mistress. If it were, we should find out for whom our friend Saint-Clair sighs.' And, while uttering these words, he filled up his own glass and those of his neighbours.

Saint-Clair felt slightly embarrassed, but was about to reply when Jules Lambert prevented him.

'I heartily approve this custom,' he said, raising his glass; 'and I adopt it. To all the milliners of Paris, with the exception of those past thirty, the one-eyed and the lame.'

'Hurrah! hurrah!' shouted the Anglomaniacs. Saint-Clair rose, glass in hand.

'Gentlemen,' said he, 'I have not such a large heart as has our friend Jules, but it is more constant – a constancy all the more faithful since I have been long separated from the lady of my thoughts. Nevertheless I am sure that you will approve of my choice, even if you are not already my rivals. To Judith Pasta, gentlemen! May we soon welcome back the first *tragédienne* of Europe.'

Thémines was about to criticise the toast, but was interrupted by acclamation. Saint-Clair, having parried this thrust, believed himself safe for the rest of the day.

The conversation turned first on theatres. From the criticism of drama they wandered to political topics. From the Duke of Wellington they passed to English horses. From English horses to women, by a natural connection of ideas; for, to young men, a good horse first, and then a beautiful mistress, are the two most desirable objects.

Then they discussed the means of acquiring these coveted treasures. Horses are bought, women also are bought; only we do not so talk of them. Saint-Clair, after modestly pleading inexperience in this delicate subject, gave as his opinion that the chief way to please a woman is to be singular, to be different from others. But he did not think it possible to give a general prescription for singularity.

'According to your view,' said Jules, 'a lame or humpbacked man would have a better chance of pleasing than one of ordinary make.'

'You push things too far,' retorted Saint-Clair, 'but I am willing to accept all the consequences of my proposition. For example, if I were humpbacked, instead of blowing out my brains I would make conquests. In the first place, I would try my wiles on those who are generally tender-hearted; then on those women – and there are many of them – who set up for being original – eccentric, as they say in England. To begin with, I should describe my pitiful condition, and point out that I was the victim of Nature's cruelty. I should try to move them to sympathy with my lot, I should let them suspect that I was capable of a passionate love. I should kill one of my rivals in a duel, and I should pretend to poison myself with a feeble dose of laudanum. After a few months they would not notice my deformity, and then I should be on the watch for the first signs of affection. With women who aspire to originality, conquest is easy. Only persuade them that it is a hard-and-fast rule that a deformed person can never have a love-affair, they will immediately then wish to prove the opposite.'

'What a Don Juan!' cried Jules.

'As we have not had the misfortune of being born deformed,' said Colonel Beaujeu, 'we had better get our legs broken, gentlemen.'

'I fully agree with Saint-Clair,' said Hector Roquantin, who was only three and a half feet high. 'We constantly see beautiful and fashionable women giving themselves to men whom you fine fellows would never dream of.'

'Hector, just ring the bell for another bottle, will you?' said Thémines casually.

The dwarf got up and everyone smiled, recalling the fable of the fox without a tail.

'As for me,' said Thémines, renewing the conversation, 'the longer I live, the more clearly I see that the chief singularity which attracts even the most obdurate, is passable features' – and he threw a complaisant glance in a mirror opposite – 'passable features and good taste in dress,' and he filliped a crumb of bread off his coat.

'Bah!' cried the dwarf, 'with good looks and a coat by Staub, there are plenty of women to be had for a week at a time, but we should be tired of them at the second meeting. More than that is needed to win what is called love . . . You must . . .'

'Stop!' interrupted Thémines. 'Do you want an apt illustration? You all know what kind of man Massigny was. Manners like an English groom, and no more conversation than his horse . . . But he was as handsome as Adonis, and could tie his cravat like Brummel. Altogether he was the greatest bore I have ever met.'

'He almost killed me with weariness,' said Colonel Beaujeu. 'Only think, I once had to travel two hundred leagues with him!'

'Did you know', asked Saint-Clair, 'that he caused the death of poor Richard Thornton, whom you all knew?'

'But', objected Jules, 'I thought he was assassinated by brigands near Fondi?'

'Granted; but Massigny was at all events an accomplice in the crime. A party of travellers, Thornton among them, had arranged to go to Naples together to avoid attacks from brigands. Massigny asked to be allowed to join them. As soon as Thornton heard this, he set out before the others, apparently to avoid being long with Massigny. He started alone, and you know the rest.'

'Thornton took the only course,' said Thémines; 'he chose the

easiest of two deaths. We should all have done the same in his place.'
Then, after a pause, 'You grant me', he went on, 'that Massigny was the
greatest bore on earth?'

'Certainly,' they all cried with one accord.

'Don't let us despair,' said Jules; 'let us make an exception in favour
of —— especially when he divulges his political intrigues.'

'You will next grant me', continued Thémines, 'that Madame de
Coursy is as clever a woman as can be found anywhere.'

A moment's silence followed. Saint-Clair looked down and fancied
that all eyes were fixed on himself.

'Who disputes it?' he said at length, still bending over his plate
apparently to examine more closely the flowers painted on the china.

'I maintain,' said Jules, raising his voice – 'I maintain that she is one
of the three most fascinating women in Paris.'

'I knew her husband,' said the Colonel, 'he often showed me her
charming letters.'

'Auguste,' interrupted Hector Roquantin, 'do introduce me to the
Countess. They say you can do anything with her.'

'When she returns to Paris at the end of autumn . . .' murmured
Saint-Clair, 'I – I believe she does not entertain visitors in the country.'

'Will you listen to me?' exclaimed Thémines.

Silence was restored. Saint-Clair fidgeted upon his chair like a
prisoner before his judges.

'You did not know the Countess three years ago because you were
then in Germany, Saint-Clair,' went on Alphonse de Thémines, with
aggravating coolness. 'You cannot form any idea, therefore, of her as she
was then; lovely, with the freshness of a rose, and as light-hearted and
gay as a butterfly. Perhaps you do not know that among all her many
admirers Massigny was the one she honoured with her favours? The
most stupid and ridiculous of men turned the head of the most fascinating amongst women. Do you suppose that a deformed person could
have done as much? Nonsense; believe me, with a good figure and a first-
rate tailor, only boldness in addition is needed.'

Saint-Clair was in a most awkward position. He longed to fling back
the lie direct in the speaker's face, but was restrained from fear of compromising the Countess. He would have liked to have said something to
defend her, but he was tongue-tied. His lips trembled with rage, and he
tried to find some indirect means of forcing a quarrel, but could not.

'What,' exclaimed Jules, with astonishment, 'Madame de Coursy gave herself to Massigny? Frailty, thy name is woman!'

'The reputation of a woman being of such small moment, it is, of course, allowable to pull it to pieces for the sake of a little sport,' observed Saint-Clair in a dry and scornful tone, 'and—'

But as he spoke he remembered with dismay a certain Etruscan vase that he had noticed a hundred times upon the mantelpiece in the Countess's house in Paris. He knew that it was a gift from Massigny, who had brought it back with him from Italy; and – overwhelming coincidence! – it had been taken by the Countess from Paris to her country house. Every evening when Mathilde took the flowers out of her dress she put them in this Etruscan vase.

Speech died upon his lips. He could neither see nor think of anything but that Etruscan vase.

'How absurd', cries a critic, 'to suspect his mistress from such a trifle!'

'Have you ever been in love, my dear critic?'

Thémines was in too good a humour to take offence at the tone Saint-Clair had used when speaking to him, and replied lightly and with great good nature:

'I can only repeat what I heard in Society. It passed as a true story while you were in Germany. However, I scarcely know Madame de Coursy. It is eighteen months since I was at her house. Very likely I am wrong, and the story was a fabrication of Massigny's. But let us return to our discussion, for whether my illustration be false or not does not affect my point. You all know that the cleverest woman in France, whose works—'

The door opened, and Théodore Néville came in. He had just returned from Egypt.

'Théodore, you have soon come back!' He was overwhelmed with questions.

'Have you brought back a real Turkish costume?' asked Thémines. 'Have you got an Arabian horse and an Egyptian groom?'

'What sort of man is the Pasha?' said Jules. 'When will he make himself independent? Have you seen a head cut off with a single stroke of the sabre?'

'And the *almées*,' said Roquantin. 'Are the Cairo women beautiful?'

'Did you meet General L——?' asked Colonel Beaujeu. 'Has he organised the army of the Pasha? Did Colonel C—— give you a sword for me?'

'And the Pyramids? The cataracts of the Nile? And the statue of Memnon? Ibrahim Pasha?' etc. They all talked at once; Saint-Clair only brooded on the Etruscan vase.

Théodore sat cross-legged. He had learned that habit in Egypt, and did not wish to lose it in France. He waited till his questioners were tired, and then spoke as fast as he could to save himself from being easily interrupted.

'The Pyramids! upon my word they are a regular humbug. They are not so high as I expected. Strasbourg Cathedral is only four yards lower. I passed by the antiquities. Do not talk to me about them. The very sight of hieroglyphics makes me faint. There are plenty of travellers who worry themselves over these things! My object was to study the nature and manners of all the strange people that jostle against each other in the streets of Alexandria and of Cairo. Turks, Bedouins, Copts, Fellahs, Maghrebins. I drew up a few hasty notes when I was in the quarantine hospital. What infamous places they are! I hope none of you fellows are nervous about infection! I smoked my pipe calmly in the midst of three hundred plague-stricken people. Ah! Colonel, you would admire the well-mounted cavalry out there. I must show you some superb weapons that I have brought back. I have a *djerid* which belonged to a famous Mourad Bey. I have a *yataghan* for you, Colonel, and a *khandjar* for Auguste. You must see my *metchlâ* and *bournous* and *hhaick*. Do you know I could have brought back any number of women with me? Ibrahim Pasha has such numbers imported from Greece that they can be had for nothing . . . But I had to think of my mother's feelings . . . I talked much with the Pasha. He is a thoroughly intelligent and unprejudiced man. You would hardly credit it, but he knows everything about our affairs. Upon my honour, he knows the smallest secrets of our Cabinet. I gleaned much valuable information from him on the state of parties in France . . . Just now he is taken up with statistics. He subscribes to all our papers. Would you believe it? – he is a pronounced Bonapartist, and talks of nothing but Napoleon. "Ah! what a great man *Bounabardo* was!" he said to me; "Bounabardo", that is how he pronounces Bonaparte.'

'Giourdina, meaning Jourdain,' murmured Thémines.

'At first', continued Théodore, 'Mohamed Ali was extremely reserved with me. All the Turks are very suspicious, you know, and he took me for a spy or a Jesuit, the devil he did! He had a perfect horror of Jesuits. But, after several visits, he recognised that I was an unprejudiced traveller, anxious to inform myself at firsthand of Eastern manners, customs and politics. Then he unbosomed himself and spoke freely to me. At the third and last audience he granted me I ventured to ask His Excellency why he did not make himself independent of the Porte. "By Allah!" he replied, "I wish it indeed, but I fear the Liberal papers which govern your country would not support me if I proclaimed the independence of Egypt." He is a fine old man, with a long white beard. He never smiles. He gave us some first-rate confections; but the gift that pleased him most of all I offered him was a collection of costumes of the Imperial Guard by Charlet.'

'Is the Pasha of a romantic turn of mind?' asked Thémines.

'He does not trouble himself much about literature; but you know, of course, that Arabian literature is entirely romantic. They have a poet called Melek Ayatalnefous-Ebn-Esraf, who has recently published a book of Meditations, compared with which Lamartine's read like classic prose. I took lessons in Arabic directly I got to Cairo, in order to read the Koran. I did not need to have many lessons before I was able to judge of the supreme beauty of the prophet's style, and of the baldness of all our translations. Look here, would you like to see Arabian handwriting? This word in gold letters is *Allah*, which means God.'

As he spoke he showed them a very dirty letter, which he took out of a scented silk purse.

'How long were you in Egypt?' asked Thémines.

'Six weeks.'

And the traveller proceeded to hold forth on everything from beginning to end. Saint-Clair left soon after his arrival, and went in the direction of his country house. The impetuous gallop of his horse prevented him from thinking logically, but he felt vaguely that his happiness in life had gone for ever, and that it had been shattered by a dead man and an Etruscan vase.

After reaching home he threw himself on the same couch upon which he had dreamed for so long and so deliciously, and analysed his happiness the evening before. His most cherished dream had been that his mistress was different from other women, that she had not loved nor ever would love anyone but himself. Now this exquisite dream must perish in the light of a sad and cruel reality. 'I have had a beautiful mistress, but nothing more. She is clever; she is therefore all the more to be blamed for loving Massigny! . . . I know she does love me now . . . with her whole soul . . . as she can love. But to be loved in the same fashion as

Massigny has been loved! . . . She has yielded herself up to my attentions, my importunities, my whims. But I have been deceived. There
has been no sympathy between us. Whether her lover were Massigny or
myself was equally the same to her. He is handsome, and she loves him
for his good looks. She amuses herself with me for a time. "I may as well
love Saint-Clair", she says to herself, "since the other is dead! And if
Saint-Clair dies, or I tire of him, who knows?"

'I firmly believe the Devil listens invisible behind a tortured wretch
like myself. The enemy of mankind is tickled by the spectacle, and as soon
as the victim's wounds begin to heal, the Devil is waiting to reopen them.'

Saint-Clair thought he heard a voice murmur in his ears:

> *The peculiar honour*
> *Of being the successor . . .'*

He sat up on the couch and threw a savage glance round him. How
glad he would have been to find someone in his room! He would have
torn him limb from limb without any hesitation.

The clock struck eight. At eight-thirty the Countess expected him.
Should he disappoint her? Why, indeed, should he ever see Massigny's
mistress again? He lay down again on the couch and shut his eyes. 'I will
try to sleep,' he said. He lay still for half a minute, then he leapt to his feet
and ran to the clock to see how the time was going. 'How I wish it were
half past eight!' he thought. 'It would be too late then for me to start.' If
only he were taken ill. He had not the courage to stop at home unless he
had an excuse. He walked up and down his room, then he sat down and
took a book, but he could not read a syllable. He sat down in front of his
piano, but had not enough energy to open it. He whistled; then he looked
out of his window at the clouds, and tried to count the poplars. At length
he looked at the clock again, and saw that he had not succeeded in
whiling away more than three minutes. 'I cannot help loving her,' he
burst out, grinding his teeth and stamping his feet. 'She rules me, and I
am her slave, just as Massigny was before me. Well, since you have not
sufficient courage to break the hated chain, poor wretch, you must obey.'

He picked up his hat and rushed out.

When we are carried away by a great passion it is some consolation to
our self-love to look down from the height of pride upon our weakness.
'I certainly am weak,' he said to himself; 'but what if I wish to be so?'

As he walked slowly up the footpath which led to the garden gate, he could see in the distance a white face standing out against the dark background of trees. She beckoned to him with her handkerchief. His heart beat violently, and his knees trembled under him; he could not speak, and he had become so nervous that he feared lest the Countess should read his ill-humour.

He took the hand she held out to him, and kissed her brow, because she threw herself into his arms. He followed her into her sitting-room in silence, though scarce able to suppress his bursting sighs.

A single candle lighted the Countess's room. They sat down, and Saint-Clair noticed his friend's coiffure; a single rose was in her hair. He had given her, the previous evening, a beautiful English engraving of Leslie's *Duchess of Portland* (whose hair was dressed in the same fashion), and Saint-Clair had merely remarked to the Countess, 'I like that single rose better than all your elaborate coiffures.' He did not like jewels, and inclined to the opinion of a noble lord who once remarked coarsely, 'The Devil has nothing left to teach women who overdress themselves and coil their hair fantastically.' The night before, while playing with the Countess's pearl necklace (he always would have something between his hands when talking), Saint-Clair had said, 'You are too pretty, Mathilde, to wear jewels; they are only meant to hide defects.' Tonight the Countess had stripped herself of rings, necklaces, earrings and bracelets, for she stored up his most trivial remarks. He noticed, above everything else in a woman's toilet, the shoes she wore; and, like many other men, he was quite mad on this point. A heavy shower had fallen at sunset, and the grass was still very wet; in spite of this, the Countess walked on the damp lawn in silk stockings and black satin slippers . . . Suppose she were to take cold?

'She loves me,' said Saint-Clair to himself.

He sighed at his folly, but smiled at Mathilde in spite of himself, tossed between his sorry mood and the gratification of seeing a pretty woman, who had sought, by those trifles which have such priceless value in the eyes of lovers, to please him.

The Countess was radiant with love, playfully mischievous and bewitchingly charming. She took something from a Japanese lacquered box and held it out to him in her little, firmly closed hand.

'I broke your watch the other night,' she said; 'here it is, mended.'

She handed the watch to him and looked at him tenderly, and yet mischievously, biting her lower lip as though to prevent herself from laughing. Oh, what beautiful white teeth she had! and how they gleamed

against the ruby red of her lips! (A man looks exceedingly foolish when he is being teased by a pretty woman, and replies coldly.)

Saint-Clair thanked her, took the watch and was about to put it in his pocket.

'Look at it and open it,' she continued. 'See if it is mended all right. You, who are so learned, you, who have been to the Polytechnic School, ought to be able to tell that.'

'Oh, I didn't learn much there,' said Saint-Clair.

He opened the case in an absent-minded way, and what was his surprise to find a miniature portrait of Madame de Coursy painted on the interior of the case? How could he sulk any longer? His brow cleared; he thought no longer of Massigny; he only remembered that he was by the side of a beautiful woman, and that this woman loved him.

'The lark, that harbinger of dawn' began to sing, and long bands of pale light stretched across the eastern clouds. At such an hour did Romeo say farewell to Juliet, and it is the classic hour when all lovers should part.

Saint-Clair stood before a mantelpiece, the key of the garden gate in his hand, his eyes intently fixed on the Etruscan vase, of which we have already spoken. In the depths of his soul he still bore it a grudge, although he was in a much better humour. The simple explanation occurred to his mind that Thémines might have lied about it. While the Countess was wrapping a shawl round her head in order to go to the garden gate with him he began to tap the detested vase with the key, at first gently, then gradually increasing the force of his blows until it seemed as though he would soon smash it to atoms.

'Oh, do be careful!' Mathilde exclaimed. 'You will break my beautiful Etruscan vase!'

She snatched the key out of his hands.

Saint-Clair was very angry, but he resigned himself and turned his back on the chimney-piece to avoid temptation. Opening his watch, he began to examine the portrait that had just been given him.

'Who painted it?' he asked.

'Monsieur R——, and it was Massigny who introduced him to my notice. (After Massigny had been in Rome he discovered that he had exquisite taste in art, and constituted himself the Maecenas of all young painters.) I really think the portrait is like me, though it is a little too flattering.'

Saint-Clair had a burning desire to fling the watch against the wall, to break it beyond all hope of mending. He controlled himself, however, and put the watch in his pocket. Then he noticed that it was daylight, and, entreating Mathilde not to come out with him, he left the house and crossed the garden with rapid strides, and was soon alone in the country.

'Massigny! Massigny!' he burst forth with concentrated rage. 'Can I never escape him? . . . No doubt the artist who painted this portrait painted another for Massigny . . . What a fool I am to imagine for a moment that I am loved with a love equal to my own! . . . just because she put aside her jewels and wore a rose in her hair! . . . Jewels! why, she has a chest full . . . Massigny, who thought of little else save a woman's *toilette*, was a lover of jewellery! . . . Yes, she has a gracious nature, it must be granted; she knows how to gratify the tastes of her lovers. Damn it! I would rather a hundred times that she were a courtesan and gave herself for money. Just because she was my mistress and unpaid I thought she loved me indeed.'

Soon another still more unhappy idea presented itself. In a few weeks' time the Countess would be out of mourning, and Saint-Clair had promised to marry her as soon as her year of widowhood was over. He had promised. Promised? No. He had never spoken of it, but such had been his intention and the Countess had understood it so. But for him this was as good as an oath. Last night he would have given a throne to hasten the time for acknowledging his love publicly; now the very thought of marrying the former mistress of Massigny filled him with loathing.

'Nevertheless, I owe it to her to marry her,' he said to himself, 'and it shall be done. No doubt she thinks, poor woman, I heard all about her former *liaison*; it seems to have been generally known. Besides, she did not then know me . . . She cannot understand me; she thinks that I am only such another lover as Massigny.'

Then he said to himself, and not without a certain pride:

'For three months she has made me the happiest man living; such happiness is worth the sacrifice of my life.'

He did not go to bed, but rode about among the woods the whole of the morning. In one of the pathways of the woods of Verrières he saw a man mounted on a fine English horse, who called him immediately by his name while he was still far off. It was Alphonse de Thémines. To a man in Saint-Clair's state of mind solitude is particularly desirable, and this encounter with Thémines changed his bad humour into a furious temper. Thémines did not notice his mood, or perhaps took a wicked pleasure in thwarting it. He talked and laughed and joked without noticing that he did not receive any response. Saint-Clair soon tried to turn his horse aside into a narrow track, hoping the bore would not follow him; but it was of no use, bores do not leave their prey so easily. Thémines pulled the bridle in the same direction, increased his horse's pace to keep by Saint-Clair's side and complacently continued the conversation.

I have said that the path was a narrow one. The two horses could hardly walk abreast. It was not, therefore, to be wondered at that even so good a horseman as Thémines should graze against Saint-Clair's foot as he walked along with him. This put the finishing touch to his anger, and he could not contain himself any longer. He rose in his stirrups and struck Thémines' horse sharply across the nose with his whip.

'What the devil is the matter with you, Auguste?' cried Thémines. 'Why do you strike my horse?'

'Why do you pursue me?' roared Saint-Clair.

'Have you lost your senses, Saint-Clair? You forget to whom you are talking.'

'I know quite well that I am talking to a puppy.'

'Saint-Clair! . . . you must be mad, I think . . . Listen to me. Tomorrow you will either apologise to me, or you will account for your insolent conduct.'

'Tomorrow, then, sir—'

Thémines stopped his horse; Saint-Clair pushed his on, and very soon disappeared among the trees.

He was calmer now. He was silly enough to believe in presentiments. He felt sure he would be killed on the morrow, and that would be a suitable ending to his condition. Only one more day of anxieties and torments to endure. He went home and sent a note by his servant to Colonel Beaujeu. He wrote several letters, after which he dined with a good appetite, and was promptly at the little garden gate by eight-thirty.

'What is the matter with you today, Auguste?' said the Countess. 'You are unusually lively, and yet your gaiety does not move me to laugh. Last night you were just a trifle dull, and I was the gay one! We have changed parts today. I have a racking headache.'

'Dear one, I admit it. Yes, I was very tedious yesterday, but today I have been out, I took exercise, and I feel quite excited.'

'On the other hand, I overslept this morning, and rose late. I had bad dreams.'

'Ah! dreams? Do you believe in dreams?'

'What nonsense!'

'I believe in them. I am sure that you had a dream which foretold some tragic event.'

'Good heavens! I never remember my dreams. Once I recollect . . . that I saw Massigny in my dream; so, you see, it was not very entertaining.'

'Massigny! But I should have thought you would have been pleased at seeing him again!'

'Poor Massigny!'

'Why "poor Massigny"?'

'Please tell me, Auguste, what is wrong with you tonight. Your smile is perfectly diabolical, and you seem to be play-acting.'

'Ah! now you are treating me as badly as your old dowager friends treat me.'

'Yes, Auguste, you wear the same expression today that you put on before people whom you do not like.'

'That is unpardonable in me. Come, give me your hand.'

He kissed her hand with ironical gallantry, and they gazed at each other studiously for a minute. Saint-Clair was the first to drop his eyes.

'How difficult it is', he exclaimed, 'to live in this world without being thought ill of! One ought really never to talk of anything but the weather and hunting, or eagerly to discuss with your old friends the reports of their benevolent societies.'

He picked up a paper from the table near him.

'Come, here is your lace-cleaner's bill. Let us discuss that, sweetheart; then you cannot say I am ill-tempered.'

'Really, Auguste, you amaze me . . .'

'This handwriting puts me in mind of a letter I found this morning. I must explain that I have fits of untidiness occasionally, and I was arranging my papers. Well, then, I found a love-letter from a dressmaker with whom I fell in love at sixteen. She had a trick of writing each word most fantastically, and her style was equal to her writing. Well, I was foolish enough then to be vexed that my mistress could not write as well as Madame de Sévigné, and I left her abruptly. In reading over this letter today I see that this dressmaker really did love me.'

'Really! a woman whom you kept?'

'In fine style on fifty francs a month. But I could not afford more, as my guardian only allowed me a little money at a time, for he said that youths who had money ruined themselves and others.'

'What became of this woman?'

'How should I know? . . . Probably she died in a hospital.'

'Auguste . . . if that were true you would not speak so flippantly.'

'Well, then, to tell you the truth, she is married to a respectable man, and when I came of age I gave her a small dowry.'

'How good of you! . . . But why do you try to make yourself out so evil?'

'Oh, I am good enough . . . The more I think of it the more I persuade myself that this woman really did care for me . . . But on the other hand, it is difficult to discern true feeling under such a ridiculous expression of it.'

'You ought to have shown me your letter. I should not have been jealous . . . We women have finer tact than you, and we can tell at a glance, from the style of a letter, whether the writer is sincere, or feigning a passion he does not really feel.'

'But what a number of times you have allowed yourself to be taken in by fools and rogues!'

As he spoke he looked at the Etruscan vase with a threatening glance, to which his voice responded, but Mathilde went on without noticing anything.

'Come, now, all you men wish to pose as Don Juans. You fancy you are making dupes when often you have encountered only Doña Juana, who is much more cunning than yourselves.'

'I perceive that with your superior wit you ladies scent out rakes in every place. Nor do I doubt that our friend Massigny, who was both stupid and a coxcomb, became, when dead, spotless and a martyr.'

'Massigny? He was not a fool; then too there are silly women to be found. I must tell you a story about Massigny. But surely have I not told it you already?'

'Never,' replied Saint-Clair tremblingly.

'Massigny fell in love with me after his return from Italy. My husband knew him and introduced him to me as a man of taste and culture. Those two were just made for each other. Massigny was most attentive to me from the first; he gave me some water-colour sketches which he had bought from Schroth, as his own paintings, and talked of music and art in the most divertingly superior manner. One day he sent me an incredibly ridiculous letter. He said, among other things, that I was the best woman in Paris; therefore he wished to be my lover. I showed the letter to my cousin Julie. We were then both very silly, and we resolved to play him a trick. One evening we had several visitors, among them being Massigny. My cousin said to me, "I am going to read you a declaration of love which I received this morning." She took the letter and read it amidst peals of laughter . . . Poor Massigny! . . .'

Saint-Clair fell on his knees uttering a cry of joy. He seized the Countess's hand and covered it with tears and kisses. Mathilde was surprised beyond measure, and thought at first he had gone mad. Saint-Clair could only murmur, 'Forgive me! forgive me!' When he rose to his feet he was radiant; he was happier than on the day when Mathilde had said to him for the first time, 'I love you.'

'I am the guiltiest and most stupid of men,' he cried; 'for two days I have misjudged you . . . and never given you a chance to clear yourself . . .'

'You suspected me? . . . And of what?'

'Oh! idiot that I was! . . . they told me you had loved Massigny, and—'

'Massigny!' and she began to laugh; then soon quickly growing more earnest, 'Auguste,' she said, 'how could you be so foolish as to harbour such suspicions, and so hypocritical as to hide them from me?'

Her eyes filled with tears.

'I implore you to forgive me.'

'Of course I forgive you, beloved . . . but let me first swear . . .'

'Oh! I believe you, I believe you; do not say any more about it.'

'But in Heaven's name what put such an improbable notion in your head?'

'Nothing, nothing in the world except my accursed temper . . . and . . . would you believe it? that Etruscan vase which I knew Massigny had given you.'

The Countess clasped her hands together in amazement, and then she burst into shouts of laughter.

'My Etruscan vase! my Etruscan vase!'

Saint-Clair was obliged to join in the laughter himself, although great tears rolled down his cheeks. He seized Mathilde in his arms. 'I will not let you go', he said, 'until you pardon me.'

'Yes, I forgive you, though you are so foolish,' she replied, kissing him tenderly. 'You make me very happy today; it is the first time I have seen you shed tears, and I thought that you could not weep.'

Then she struggled from his embrace, and, snatching the Etruscan vase, broke it into a thousand pieces on the floor. It was a valuable and unique work, painted in three colours, and represented the fight between a Lapithe and a Centaur.

For several hours Saint-Clair was the happiest and the most ashamed of men.

'Well,' said Roquantin to Colonel Beaujeu, when he met him in the evening at Tortoni's, 'is this news true?'

'Too true, my friend,' answered the Colonel sadly.

'Tell me, how did it come about?'

'Oh! just as it should. Saint-Clair began by telling me he was in the wrong, but that he wished to draw Thémines' fire before begging his pardon. I could do no other than accede. Thémines wished to draw lots who should fire first. Saint-Clair insisted that Thémines should. Thémines fired; and I saw Saint-Clair turn round once and then fall stone-dead. I have often remarked, in the case of soldiers when they have been shot, this strange turning round which precedes death.'

'How very extraordinary!' said Roquantin. 'But Thémines, what did he do?'

'Oh, what is usual on these occasions: he threw his pistol on the ground remorsefully, with such force that he broke the hammer. It was an English pistol of Manton's. I don't believe there is a gun-maker in Paris who could make such another.'

The Countess shut herself up in her country house for three whole years without seeing anyone; winter and summer, there she lived, hardly going out of her room. She was waited upon by a mulatto woman who knew of the attachment between Saint-Clair and herself. She scarcely spoke a word to her day after day. At the end of three years her cousin Julie returned from a long voyage. She forced her way into the house and found poor Mathilde thin and pale, the very ghost of the beautiful and fascinating woman she had left behind. By degrees she persuaded her to come out of her solitude, and took her to Hyères. The Countess languished there for three or four months, and then died of consumption brought on by her grief – so said Dr M——, who attended her.

Charles de Bernard

Charles de Bernard was the pseudonym of Charles-Bernard du Grail de la Villette (1805–50). He was a journalist and novelist, and is best known for his novel *Gerfaut* (1838). A friend of Balzac, who influenced him considerably, he also produced collections of short stories, *Le Noeud gordien* in 1838 and *Paravent* the following year.

Medical Advice

A MONG THE PEOPLE ASSEMBLED, AT THE BEGINNING OF LAST autumn, in Dr Magnian's waiting-room, was a thin, sallow-faced man of about forty, with fair hair and stooping shoulders, so sickly in appearance, in a word, that the mere sight of him was sufficient to make you realise you were at a doctor's. On entering, this delicate-looking person went and sat down in a corner with a harassed air; he stayed there meekly until all the other patients had been received by the master of the house, who, after giving his last consultation, came towards him, with a cordial smile. 'How do you do, Bouchereau?' said the doctor. 'Many apologies for keeping you so long; you know my time belongs to my patients in the first place, and I hope you lay no claim to it on those grounds?'

'Mental sufferings are worse than bodily ones,' answered Bouchereau, stifling a sigh.

'Why, what is wrong?' continued the doctor; 'you look done up! Madame Bouchereau isn't ill, is she?'

'My wife is as strong as a horse,' answered Bouchereau, accompanying his words with a bitter smile.

'Then tell me why you are so upset. You mentioned sufferings of the mind, didn't you? If you don't explain yourself, how can you expect me to guess what is going on in yours? Come, now, what can I do for you?'

'My dear Doctor,' answered the other, sitting down with an air of deep depression, 'we have known each other for more than twenty years. I regard you as one of my best friends, and I have unlimited confidence in you.'

'Let's omit the flattery!'

'It's not flattery. I am revealing my most secret thoughts to you. Besides, the strange confession I have made up my mind to make to you will be a proof of the esteem I have for your character.'

'Let us get to the point,' said the doctor, with a touch of impatience.

'The point is disastrous for me, and may even seem ridiculous; that is why I hesitate to broach it; but first promise not to reveal what I am going to tell you to any living person.'

'The secret of the confessional is as sacred to a doctor as to a priest,' said Dr Magnian, gravely.

Bouchereau sighed again, bit his lip, and raised his eyes to the ceiling.

'You know Pelletier, don't you?' he said at last, looking gloomily at his interlocutor.

'The staff officer? Of course I do. A fellow of sanguine temperament, short in the neck, stronger in the shoulders than in the head, the constitution of an ox! I predicted he would die of apoplexy a long time ago.'

'God grant it be so!'

'You surprise me: I thought you were friends.'

'Friends!' repeated Bouchereau, with a mixture of irony and indignation.

'Confound you! Either speak clearly or hold your tongue. I'm no Oedipus to guess your riddles!'

The impatience that glittered in the doctor's dark eyes prevented his doleful friend from evading the main point of his confession any longer.

'Well, my dear Magnian, here's my story in a few words,' he said, in a shaky voice. 'Pelletier is making love to my wife.'

The doctor pursed his nether lip to conceal a smile, and nodded his head several times with affected gravity.

'Well I never!' he then exclaimed. 'I wouldn't have thought that great fat fellow had such good taste. But are you sure? Usually husbands are the last to learn of this sort of thing.'

'I am only too sure; and I'll tell you why. My wife went to spend a few days at Fontainebleau with her mother. The day before yesterday, as I happened to be ferreting around in her bedroom, I noticed that the key of my bureau fitted her wardrobe too. Mechanically, I opened the door, and in a rather mysterious drawer at the back I found several letters from Pelletier.'

'Yes, but, hang it all, what reason had you to open a wardrobe belonging to your wife?'

'I had the right to do so; but don't pass judgement so quickly. From the tenor of these letters I got absolute proof of Virginie's innocence, and no blame attaches to her, except for making such a secret of this correspondence. She has never given him any encouragement, I am practically certain of that. So I am less annoyed with her than with Pelletier;

but, as for him, I know I shall never forgive him. A man I welcomed to my house! We were at school together at Sainte-Barbe! A friend, or so at least I thought!'

'Are you forgetting that only our friends play us false?'

'Yesterday, I went to his house.'

'Oh, did you!'

'Yes, and I upbraided him for his infamous conduct: and do you know what he said?'

'He denied everything.'

'Yes, at first. But when he saw his letters, he understood that all his denials were useless. "My dear Bouchereau," he said then, with the impertinent air you know so well, "since you're so well informed, I won't put myself to the trouble of telling lies. It is quite true that I am in love with your wife; I have already told her so, and I won't promise not to tell her so again, as it's not probable I should keep my word. I understand quite well that this conduct must annoy and wound you; but you know I am a man of honour, and that it is my habit to accept the responsibility of my actions. So if you consider yourself insulted, I am at your disposal, and ready to give you satisfaction where, when, and how you wish."'

'What cheek!' said the doctor, trying to keep a serious face. 'Did he really dare to say that?'

'Word for word.'

'And what answer did you make?'

'That he should hear from me shortly. Thereupon I took my leave, for it did not suit me to carry the discussion any farther. That's how things stand.'

A grave look passed over the doctor's face. He walked round the room, with his head bent and his hands behind his back; then going up to his visitor, he said with his eyes fixed steadily on him: 'Now, what do you intend to do?'

'What do you advise?'

'I can understand that you find it hard to put up with his behaviour; on the other hand, I should be sorry to see you engaged in a duel with a swashbuckler like Pelletier.'

'A swashbuckler!' cried Bouchereau, his eyes dilating more and more. 'You should say a fire-eater, a prizefighter, a man who spends all his mornings at Lepage's shooting-range or at the fencing school, and has a duel every three months!'

'And have you ever fought a duel yourself?' enquired the doctor, with a penetrating glance.

'Never,' answered the husband, more livid than before. 'Not that I have not had the chance several times, but duelling is against my principles. The idea of shedding blood fills me with repulsion; it is a barbarous custom, which has always seemed to me to be a monstrous anomaly in our modern civilisation.'

'In short, you have no burning desire to fight a duel?'

'If I were actually wronged, if I had to avenge a deadly insult, the voice of passion would perhaps speak louder than the voice of humanity; for, in certain circumstances, the most reasonable of men cannot be sure of himself. But in this case, as things have not yet reached a crisis, if Pelletier, instead of affecting this arrogant talk, had offered me the apology which I believe I have the right to expect, and promised to behave himself in the future, it seems to me that in that case . . . in the interests of everyone concerned . . . to avoid a scandal . . . do you not agree with me that it would have been possible and honourable—'

'Not to fight? Certainly,' interrupted Magnian. 'If you have a duel with him, it's ten to one Pelletier will bleed you like a chicken, and you wouldn't like that.'

'Doctor, you don't see my point.'

'Oh, yes, indeed I do, admirably; and the proof is that you won't fight, and the captain will make you satisfactory apologies. Isn't that what you are after?'

The doctor's perspicacity brought a pale-red glow into the cheeks of this lover of peace.

'Pelletier is a brute,' resumed the doctor, as if speaking to himself. 'Usually staff officers have more knowledge of the world than that. It's all right for him to make love to the wives, but he breaks all the rules of decorum when he goes and provokes their husbands.'

'So you advise me to let the affair be smoothed over?' asked Bouchereau in an insinuating tone of voice.

'Yes, indeed,' answered the doctor, laughing, 'and, what is more, I am prepared to do the negotiating myself. I assure you that tomorrow Pelletier will withdraw his challenge; he will send you a formal apology and give you his word not to try and upset your conjugal peace. I make that my business; the rest concerns you.'

'The rest?'

'To promise is one thing, and keeping one's promise is another, as you know; it would, I think, be very wise, on your part, to make it easier for the captain to keep his promise by taking Madame Bouchereau away for a few months. His post keeps him in Paris; but you are free. What is there to prevent you from going to spend the winter in the Midi: at Nice, for instance?'

'It had already occurred to me that a journey would be a good thing, and I am glad you agree with me on this point. But why Nice in preference to another town?'

'Because the climate is very healthy, especially for people with weak lungs.'

'But my lungs are in excellent condition . . . at any rate, I think so,' interrupted Bouchereau, casting an anxious glance of enquiry at the doctor.

'No doubt, I don't say they're not,' the doctor added seriously. 'It is not for that reason especially that I give you this advice; but precautions never do any harm, and prevention is better than cure.'

'So you really think I may be threatened with some lung complaint?' said the married man, turning pale; as you see, he had vowed the greatest attachment to his own person.

'I've said nothing of the sort,' answered Dr Magnian, looking as though he was secretly regretting having said too much. 'Do you want to know why I mentioned Nice? Pure selfishness. Possibly I shall spend part of the winter there myself; and if you and your wife were there, I should certainly have a much better time.'

'Well, we'll see; we may be able to arrange it,' answered Bouchereau, taking leave of the doctor considerably more worried than when he came, for to the apprehension he felt at the prospect of a duel, was added the equally keen fear of a disease which was often fatal, and which he had never bothered about till then.

At six o'clock Dr Magnian went to the Café Anglais, where he was almost certain to see Pelletier. The officer was indeed there already, sitting alone at a small table and dining with a good appetite, taking his wine undiluted. He was a great, burly, red-faced individual, broad at the shoulders and slim about the hips, with staring eyes and a glossy moustache, a man of powerful build with a grip of iron, who, if he had not been in the Army, would have seemed to have missed his vocation; his very demeanour inspired restraint and modesty in the most overbearing of his fellows. Others than the sickly-looking Bouchereau would have thought it a real catastrophe to have a bone to pick with such a lion.

The doctor and the officer greeted each other cordially, and, after exchanging a few remarks, dined each at his own table. They left the restaurant at the same time, met at the door, and, taking each other's arm simultaneously, they strolled down the Boulevard together in the direction of the Madeleine church.

'Well, Doctor,' said Pelletier, jocosely, 'have you found me what I've asked you for at least ten times: a nice wife (girl or widow, dark or fair, short or tall, it's all the same to me) who will be ready to make me a happy man by joining her lot to mine? I only ask for a modest dowry of a hundred thousand crowns. Hang it all! I'm reasonable enough, I think.'

'Too reasonable! you're worth more than that.'

'You're laughing at me, aren't you?'

'Not at all; besides, this is no time for joking, for I want to talk to you about something serious, so we'll leave the fiancée with the hundred thousand crowns out of the question for the time being. Bouchereau has asked me to speak to you.'

'And you call that serious?' asked the captain, laughing scornfully.

'All affairs seem serious to me when they may end in bloodshed,' said the doctor with affected gravity.

'Oh, so Monsieur Bouchereau's thirsting for my blood, is he?' continued Pelletier, laughing still louder. 'I'd always thought him herbivorous rather than carnivorous. What's the sauce he's going to eat me with? Sword or pistol?'

'He leaves the choice of weapon to you,' said Dr Magnian with imperturbable gravity.

'It's all the same to me, I've told him so already. Look here, tomorrow I'm lunching with some of my pals; it's a sort of banquet for our corps, and I shouldn't like to miss it; but I'm at your service on the morning of the next day. Will that suit you?'

'Perfectly. The day after tomorrow, at seven a.m., at the entrance to the Bois de Vincennes.'

'Right you are!' cried the captain, patting his companion's arm in a friendly fashion with his big hand. 'Well, Doctor, who'd have thought you were keen on duelling? Yet it's a rival you might have good cause to take objection to!'

The doctor answered this well-worn joke with a mischievous smile that he suppressed immediately.

'As a matter of fact you've touched me on one of my sore spots with your jesting,' he said after a moment's silence. 'I wonder if I can trust you with a secret, a queer idea, even a monstrous one, that has just occurred to me?'

'Out with it! I'm rather fond of monstrous ideas.'

'I was thinking that, in the interests of my reputation, I have good reason to hope that this duel will prove fatal to Bouchereau.'

'Why on earth?' asked the officer in surprise.

'Well, if you don't kill him, I shall be considered responsible for his death in less than a year's time.'

'I don't understand you. Do you want to have a duel with him yourself?'

'No, indeed; but I'm his doctor, and so responsible for his life in the eyes of many people who expect medical science to endow patients with the health Nature has refused them. Now, as Bouchereau, to all appearances, cannot live another year—'

'Why, what's wrong with him?' cried Pelletier, opening his big eyes wide.

'Consumption!' answered the doctor with a touch of compassion in his voice, 'a chronic disease, and there's no cure! I meant to send him to Nice. You know, when we doctors are at our wits' end what to prescribe for our patients, we send them to some watering-place, or to the Midi. If no harm comes to him the day after tomorrow, he will go there. Will he ever come back? There's no knowing!'

'Consumption! Why, his face is as white as a Pierrot's!'

'That means nothing.'

'And do you think his life is in danger?'

'I think he cannot live more than a year, perhaps not six months.'

The two men walked on in silence for some time, looking grave.

'Yes, Captain,' said the doctor, resuming the conversation, 'poor Bouchereau may be regarded as a man under sentence of death, quite apart from the danger your sword will expose him to. Certainly before this time next year, his wife will be free to think of taking another husband. She'll be an attractive widow, there's no getting away from it, and won't be short of suitors.'

Pelletier cast a sidelong glance at his companion. The doctor's simple, good-natured air destroyed the feeling of suspicion roused by his words.

'If Bouchereau died, would his wife be well-off?' asked the captain in a half-whisper, but with a note of enquiry in his voice.

'By Gad, yes!' answered the doctor, 'her fortune would not be reckoned at a hundred thousand crowns, but at two hundred thousand.'

'You're exaggerating,' cried the captain, his eyes gleaming with a sudden light.

'It's easily reckoned,' answered Dr Magnian with assurance. 'Madame Bouchereau inherited a hundred thousand francs from her father, she expects another hundred and fifty thousand from her mother, and her husband will leave her at least three hundred and fifty thousand; add that up.'

'So he made everything over to her in the marriage settlement?' asked Pelletier, growing more and more excited at each figure mentioned by his companion.

'Yes, everything,' answered the doctor solemnly.

These few syllables were as effective as a long speech. If he had been talking to someone whose intelligence he respected, Dr Magnian would not have added another word; but judging the captain better provided with strength of body than of mind, as he had said a few hours before, he did not hesitate to lay great stress on the ideas which he hoped would have a magical result.

'Your matrimonial bump is well developed,' he went on jocosely. 'Here's a match that would just suit you; a pretty, charming young woman and six hundred thousand francs dowry. It is certain that, to win the prize, you should not begin by killing the husband.'

Pelletier gave an affected laugh, although his face had assumed a thoughtful expression during the last few minutes, then he changed the subject. Feeling certain he had achieved his end, the doctor said he had a patient to see and left his companion on the Boulevard, smitten by the six hundred thousand francs of the future widow.

Without stopping an instant or taking a bus, the captain went from the Madeleine to the Bastille with the headlong speed of a wounded boar. On reaching the Porte Saint-Martin, his mind was made up.

'Without knowing it,' he thought, 'the doctor has given me excellent advice. I'm not such a fool as to fight a duel with Bouchereau; I should kill him; I've an unlucky aim! How dare I show myself before Virginie then? She has rather a soft spot for me: fortunately I've helped things on by making love to her for the last six months, so when the great day arrives, she can't think I'm after her fortune. It would be idiotic to kill Bouchereau! Let the dear fellow die a natural death, I'll do nothing to prevent it. To all appearances, I'll have plenty of opportunities for duels with my rivals as soon as his wife is a widow. Six hundred thousand francs! There'll be crowds of them; but the others had better be careful: I'm first on the list, and I'm not the sort to let anyone stand in my way.'

The next morning, the captain arrived at Dr Magnian's long before his consultation hour.

'Doctor,' he said, with military frankness, 'what you told me yesterday about Bouchereau's illness has made me think things over very seriously. I don't feel I can loyally fight a man who has only six months to live. Suppose I wound him. A sword-scratch from which another would recover, in his case might prove fatal; and then I should have it on my conscience for the rest of my life that I had killed an old friend for a silly trifle. Has he told you the cause of our quarrel?'

'No,' said the doctor, considering that his role of arbitrator entitled him to tell a lie.

'A few sharp words on both sides,' continued the officer, deceived by the doctor's air of innocence. 'To tell you the truth, I believe I was in the wrong. You know how fiery I am; for some trifle or other I insulted poor Bouchereau, and I am sorry for it now. In short, I've had enough duels to be able to settle one peacefully without people thinking I'm showing the white feather. So, if you'll advise Bouchereau to let things slide, I give you a free hand. Between ourselves I think he'll jump at the proposal.'

'You may be mistaken, Captain,' said the doctor, who had an admirable talent for keeping a straight face; 'yesterday Bouchereau was in a fury: although he is a lover of peace, he's like a tiger when his blood is up. It seems you offended him deeply in your altercation, and unless you offer him a formal apology—'

'That's not difficult,' interrupted Pelletier, 'it's not usual for me to make excuses; it will be the first time such a thing has happened; but one must not be too fastidious with an old friend. Besides I'd sooner make concessions than have anything on my conscience afterwards. Come, shall we go to Bouchereau's together?'

'Yes, come along,' said the doctor, striving not to smile on seeing how humane, sensitive, and delicate fortune-hunting could render even a professional duellist.

When he saw the doctor enter his drawing-room, followed by the captain, Bouchereau, who had not slept a wink all night, experienced an emotion similar to that of a condemned man when the Clerk of the Court reads a judgement remitting a sentence of capital punishment.

His heart, which seemed to have stood still, began to beat again at the first words they exchanged. The captain gave utterance to the most formal and explicit apologies, and took his leave immediately after shaking the hand of his old friend, who was so overjoyed at his escape that it did not occur to him to make any objections.

'Doctor, you're a sorcerer!' exclaimed Bouchereau as soon as he was alone with the physician.

'Yes, that's my calling, in a way,' said the latter with a laugh. 'So now this terrible business is practically settled. I've done my share, will you do yours? When do you start for the Midi?'

The satisfaction beaming on Bouchereau's countenance vanished immediately, and gave way to a worried and gloomy expression.

'Doctor,' he said, in a tremulous voice, 'you must tell me the truth; I have enough self-control to hear my sentence; my lungs are affected, aren't they?'

'Your head, you should say!'

'My head too!' exclaimed Bouchereau, turning paler than ever.

'You're out of your senses,' continued the doctor, shrugging his shoulders; 'I'd gladly exchange my lungs for yours.'

'You're deceiving me. I can't forget what you said yesterday. I coughed the whole of the night, and I have a pain between my shoulders that I had not noticed till now.'

'Pure fancy!'

'I know what I feel,' said Bouchereau in a lugubrious voice. 'I am not afraid of death, but I confess I should be sorry to bid an eternal farewell to my wife and family when I'm only in my prime. It's my duty to look after myself, for their sakes if not for my own. Instead of writing to tell Virginie to return here, I'll go and fetch her at Fontainebleau, and we'll go straight to Nice.'

'Yes, that's right,' said the doctor, 'the journey can do you no harm.'

'But do you think it will do me any good?'

'Yes, sure to.'

'And it's not too late to fight this terrible disease?'

'Oh, we'll cure you all right,' said Magnian with mock gravity. 'In about six weeks I shall be in Nice myself, so you're sure of being in the hands of a doctor you have confidence in, if, contrary to all appearances, you should get worse.'

The two friends separated: the doctor laughing at his patient's fears, while the latter imagined he could already feel death in his lungs, and wondered if, after all, it would not have been better to brave Captain

Pelletier's sword than go and die in foreign parts in the flower of his age. Haunted by this gloomy vision, Bouchereau obtained his passport in two days, put his affairs in order, and completed the preparations for his journey. He jumped into a post-chaise, and arrived like a bomb at Fontainebleau, where he was not expected. Asserting his marital rights as he had never dared to before, he carried off his wife, who was bewildered by such unusual behaviour and annoyed at going so far from Paris, where she had been finding life more amusing than usual for some time past, owing to the officer's love-letters. At the end of the week the pair arrived at Nice, and were joined by Dr Magnian at the end of the autumn; the doctor was scrupulously exact in keeping his promise.

In the following April, *Horace* was being acted at the Théâtre Français. The house was packed, owing more to the youthful talent of Mademoiselle Rachel than to the genius of old Corneille. In the middle of the dress circle to the right sat Captain Pelletier with several brawlers of his set, talking and laughing loudly, criticising the actors, staring at the women, and being a nuisance to everyone near them, without a single person daring to remonstrate, so great in certain cases is the prestige of an insolent eye, a ferocious moustache, and elephantine shoulders.

Letting his eyeglass wander all over the theatre, from the stalls to the top of the roof, the captain suddenly noticed in one of the boxes a group that absorbed his attention completely. Right in the front sat Monsieur and Madame Bouchereau, and at the back, behind the young woman, Dr Magnian. The attitude of these three persons was characteristic. With pale cheeks, looking as usual overdosed with physic, wearing a pair of coloured spectacles – a new adornment due to imaginary ophthalmia – the peace-loving husband was holding the programme in his hand and reading it during the intervals, and he listened conscientiously to the tragedy, even to Corneille interpreted by Arsène and Fonta. Madame was toying with a pretty bouquet, raising it frequently to her nose, and the crimson flowers suited her white complexion so well that one could not help thinking that this gesture, made with an air of detachment, was not quite exempt of coquetry. Leaning carelessly against the back of her seat, the young woman turned her head occasionally to catch the remarks the doctor was whispering with a smile, but her husband took no part in this conversation, nor did he seem to notice its intimate and confidential nature.

'Who's that you've been staring at for the last quarter of an hour?'

one of his neighbours asked the captain. 'Isn't it your old flame, Madame Bouchereau? I thought you had thrown her over long ago.'

'I did not know she was back from Nice,' answered Pelletier, with an air of reserve.

'She's been back in Paris a fortnight.'

'Bouchereau looks ill, doesn't he? The climate of Nice doesn't seem to have done him much good. He's twice as pale as when he went. Poor Bouchereau!'

'By Jove,' said another, 'do you believe the yarn that he's consumptive, too? What a joke!'

'What's a joke?' asked the captain testily.

'The trick that wily fellow Magnian has played on Bouchereau and you, for, judging from your bewilderment, you're involved in the mystification.'

'Berton, you're getting on my nerves,' said Pelletier crossly.

'Wolves don't devour each other,' cried Berton, laughing. 'So don't let's lose our tempers. I'll tell you the story: all Paris, except you, has been cracking its sides over it for the last week. It appears, on the one hand, that the said Magnian was in love with Madame Bouchereau, and on the other, that he thought it wise to spend the winter in a warmer climate, as he had been suffering with his lungs for some time past. So he persuades poor simple Bouchereau that it is he, Bouchereau, who has lung trouble; he made him go to Nice with his charming wife; then he joined them when it suited him, taking his time about it. The picture they form at present leaves no doubt as to the end of the story; the very sight of them enables you to guess that the title of one of Paul de Kock's latest novels – *Husband, Wife and Lover* – could be inscribed on the front of their box, without risk of calumny. Magnian's a clever chap and has ingenious ideas. Not wanting her husband to see too much, he threatened him with ophthalmia and persuaded him to wear smoked glasses. He's played his cards well, and it's an amusing affair, isn't it?'

'Charming, delightful,' answered the captain with a smile that was rather like a snarl.

The play was over. Dr Magnian left the box, Pelletier followed his example. A moment later the two men met in the foyer.

'A word with you, Doctor,' said the officer gravely.

'Two if you like, Captain,' answered Magnian jovially.

'It appears Bouchereau is in excellent health in spite of your prognostics.'

'Would you have him die?'asked the doctor, parodying the accents of Joanny, who had just played the part of the father of the Horatii.

'I know you're very witty,' retorted the captain, whose annoyance was beginning to blaze into real anger; 'but you must know I won't stand being made a fool of. Will you please answer me seriously: is it true that Bouchereau's life has never been in danger?'

'On the contrary, in great danger. Wasn't he to fight a duel with you?'

'So when you sent him to Nice—'

'It was to prevent the duel. As a medical man I am used to looking after my patients' health, and it was my duty to rescue Bouchereau from the point of your sword, which is said to be a terrible ailment.'

'An ailment you'll perhaps have to be treating yourself for shortly,' said the captain, exasperated by the doctor's offhand manner. 'Whether that fool Bouchereau dies of fright or something else, I won't do him the honour of having a hand in it; but you, my dear fellow, who are so good at having a joke, I should be glad to see if your courage is equal to your wit.'

The part of unsuccessful and mystified lover is so humiliating that Pelletier's vanity prevented him from making any reference to his real grievance and to Madame Bouchereau during this discussion. The doctor showed the same reticence, which indeed his position as successful lover rendered obligatory. He received the officer's challenge with the same careless smile that had never left his lips.

'My dear Captain,' he said, 'I can see it would give you great pleasure at the present moment to run your sword through my heart, or fire a bullet into my thigh (I assume you would spare my head on account of our long friendship), and it's a whim you can indulge if you really want to. But if you kill me, who'll arrange your marriage with Mademoiselle Nanteuil?'

Pelletier stared at his adversary with a dazed expression, which increased the latter's high spirits.

'Who's Mademoiselle Nanteuil?' he then asked, softening his voice in spite of himself.

'A charming heiress, a patient of mine, although she is in perfect health; she has two hundred thousand francs, and will probably come into as much again; and if an intelligent friend were to undertake the negotiations, I think she would be ready to make a fine fellow like you happy.'

'What the deuce of a chap you are, Magnian!' cried the captain, taking the doctor's arm. 'It's impossible to lose one's temper with you!'

Jules Barbey d'Aurevilly

The legacy of Romanticism can be traced in the strange writings of Barbey d'Aurevilly (1808–89). A journalist and critic, he was a tempestuous, flamboyant character with a flair for sadistic melodrama and a Baudelairean distaste for humanity. After the early *L'Amour impossible* (1841), which offered readers the piquancy of blasphemous transgression, he wrote several novels, notably *L'Ensorcelée* (1854) and *Le Chevalier des Touches* (1864). His short stories, *Les Diaboliques*, were suppressed by the police when they first appeared in 1874, but enjoyed notorious success when the engraver Félicien Rops reissued them in 1886. His rigorous, far-seeing criticism, although coloured by his reactionary Catholicism, has influenced writers like Léon Bloy and Joris-Karl Huysmans and his reputation has grown considerably since his death.

The Greatest Love of Don Juan

The Devil's primest fare is innocence

'HE IS STILL ALIVE THEN, THAT HOARY OLD REPROBATE?'
'Still alive! I should rather think he was – by God's grace,' I took care to add, remembering Madame's piety, 'and of the most distinguished and aristocratic parish of Sainte-Clotilde – *Le roi est mort! vive le roi!* is what they used to say under the old monarchy, in the days when their fine old piece of Sèvres porcelain was yet unbroken. But Don Juan, in spite of all your democracies, is a monarch they will never break.'

'Yes! yes! no doubt the Devil is among the immortal!' she returned in a self-approving tone.

'As a matter of fact, he . . .'

'Who? . . . the Devil? . . .'

'No! no! Don Juan. He supped, I say, only three days ago in pleasant company . . . Guess where . . .'

'At your horrid Maison d'Or, of course . .'

'My dear madame! Don Juan *never* goes there now . . . they've no fish fit to fry for His Highness's palate. The Señor Don Juan has always been a bit like Arnold of Brescia's famous monk who, the chronicles tell us, lived only on the blood of souls. That is what he loves to colour his champagne with, and it's many a long day since it was to be had at the rendezvous of the commonplace *cocotte!*'

'You'll be telling me next', she interrupted, in the ironic vein, 'he supped at the Benedictine nunnery with the holy ladies . . .'

'Yes! ladies of the Perpetual Adoration; why, certainly, madame. For indeed I do think the adoration he has once inspired, our redoubtable Lovelace, seems to last for good and all.'

'And I think that for a good Catholic you are a trifle profane, sir!' – this she said slowly, but not without a touch of irritation – 'and I must beg you to spare me the details of your naughty suppers. I suppose this is a new way of telling me about your disreputable lady-friends, this harping on Don Juan and his doings tonight.'

'I merely state the facts, madame. The disreputable persons present at the supper in question, if they are disreputable, are not my friends at all . . . unfortunately . . .'

'Enough! enough!'

'Forgive my modest disclaimer . . . They were . . .'

'The *mille e tre*? . . .' she interrupted again, thinking better of it, and all but recovering her good temper under the stress of curiosity.

'Oh! not all of them . . . A round dozen merely. With as many as that, nothing could be more respectable, you know.'

'Or more disreputable,' she put in tartly.

'Besides, you know as well as I do the Comtesse de Chiffrevas's boudoir will not hold a crowd. Everything was done that could be done; but, after all, it's only a small room, her boudoir.'

'What!' – raising her voice in astonishment. 'They had supper in the boudoir?'

'Yes! in the boudoir. And why not? A battlefield makes a famous place to dine in. They wished to give a very special and particular supper to Señor Don Juan, and it seemed better worthy of his exploits to give it on the scene of his former triumphs, where fond memories bloom instead of orange blossoms. A pretty notion, at once tender and sad! *'Twas no victims' ball!* it was a victims' supper-party!'

'And Don Juan?' she asked in the tone of Orgon, in the play, saying: 'And Tartuffe?'

'Don Juan took it in excellent part, and made an excellent supper,

> . . . *He, he alone before them all,*

as the poet sings – in the person of someone you know very well indeed – none other than the Comte Jules-Amédée-Hector de Ravila de Ravilès.'

'Comte de Ravilès! Why, yes! He was a Don Juan . . .'

So saying, the pious lady, case-hardened in her narrow bigotry as she was, and long past the age of day-dreams, lapsed then and there into a fond reverie of which Comte Jules-Amédée was the theme – that man of the old Don Juan breed, to which God has not indeed given 'all the world and glory thereof', but has suffered the Devil to do it for Him.

II

What I had just told the aged Marquise Guy de Ruy was the unvarnished truth. Hardly three days had elapsed since a dozen ladies of the virtuous Faubourg Saint-Germain (rest them easy, I will never damage their noble names!), who, every one, the whole dozen, if we are to believe the cackling dowagers of the quarter, had been 'on the best of good terms' (a really charming old-fashioned locution) with the Comte Ravila de Ravilès, had conceived the idea of offering him a supper – he being the only male guest – in pious memory of . . . well! they did not say of what. A bold thing to do, but women, while timid individually, are as bold as brass when banded together. Probably not one of the whole party would have ventured to invite the comte to a *tête-à-tête* supper at her own house; but all together, each backing up the other, they feared not to weave a chain, like mesmerists round their mystic tub, round this magnetic and most compromising individual, the Comte de Ravila de Ravilès . . .

'What a name!'

'A providential name, madame.'

The Comte de Ravila de Ravilès, who, by the bye, had always lived up to his high-sounding and picturesque title, was the perfect incarnation of all the long line of Lovelaces Romance and History tell of, and even the old Marquise Guy de Ruy – a discontented old lady, with light blue eyes, cold and keen, but not so cold as her heart, or so keen as her tongue – allowed that in these times, when women and women's concerns grow day by day less important, if there *was* anyone who could recall Don Juan, it must surely be he! Unfortunately it was Don Juan in the Fifth Act. The witty Prince de Ligne said he could *not* make himself believe Alcibiades ever grew to be fifty; and here again the Comte de Ravila was to be a true Alcibiades to the end of the chapter. Like d'Orsay, a dandy hewn out of the marble of Michelangelo, who was the handsomest of men down to his last hour, Ravila had possessed the good looks especially belonging to the Don Juan breed – that mysterious race which does not proceed from father to son, like other races, but appears here and there at recurring intervals in the families of mankind.

His beauty was beyond dispute – of the gay, arrogant, imperial sort, *Juanesque* in fact (the word is a picture, and makes description heedless); and – had he made an unholy bargain with the Devil? – it was his still . . . Only, God was beginning to exact His penalty; life's cruel tiger-claws already seamed that 'front divine', crowned with the roses of so many kisses, and on his wide and wicked temples appeared the first white hairs that proclaim the impending invasion of the barbarian hosts and the fall of the empire . . . He wore them, it is true, with the calm insouciance of pride surfeited with power; but women who had loved him would sometimes gaze at them with sad eyes. Who knows? perhaps they had read what hour of day it was for themselves in that whitening brow? Alas and alas! for them as for him, 'twas the hour for the grim supper with the cold white-marble Commendatore, after which only Hell is left – first the Hell of old age, then the other! And this perhaps is why, before sharing with him this last, bitter meal, they planned to offer him this supper of their own, and made it the miracle of art it was.

Yes, a miracle of good taste and refinement, of patrician luxury, elegance, and pretty conceits; the most charming, the most delicious, the most toothsome, the most heady, and, above all, the most original of suppers. How original, just think for a moment! Commonly it is love of merriment, the thirst for amusement, that supply motives for a supper-party; but this one was dedicated only to fond memories and sad regrets, we might almost say to despair – but despair in full dress, despair hidden beneath smiles and laughter, despair that craved just one more merry night, one more escapade, one last hour of youth, one last intoxication – and so an end of it all for ever.

The fair Amphitryons of this incredible supper, so far removed from the timid habits of the society to which they belonged, must surely have experienced something of the feelings of Sardanapalus on his funeral pyre when he heaped upon it, to perish with him, wives, slaves, horses, jewels, all the splendid trappings of his life. They too collected at this last supper of farewell all the splendid trappings of their past. To it they brought all their stores of beauty, of wit and wisdom, of magnificence and power, to pour them forth once and for all in one supreme and final conflagration.

The hero before whom they wrapped and robed themselves in this garment of consuming fire counted for more in their eyes than all Asia did for Sardanapalus. They flirted with him as never women flirted with any man before, or with any roomful of men; and their keen coquetry was yet further inflamed by jealousy, which is concealed in good society, but which they had no cause to dissemble here, for they all knew that he had been the lover of each and all of them, and shame shared among so many ceases to be shame at all . . . The sole and only rivalry between

them was, which should carve his epitaph deepest in her heart?

That night he enjoyed the rich, sovereign, nonchalant, ruminating pleasure of a father confessor and a sultan. There he sat, monarch and master, in the centre of the table, facing the Comtesse de Chiffrevas, in her boudoir with its peach-blossom hangings – or was it the fruit of the tree of the knowledge of evil? – this has always been a moot point. The fiery gaze of his blue eye – heavenly blue, many a poor creature has deemed to her cost, to find it later of quite another sort – was fixed on his fair companions. All twelve were beautiful, all were dressed to perfection; and, seated round the festive board, which glistened with crystal lights and flowers, they displayed, from the scarlet of the open rose to the soft gold of the mellow grape, every nuance of ripe and opulent charms.

Only the crude green of extreme youth was absent, the little girls Byron loathed, smelling of bread and butter, thin, weedy, undeveloped creatures. Fine, full-flavoured summer, rich and generous autumn, these were the seasons represented – full curves and ample proportions, dazzling bosoms, beating in majestic swell above liberally-cut corsages, and below the clear modelling of the naked shoulder, arms of every type of beauty, but mostly powerful arms, Sabine biceps, that have struggled against the Roman ravisher, vigorous enough, you would think, to grasp the wheels of the chariot of life and twine around the spokes and stop its course by sheer force.

I have spoken of happy ideas. One of the happiest at this supper was to have all the waiting done by maidservants, that nothing might disturb the harmony of a celebration where women were the only queens, and did all the honours . . . Señor Don Juan then was able to bathe his burning gaze in a sea of living and dazzling flesh, such as Rubens delights to flaunt in his strong, fleshy pictures, but, besides, he could plunge his pride in the ether, more or less transparent, more or less turgid, of all these hearts. The fact is, at bottom, and despite all appearances to the contrary, Don Juan is an ardent idealist! He is like the Devil, his master, who loves men's souls better than their bodies, and actually traffics in the former by choice, the hellish slave-driver!

Witty, high-bred, and aristocratic, but for the nonce as recklessly gay as pages of the household – when there was a king's household and pages of it – they exhibited a scintillating brilliance, a dash, a verve, a *brio*, that were beyond compare. They felt themselves in better form than they had ever been in their most palmy days; they felt a new and mysterious power in their inmost being which they had never suspected the existence of before.

Joy at this discovery, a sensation of tripled intensity in the vital powers, still more the physical incitements, so stimulating to highly-strung temperaments, the flashing lights, the penetrating odour of many flowers dying in an atmosphere overheated with the emanations of all these lovely bodies, the sting of heady wines, all acted together. Then the mere thought of this supper, which had just the piquancy of naughtiness the fair Neapolitan asked for in her lemonade to make it perfectly delicious, the intoxicating notion of complicity in this wild, wicked feast – not that it condescended for an instant to any of the vulgar incidents of the Regent's suppers; it remained throughout true to the tone of the Faubourg Saint-Germain and the nineteenth century, and of all these lovely bosoms, with hearts beating beneath that had been under fire and still loved to tempt the fray, not one lost so much as a pin or a knot of ribbon – all these things together helped to tune the magic harp which all of them carried within themselves, and to stretch the strings wellnigh to breaking-point, till they quivered again in passionate octaves and ineffable diapasons of emotion . . . A curious page it will make of his Secret Memoirs, this, if Ravila ever writes them! . . . As I told the Marquise Guy de Ruy, I was not at the supper myself, and if I am able to report some of its incidents and the narrative with which it concluded, I owe them to no other than Ravila himself who, faithful to the traditional indiscretion of all the Don Juan breed, took the trouble one evening to tell me the whole story.

III

It was getting late – or, rather, early – and dawn was near. On the ceiling, and at one spot in the pink silk curtains of the boudoir, otherwise hermetically closed, there grew and increased a splash of opalescent light, like an ever-enlarging eye, the eye of day, as if it wanted to look in through the crevice and see what was doing in the brilliantly lighted room. A certain languor was in the air, assailing these champions of the Round Table, these merry-makers who had been so animated but a moment ago.

The crisis is familiar at every supper-party, the instant when, wearied with the gaiety and emotional stress of the night, everything seems to languish at once, drooping heads, burning cheeks, reddened or paled by excitement, tired eyes under heavy, darkened lids, even the candles themselves, which seem to quiver and grow larger in the many-branched candelabra, fiery flowers with stems of chiselled bronze and gold.

The conversation, hitherto general and vivacious, a game of shuttle-cock, where each had put in her stroke, had grown fragmentary and broken, and no distinct word was now audible amid the general confusion of voices which, with their aristocratic tones, mingled in a pretty babble, like birds at break of day on the confines of a wood, when one of them – a high-pitched voice, imperious, almost insolent, as a duchess's should be – cried suddenly above all the rest to the Comte de Ravila what was evidently the conclusion of a previous whispered conversation between the two, which none of the others, each engaged in talk with her immediate neighbour, had heard.

'You are the reputed Don Juan of our day: well! you should tell us the history of the conquest of all others which most flattered your pride as a ladies' man, and which you judge, in the light of the present moment, the greatest love of your life . . .'

And the question, no less than the voice in which it was uttered, instantly cut short the scattered conversations that were buzzing round the table, and imposed a sudden silence.

The voice was that of the Duchesse de *** – I will not lift the veil of asterisks, but you will very likely know who it was when I tell you she is the fairest of all fair women, both complexion and hair, with the darkest eyes under long golden eyebrows in all the Faubourg Saint-Germain. She was seated, like a Saint at God's right hand, at the right hand of the Comte de Ravila, the God of the Feast, a god that, for the moment, waived his right to use his enemies as his footstool; slender and spiritual, like an arabesque and a fairy, in her dress of green velvet, with glints of silver, the long train twining round her chair, no bad imitation of the serpent's tail in which the alluring shape of the sea-nymph Melusina terminates.

'A happy thought!' put in the Comtesse de Chiffrevas, seconding as mistress of the house the wish expressed by the duchess. 'Yes! the love of all loves, inspired or felt, you would most gladly live again, were such a thing possible.'

'Oh, I would be glad to live them all again!' cried Ravila, with the unquenchable gusto of a Roman Emperor, the insatiable craving your utterly *blasé* man of pleasure sometimes retains. And he flourished aloft his champagne glass, the glass our fathers drank from, tall and slender,

and called by them a *flûte*, perhaps from the celestial harmonies in
which it often bathes our heart! Then he embraced in one sweeping look
the whole circle of fair women that wreathed the board so royally. 'And
still,' he went on, replacing his glass before him with a sigh that sounded
strange from such a Nebuchadnezzar, whose only experience as yet
of the grass of the field as an article of diet had been the tarragon salads
at the Café Anglais – 'and still, how true it is there is always *one* among
all the emotions of a lifetime that shines ever in the memory more
brightly than the rest, as life advances – one for which we would gladly
exchange them all.'

'The brightest diamond of the casket,' murmured the Comtesse de
Chiffrevas in a dreamy tone, perhaps looking back at the sparkling facets
of her own career.

'. . . The legends of my country', broke in the Princess Jable – who is
from the foothills of the Ural Mountains – 'tell of a famous and fabulous
diamond, rose-coloured at first, but which turns black presently, yet
remains a true diamond all the time, and sparkles the more brilliantly
for the change . . .' She said it with the strange exotic charm peculiar to
her, this Gipsy Princess. For a true gipsy she is, married for love by the
handsomest prince of all the exiled Polish nobility; yet having as much
the air of a high-born princess as if she had first seen the light in the
palace of the Jagellons.

A regular explosion followed. 'Yes! yes!' they clamoured with one
voice. 'Tell us, Comte!' they urged in a tone already vibrating with
a passionate supplication, curiosity quivering in the very curls that
fringed the back of their necks. They drew together, shoulder to shoulder; some with cheek on hand and elbow on the board, some leaning
back in their chairs, with open fans before their mouths, all challenging
him with wide, inquisitive eyes.

'If you are bent on hearing the story . . .' said the comte with the non-
chalance of a man well aware how much procrastination adds to the
keenness of desire.

'We are, we are!' cried the duchesse, gazing, as a Turkish despot
might at his sabre's edge, at the gold dessert knife she held in her fingers.

'Well, listen then,' he said finally, still with the same fine air of indifference.

They fell into attitudes of profound attention, and, fixing their gaze
on his face, devoured him with their eyes. Every love-story is interesting
to a woman; but here, perhaps – who knows? – the chief charm lay for

each one of his audience in the thought that the tale he was about to unfold might be her own . . . They knew him to be too much of a gentleman and too well-bred not to be sure he would suppress all names and, where necessary, slur over indiscreet details; and their conviction of this fact made them so much the more eager to hear the story. They not only desired but, what is more, they hoped – each for a special and particular sop to her own vanity.

Yet this same vanity was on the qui vive to scent a rival in this reminiscence called up as the tenderest in a life that must have been so full of them. The old sultan was going once more to throw the handkerchief . . . that no hand would stoop to pick up, but which the favoured *one* it should have fallen to would silently and gratefully receive into her heart.

Knowing what his fair audience expected, you will now be able to realise the utterly unexpected thunderclap he called down on all those listening heads.

IV

'I have often heard moralists declare – men who have had deep experience of life,' began the Comte de Ravila, 'that the strongest of all our loves is neither the first nor yet the last, as many think, but the second. But in these matters everything is uncertain, and at any rate it was not so with me . . . What you ask me about, ladies, the story I am about to tell you tonight, dates from the best period of my youth. I was not then what is technically called a "young man", but I was young, albeit I had already, as an old uncle of mine, a knight of Malta, used to say to describe this epoch of life, sown my wild oats. I was in the full vigour of my prime, and I was in full *relations* (to use the pretty Italian phrase) with a woman you all know well, and have all admired . . .'

At this the look which each of the group simultaneously cast at all the rest, one and all eagerly drinking in the old serpent's honeyed words, was a thing to have seen – for, indeed, it is indescribable.

'The woman in question', Ravila went on, 'had every element of "distinction" you can imagine, in every sense of the word. She was young, rich, of noble name, beautiful, witty, and artistic – simple, too, and unaffected, with the genuine unaffectedness to be found only in well-bred circles, and not always there – to crown all, without another thought or inspiration but to please me, to be my devoted slave, at once the fondest of mistresses, and the best of comrades.

'I was not, I have reason to believe, the first man she had loved . . . She had given her affections once before – and it was not to her husband; but the whole affair had been virtuous, platonic, utopian – the sort of love that exercises rather than satisfies a woman's heart, that trains its powers for another and fuller passion, which is bound to supervene before long. It is prentice love, in fact, something like the *messe blanche* young priests repeat by way of rehearsal, that they may not blunder in the genuine solemn Mass that is to follow . . . When I came into her life she was only at the "white Mass"; I was her genuine Mass – and she went through it with every circumstance of pomp and ceremony, like a very cardinal.'

At this the prettiest smile flashed out on the twelve sweet mouths that listened round, like a circling eddy on the limpid surface of a pool . . . It was gone in an instant, but entrancing while it lasted.

'She was indeed one in a thousand!' the comte resumed. 'Rarely have I known more real good-heartedness, more gentle compassion, more justness of feeling – and this, even in love, which is, you know, a passion made up of evil as well as good . . . Nowhere have I seen less manoeuvring, or less prudishness and vanity, two things so often entangled in the web of feminine character, like a skein clawed over by a mischievous cat . . . The cat had no part in her composition . . . She was what those confounded romance-writers who poison our minds with phrases would call a "simple, primitive nature, complicated and embellished by civilisation"; but she had borrowed of it only the pretty luxury of her habits, and not one of those little vices that sometimes seem even more alluring than the luxuries.'

'Was she dark or fair?' suddenly interrupted the duchesse, with a startling directness, tired out with so much metaphysics.

'Ah! you miss my point!' exclaimed Ravila keenly. 'Well, I will tell you; her hair was dark, black as the blackest jet, the most perfect ebony mirror I have ever seen flash back the light from a woman's head, but her complexion was fair – and it is by complexion, not hair, you should pronounce a woman brunette or blonde,' added this student of the sex, who had observed women for something else than just to paint their portraits afterwards . . . 'She was blonde with black hair . . .'

Each blonde head around the table (alas, only blonde-*haired* they!) betrayed an almost imperceptible movement of disappointment. For them clearly the tale had henceforth lost something of its interest.

'She had the ebony locks of Night,' resumed Ravila, 'but crowning the face of Aurora, for indeed her face glowed with a rosy freshness of dawn, as dazzling as rare, that had triumphantly resisted years of Paris life with its hot rooms and artificial light, that burns up so many roses in the flames of its candelabra. *Her* roses seemed but to win a richer hue, so brilliant was the carmine that mantled on cheek and lip! Indeed, this twofold radiance accorded well with the ruby she always wore on her forehead (the frontlet was still in fashion in those days), which, in combination with her flashing eyes, whose very brilliancy made it impossible to distinguish their colour, formed a triangle, as it were, of three bright jewels in her face! Tall, but robust, and even majestic in figure, cut out for the helpmate of a colonel of Dragoons – her husband at that time was only a major in the Light Horse – she enjoyed, for all her fine ladyhood, a peasant woman's vigorous health, who drinks in the sun at every pore. And she had all the heat and ardour of the sun in her veins, and in her very soul as well – ever present, and ever ready . . . But – and this was the strange part of it – this being, so strong and simple and unspoiled, as generous and as pure as the red blood that mantled on her cheeks and dyed her rosy arms, was – can you credit it? – maladroit and awkward in a lover's arms . . .'

Here one or two fair auditors dropped their eyes, only to raise them again directly with a look of demure mischief in their depths . . .

'Yes! awkward in this respect as she was reckless in her regard for appearances,' continued Ravila, and vouchsafed no further information on this delicate point. 'In fact, the man who loved her had to be incessantly teaching her two lessons, neither of which she ever really learned – not to affront needlessly public opinion, a foe that is always under arms and always merciless, and to practise in the intimacy of private life those all-important acts of love that guard passion from dying of satiety. Love she had in abundance, but the art and mystery of its skilled exponents were beyond her ken . . . She was the antipodes of most women, who possess the latter qualifications to perfection, but of the other not a whit. Now to comprehend and apply the cunning maxims of *Il Principe*, you must be a Borgia to begin with. Borgia comes first, Machiavelli second; one is the poet, the other the critic. No Borgia was she, but just a good woman in love, as simple-minded, with all her monumental beauty, as the little maid in the rustic picture who tries to take up a handful of spring water from the fountain to quench her thirst, but in her trembling haste lets it trickle away every drop between her fingers, and stands there an image of embarrassment and confusion . . .

'Yet in a way the contrast was piquant and almost delightful between this embarrassed awkwardness and the grand, passion-fraught personality of the woman, who would have deceived the most acute observer when seen in society – who knew love, and even love's bliss, but had not the faculty to pay back half of what she received. Only, unfortunately, I was not artist enough to be content with this mere delight of contrast; hence now and again displays on her part of disquiet, jealousy, and even violence. But all this jealousy, disquiet, violence, was swallowed up in the inexhaustible kindness of her heart at the first sign of pain she thought she had inflicted – as awkward at wounding as she was at caressing! Tigress of an unknown species, she fondly imagined she had claws, but lo! when she would show them, none were to be found within the sheath of her beautiful velvet paws. Her very scratches were velvet-soft!'

'What is the man driving at?' whispered the Comtesse de Chiffrevas to her neighbour. 'This surely cannot be Don Juan's proudest triumph!'

All these complex natures could not understand such simplicity, and remained incredulous.

'Thus we lived', Ravila went on, 'on terms of friendship, now and then interrupted by storms, yet never shipwrecked, a friendship that, in the little village they call Paris, was a mystery to none . . . The marquise – she was a marquise . . .'

There were three at the table, and raven-locked too. But they made no sign. They knew only too well it was not of them he spoke . . . The only velvet about the trio was on the upper lip of one of the three – a lip bearing a voluptuous shadowing of down, and for the moment, I can assure you, a well-marked expression of disdain.

'. . . And a marquise three times over, just as pashas may be pashas of three tails,' continued Ravila, who was getting into the swing of his narrative. 'The marquise was one of those women who have no idea of hiding anything, and who, if they had, could never do it. Her daughter even, a child of thirteen, for all her youth and innocence, saw only too clearly the nature of the feeling the mother had for me. I know not which of our poets has asked what the girls think of us, the girls whose mothers we have loved. A deep question I often put to myself when I caught the child's inquisitive gaze fixed black and menacing upon me from the ambush of her great, dark eyes . . . A shy reserved creature, she would, more often than not, leave the drawing-room when I entered and, if obliged to remain, would invariably station herself as far away from me as possible; she had an almost convulsive horror of my person – which she strove to hide in her own bosom, but which was too strong for her, and betrayed itself against her will by little almost imperceptible signs. I noticed every one. The marquise, though anything but an observant woman, was forever warning me: "You must take care, dearest, I think my girl is jealous of you . . ."

'But I was taking much better care all the while than she was.

'Had the little girl been the Devil himself I would have defied her to decipher my game . . . But her mother's was as clear as day. Everything was visible in the rosy mirror of her beautiful face, so often troubled by passing clouds! From the strange dislike the girl showed, I could not help thinking she had surprised her mother's secret through some indiscreet burst of feeling, some involuntary look fraught with excess of tenderness. I may tell you she was a funny-looking child, quite un-worthy of the glorious mould she had issued from, an ugly child, even by her mother's admission, who only loved her the more for it. A little rough-cut topaz – how shall I describe it? – a half-finished sculptor's study in bronze – but with eyes black as night, and having a strange, uncanny magic of their own. Later on . . .'

But here he stopped dead, as if regretting his burst of confidence, and fearful of having said too much . . . Every face once more expressed an open, eager, vivid curiosity, and the comtesse, with a knowing air of pleased expectancy, actually dropped from between her lovely lips an expressive 'At last!'

'In the earlier days of my liaison with her mother,' the Comte de Rav-ila resumed, 'I had shown the child all the little fondling familiarities one has with children . . . I used to bring her bags of sugared almonds; I used to call her my "little witch", and very often, when talking to her mother, I would amuse myself with fingering the curls that hung over her temple – thin, sickly-looking curls, like black tow – but the "little witch", whose big mouth had a pretty smile for everybody else, at once waxed pensive, her little face grew tense and rigid, the wrinkled mask of an overburdened caryatid, and as my hand brushed her forehead, it looked for all the world as though it bore the crushing weight of some vast entablature.

'After a while, meeting invariably the same sullenness and apparent hostility, I took to leaving this sensitive plant alone, which drew in its sad-coloured petals so violently at the least touch of a caress . . . I even left off speaking to her! "She feels you are robbing her," the marquise would say to me. "Her instinct tells her you are appropriating a portion of her mother's love." Sometimes she would add outright: "The child is my conscience, and her jealousy my remorse."

'Once, the marquise had tried to question her as to the profound disfavour in which she held me, but she had got nothing out of her but the broken, obstinate, stupid answers you have to drag out with a corkscrew of reiterated questions from a child that prefers not to speak . . . "Nothing is the matter. . . . I don't know . . ." and so on. Finally, seeing how hard and obstinate the little image was, she had left off questioning her, and turned away in sheer weariness.

'I forgot, by the bye, to tell you one thing. The queer child was profoundly religious, in a gloomy, medieval, Spanish, superstitious sort of way. She twined around her meagre little person all kinds of scapularies and stuck on her bosom, which was as flat as the back of your hand, and round her swarthy throat a whole heap of crosses, Blessed Virgins, and Holy Spirits. "You are a free-thinker, you know," the marquise would say to me, "worse luck; perhaps you have shocked her feelings some time with your talk. Be very careful of anything you say before her; and do not add to my sins in the eyes of my child, towards whom I already feel myself so guilty!" Then, later on, the girl's behaviour showing no change or improvement whatever: "You will end by hating the child," the marquise would complain anxiously, "and I cannot blame you." But she was wrong in this; my feeling towards the sullen child was one of simple indifference, when I took the trouble to think of her at all.

'I treated her with the ceremonious politeness usual between grown-up people who do not like each other. I addressed her formally as Mademoiselle, and she returned the compliment with a freezing "Monsieur" . . . She would do nothing when I was there to attract admiration or even notice . . . Her mother could never persuade her to show me one of her drawings or play a piece on the piano in my presence. If ever I came upon her seated at the instrument practising eagerly and industriously, she would stop dead, get up from the music-stool, and refuse utterly to go on . . .

'Once only, when there was company, and her mother desired her to play, she consented to take her place at the open keyboard, with a look of being victimised that was anything but propitiating, I can tell you, and began some drawing-room piece with abominably difficult fingering. I was standing by the fireplace, and enfiladed her with my gaze. Her back was towards me, and there was no mirror in front of her in which she could see I was looking at her . . . All of a sudden her back – she always held herself ill, and many a time her mother would tell her: "If you *will* hold yourself like that, you'll end by getting consumption" – well, all of a sudden her back straightened as if my look had broken her spine like a bullet; and, slamming down the lid of the piano with a resounding crash, she rushed out of the room . . . They went to look for her, but for that evening, at any rate, nothing would induce her to come back.

'Well, vain as men are, it would seem their vanity is often blind, and, for all her strange behaviour (and indeed I gave it very little attention), I had never a suspicion of the true feeling the mysterious creature entertained for me. Nor yet had her mother; jealous as the latter was of every woman who entered her drawing-room, in this case her jealousy was as fast asleep as my own vanity. The truth was eventually revealed in a sufficiently startling fashion. The marquise, who could keep nothing from her intimates, told me the story, her face still pale with the fright she had had, though bursting with laughter at the notion of having been frightened at all. In doing so she was ill-advised.'

The word 'ill-advised' the count had marked with just that touch of emphasis a clever actor knows how to throw into his voice when he has a point to make. This was the thread, he was perfectly aware of the fact, on which the whole interest of his story now hung.

The mere hint was enough apparently, for all twelve faces flushed once more with an intensity of emotion comparable only to the cherubim's countenances before the throne of the Almighty! Is not curiosity in a woman's heart as intense an emotion as ever adoration among the angels of God? . . . For his part, he marked them all, those cherub faces (which were a good deal more than mere head and shoulders, though), and, finding them doubtless primed for what he had to say, quickly resumed and went on without further pause.

'Yes, she could not help bursting with laughter, merely to think of it! – so the marquise told me a while after, when she came to relate the story; but she had been in no laughing mood at first! – "Only picture the scene," she began (I will endeavour to recall her exact words); "I was seated just where we are now."

'This was one of those small double sofas known as *dos-à-dos*, of all contrivances in the way of furniture surely the best-designed for a pair of lovers to quarrel and make it up again, without leaving their seats.

' "But you were not where you are now – thank goodness – when, who do you think was announced? – you would never guess – who but

the respected *curé* of Saint-Germain-des-Prés? Do you know him? . . .
No, you never go to church, you bad man! . . . So how should you know
the poor old *curé*, who is a saint, and who never sets foot inside the doors
of any woman in his parish unless it is a question of raising money for his
poor or his church? For a moment I thought this was what he had come
for now.

' "He had prepared my daughter at the proper time for her first communion; and as she went regularly to communion, subsequently, she
had retained him as her confessor. For this reason, over and over again
since then, I had invited the good priest to dine with us, but always in
vain. On entering the room he displayed the greatest agitation, and I
read in his usually placid features manifest signs of an embarrassment so
extreme and so uncontrollable, I could not set it down to the account of
mere shyness. Involuntarily the first words that escaped me were: 'Good
heavens, Father! What is the matter?'

' " 'The matter, dear madame,' he began, '. . . the matter is, you see
before you the most embarrassed man in Europe. For fifty years I have
been a minister in God's service, and all that time I have never had a
more delicate mission to perform, or one that baffled me more completely to understand . . .'

' "Then he sat down, asking me to have the door shut against all
comers throughout our interview. As you may suppose, all these solemn
preliminaries began rather to frighten me . . .

' "Noticing this, he added: 'Nay! do not be frightened, I beg of you;
you will need all your calmness to attend to my story, and to account, to
my satisfaction, for the unheard-of circumstance we have to deal with,
and which even now I cannot believe authentic . . . Your daughter,
madame, on whose behalf I am here, is – you know it as well as I do – an
angel of purity and goodness. I know her very soul. I have held it
between my hands since she was a child of seven, and I am convinced
she is deceiving herself – through sheer innocence of heart, it may be
. . . But this morning she came to me to avow in confession – you will
not believe it, nor can I, but the word must come out – that she was
pregnant!'

' "A cry escaped me of wonder and incredulity . . .

' " 'I did the very same thing this morning in my confessional,' the
priest declared, 'on hearing her make this assertion, accompanied as it
was by every mark of the most genuine and terrible despair. I know the
child thoroughly; she is absolutely ignorant of the world and its wicked-

ness . . . Of all the young girls, I confess, she is undoubtedly the one I could most unhesitatingly answer for before God. There is no more to tell! We priests are the surgeons of souls, and it is our duty to deliver them of shameful secrets they would rather conceal, with hands careful neither to wound nor pollute. I therefore proceeded, with all possible guardedness, to interrogate, question, and cross-question the desperate girl. But, the avowal once made, the fault once confessed – she calls it a crime herself, and her eternal damnation, fully believing herself, poor girl, a lost soul – she thenceforth refused to say another word, maintaining an obstinate silence which she broke only to beseech me to come to you, madame, to inform you of the crime – "for mamma *must* know", she said, "and I shall never, never be brave enough to tell her." '

' "You may easily imagine with what mingled feelings of amazement and anxiety I listened to the *curé* of Saint-Germain-des-Prés. I was just as sure as he was, surer, in fact, of my little girl's innocence; but do not the innocent sometimes fall, out of very innocence? . . . And what she had told the confessor was not in the nature of things impossible . . . I did not believe it! . . . could not believe it! but still it was not in itself impossible! . . . She was only thirteen, but she was a woman, and the very fact of her precocity had startled me before now . . . A fever, a frenzy of curiosity came over me.

' " 'I must and will know all!' I cried excitedly to the worthy priest as he stood there listening to me with a bewildered air, plucking his hat to pieces in his agitation. 'Leave me, Father. She would not speak before you; but I am certain she will tell me everything . . . I am certain I can drag everything out of her. Then we shall understand what is now so utterly incomprehensible.'

' "On this the good priest took his departure. The instant he was gone I sprang upstairs to my daughter's room, not having patience enough to send for her and wait till she came.

' "I found her kneeling – no! not kneeling, prostrate – before her crucifix, pale as death, her eyes dry and very red, like eyes that have wept many bitter tears. I took her in my arms, seated her by my side, and presently on my knees, and told her I could not believe what her confessor had just been telling me was true.

' "But here she interrupted me to assure me with a heartbroken voice and look that it *was* true, what he had said; and at this point, more and more anxious and wondering, I asked her who it was that . . .

' "I left the sentence unfinished . . . The terrible moment was come! She had her head and face on my shoulder . . . but I could see the blush of shame burning on her neck behind, and feel her shudder. The same leaden silence she had opposed to her father confessor, she now opposed to me. She was impenetrable.

' " 'It must be someone very much beneath you, since you are so deeply ashamed? . . .' I said, trying to make her speak in self-exculpation, for I knew she had plenty of pride.

' "But still the same silence, the same burying of her head on my shoulder. This lasted what seemed to me an infinity of time, when suddenly she said, without lifting her head: 'Swear you will forgive me, mother!'

' "I swore everything she asked me, at the risk of perjuring myself a hundred times over – little I cared! I was boiling with impatience – boiling . . . I thought my skull would burst and let my brains out . . .

' " 'Well, then! it was Monsieur de Ravila,' she whispered, without changing her position in my arms.

' "Oh! the shock of hearing that name, Amédée! At one fell swoop I was receiving full and condign punishment for the great fault of my life, and my heart quailed within me! You are so terrible a man where women are concerned, you have made me so fearful of rivals, that those fatal words of doubt, 'why not?' – so heart-rending when spoken of the man you love, yet suspect – rose involuntarily to my lips. What I felt, however, I had resolution enough left to hide from the cruel child, who had, it may be, guessed her mother's guilty secret.

' " 'Monsieur de Ravila!' I ejaculated in a tone I feared must betray everything; 'why, you never even speak to him!' – 'You avoid him,' I was going to add, for my anger was rising, I felt it was . . . 'You are surely very deceitful, the pair of you!' – But I refrained: was I not bound to learn the details, one by one, of this vile tale of seduction? . . . I began to question her with an enforced gentleness I thought would have killed me, when she released me from the torture of the rack, saying with perfect *naïveté*:

' " 'It was one evening, Mother. He was in the big armchair by the fireside, facing the sofa . . . He sat there ever so long, then presently got up, and I – I had the misfortune to go and sit down in the same chair after him. Oh! Mamma . . . it was just as if I had fallen into a flame of fire. I wanted to get up, but I could not . . . for my heart had stopped beating! and I felt . . . Oh! Mamma, Mamma, I felt . . . that what hurt me so . . . was a baby! . . .' " '

The marquise laughed, Ravila said, when she told him the story; but not one of the twelve women surrounding the table as much as thought of laughing – nor Ravila either.

'And this, ladies, believe me or not, as you please,' he added by way of conclusion, 'I consider the greatest triumph of my life, the passion I am proudest of having inspired.'

And with this he fell silent – a silence they left unbroken one and all. His auditors were pensive . . . Had they understood his meaning?

When Joseph was a slave in the Lady Potiphar's household, he was so handsome, says the Koran, that, in their dreamy state, the women he waited on at table used to cut their fingers with their knives as they gazed at him. But we have travelled far since Joseph's time, and the pre-occupations we experience at dessert are not so absorbing nowadays.

'But there, what a consummate idiot, with all her cleverness, your marquise was, to have told you about such a thing!' at last said the duchesse, who condescended to be cynical, but who cut neither her fingers nor anything else with the gold dessert knife she still held in her hand.

Meanwhile the Comtesse de Chiffrevas was gazing fixedly into the depths of a glass of Rhine wine, a green crystal glass, as profound and mysterious as her own reverie.

'And the little witch?' she asked.

'Oh, she was dead – she died quite young – married to somebody in the country – when her mother told me the story,' Ravila quietly replied.

'But for that . . .' said the duchesse thoughtfully.

Alfred de Musset

Alfred de Musset (1810–57), poet, novelist and dramatist, is associated with the Romantic movement, but his best writing often displays other concerns. Born into a respectable Parisian family, Musset tried several 'serious' careers before yielding to his literary vocation. In 1828 he translated De Quincey's *Confessions of an English Opium Eater*, and the publication in 1830 of *Contes d'Espagne et d'Italie* – a series of often Byronic narrative poems – established his position amongst the Romantics. Following the failure of his early comedy *La Nuit vénitienne* (1830), Musset turned away from the stage and began, instead, to write his *Un Spectacle dans un fauteuil* (1833–4), a series of dramatic works intended to be read rather than performed. These display a concern for the *mal du siècle*, the worldweariness of the Romantic individual born too late to define his masculinity in a Napoleonic army and unable to fix his sense of self. Such ideas are developed in the novel *La Confession d'un enfant du siècle* (1836) whose account of amorous disillusionment echoes Musset's own relationship with George Sand.

Mimi Pinson

A MONG THE STUDENTS WHO ATTENDED THE LECTURES, LAST
year, at the School of Medicine, there was one called Eugène
Aubert. He was a young man of good family, about nineteen years
of age. His parents lived in the country and made him a small but sufficient allowance. He lived a quiet life and was considered to have a mild
character. His friends loved him; always finding him kind and helpful,
generous and open-hearted. The only fault with which he could be
reproached was a singular liking for reverie and solitude, and he had
such an excessive reserve in his conversation and his smallest actions
that he was nicknamed the 'Little Girl', a description, moreover, at
which he laughed himself, and on which his friends did not place any
construction that could offend him, believing him to be as courageous
as anyone else when necessary; but it must be admitted that his conduct
justified, in a small way, this appellation, particularly by the way it contrasted with the habits of his companions. As long as it was a question
of work, he was the first; but if it was a suggestion of a pleasure party, a
dinner at the Moulin de Beurre, or a dance at the Chaumière, the 'Little
Girl' shook his head and returned to his room. This was a monstrous
state of affairs to the students; not only had Eugène no mistress,
although his youth and his appearance would have helped him considerably, but he had never been seen flirting at a bar with a grisette, an
immemorial custom in the Quartier Latin. The beauties who thronged
the Montagne Sainte-Geneviève, and shared among themselves the
love-affairs of the schools, inspired him with such a repugnance that it
almost amounted to aversion. He regarded them as a species apart,
dangerous, ungrateful, and depraved, born to disseminate illness and
misfortune in exchange for a few pleasures. Avoid all the women there,
he said to himself, they are bad lots.

And unfortunately he found too many examples to justify the horror with which they inspired him. The quarrels, the dissipations,

sometimes even the ruin which followed these transient liaisons, with their outward aspect of happiness, were only too easy to name; last year like today, and probably the same as next year.

Naturally Eugène's friends laughed continually at his morals and scruples.

'What do you mean?' one of his friends called Marcel often asked him, who pretended to be a jovial fellow; 'what does one fault prove, or one accidental happening?'

'That one should abstain,' replied Eugène, 'for fear of it happening a second time.'

'Wrong reasoning,' rejoined Marcel; 'the argument of a *capucin de carte*, who falls if his neighbour stumbles. What are you worrying yourself about? Which of us has not lost at the game? Is that a reason for turning monk? One has no money and another only drinks water; is that a reason for Élise to lose her appetite? Whose fault is it if your neighbour pawns his watch so that he may go to Montmorency and cut a caper? No one is hurt by it. You make love to Rosalie and get a sword thrust through you; she turns her back on you, quite naturally: does she suffer by it? They are the little inconveniences of which life is full, and even so they are much less common than you suppose. Take a Sunday, when it is fine, and there are many friendly couples in the cafés in the gardens, and the public-houses. Look at those great omnibuses, crowded with grisettes, going to Ranelagh or Belleville. Count those who go out, on a fête day, from the Quartier Saint-Jacques: the battalions of dressmakers, the armies of sempstresses, the crowds of tobacconists; they all amuse themselves, they all have their love-affairs, they all go to lie down around Paris under the arbours of the countryside, like flocks of sparrows. If it rains they all go to the play, eat oranges and weep; for these people eat a lot, it is true, and weep readily; which goes to show a good disposition. But what harm do those poor women do, who have sewn, basted, hemmed and mended all the week, in showing an example, on Sundays, of forgetting troubles and looking to the future? And what could an honest man do better, who on his part, having spent a week dissecting things unpleasant, clears his eyes by looking at a pretty face, a rounded leg, and life?'

'Whited sepulchres,' said Eugène.

'I say and maintain', continued Marcel, 'that one must and should sing the praises of the grisettes, and that friendship with them does no harm. First, they are virtuous, for they spend the day in making garments indispensable to modesty and decency; secondly, they are courteous, for there is no proprietress of a shop who does not see that her shop-girls speak politely to customers; thirdly, they are very careful and very clean, inasmuch as they constantly have in their hands lingerie which they must not soil, under penalty of being fined; fourthly, they are sincere, because they drink ratafia; in the fifth place, they are economical and frugal, for they have to work hard to make thirty sous, and if on occasions they show themselves greedy and extravagant, it is never with their own money; sixthly, they are very cheerful, because the work they do is in general deadly tedious, so they frisk like a fish in water as soon as their work is done. Another thing that one finds in them is that they are not at all exacting; for as they spend their life pinned to a chair from which they cannot move, they can't run after their lovers like ladies of good society. Besides, they are not loquacious, for they have to count their stitches. They do not spend much on their shoes, because they do not walk much, nor for their dress, for hardly anyone gives them credit. If they are accused of inconstancy, it is not from natural naughtiness; but from the temptation of the great number of different people who pass their shops. From another angle they prove convincingly that they are capable of genuine passion, by the great number of them who throw themselves daily into the Seine or out of the window, or asphyxiate themselves in their homes. It is true, they have the misfortune of being nearly always hungry and thirsty precisely because of their temperance; for it is notorious that they can be satisfied with a glass of beer and a cigarette for a meal; a valuable quality that is rarely met with at home. In short, I maintain that they are good, lovable, faithful, and impartial, and it is regrettable when they finish in a hospital.'

Whilst Marcel was talking like this, as they were seated at a café, he became rather heated, and filling his friend's glass, asked him to drink the health of Mademoiselle Pinson, who was their neighbour; but Eugène, while Marcel continued to harangue his comrades, took his hat and stole away quietly.

II

Mademoiselle Pinson could not exactly be described as a *jolie femme*. There is a great deal of difference between a *jolie femme* and a *jolie grisette*. If a *jolie femme*, recognised as such, in Parisian terms, bethinks herself of wearing a small bonnet, a dress of gingham, and a silk apron, she will be dressed, it is true, like a *jolie grisette*. But if a grisette puts on a hat, a velvet mantle and a silk dress, she does not become a *jolie femme*; on the contrary, it is probable she would look like a portmanteau, and deceive no one. The difference arises from the conditions in which these two beings live, and principally in that cardboard wheel, covered with material and called a hat, which women consider correct to apply to all sides of the head, rather resembling a horse's blinkers. (It should be noted meanwhile that the blinkers prevent the horses from seeing one side or the other, and that the piece of cardboard does not stop anything!)

Whatever it is made of, a small bonnet demands a snub nose, which in its turn should be above a well-cut mouth, in which are good teeth, with a round face as frame. A round face should have sparkling eyes; it is better that they should be as black as possible, and the eyebrows well defined. The hair must be *ad libitum* and in keeping with the black eyes. Such an appearance is far from beauty as generally understood. One would rather describe it as a doll's face, the typical face of the grisette, who would perhaps be ugly under the wheel of cardboard, but whom the bonnet can somehow make charming, more pretty than beautiful. Such was the appearance of Mademoiselle Pinson.

Marcel resolved in his mind that Eugène should pay his addresses to this young lady. Why? Either I know nothing about it, or else because he himself was the admirer of Mademoiselle Zelia, the intimate friend of Mademoiselle Pinson, and it seemed to him natural and proper to arrange matters to suit himself, and to make love in couples. Such plans are not uncommon, and succeed fairly often, opportunity being, since the world existed, the greatest of all temptations. Who can say what events are brought about, happy or unhappy, of love, of quarrels, of joys or of sorrows, by communicating doors, a secret staircase, a corridor, or a broken-down wheel?

Nevertheless, there are certain characters who deny themselves these opportunities. They prefer to work for their enjoyments, not to win them by chance, and they are not disposed to make love just because they find themselves next to a pretty woman in a carriage. Such was Eugène, and Marcel knew it; however, he had long ago formulated a fairly simple plan, that he believed to be admirable, and above all in-fallible, to break down the resistance of his friend.

He made up his mind to give a supper, and could not think of any more appropriate day than his own birthday. He ordered two dozen bottles of beer to be sent to his rooms, a large piece of cold veal with a salad, an enormous *galette de plomb*, and a bottle of champagne.

First he invited two students of his acquaintance, then he told Mademoiselle Zelia that he was giving a party in his rooms, and that she was to bring Mademoiselle Pinson. They were on no account to fail to come. Marcel had the reputation, quite justly, of being one of the 'bloods' of the Quartier Latin, one of those people whom one does not refuse. Scarcely had the clock struck seven when the two grisettes knocked at the door of the student's room: Mademoiselle Zelia in a short dress, grey boots and a flower-trimmed bonnet; Mademoiselle Pinson, more modest, dressed in a black coat which she did not remove, and which gave her, so it was said, a slightly Spanish air, of which she was very proud. Both of them were ignorant, it is hoped, of their host's secret designs.

Marcel had not made the mistake of asking Eugène beforehand; he was too certain of a refusal in that case. It was only after the ladies had sat down to table, and after the first glass had been emptied, that he asked permission to absent himself for a few minutes to go and fetch a friend, and went to the house where Eugène lived. He found him, as usual, at his work, alone, surrounded by his books. After a few remarks, he started gently his usual expostulations; that he was overtiring himself, that he was wrong in not taking any kind of distraction, then he suggested a short walk. Eugène accepted, he was a little tired, in fact, as he had been working all day; the two young men went out together, and after strolling in the Luxembourg Gardens, it was not difficult for Marcel to persuade his friend to return with him to his rooms.

The two grisettes, left alone, and probably tired of waiting, had begun to make themselves at home; they had taken off their bonnets and shawls, and singing, danced a country dance, not without helping themselves to the refreshments, from time to time. With bright eyes and animated faces they ceased their dance, slightly out of breath, as Eugène bowed to them somewhat timidly, looking surprised. Because of his solitary habits, he was scarcely known to them; they had soon taken in his appearance, from head to feet, with that unabashed curiosity which is the privilege of their type; then going on with their singing and dancing, as if nothing had happened. The newcomer, somewhat disconcerted, took a few steps backwards, when Marcel, having closed and locked the door, threw the key noisily on the table.

'No one else yet,' he exclaimed. 'What are my friends doing? But never mind, the wild man is ours. Ladies, allow me to present to you the most virtuous young man in France and Navarre, who has long wished to make your acquaintance, and is, particularly, a great admirer of Mademoiselle Pinson.'

The country dance ceased once more; Mademoiselle Pinson bowed slightly and replaced her bonnet.

'Eugène,' cried Marcel, 'today is my birthday; these two ladies have very kindly come here to celebrate it with us. It is true I nearly brought you here by force; but I hope that, at our united request, you will stay here willingly. It is now nearly eight o'clock; we have time to smoke a pipe whilst waiting for our appetites.'

Speaking thus, he threw a significant look at Mademoiselle Pinson, who, understanding it, bowed once more, smiling, and said gently to Eugène:

'Yes, monsieur, we beg you to.' At this moment the two students invited by Marcel knocked at the door. Eugène, realising that he could not withdraw without being ungracious, resignedly took his seat with the others.

III

The supper was long and noisy. The men, having commenced by filling the room with a fog of smoke, drank the more to refresh themselves. The ladies made most of the conversation, and amused the company with tales more or less scandalous, at the expense of their friends and acquaintances, and adventures more or less true, from the workroom. If the stories lacked probability, they did not lack spice. Two lawyers' clerks, if they were to be believed, had made a profit of twenty thousand francs by dealing in Spanish Funds, and had spent it in six weeks on two girls in a glove shop. The son of one of the richest bankers in Paris offered a well-known dressmaker a box at the opera and a house in the country, which she had refused, preferring to look after her parents and remain faithful to a clerk at the Deux-Magots. A certain personage, who must not be named, and whose rank obliged him to keep the greatest secrecy, went incognito to visit an embroideress in the Passage Pont-Neuf; the latter had been suddenly carried away by the authorities in a post-chaise, at midnight, given a pocketbook full of banknotes and shipped to the United States, etc.

'Enough,' said Marcel, 'we know that. Zelia invents, and as to Mademoiselle Mimi' (as Mademoiselle Pinson was called familiarly) 'her information is not correct. Your lawyers' clerks only got swindled; your banker offered an orange, and your embroideress is so far from the United States that she is to be seen daily, from twelve to four, at the hospital of La Charité, where she has gone to live owing to lack of food.'

Eugène was seated near to Mademoiselle Pinson. He thought he saw her turn pale at this last word, spoken with such indifference. But, almost immediately, she rose, lit a cigarette, and said easily:

'Silence in your turn . . . I claim to speak. As Monsieur Marcel does not believe in fables, I will tell you a true story, "*et quorum pars magna fui*".'

'Do you speak Latin?' said Eugène.

'As you see,' Mademoiselle Pinson replied; 'that sentence comes to me from an uncle, who served under the great Napoleon, and never failed to use it when telling the story of a battle. If you do not know the meaning of these words you may learn without payment. They mean, "I give you my word of honour." You know that I went last week, with one of my friends, to the Odéon . . .'

'Wait a minute,' said Marcel, 'until I cut the cake.'

'Cut, but listen,' replied Mademoiselle Pinson. 'I had gone with Blanchette and Rougette to the Odéon to see a tragedy. Rougette, as you know, has just lost her grandmother; she inherited four hundred francs. We took a box; three students were in the stalls; these young men noticed us, and, with the excuse of our being alone, invited us to supper.'

'Outright – directly?' asked Marcel; 'really it was kind. And I suppose you refused?'

'No, sir!' said Mademoiselle Pinson; 'we accepted and, at the interval, without waiting for the end of the piece, we went to Viot.'

'With your beaux?'

'With our beaux. The waiter, to be sure, began by telling us that there was nothing left; but such a state of affairs could not stop us. We insisted that they should send out and get what was wanting. Rougette ordered a regular wedding feast: prawns, a sweet omelette, mussels, fritters, eggs *à la neige*, everything there was to be had for a good dinner. To tell the truth, our young acquaintances looked rather sour . . .'

'I should think so,' said Marcel.

'We did not mind. The supper brought, we began to imitate fine ladies. We did not like anything, everything displeased us. As soon as one dish was tasted we sent it away and insisted on another being brought. "Waiter, take that away . . . it won't do at all . . . Where did you get such stuff from?" Our friends wanted to eat, but were not allowed to. In short, we supped as Sancho dined, and anger made us even break some crockery.'

'Good behaviour! And what about paying?'

'Precisely the question the three strangers were asking themselves. It seemed to us, from what we heard of a whispered conversation they had together, that one of them possessed six francs, another very much less, and the third only had a watch, which he generously drew from his pocket. In this condition the three unfortunates went to the cashier, with the object of getting some kind of credit. And what do you think the reply was?'

'I should think', said Marcel, 'that they kept you as security, and sent them to the police station.'

'You are wrong,' said Mademoiselle Pinson. 'Before going up to the supper-room, Rougette had taken their measure and paid for everything in advance. Imagine the sensation when Viot said to them: "Gentlemen, the account is already settled!" Our unknown friends looked at us dumbfounded with woeful stupefaction mingled with pure gratitude. We, in the meantime, pretending not to notice anything, walked down and had a cab called.

' "Dear Marquise," said Rougette to me, "we must take these gentlemen to their homes ..." "Willingly, dear Comtesse," I replied. Our poor lovers did not know what to say. Can you imagine how put out they were ... they declined our offer, not wishing us to take them home, and would not give their addresses ... I really believe that they thought we were society ladies, and they lived in the Rue du Chat-qui-pêche!'

The two student friends of Marcel, who, up to the present, had only smoked and drunk in silence, did not seem at all pleased with this story. They looked black; perhaps they knew as much as Mademoiselle Pinson did about this unlucky supper, for they looked at her uneasily as Marcel said to them, laughing:

'Give their names, Mademoiselle Mimi. As it was last week it will not hurt anyone.'

'Never, monsieur,' replied the grisette. 'One may laugh at any man, but damage his career, never ...'

'You are right,' said Eugène, 'and in this case you are perhaps acting more wisely than you think. Among all the young men who fill these schools, there is scarcely one who has not at some time or other made some mistake, or done some foolish thing, and yet the most respectable and distinguished men in France come from them: doctors, magistrates ...'

'Yes,' responded Marcel, 'that is true. There are peers of France who dine at Flicoteaux and do not always have the means to pay their bill.

But', he added, winking, 'have you never seen your friends again?'

'Who do you take us for?' replied Mademoiselle Pinson, in a serious and almost offended manner; 'do you know Blanchette and Rougette? And do you suppose that I . . . ?'

'That's all right,' said Marcel, 'don't be annoyed. But, listen, here is a nice trick. Three scatterbrains who have not perhaps sufficient to pay for their next day's dinner, and throw money away in order to mystify three poor devils as poor as themselves . . .'

'Then why did they invite us to supper?' said Mademoiselle Pinson.

IV

With the cake appeared, in all its glory, the single bottle of champagne as dessert. With the wine the talk turned to singing. 'I hear,' said Marcel, 'as Cervantes said, I hear Zelia coughing; that is a sign that she wants to sing. But, if these gentlemen agree, it is I who am being fêted, and give myself the pleasure of asking Mademoiselle Mimi, if telling her anecdote has not made her hoarse, to give us a song. Eugène,' he added, 'be agreeable and take a glass of wine with your neighbour, and beg her to sing a song for me.'

Eugène blushed and obeyed. Just as Mademoiselle Pinson had not disdained to induce him to remain, he bowed and said to her: 'Yes, Mademoiselle, we beg you to.'

At the same time he raised his glass and touched that of the grisette. From this light contact arose a clear and silver note; Mademoiselle Pinson caught this note and sang it with a pure fresh voice.

'Yes, I will,' she said, 'for my glass has given me the "la". But what do you wish me to sing? I am not conceited, I would have you know, but I do not know any song of the *corps de garde*. I do not fill my memory with such stuff . . .'

'We know that,' said Marcel, 'you are above such stuff; go your own way, opinions are free.'

'Well,' resumed Mademoiselle Pinson, 'I will sing you, to show there's no ill-feeling, some verses written on me.'

'One minute . . . Who is the author?'

'My colleagues in the shop. It is what we compose while we are sewing, so you must not be too critical.'

'Is there a chorus to your song?'

'Certainly; such a thing is always expected.'

'In that case,' said Marcel, 'take your knives, and when the chorus comes beat on the table, but take care to do so in time. Zelia need not if she does not want to.'

'Why not, rude boy?' demanded Zelia, angrily.

'For a very good reason,' replied Marcel; 'but if you wish to join in, take a cork, that will be less painful for our ears and your white hands.'

Marcel had arranged all the glasses and plates in a circle and seated himself in the middle of the table, his knife in his hand. The two students, guests at Rougette's supper, a little more cheerful, removed the bowls of their pipes so as to beat with the wooden mouthpieces; Eugène dreamed, Zelia pouted. Mademoiselle Pinson took a plate and requested permission to break it, to which Marcel replied with a gesture of consent, so the singer, taking some pieces to use as castanets, began the song which her companions had composed, after having apologised for anything it contained flattering to herself . . .

The knives and the pipes, even the chairs, had contributed their noise, of course, at the end of each verse. The glasses danced on the table and the bottles, half-full, rocked joyously, tapping each other's necks.

'And so your good friends', said Marcel, 'composed that song for you? For my part I think it is too affected. Give me those good old songs in which they don't mind what they say . . .' And he tuned up in a loud voice:

> '*Nanette n'avait pas encore quinze ans . . .*'

'Enough, enough,' said Mademoiselle Pinson; 'let us dance; let us have a waltz. Can anyone here play?'

'I have what you want,' said Marcel; 'I have a guitar; but', he continued, while undoing the instrument, 'my guitar is not all it should be; it lacks three of its strings.'

'But here is a piano,' said Zelia; 'Marcel will play for our dance!'

Marcel glared at his mistress as if she had accused him of a crime. It was true he knew enough to play for a country dance; but it was for him, as for many others, a species of torture to which he submitted very unwillingly.

Zelia, in betraying him, took her revenge for the cork.

'Are you mad?' said Marcel. 'You know that that piano is only there for ornament, and God knows you are the only one who can get anything out of it. Where did you get the idea that I could play dance music?

I only know the "Marseillaise", which I play with one finger. If you asked Eugène it would be much better; there is a boy who understands it, I am quite certain. You are the only one here sufficiently indiscreet to *do* such a thing without warning.'

For the third time Eugène blushed and prepared, politely and tactfully, to do what he was asked. He sat down at the piano and a quadrille was arranged. This lasted nearly as long as the supper. After the quadrille came a waltz, after the waltz, the galop, for one still galops in the Quartier Latin. The ladies especially were indefatigable, gambolling and shouting with laughter enough to wake the neighbourhood. Soon Eugène, doubly tired by the noise and the late hour, fell into a sort of half-sleep, still playing mechanically, like the postilions who slumber whilst riding. The dancers moved to and fro in front of him like phantoms in a dream; and as there is nothing which makes a man melancholy so easily as listening to the laughter of others, melancholy, to which he was subject, took possession of him. Sorrowful joy, he thought, miserable pleasures . . . moments that one imagines snatched from sorrow . . . And who knows which one of those five people dancing so gaily in front of me is certain of the wherewithal for tomorrow's dinner?

As he was thus reflecting, Mademoiselle Pinson passed near him; he thought he saw her, whilst dancing, take a piece of cake from the table and surreptitiously put it in her pocket.

V

It was nearly daybreak when the company separated. Eugène, before going home, walked about the streets for a short time to get some fresh air. Still possessed by his melancholy thoughts, he repeated quietly to himself the words of the grisette's song:

'*Elle n'a qu'une robe au monde*
Et qu'un bonnet . . .'

'Is it possible?' he said to himself. 'Can misery get to such a pitch as to be freely shown and laughed at by one's own self? Can one laugh at one's lack of bread?'

The piece of cake that had been taken was a suspicious sign. Eugène could not help smiling and at the same time being moved with pity.

'Yet', he thought, 'she took a piece of cake and not a piece of bread; perhaps this was greediness. Who knows? Perhaps it is a neighbour's

child to whom she is taking a piece of cake, perhaps a talkative
concierge, who would tell of her having passed a night out, a Cerberus
to be appeased.'

Not noticing where he was going, Eugène had wandered into that
labyrinth of small streets behind the Carrefour Bucy, through which a
carriage can scarcely pass. Just as he was retracing his steps, a woman
came out of an old house, wrapped in an old dressing-gown, bare-
headed, hair untidy, pale and wasted. She seemed so weak as to be
scarcely able to walk; her knees bent; she leaned against the wall and
seemed to want to go to a neighbouring door where there was a letter-
box, in which to post a letter that she held in her hand. Surprised and
shocked, Eugène approached her and asked where was she going, what
was she looking for, and could he help her. At the same time he put out
his arm to support her, as she seemed about to fall to the ground. But
without answering him, she drew back with a mixture of fear and pride.
She placed her letter on a wall, pointed with her finger to the box, and
seeming to summon all her strength, said: 'There!' Then, still clinging
to the wall, she returned to her house. Eugène vainly tried to make her
take his arm and answer his questions. She returned slowly to the dark
and narrow alley from which she had come.

Eugène had picked up the letter; he started to walk to the box to post
it, but he hesitated. This strange encounter had troubled him greatly,
and he felt overcome with a kind of horror mingled with a feeling of pity,
so strong that without thinking, he broke the seal almost involuntarily. It
seemed to him hateful and impossible not to try, no matter how, to
unravel such a mystery. Evidently that woman was dying; was it from
illness or hunger? In all probability from misery. Eugène opened the
letter: it was addressed: *A Monsieur le Baron de X.*, and contained the
following:

Read this letter, monsieur, and for pity's sake do not reject my appeal.
You can save me, and you only. Believe me when I say to you, save me,
and you will have done a good action, which will bring you happiness. I
am suffering from a severe illness, which has deprived me of that small
amount of strength and courage that I once had. In August last I
returned to the shop; my belongings have been seized by my former
landlady, and I am practically certain that before Saturday I shall find
myself without shelter. I have such a horror of dying of starvation that I
resolved this morning to drown myself, for I have had no food for nearly

twenty-four hours. As soon as I thought of you, a ray of hope lit up in my heart. I pray that I have not deceived myself. Monsieur, on my knees I beseech you, however little you may do for me, let me live for a few more days; I am afraid of dying, for I am only twenty-three years old . . . I shall perhaps, with a little help, succeed in surviving until the first of the next month. If I only knew with what words to arouse your pity, I would write them, but none come into my thoughts. I can only deplore my inability, for I am afraid you will treat my letter as is usually done when such are received: you will destroy it without thinking that a poor woman is there, watching the hours and the minutes go by in the hope that you would have thought it too cruel to leave her in such suspense. It is not the idea of giving a louis, a small thing for you, that will restrain you, I am quite sure; it seems to me that nothing is simpler for you than to place your alms in an envelope and address it: 'A Mademoiselle Bertin, 7, Rue de l'Éperon.' I have changed my name since going to work in a shop, as mine was my mother's. On leaving your house, give the letter to a commissionaire. I shall wait Thursday and Friday and pray fervently that something will soften your heart.

It occurs to me that you have no idea of such misery; but if you would see me you would be convinced.

ROUGETTE

If Eugène had at first been touched on reading these lines, one can well believe his astonishment when he saw the signature. So this was the same girl who had foolishly wasted her money on pleasure parties; and think of that ridiculous supper mentioned by Mademoiselle Pinson; it was she, reduced by misfortune to such suffering, and such an appeal . . . So much improvidence and folly appeared to Eugène as an unbelievable dream. But undoubtedly the signature was there; and Mademoiselle Pinson, in the course of the evening, had mentioned the *nom de guerre* of her friend Rougette, now become Mademoiselle Bertin. How was it that she found herself suddenly abandoned, without help, without bread, almost without shelter? What were her friends of yesterday doing, whilst she was perhaps dying in some attic of that house? And what kind of house was it in which one could exist in such a manner?

This was not the time for indulging in such surmises; it was most urgent to go and relieve the poor creature's starvation.

Eugène began by entering a provision shop, which had just been opened, and buying what he could find. That done, he proceeded, followed by a waiter, towards the lodging of Rougette; but he experienced a feeling of embarrassment at the thought of presenting himself so abruptly. The poor girl's pride, which he had discovered, made him fear, if not a refusal, at least a wound to her vanity; how to admit that he had read her letter? When he arrived at the door, he said to the waiter: 'Do you know a young lady living in this house called Mademoiselle Bertin?'

'Oh yes, monsieur,' replied the waiter. 'It is we who habitually serve her. But if monsieur is going there, it is not the day. She is now in the country.'

'Who told you that?' asked Eugène.

'*Pardi*, monsieur . . . it was the concierge. Mademoiselle Rougette likes to dine well, but she does not like paying. She would as soon order roast chicken and lobsters as anything; but to get her money is a question of several visits . . . We also know, in this neighbourhood, when she is here and when she is away . . .'

'She has returned,' rejoined Eugène. 'Go up to her room, deliver what you are carrying, and if she owes you anything, do not ask for it today. Should she wish to know who has sent her this, you will say it is the Baron de X.'

With these words Eugène departed. On his way he readjusted, as well as he could, the seal of the letter and posted it. 'After all,' he thought, 'Rougette will not refuse, and if she finds the answer to her letter somewhat prompt, she can get the explanation from her baron.'

VI

But students, any more than grisettes, are not rich every day. Eugène understood full well that, to give an air of likelihood to the story that the waiter had to tell, he should have added the louis which Rougette had asked for to his gift; but there was the difficulty. Louis are not precisely common currency in the Rue St-Jacques. On the other hand, Eugène had promised to pay the restaurant, but unfortunately at this moment his drawer was not better furnished than his pocket. That is why it was that, without any delay, he went on his way to the Place du Panthéon.

At this time there lived in this Place that famous barber who by going bankrupt ruined himself whilst ruining others. There, in the back shop, was carried on in secret large and small usury, where students poor and careless, perhaps in love, borrowed money at enormous interest, spending it gaily in the evening and paying dearly for it next morning. Grisettes entered there furtively, with lowered head and shamed look, borrowing, in order to go to a country party, on a faded hat, a dyed shawl, a chemise bought at the pawnshop. There, young men of good family, having need of twenty-five louis, signed bills for two or three thousand francs. Minors spent their fortune before they had got it; the imprudent ruined their families and threw away their future. From the titled courtesan, longing for a bracelet, to the necessitous college servant coveting a hare or a plate of lentils, all went there as if to the springs of Pactolus, and the usurious barber, proud of his clients and his exploits to the point of boasting about them, kept the prison of Clichy in repair pending his own visit there.

This was the dismal resort to which Eugène went, though with much repugnance, to get the means to help Rougette, or to be in the position to do so; because it did not seem certain to him that the appeal addressed to the baron would produce the desired result. To run into debt for someone unknown was really an act of great charity on the part of the student; but as Eugène believed in God, every good action was a duty to Him.

The first face he saw on entering was that of his friend Marcel, seated in front of a mirror, a towel round his neck, pretending to be having his hair done. The poor fellow had probably come to procure the wherewithal to pay for his supper of the previous evening; he seemed very preoccupied and frowned with an air of dissatisfaction, whilst the barber, pretending on his part to curl his hair with a cold instrument, talked to him in a subdued Gascon accent. Facing another mirror in a small cabinet, a very restless stranger was seated, also wrapped in a towel, looking ceaselessly round about him, and one saw, through the partly opened door of the back shop, in an old cheval-glass, the somewhat thin silhouette of a young woman who, aided by the wife of the barber, was trying on a dress of Scotch plaid.

'What are you doing here at this hour of the day?' cried Marcel, whose face regained its customary expression of good humour as soon as he recognised his friend.

Eugène sat himself by the mirror and explained in a few words the encounter he had had and the purpose that had brought him here.

'*Ma foi!*' said Marcel, 'you are really sincere? As there is a baron, why mix yourself up in it? You saw an interesting young lady apparently in need of food; you bought her a cold chicken, which was worthy of you; there is nothing more to be said. You do not ask any gratitude from her, you are pleased to remain incognito; this is heroic, to go a little further, it is chivalrous. To pledge one's watch or signature for a semp-stress kept by a baron, and whom one has not the honour of visiting, has never been done in human memory, except in the Bibliothèque Bleue.'

'Laugh at me if you like,' said Eugène. 'I know that there are many more unfortunates in the world than I can help. Those that I cannot help have my pity; but if I meet one I must help. Whatever I do, it is imposs-ible for me to remain indifferent in the face of suffering. My charity does not go so far as to look for cases, I am not rich enough for that; but when I find a case I give.'

'In that event,' said Marcel, 'you have much to do; you will find no lack of applicants in this country.'

'What does it matter?' said Eugène, still moved by the incident of which he had just been a witness; 'is it better to let these people die and pass on one's way? That unfortunate girl is scatterbrained, flippant, anything you like to call her; she does not perhaps deserve the compass-ion which she evokes; but this compassion, I feel it sincerely. Is it better to act like her intimates, who hardly seem to worry about her any more than if she were dead, and who yesterday were only too pleased to lend a hand in her downfall?

'To whom could she turn to help? To a stranger who would light his cigar with her letter, or to Mademoiselle Pinson, I suppose, who is always dining out and going the pace, whilst her friend just – starves? I must say, my dear Marcel, that all that upsets me profoundly. That thoughtless little creature of yesterday evening, with her snatches of song and vulgar jokes, laughing and babbling at your party, at the time when the other, the heroine of her story, is dying in a loft. It makes my heart sick. To live in that way, as friends, almost as sisters, for days and weeks, going the round of theatres, dances, cafés, and not to know from one day to another whether one is dead or the other alive, it is worse than the indifference of the *égoïstes*, it is the indifference of an animal. Your Mademoiselle Pinson is a monster, and your grisettes that you boast about, their shameless manners, their butterfly friendships, I know nothing so contemptible!'

The barber, who during this discourse had listened in silence, con-tinuing to manipulate his cold tongs over Marcel's head, smiled mali-ciously as Eugène stopped talking.

In this way, chattering like a magpie, or rather like the barber that he was, when it was a question of something being said with an ulterior motive, taciturn and laconic, like a Spartan, as soon as things were moving, it was his habit always to let his clients speak first before joining in the conversation. The indignation which Eugène expressed in such violent terms nevertheless made him break his habitual silence.

'You are severe, m'sieur,' said he, smiling rather boastfully. 'I have the honour to *coiffer* Mademoiselle Mimi, and I believe she is a very kind-hearted creature.'

'Yes,' said Eugène, 'excellent, as far as that goes, when it's a question of drinking or smoking!'

'Possibly,' retorted the barber, 'I do not deny it; these youngsters, they laugh, they sing, they smoke; but they are mostly very good-hearted.'

'What are you trying to make out, *père* Cadedis?' asked Marcel. 'Not so much tact; come to the point!'

'I'll prove it to you', replied the barber, pointing to the back shop, 'that there is there, hanging on a hook, a little black silk dress that you gentlemen doubtless know, if you know the owner, for she does not possess a very extensive wardrobe. Mademoiselle Mimi sent me this dress early this morning; and I presume that, if she has not helped *la petite* Rougette, it is that she herself is not too well off.'

'That's a strange thing,' said Marcel, rising and going into the back shop, without consideration for the poor girl who was still trying on her tartan dress. 'Mimi's song was hardly true to fact, as she has been forced to pawn her frock. But in the devil's name in what does she go visiting now? Isn't she calling on anybody now, then?'

Eugène had followed his friend.

The barber had not deceived them: in a dim corner, mixed up with all sorts and kinds of clothes, Mademoiselle Pinson's only dress was drooping humbly and sadly.

'That's actually it,' said Marcel; 'I recognise the frock, having seen it when it was quite new, eighteen months ago. It is the working dress, riding habit and afternoon frock of Mademoiselle Mimi. There should be on the left cuff a little stain about the size of a franc, caused by a drop of champagne. And how much have you lent on that, *père* Cadedis? For I suppose that that dress is not sold, and is only to be found in this boudoir as a pledge?'

'I have lent four francs,' replied the barber, 'and I assure you, m'sieur, that it was pure charity. To any other I would not have advanced more than forty sous; the dress is worn out, one can see through it, the whole thing's transparent. But I know that Mademoiselle Mimi will pay me; she is always good for four francs.'

'Poor Mimi!' sighed Marcel; 'I'll eat my hat if she's not borrowed this trifling sum to send to Rougette.'

'Or to pay some pressing debt,' said Eugène.

'No,' said Marcel, 'I know Mimi; I don't think she'd strip herself for a creditor.'

'That may be true,' said the barber. 'I knew Mademoiselle Mimi in a better position than that in which she now finds herself; she had then a quantity of debts. One arrived daily to seize what she possessed, and one finished, as far as that goes, by taking all her furniture, except her bed, for you gentlemen will doubtless be aware that a debtor's bed cannot be seized. But Mademoiselle Mimi had at this time four very nice dresses. She put all four of them one on top of the other, and she went to bed on top of them so as to prevent their being seized; that is why I was surprised that, not having more than one dress now, she pledged it to pay somebody.'

'Poor Mimi,' repeated Marcel; 'but how does she actually manage? Has she been gulling her friends? Has she got a dress we know nothing about? Has she made herself ill through eating too much sticky cake? As far as that goes, if she is in bed there's no necessity for her to dress. That's no matter, *père* Cadedis, the sight of that dress hurts me, with its dangling cuffs which seem to ask for help; here, take back four francs from the thirty-five livres that you were going to advance me, and wrap up the dress, and I will return it to the poor child. Well, Eugène,' he continued, 'what does your Christian charity say to that?'

'That you are right', responded Eugene, 'to talk and act as you do, but perhaps for my part I am not wrong; I will have a bet on it if you like.'

'Right,' said Marcel, 'let us have a cigar on it, like the members of the Jockey Club. You have nothing more to do here. I have thirty-one francs – we are rich! Let us go and see Mademoiselle Pinson; I am anxious to call on her.'

He put the dress under his arm, and the two of them went out of the shop.

VII

'Mademoiselle has gone to Mass,' the concierge informed the two students, when they arrived at the lodging of Mademoiselle Pinson.

'To Mass!' exclaimed Eugène in surprise.

'To Mass!' repeated Marcel. 'It is impossible, she has not gone out; let us go in; we are old friends.'

'I assure you, m'sieur,' replied the concierge, 'that she has actually gone out to Mass, about three-quarters of an hour ago.'

'And which church has she gone to?'

'To St-Sulpice, as she always does; she never misses a day.'

'Yes, yes, I know she prays to *le bon Dieu*; but it seems strange to me that she has gone out today.'

'Here she is coming back, m'sieur; she is just coming down the street; you can see her for yourself.'

In fact Mademoiselle Pinson, having left the church, was returning home.

Marcel had no sooner caught sight of her than he ran towards her, impatient to see her rig-out from close to. She had for a dress a skirt of dark Indian print, partially covered by a green serge curtain; out of which she had contrived a sort of shawl. Her graceful head, set off by a white bonnet, emerged from this singular garb, which owing to its sombre colour passed without comment, and her tiny feet were shod in dainty little boots.

She had draped herself in her curtain with such care and art that it really looked like a genuine old shawl, so that one scarcely saw the bound edge of it. In short, she had found the means of pleasing the eye in this contrivance, and of proving again to the world that a pretty woman is a pretty woman anyhow.

'How do you like me?' she said to the two young men, slightly parting her 'curtain', and letting them have a glimpse of her finely-moulded figure, modelled by her corsets. 'It is a morning *déshabillé* that Palmir has just sent me.'

'You are charming,' said Marcel. '*Ma foi*, I would not have believed that anyone could look so effective in a window-curtain!'

'Really,' replied Mademoiselle Pinson, 'in spite of the fact that I feel rather like a tied-up sachet.'

'Sachet of roses,' responded Marcel. 'I almost regret now having brought you your dress.'

'My dress? Where did you find it?'

'Where it was, apparently.'

'Then you have liberated it from slavery?'

'Yes, indeed, I have ransomed it. Are you annoyed with me for my temerity?'

'Certainly not, if I may recoup you. I am very pleased indeed to see my dress again; for, to tell you the truth, the two of us have lived together for so long that I have become unconsciously very attached to it.'

So speaking, Mademoiselle Pinson tripped briskly up the five flights of stairs which led to her little room, which the two friends entered with her.

'I can only return you this dress on one condition,' said Marcel.

'How shameful,' ejaculated the grisette. 'What nonsense! Conditions? I'll have nothing to do with them.'

'I have made a bet,' said Marcel; 'you must tell us frankly why this dress was pawned,'

'Let me first of all put it on,' replied Mademoiselle Pinson; 'I will then give you the reason. But I must warn you that if you will not use my wardrobe, or the gutter, as an antechamber you must cover your face like Agamemnon.'

'We can't agree to that; we're better behaved than you think, and wouldn't even steal a glimpse.'

'Wait,' replied Mademoiselle Pinson. 'I have every confidence in you, but experience tells us that two precautions are better than one.'

Saying this she took off her curtain and put it gently over the heads of the two friends, and in such a way as to render them completely blind.

'Don't move,' she said to them, 'it's only for a second.'

'Take care of yourself,' said Marcel; 'if there's a hole in the curtain I will answer for nothing. You will not be satisfied with our word, consequently it is withdrawn.'

'Happily, so is my dress,' said Mademoiselle Pinson; 'and my figure as well,' she added, laughing, and throwing the curtain on the floor. 'Poor little dress! It seems to me quite new. It gives me great pleasure to snuggle in it again!'

'And your secret – you will tell it to us now? Listen! The truth! We're not given to gossiping. How and why a young person like you, knowing, experienced, virtuous and modest, could all at once put the whole of her wardrobe in pawn, at one fell swoop.'

'Why, why?' replied Mademoiselle Pinson, seeming to hesitate. Then, taking the two young men, each by an arm, she said to them, pushing them towards the door: 'Come with me and you shall see.'

As Marcel expected, she took them to the Rue de l'Éperon.

VIII

Marcel had won his bet. The four francs and Mademoiselle Pinson's piece of cake were on Rougette's table, with the remains of Eugène's chicken.

The poor invalid was a bit better, but still confined to her bed; and whatever her gratitude was towards her unknown benefactor, she made her friend tell these gentlemen that she asked to be excused, but she was not in a condition to receive them.

'How well I know that touch,' said Marcel; 'she would die on the straw in an attic, but she would still behave like a duchess in front of her water-jug.'

The two friends, with much regret, were then obliged to return home as they had come, not without laughing together at the pride and discretion so strangely manifested in a garret.

After having been to the School of Medicine for their daily lecture they dined together, and the evening having set in they took a turn up and down the Boulevard des Italiens. There, still smoking the cigar he had won in the morning:

'With all this,' said Marcel, 'are you not obliged to admit that I have at heart reason to love and also to esteem these poor creatures? Let us consider temperately these matters from a philosophic point of view. This little Mimi, whom you have abused so, has she not, in depriving herself of her dress, done an action more praiseworthy, more meritorious, I even venture to say more Christian, than the good King Robert in allowing a poor creature to cut a piece off his mantle? The good King Robert, on the one hand, had no doubt plenty of mantles; on the other hand, he was seated at table, said the historian, when a beggar approached him, dragging himself along on hands and knees, and with a pair of scissors cut the gold fringe from his sovereign. This the queen considered was taking a liberty, but the dignified monarch actually pardoned the thief; perhaps he had dined well! Reflect, what a difference between him and Mimi! Mimi, when she had learned of Rougette's misfortune, was undoubtedly fasting, for you can rest assured that the piece of cake she took away from my supper was destined in advance to form her own breakfast. But, what did she do? Instead of breakfasting, she goes to Mass, and in so doing she shows herself once more the equal of King Robert, who was very pious, I admit it, but who wasted his time singing to the lute whilst the Normans ran wild. King Robert let his friends go hang, and actually he retained the mantle. Mimi sent her complete wardrobe to *père* Cadedis, an incomparable action in that Mimi is a woman, young, pretty, coquettish and poor; and take special note, that this dress is necessary to her so that she can go as usual to her shop, to earn her daily bread. Not only then does she deprive herself of the piece of cake which she was going to feast on, but she voluntarily puts herself into the position of not being able to dine. Moreover, notice that *père* Cadedis is far from being a beggar, and dragging himself on all fours under the table. King Robert, giving up his fringe, did not make any great sacrifice, because it was cut off before he noticed it. It is not known whether this fringe was cut across or not, and if it was possible to mend it; whilst Mimi, voluntarily, far from expecting that she would have her dress stolen, herself tears this covering from her poor body, more precious, more useful than the tinsel of all the lace-makers in Paris. She goes out draped in a curtain; but rest assured that she would not have gone out in this garb to any other place than the church. She would sooner have an arm cut off than show herself arrayed in a bundle of rags at the Luxembourg or the Tuileries; but she dares to show herself to God, because it is the time for her daily prayer. Believe me, Eugène, there is more courage and real religion in Mimi crossing in her curtain the Place Saint-Michel, Rue de Tournon and Rue de Petit Lion, where she is known to everybody, than in all the hymns of good King Robert, of which all the world talked, from the fat Bossuet to the thin Anquetil, whereas Mimi will die unknown in her fifth storey between a jar of flowers and a half-finished dress.'

'All the better for her,' said Eugène.

'If I wished', resumed Marcel, 'to continue to make comparisons, I could draw you a parallel between Mucius Scaevola and Rougette. Do you believe, as far as that goes, that it would be more difficult for a Roman of the time of Tarquin to keep his arm for five minutes over a lighted fire than for a present-day grisette to go without food for twenty-four hours? Neither one nor the other made any plaint, but look into their reasons. Mucius was in the middle of a camp, in the presence of an Etruscan king whom he had tried to assassinate; he failed lamentably, he was in the hands of the soldiery. What was going through his mind? Bravado? So that he should be admired before he was hanged? He burnt his fingers with a brand, but it has not been proved that the brazier was really hot, nor that the finger was incinerated. Upon which, the digni-fied Porsenna, astounded by this high-flown gesture, pardoned him and

sent him home. It is debatable if the said Porsenna, capable of such generosity, cut a good figure, and whether Scaevola had reason to suppose
that in sacrificing his arm he would save his head. Rougette, on the contrary, endures patiently the most horrible, the most tedious of tortures,
that of hunger; no one was taking any notice of her. She is alone in the
corner of a garret, she has neither Porsenna to admire her, that is to say
the baron, nor the Romans, that is to say the neighbours, nor the Et-
ruscans, that is to say her creditors, nor even the brazier, for her stove
was out. But why did she suffer without complaint? First, from vanity,
that is certain; but the case of Mucius was the same; from nobility of
soul, then, and that constitutes her glory; for if she remained quiet
behind her locked door it is precisely in order that her friends should
not know she was dying, so that she should be spared the humiliation of
pity, so that her friend Pinson, whom she knew to be kind-hearted and
thoroughly devoted, should not be obliged, as she had done previously,
to give her her dress and her food. Mucius, in Rougette's place, would
have pretended to die in silence, but that would have been at the cross-
roads or some other public place. His taciturn and sublime vanity would
have found a delicate way of hinting for a glass of wine and a crust. It is
true Rougette asked the baron, whom I insist on comparing with Porsenna, for a louis, but you must realise that the baron was really indebted
to Rougette for many kindnesses. That is clear to the least observant. As
you have, moreover, wisely remarked, it was possible that the baron was
in the country, and if this were so Rougette was lost. And do not think
that you can confound me with the usual platitude with which one
refers to all the good deeds of women, that they do not know what they
are doing, and that they run towards danger as cats make for the tiles.
Rougette knows what death means; she has seen it at first hand on the
Pont d'Jena, for she has already thrown herself in the water once, and I
asked her if she had suffered. She said, no, that she had felt nothing,
except at the moment when she was hauled out, for the boatmen had
dragged her by the legs, and they had, so she said, grazed her head on
the side of the boat.'

'Enough!' said Eugène, 'spare me your gruesome pleasantries.
Answer me seriously: do you believe that such horrible instances, often
repeated, always menacing, can eventually have any good result? These
poor girls, living alone, with nothing behind them, without advice, have
they enough native good sense to counterbalance their lack of experience? Is there a familiar spirit in attendance on them, who condemns

them always to ill-luck and misfortune, but, in spite of such vagaries, can they return to better things? Here is one who prays to God, you say; she goes to church, performs her devotions, lives honestly by her work; her friends appear to hold her in esteem; and you other blackguards, you do not treat her yourselves with your usual thoughtlessness. Here is another who goes from one blunder to another, from prodigality to the pangs of hunger. Indeed, she will always have in mind the cruel lessons she has learned. Do you believe that with wise counsel, regular habits, a little help, one could make such women into reasonable beings? If there are any such, tell me. An opportunity is presented to us; let us make our way to poor Rougette; she is doubtless still suffering a great deal, and her friend watches by her bedside. Do not discourage me, let me take action; I would like to guide them back to the straight path, to speak to them in all sincerity; I do not wish to preach to or reproach them. I want to go to them, take their hands, and say to them . . .'

At this moment the two friends passed in front of the Café Tortoni. The silhouettes of the two young women, who were eating ices in front of a window, were thrown up by the bright lights. One of them waved her handkerchief and the other one burst out laughing.

'By jingo,' exclaimed Marcel, 'if you wish to speak to them, we've only to cross the road, for there they are, God bless me! I recognise Mimi by her dress, and Rougette by her white feather, always to be found where there is something good to eat! It appears that M'sieur le Baron has done his part handsomely!'

'Does not such irresponsibility frighten you?' said Eugène.

'Undoubtedly,' replied Marcel; 'but I beg of you, when you speak disparagingly of grisettes, make an exception of the little Pinson. She recited to us the history of a supper, she pawned her dress for four francs, she made herself a mantle out of a curtain; and who says what he knows, who gives what he has, who does what he can, is not called upon to do more.'

Théophile Gautier

The many and varied writings of Théophile Gautier (1811–72) first
came to the attention of the English-speaking public during the *fin de
siècle*. Gautier began his career amongst the dandyish young aesthetes of
the Petit Cénacle, and their concern with the theory of *l'art pour l'art* is
apparent in the preface to *Mademoiselle de Maupin* (1835–6), a novel
written to scandalise the despised middle class. His *Histoire du roman-
tisme* (1827) shows his commitment to Hugo's beliefs, but his 'Romanticism' is more often macabre and fantastic, notably in his famous
vampire story 'La Mort amoureuse' (1836). He had many interests and
wrote on fine art, theatre, pantomime, ballet and dance, and travel. He
was a skilled poet, commemorated – however ironically – in the dedica-
tion to Baudelaire's *Les Fleurs du mal*, and his later desire to transcend
Romanticism is evident in the coolly chiselled architecture of poetic
form which characterises *Émaux et Camées* (1852).

The Mummy's Foot

I HAD ENTERED, IN AN IDLE MOOD, THE SHOP OF ONE OF THOSE curiosity vendors who are called *marchands de bric-à-brac* in that Parisian *argot* which is so perfectly unintelligible elsewhere in France.

You have doubtless glanced occasionally through the windows of some of these shops, which have become so numerous now that it is fashionable to buy antiquated furniture, and that every petty stock-broker thinks he must have his *chambre au moyen âge*.

There is one thing there which clings alike to the shop of the dealer in old iron, the ware-room of the tapestry-maker, the laboratory of the chemist, and the studio of the painter: in all those gloomy dens where a furtive daylight filters in through the window-shutters the most mani-festly ancient thing is dust. The cobwebs are more authentic than the gimp laces, and the old pear-tree furniture on exhibition is actually younger than the mahogany which arrived but yesterday from America.

The warehouse of my bric-à-brac dealer was a veritable Caphar-naum. All ages and all nations seemed to have made their rendezvous there. An Etruscan lamp of red clay stood upon a Boule cabinet, with ebony panels, brightly striped by lines of inlaid brass; a duchess of the court of Louis XV nonchalantly extended her fawn-like feet under a massive table of the time of Louis XIII, with heavy spiral supports of oak, and carven designs of chimeras and foliage intermingled.

Upon the denticulated shelves of several sideboards glittered immense Japanese dishes with red and blue designs relieved by gilded hatching, side by side with enamelled works by Bernard Palissy, rep-resenting serpents, frogs, and lizards in relief.

From disembowelled cabinets escaped cascades of silver-lustrous Chinese silks and waves of tinsel, which an oblique sunbeam shot through with luminous beads, while portraits of every era, in frames more or less tarnished, smiled through their yellow varnish.

The striped breastplate of a damascened suit of Milanese armour glittered in one corner; loves and nymphs of porcelain, Chinese grotesques, vases of *céladon* and crackle-ware, Saxon and old Sèvres cups encumbered the shelves and nooks of the apartment.

The dealer followed me closely through the tortuous way contrived between the piles of furniture, warding off with his hand the hazardous sweep of my coat-skirts, watching my elbows with the uneasy attention of an antiquarian and a usurer.

It was a singular face, that of the merchant; an immense skull, polished like a knee, and surrounded by a thin aureole of white hair, which brought out the clear salmon tint of his complexion all the more strikingly, lent him a false aspect of patriarchal *bonhomie*, counteracted, however, by the scintillation of two little yellow eyes which trembled in their orbits like two louis d'or upon quicksilver. The curve of his nose presented an aquiline silhouette, which suggested the Oriental or Jewish type. His hands – thin, slender, full of nerves which projected like strings upon the finger-board of a violin, and armed with claws like those on the terminations of bats' wings – shook with senile trembling; but those convulsively agitated hands became firmer than steel pincers or lobsters' claws when they lifted any precious article – an onyx cup, a Venetian glass, or a dish of Bohemian crystal. This strange old man had an aspect so thoroughly rabbinical and cabalistic that he would have been burnt on the mere testimony of his face three centuries ago.

'Will you not buy something from me today, sir? Here is a Malay kreese with a blade undulating like flame. Look at those grooves contrived for the blood to run along, those teeth set backwards so as to tear out the entrails in withdrawing the weapon. It is a fine character of ferocious arm, and will look well in your collection. This two-handed sword is very beautiful. It is the work of Josepe de la Hera; and this *coliche-marde*, with its fenestrated guard – what a superb specimen of handicraft!'

'No; I have quite enough weapons and instruments of carnage. I want a small figure, something which will suit me as a paperweight, for I cannot endure those trumpery bronzes which the stationers sell, and which may be found on everybody's desk.'

The old gnome foraged among his ancient wares, and finally arranged before me some antique bronzes, so-called at least; fragments of malachite, little Hindoo or Chinese idols, a kind of poussah-toys in jade-stone, representing the incarnations of Brahma or Vishnoo, and

wonderfully appropriate to the very undivine office of holding papers
and letters in place.

I was hesitating between a porcelain dragon, all constellated with
warts, its mouth formidable with bristling tusks and ranges of teeth, and
an abominable little Mexican fetish, representing the god Vitzi-liputzili
au naturel, when I caught sight of a charming foot, which I at first took
for a fragment of some antique Venus.

It had those beautiful ruddy and tawny tints that lend to Florentine
bronze that warm, living look so much preferable to the grey-green
aspect of common bronzes, which might easily be mistaken for statues
in a state of putrefaction. Satiny gleams played over its rounded forms,
doubtless polished by the amorous kisses of twenty centuries, for it
seemed a Corinthian bronze, a work of the best era of art, perhaps
moulded by Lysippus himself.

'That foot will be my choice,' I said to the merchant, who regarded
me with an ironical and saturnine air, and held out the object desired
that I might examine it more fully.

I was surprised at its lightness. It was not a foot of metal, but in sooth
a foot of flesh, an embalmed foot, a mummy's foot. On examining it still
more closely the very grain of the skin, and the almost imperceptible
lines impressed upon it by the texture of the bandages, became percept-
ible. The toes were slender and delicate, and terminated by perfectly
formed nails, pure and transparent as agates. The great toe, slightly
separated from the rest, afforded a happy contrast, in the antique style,
to the position of the other toes, and lent it an aerial lightness – the grace
of a bird's foot. The sole, scarcely streaked by a few almost imperceptible cross-lines, afforded evidence that it had never touched the bare
ground, and had only come in contact with the finest matting of Nile
rushes and the softest carpets of panther skin.

'Ha, ha, you want the foot of the Princess Hermonthis!' exclaimed
the merchant, with a strange giggle, fixing his owlish eyes upon me.
'Ha, ha, ha! For a paperweight! An original idea! – artistic idea! Old
Pharaoh would certainly have been surprised had someone told him that
the foot of his adored daughter would be used for a paperweight after he
had a mountain of granite hollowed out as a receptacle for the triple
coffin, painted and gilded, covered with hieroglyphics and beautiful
paintings of the Judgement of Souls,' continued the queer little merchant, half audibly, as though talking to himself.

'How much will you charge me for this mummy fragment?'

'Ah, the highest price I can get, for it is a superb piece. If I had the match of it, you could not have it for less than five hundred francs. The daughter of a Pharaoh! Nothing is more rare.'

'Assuredly that is not a common article, but still, how much do you want? In the first place, let me warn you that all my wealth consists of just five louis. I can buy anything that costs five louis, but nothing dearer. You might search my jacket pockets and most secret drawers without even finding one poor five-franc piece more.'

'Five louis for the foot of the Princess Hermonthis! That is very little, very little indeed. 'Tis an authentic foot,' muttered the merchant, shaking his head, and imparting a peculiar rotary motion to his eyes. 'Well, take it, and I will give you the bandages into the bargain,' he added, wrapping the foot in an ancient damask rag. 'Very fine! Real damask – Indian damask which has never been re-dyed. It is strong, and yet it is soft,' he mumbled, stroking the frayed tissue with his fingers, through the trade-acquired habit which moved him to praise even an object of such little value that he himself deemed it only worth the giving away.

He poured the gold coins into a sort of medieval alms-purse hanging at his belt, repeating:

'The foot of the Princess Hermonthis to be used for a paperweight!'

Then turning his phosphorescent eyes upon me, he exclaimed in a voice strident as the crying of a cat which has swallowed a fishbone:

'Old Pharaoh will not be well pleased. He loved his daughter, the dear man!'

'You speak as if you were a contemporary of his. You are old enough, goodness knows! but you do not date back to the Pyramids of Egypt,' I answered, laughingly, from the threshold.

I went home, delighted with my acquisition.

With the idea of putting it to profitable use as soon as possible, I placed the foot of the divine Princess Hermonthis upon a heap of papers scribbled over with verses, in themselves an undecipherable mosaic-work of erasures; articles freshly begun; letters forgotten, and posted in the table drawer instead of the letter-box, an error to which absent-minded people are peculiarly liable. The effect was charming, bizarre, and romantic.

Well satisfied with this embellishment, I went out with the gravity and pride becoming one who feels that he has the ineffable advantage over all the passers-by whom he elbows, of possessing a piece of the Princess Hermonthis, daughter of Pharaoh.

I looked upon all who did not possess, like myself, a paperweight so authentically Egyptian as very ridiculous people, and it seemed to me that the proper occupation of every sensible man should consist in the mere fact of having a mummy's foot upon his desk.

Happily I met some friends, whose presence distracted me in my infatuation with this new acquisition. I went to dinner with them, for I could not very well have dined with myself.

When I came back that evening, with my brain slightly confused by a few glasses of wine, a vague whiff of Oriental perfume delicately titillated my olfactory nerves. The heat of the room had warmed the natron, bitumen, and myrrh in which the *paraschistes*, who cut open the bodies of the dead, had bathed the corpse of the princess. It was a perfume at once sweet and penetrating, a perfume that four thousand years had not been able to dissipate.

The Dream of Egypt was Eternity. Her odours have the solidity of granite and endure as long.

I soon drank deeply from the black cup of sleep. For a few hours all remained opaque to me. Oblivion and nothingness inundated me with their sombre waves.

Yet light gradually dawned upon the darkness of my mind. Dreams commenced to touch me softly in their silent flight.

The eyes of my soul were opened, and I beheld my chamber as it actually was. I might have believed myself awake but for a vague consciousness which assured me that I slept, and that something fantastic was about to take place.

The odour of the myrrh had augmented in intensity, and I felt a slight headache, which I very naturally attributed to several glasses of champagne that we had drunk to the unknown gods and our future fortunes.

I peered through my room with a feeling of expectation which I saw nothing to justify. Every article of furniture was in its proper place. The lamp, softly shaded by its globe of ground crystal, burned upon its bracket; the water-colour sketches shone under their Bohemian glass; the curtains hung down languidly; everything wore an aspect of tranquil slumber.

After a few moments, however, all this calm interior appeared to become disturbed. The woodwork cracked stealthily, the ash-covered log suddenly emitted a jet of blue flame, and the discs of the paterae seemed like great metallic eyes, watching, like myself, for the things which were about to happen.

My eyes accidentally fell upon the desk where I had placed the foot of the Princess Hermonthis.

Instead of remaining quiet, as behoved a foot which had been embalmed for four thousand years, it commenced to act in a nervous manner, contracted itself, and leapt over the papers like a startled frog. One would have imagined that it had suddenly been brought into contact with a galvanic battery. I could distinctly hear the dry sound made by its little heel, hard as the hoof of a gazelle.

I became rather discontented with my acquisition, inasmuch as I wished my paperweights to be of a sedentary disposition, and thought it very unnatural that feet should walk about without legs, and I commenced to experience a feeling closely akin to fear.

Suddenly I saw the folds of my bed-curtain stir, and heard a bumping sound, like that caused by some person hopping on one foot across the floor. I must confess I became alternately hot and cold, that I felt a strange wind chill my back, and that my suddenly rising hair caused my nightcap to execute a leap of several yards.

The bed-curtains opened and I beheld the strangest figure imaginable before me.

It was a young girl of a very deep coffee-brown complexion, like the bayadère Amani, and possessing the purest Egyptian type of perfect beauty. Her eyes were almond-shaped and oblique, with eyebrows so black that they seemed blue; her nose was exquisitely chiselled, almost Greek in its delicacy of outline; and she might indeed have been taken for a Corinthian statue of bronze but for the prominence of her cheekbones and the slightly African fullness of her lips, which compelled one to recognise her as belonging beyond all doubt to the hieroglyphic race which dwelt upon the banks of the Nile.

Her arms, slender and spindle-shaped like those of very young girls, were encircled by a peculiar kind of metal bands and bracelets of glass beads; her hair was all twisted into little cords, and she wore upon her bosom a little idol-figure of green paste, bearing a whip with seven lashes, which proved it to be an image of Isis; her brow was adorned with a shining plate of gold, and a few traces of paint relieved the coppery tint of her cheeks.

As for her costume, it was very odd indeed.

Fancy a *pagne*, or skirt, all formed of little strips of material bedizened with red and black hieroglyphics, stiffened with bitumen, and apparently belonging to a freshly unbandaged mummy.

In one of those sudden flights of thought so common in dreams I heard the hoarse falsetto of the bric-à-brac dealer, repeating like a monotonous refrain the phrase he had uttered in his shop with so enigmatical an intonation:

'Old Pharaoh will not be well pleased. He loved his daughter, the dear man!'

One strange circumstance, which was not at all calculated to restore my equanimity, was that the apparition had but one foot; the other was broken off at the ankle!

She approached the table where the foot was starting and fidgeting about more than ever, and there supported herself upon the edge of the desk. I saw her eyes fill with pearly gleaming tears.

Although she had not as yet spoken, I fully comprehended the thoughts which agitated her. She looked at her foot – for it was indeed her own – with an exquisitely graceful expression of coquettish sadness, but the foot leapt and ran hither and thither, as though impelled on steel springs.

Twice or thrice she extended her hand to seize it, but could not succeed.

Then commenced between the Princess Hermonthis and her foot – which appeared to be endowed with a special life of its own – a very fantastic dialogue in a most ancient Coptic tongue, such as might have been spoken thirty centuries ago in the syrinxes of the land of Ser. Luckily I understood Coptic perfectly well that night.

The Princess Hermonthis cried, in a voice sweet and vibrant as the tones of a crystal bell:

'Well, my dear little foot, you always flee from me, yet I always took good care of you. I bathed you with perfumed water in a bowl of alabaster; I smoothed your heel with pumice-stone mixed with palm oil; your nails were cut with golden scissors and polished with a hippopotamus tooth; I was careful to select *tatbebs* for you, painted and embroidered and turned up at the toes, which were the envy of all the young girls in Egypt. You wore on your great toe rings bearing the device of the sacred Scarabaeus, and you supported one of the lightest bodies that a lazy foot could sustain.'

The foot replied in a pouting and chagrined tone:

'You know well that I do not belong to myself any longer. I have been bought and paid for. The old merchant knew what he was about. He bore you a grudge for having refused to espouse him. This is an ill turn which he has done you. The Arab who violated your royal coffin in the subterranean pits of the necropolis of Thebes was sent thither by him. He desired to prevent you from being present at the reunion of the shadowy nations in the cities below. Have you five pieces of gold for my ransom?'

'Alas, no! My jewels, my rings, my purses of gold and silver were all stolen from me,' answered the Princess Hermonthis, with a sob.

'Princess,' I then exclaimed, 'I never retained anybody's foot unjustly. Even though you have not got the five louis which it cost me, I present it to you gladly. I should feel unutterably wretched to think that I were the cause of so amiable a person as the Princess Hermonthis being lame.'

I delivered this discourse in a royally gallant, troubadour tone which must have astonished the beautiful Egyptian girl.

She turned a look of deepest gratitude upon me, and her eyes shone with bluish gleams of light.

She took her foot, which surrendered itself willingly this time, like a woman about to put on her little shoe, and adjusted it to her leg with much skill.

This operation over, she took a few steps about the room, as though to assure herself that she was really no longer lame.

'Ah, how pleased my father will be! He who was so unhappy because of my mutilation, and who from the moment of my birth set a whole nation at work to hollow me out a tomb so deep that he might preserve me intact until that last day, when souls must be weighed in the balance of Amenthi! Come with me to my father. He will receive you kindly, for you have given me back my foot.'

I thought this proposition natural enough. I arrayed myself in a dressing-gown of large-flowered pattern, which lent me a very Pharaonic aspect, hurriedly put on a pair of Turkish slippers, and informed the Princess Hermonthis that I was ready to follow her.

Before starting, Hermonthis took from her neck the little idol of green paste, and laid it on the scattered sheets of paper which covered the table.

'It is only fair', she observed, smilingly, 'that I should replace your paperweight.'

She gave me her hand, which felt soft and cold, like the skin of a serpent, and we departed.

We passed for some time with the velocity of an arrow through a fluid

and greyish expanse, in which half-formed silhouettes flitted swiftly by us, to right and left.

For an instant we saw only sky and sea.

A few moments later obelisks commenced to tower in the distance; pylons and vast flights of steps guarded by sphinxes became clearly outlined against the horizon.

We had reached our destination.

The princess conducted me to a mountain of rose-coloured granite, in the face of which appeared an opening so narrow and low that it would have been difficult to distinguish it from the fissures in the rock, had not its location been marked by two stelae wrought with sculptures.

Hermonthis kindled a torch and led the way before me.

We traversed corridors hewn through the living rock. Their walls, covered with hieroglyphics and paintings of allegorical processions, might well have occupied thousands of arms for thousands of years in their formation. These corridors of interminable length opened into square chambers, in the midst of which pits had been contrived, through which we descended by cramp-irons or spiral stairways. These pits again conducted us into other chambers, opening into other corridors, likewise decorated with painted sparrowhawks, serpents coiled in circles, the symbols of the *tau* and *pedum* – prodigious works of art which no living eye can ever examine – interminable legends of granite which only the dead have time to read through all eternity.

At last we found ourselves in a hall so vast, so enormous, so immeasurable, that the eye could not reach its limits. Files of monstrous columns stretched far out of sight on every side, between which twinkled livid stars of yellowish flame; points of light which revealed further depths incalculable in the darkness beyond.

The Princess Hermonthis still held my hand, and graciously saluted the mummies of her acquaintance.

My eyes became accustomed to the dim twilight, and objects became discernible.

I beheld the kings of the subterranean races seated upon thrones – grand old men, though dry, withered, wrinkled like parchment, and blackened with naphtha and bitumen – all wearing *pshents* of gold, and breastplates and gorgets glittering with precious stones, their eyes immovably fixed like the eyes of sphinxes, and their long beards whitened by the snow of centuries. Behind them stood their peoples, in the stiff and constrained posture enjoined by Egyptian art, all eternally preserving the attitude prescribed by the hieratic code. Behind these nations, the cats, ibises, and crocodiles contemporary with them – rendered monstrous of aspect by their swathing bands – mewed, flapped their wings, or extended their jaws in a saurian giggle.

All the Pharaohs were there – Cheops, Chephrenes, Psammetichus, Sesostris, Amenotaph – all the dark rulers of the pyramids and syrinxes. On yet higher thrones sat Chronos and Xixouthros, who was contemporary with the deluge, and Tubal Cain, who reigned before it.

The beard of King Xixouthros had grown seven times around the granite table upon which he leaned, lost in deep reverie, and buried in dreams.

Farther back, through a dusty cloud, I beheld dimly the seventy-two pre-Adamite kings, with their seventy-two peoples, forever passed away.

After permitting me to gaze upon this bewildering spectacle a few moments, the Princess Hermonthis presented me to her father Pharaoh, who favoured me with a most gracious nod.

'I have found my foot again! I have found my foot!' cried the princess, clapping her little hands together with every sign of frantic joy. 'It was this gentleman who restored it to me.'

The races of Kemi, the races of Nahasi – all the black, bronzed, and copper-coloured nations repeated in chorus:

'The Princess Hermonthis has found her foot again!'

Even Xixouthros himself was visibly affected.

He raised his heavy eyelids, stroked his moustache with his fingers, and turned upon me a glance weighty with centuries.

'By Oms, the dog of Hell, and Tmei, daughter of the Sun and of Truth, this is a brave and worthy lad!' exclaimed Pharaoh, pointing to me with his sceptre, which was terminated with a lotus flower.

'What recompense do you desire?'

Filled with that daring inspired by dreams in which nothing seems impossible, I asked him for the hand of the Princess Hermonthis. The hand seemed to me a very proper antithetic recompense for the foot.

Pharaoh opened wide his great eyes of glass in astonishment at my witty request.

'What country do you come from, and what is your age?'

'I am a Frenchman, and I am twenty-seven years old, venerable Pharaoh.'

'Twenty-seven years old, and he wishes to espouse the Princess Hermonthis who is thirty centuries old!' cried out at once all the Thrones and all the Circles of Nations.

Only Hermonthis herself did not seem to think my request unreasonable.

'If you were even only two thousand years old', replied the ancient king, 'I would willingly give you the princess, but the disproportion is too great; and, besides, we must give our daughters husbands who will last well. You do not know how to preserve yourselves any longer. Even those who died only fifteen centuries ago are already no more than a handful of dust. Behold, my flesh is solid as basalt, my bones are bars of steel!

'I will be present on the last day of the world with the same body and the same features which I had during my lifetime. My daughter Hermonthis will last longer than a statue of bronze.

'Then the last particles of your dust will have been scattered abroad by the winds, and even Isis herself, who was able to find the atoms of Osiris, would scarce be able to recompose your being.

'See how vigorous I yet remain, and how mighty is my grasp,' he added, shaking my hand in the English fashion with a strength that buried my rings in the flesh of my fingers.

He squeezed me so hard that I awoke, and found my friend Alfred shaking me by the arm to make me get up.

'Oh, you everlasting sleeper! Must I have you carried out into the middle of the street, and fireworks exploded in your ears? It is afternoon. Don't you recollect your promise to take me with you to see M. Aguado's Spanish pictures?'

'God! I forgot all, all about it,' I answered, dressing myself hurriedly. 'We will go there at once. I have the permit lying there on my desk.'

I started to find it, but fancy my astonishment when I beheld, instead of the mummy's foot I had purchased the evening before, the little green paste idol left in its place by the Princess Hermonthis!

Gustave Flaubert

Gustave Flaubert (1821–80) was born in Rouen, where his father was a surgeon. Expelled from school, and privately educated, he revealed a startling talent for literary 'dissection' of human behaviour in his early writings. Though he is famed as the 'hermit of Croisset', a number of key friendships illuminated his life. These friends included fellow-writers such as George Sand, Maxime du Camp, Louis Bouilhet and Louise Colet. His first novel for publication was the momentous *Madame Bovary* (1857) which recounts the path to suicide of a provincial housewife who 'finds in adultery all the platitudes of marriage'. Typically, Flaubert transcends the potential banality of the plot by the ironic playfulness of an elusive narrative voice. The writing of the first *L'Education sentimentale* was interrupted when Flaubert suffered an epileptic fit in 1844, and when he returned to it in 1869, the plot was to change. Flaubert called this tale of an adulterous passion which remains unconsummated 'a book about nothing', although it provides a vivid representation of the social and political upheaval of the 1848 Revolution and the 1851 *coup d'état*. 'A Simple Heart' belongs to his final completed work *Trois contes* (1877) and expresses his characteristic mixture of pathos and absurdity.

A Simple Heart

FOR HALF A CENTURY THE WOMEN OF PONT-L'ÉVÊQUE ENVIED Madame Aubain her maidservant Félicité.

In return for a hundred francs a year she did all the cooking and the housework, the sewing, the washing, and the ironing. She could bridle a horse, fatten poultry, and churn butter, and she remained faithful to her mistress, who was by no means an easy person to get on with.

Madame Aubain had married a young fellow who was good-looking but badly-off, and who died at the beginning of 1809, leaving her with two small children and a pile of debts. She then sold all her property except for the farms of Toucques and Geffosses, which together brought in five thousand francs a year at the most, and left her house at Saint-Melaine for one behind the covered market which was cheaper to run and had belonged to her family.

This house had a slate roof and stood between an alleyway and a lane leading down to the river. Inside there were differences in level which were the cause of many a stumble. A narrow entrance-hall separated the kitchen from the parlour, where Madame Aubain sat all day long in a wicker easy-chair by the window. Eight mahogany chairs were lined up against the white-painted wainscoting, and under the barometer stood an old piano loaded with a pyramid of boxes and cartons. On either side of the chimney-piece, which was carved out of yellow marble in the Louis Quinze style, there was a tapestry-covered armchair, and in the middle was a clock designed to look like a temple of Vesta. The whole room smelt a little musty, as the floor was on a lower level than the garden.

On the first floor was 'Madame's' bedroom – very spacious, with a patterned wallpaper of pale flowers and a portrait of 'Monsieur' dressed in what had once been the height of fashion. It opened into a smaller room in which there were two cots, without mattresses. Then came the drawing-room, which was always shut up and full of furniture covered with dust-sheets. Next there was a passage leading to the study, where books and papers filled the shelves of a bookcase in three sections built round a big writing-table of dark wood. The two end-panels were hidden under pen-and-ink drawings, landscapes in gouache, and etchings by Audran, souvenirs of better days and bygone luxury. On the second floor a dormer window gave light to Félicité's room, which looked out over the fields.

Every day Félicité got up at dawn, so as not to miss Mass, and worked until evening without stopping. Then, once dinner was over, the plates and dishes put away, and the door bolted, she piled ashes on the log fire and went to sleep in front of the hearth, with her rosary in her hands. Nobody could be more stubborn when it came to haggling over prices, and as for cleanliness, the shine on her saucepans was the despair of all the other servants. Being of a thrifty nature, she ate slowly, picking up from the table the crumbs from her loaf of bread – a twelve-pound loaf which was baked specially for her and lasted her twenty days.

All the year round she wore a kerchief of printed calico fastened behind with a pin, a bonnet which covered her hair, grey stockings, a red skirt, and over her jacket a bibbed apron such as hospital nurses wear.

Her face was thin and her voice was sharp. At twenty-five she was often taken for forty; once she reached fifty, she stopped looking any age in particular. Always silent and upright and deliberate in her movements, she looked like a wooden doll driven by clockwork.

II

Like everyone else, she had had her love-story.

Her father, a mason, had been killed when he fell off some scaffolding. Then her mother died, and when her sisters went their separate ways, a farmer took her in, sending her, small as she was, to look after the cows out in the fields. She went about in rags, shivering with cold, used to lie flat on the ground to drink water out of the ponds, would be beaten for no reason at all, and was finally turned out of the house for stealing thirty sous, a theft of which she was innocent. She found work at another farm, looking after the poultry, and as she was liked by her employers the other servants were jealous of her.

One August evening – she was eighteen at the time – they took her off to the fête at Colleville. From the start she was dazed and bewildered by the noise of the fiddles, the lamps in the trees, the medley of gaily-coloured dresses, the gold crosses and lace, and the throng of people jig-ging up and down. She was standing shyly on one side when a smart young fellow, who had been leaning on the shaft of a cart, smoking his pipe, came up and asked her to dance. He treated her to cider, coffee, girdle-cake and a silk neckerchief, and imagining that she knew what he was after, offered to see her home. At the edge of a field of oats, he pushed her roughly to the ground. Thoroughly frightened, she started screaming for help. He took to his heels.

Another night, on the road to Beaumont, she tried to get past a big, slow-moving wagon loaded with hay, and as she was squeezing by she recognised Théodore.

He greeted her quite calmly, saying that she must forgive him for the way he had behaved to her, as 'it was the drink that did it'.

She did not know what to say in reply and felt like running off.

Straight away he began talking about the crops and the notabilities of the commune, saying that his father had left Colleville for the farm at Les Écots, so that they were now neighbours.

'Ah!' she said.

He added that his family wanted to see him settled but that he was in no hurry and was waiting to find a wife to suit his fancy. She lowered her head. Then he asked her if she was thinking of getting married. She answered with a smile that it was mean of him to make fun of her.

'But I'm not making fun of you!' he said. 'I swear I'm not!'

He put his left arm round her waist, and she walked on supported by his embrace. Soon they slowed down. There was a gentle breeze blow-ing, the stars were shining, the huge load of hay was swaying about in front of them, and the four horses were raising clouds of dust as they shambled along. Then, without being told, they turned off to the right. He kissed her once more and she disappeared into the darkness.

The following week Théodore got her to grant him several ren-dezvous.

They would meet at the bottom of a farmyard, behind a wall, under a solitary tree. She was not ignorant of life as young ladies are, for the an-imals had taught her a great deal; but her reason and an instinctive sense of honour prevented her from giving way. The resistance she put up inflamed Théodore's passion to such an extent that in order to satisfy it (or perhaps out of sheer naïvety) he proposed to her. At first she refused to believe him, but he swore that he was serious.

Soon afterwards he had a disturbing piece of news to tell her: the year before, his parents had paid a man to do his military service for him, but now he might be called up again any day, and the idea of going into the Army frightened him. In Félicité's eyes this cowardice of his appeared to be a proof of his affection, and she loved him all the more for it. Every night she would steal out to meet him, and every night Théodore would plague her with his worries and entreaties.

In the end he said that he was going to the Prefecture himself to make enquiries, and that he would come and tell her how matters stood the following Sunday, between eleven and midnight.

At the appointed hour she hurried to meet her sweetheart, but found one of his friends waiting for her instead.

He told her that she would not see Théodore again. To make sure of avoiding conscription, he had married a very rich old woman, Madame Lehoussais of Toucques.

Her reaction was an outburst of frenzied grief. She threw herself on the ground, screaming and calling on God, and lay moaning all alone in the open until sunrise. Then she went back to the farm and announced her intention of leaving. At the end of the month, when she had received her wages, she wrapped her small belongings up in a kerchief and made her way to Pont-l'Évêque.

In front of the inn there, she sought information from a woman in a widow's bonnet, who, as it happened, was looking for a cook. The girl did not know much about cooking, but she seemed so willing and expected so little that finally Madame Aubain ended up by saying: 'Very well, I will take you on.'

A quarter of an hour later Félicité was installed in her house.

At first she lived there in a kind of fearful awe caused by 'the style of the house' and by the memory of 'Monsieur' brooding over everything. Paul and Virginie, the boy aged seven and the girl barely four, seemed to her to be made of some precious substance. She used to carry them about pickaback, and when Madame Aubain told her not to keep on kissing them she was cut to the quick. All the same, she was happy now, for her pleasant surroundings had dispelled her grief.

On Thursdays, a few regular visitors came in to play Boston, and Félicité got the cards and the foot-warmers ready beforehand. They always arrived punctually at eight, and left before the clock struck eleven.

Every Monday morning the second-hand dealer who lived down the alley put all his junk out on the pavement. Then the hum of voices began to fill the town, mingled with the neighing of horses, the bleating of lambs, the grunting of pigs, and the rattle of carts in the streets.

About midday, when the market was in full swing, a tall old peasant with a hooked nose and his cap on the back of his head would appear at the door. This was Robelin, the farmer from Geffosses. A little later, and Liébard, the farmer from Toucques, would arrive – a short, fat, red-faced fellow in a grey jacket and leather gaiters fitted with spurs.

Both men had hens or cheeses they wanted to sell to 'Madame'. But Félicité was up to all their tricks and invariably outwitted them, so that they went away full of respect for her.

From time to time Madame Aubain had a visit from an uncle of hers, the Marquis de Grémanville, who had been ruined by loose living and was now living at Falaise on his last remaining scrap of property. He always turned up at lunch-time, accompanied by a hideous poodle which dirtied all the furniture with its paws. However hard he tried to behave like a gentleman, even going so far as to raise his hat every time he mentioned 'my late father', the force of habit was usually too much for him, for he would start pouring himself one glass after another and telling bawdy stories. Félicité used to push him gently out of the house, saying politely: 'You've had quite enough, Monsieur de Grémanville. See you another time!' and shutting the door on him.

She used to open it with pleasure to Monsieur Bourais, who was a retired solicitor. His white tie and his bald head, his frilled shirt-front and his ample brown frock-coat, the way he had of rounding his arm to take a pinch of snuff, and indeed everything about him made an overwhelming impression on her such as we feel when we meet some outstanding personality.

As he looked after 'Madame's' property, he used to shut himself up with her for hours in 'Monsieur's' study. He lived in dread of compromising his reputation, had a tremendous respect for the Bench, and laid claim to some knowledge of Latin.

To give the children a little painless instruction, he made them a present of a geography book with illustrations. These represented scenes in different parts of the world, such as cannibals wearing feather head-dresses, a monkey carrying off a young lady, Bedouins in the desert, a whale being harpooned, and so on.

Paul explained these pictures to Félicité, and that indeed was all the education she ever had. As for the children, they were taught by Guyot, a poor devil employed at the Town Hall, who was famous for his beautiful handwriting, and who had a habit of sharpening his penknife on his boots.

When the weather was fine the whole household used to set off early for a day at the Geffosses farm.

The farmyard there was on a slope, with the house in the middle; and the sea, in the distance, looked like a streak of grey. Félicité would take some slices of cold meat out of her basket, and they would have their lunch in a room adjoining the dairy. It was all that remained of a country house which had fallen into ruin, and the wallpaper hung in shreds, fluttering in the draught. Madame Aubain used to sit with bowed head, absorbed in her memories, so that the children were afraid to talk. 'Why don't you run along and play?' she would say, and away they went.

Paul climbed up into the barn, caught birds, played ducks and drakes on the pond, or banged with a stick on the great casks, which sounded just like drums.

Virginie fed the rabbits, or scampered off to pick cornflowers, showing her little embroidered knickers as she ran.

One autumn evening they came home through the fields. The moon, which was in its first quarter, lit up part of the sky, and there was some mist floating like a scarf over the winding Toucques. The cattle, lying out in the middle of the pasture, looked peacefully at the four people walking by. In the third field a few got up and made a half-circle in front of them.

'Don't be frightened!' said Félicité, and crooning softly, she stroked the back of the nearest animal. It turned about and the others did the same. But while they were crossing the next field they suddenly heard a dreadful bellowing. It came from a bull which had been hidden by the mist, and which now came towards the two women.

Madame Aubain started to run.

'No! No!' said Félicité. 'Not so fast!'

All the same they quickened their pace, hearing behind them a sound of heavy breathing which came nearer and nearer. The bull's hoofs thudded like hammers on the turf, and they realised that it had broken into a gallop. Turning round, Félicité tore up some clods of earth and flung them at its eyes. It lowered its muzzle and thrust its horns forward, trembling with rage and bellowing horribly.

By now Madame Aubain had got to the end of the field with her two children and was frantically looking for a way over the high bank. Félicité was still backing away from the bull, hurling clods of turf which blinded it, and shouting: 'Hurry! Hurry!'

Madame Aubain got down into the ditch, pushed first Virginie and then Paul up the other side, fell once or twice trying to climb the bank, and finally managed it with a valiant effort.

The bull had driven Félicité back against a gate, and its slaver was spurting into her face. In another second it would have gored her, but she just had time to slip between two of the bars, and the great beast halted in amazement.

This adventure was talked about at Pont-l'Évêque for a good many years, but Félicité never prided herself in the least on what she had done, as it never occurred to her that she had done anything heroic.

Virginie claimed all her attention, for the fright had affected the little girl's nerves, and Monsieur Poupart, the doctor, recommended sea-bathing at Trouville.

In those days the resort had few visitors. Madame Aubain made enquiries, consulted Bourais, and got everything ready as though for a long journey.

Her luggage went off in Liébard's cart the day before she left. The next morning he brought along two horses, one of which had a woman's saddle with a velvet back, while the other carried a cloak rolled up to make a kind of seat on its crupper. Madame Aubain sat on this, with Liébard in front. Félicité looked after Virginie on the other horse, and Paul mounted Monsieur Lechaptois's donkey, which he had lent them on condition they took great care of it.

The road was so bad that it took two hours to travel the five miles to Toucques. The horses sank into the mud up to their pasterns and had to jerk their hindquarters to get out; often they stumbled in the ruts, or else they had to jump. In some places, Liébard's mare came to a sudden stop, and while he waited patiently for her to move off again, he talked about the people whose properties bordered the road, adding moral reflections to each story. For instance, in the middle of Toucques, as they were passing underneath some windows set in a mass of nasturtiums, he shrugged his shoulders and said:

'There's a Madame Lehoussais lives here. Now instead of taking a young man, she . . .'

Félicité did not hear the rest, for the horses had broken into a trot and the donkey was galloping along. All three turned down a bridle-path, a gate swung open, a couple of boys appeared, and everyone dismounted in front of a manure-heap right outside the farmhouse door.

Old Mother Liébard welcomed her mistress with every appearance of pleasure. She served up a sirloin of beef for lunch, with tripe and black pudding, a fricassée of chicken, sparkling cider, a fruit tart and brandy plums, garnishing the whole meal with compliments to Madame, who seemed to be enjoying better health, to Mademoiselle, who had turned into a 'proper little beauty', and to Monsieur Paul, who had 'filled out a lot'. Nor did she forget their deceased grandparents, whom the Liébards had known personally, having been in the family's service for several generations.

Like its occupants, the farm had an air of antiquity. The ceiling beams were worm-eaten, the walls black with smoke, and the window-panes grey with dust. There was an oak dresser laden with all sorts of odds and ends – jugs, plates, pewter bowls, wolf traps, sheep shears, and an enormous syringe which amused the children. In the three yards outside there was not a single tree without either mushrooms at its base or mistletoe in its branches. Several had been blown down and had taken root again at the middle; all of them were bent under the weight of their apples. The thatched roofs, which looked like brown velvet and varied in thickness, weathered the fiercest winds, but the cart-shed was tumbling down. Madame Aubain said that she would have it seen to, and ordered the animals to be reharnessed.

It took them another half-hour to reach Trouville. The little caravan dismounted to make their way along the Écores, a cliff jutting right out over the boats moored below; and three minutes later they got to the end of the quay and entered the courtyard of the Golden Lamb, the inn kept by Mère David.

After the first few days Virginie felt stronger, as a result of the change of air and the sea-bathing. Not having a costume, she went into the water in her chemise and her maid dressed her afterwards in a Customs officer's hut which was used by the bathers.

In the afternoons they took the donkey and went off beyond the Roches-Noires, in the direction of Hennequeville. To begin with, the path went uphill between gentle slopes like the lawns in a park, and then came out on a plateau where pastureland and ploughed fields alternated. On either side there were holly bushes standing out from the tangle of brambles, and here and there a big dead tree spread its zigzag branches against the blue sky.

They almost always rested in the same field, with Deauville on their left, Le Havre on their right, and the open sea in front. The water glittered in the sunshine, smooth as a mirror, and so still that the murmur it made was scarcely audible; unseen sparrows could be heard twittering, and the sky covered the whole scene with its huge canopy. Madame Aubain sat doing her needlework, Virginie plaited rushes beside her, Félicité gathered lavender, and Paul, feeling profoundly bored, longed to get up and go.

Sometimes they crossed the Toucques in a boat and hunted for shells. When the tide went out, sea urchins, ormers and jellyfish were left behind; and the children scampered around, snatching at the foam flakes carried on the wind. The sleepy waves, breaking on the sand, spread themselves out along the shore. The beach stretched as far as the eye could see, bounded on the land side by the dunes which separated it from the Marais, a broad meadow in the shape of an arena. When they came back that way, Trouville, on the distant hillside, grew bigger at every step, and with its medley of oddly assorted houses seemed to blossom out in gay disorder.

On exceptionally hot days they stayed in their room. The sun shone in dazzling bars of light between the slats of the blind. There was not a sound to be heard in the village, and not a soul to be seen down in the street. Everything seemed more peaceful in the prevailing silence. In the distance caulkers were hammering away at the boats, and the smell of tar was wafted along by a sluggish breeze.

The principal amusement consisted in watching the fishing-boats come in. As soon as they had passed the buoys, they started tacking. With their canvas partly lowered and their foresails blown out like balloons they glided through the splashing waves as far as the middle of the harbour, where they suddenly dropped anchor. Then each boat came alongside the quay, and the crew threw ashore their catch of quivering fish. A line of carts stood waiting, and women in cotton bonnets rushed forward to take the baskets and kiss their men.

One day one of these women spoke to Félicité, who came back to the inn soon after in a state of great excitement. She explained that she had found one of her sisters – and Nastasie Barette, now Leroux, made her appearance, with a baby at her breast, another child holding her right hand, and on her left a little sailor-boy, his arms akimbo and his cap over one ear.

Madame Aubain sent her off after a quarter of an hour. From then on they were forever hanging round the kitchen or loitering about when the family went for a walk, though the husband kept out of sight.

Félicité became quite attached to them. She bought them a blanket, several shirts, and a stove; and it was clear that they were bent on getting all they could out of her.

This weakness of hers annoyed Madame Aubain, who in any event disliked the familiar way in which the nephew spoke to Paul. And so, as Virginie had started coughing and the good weather was over, she decided to go back to Pont-l'Évêque.

Monsieur Bourais advised her on the choice of a school; Caen was considered the best, so it was there that Paul was sent. He said goodbye bravely, feeling really rather pleased to be going to a place where he would have friends of his own.

Madame Aubain resigned herself to the loss of her son, knowing that it was unavoidable. Virginie soon got used to it. Félicité missed the din he used to make, but she was given something new to do which served as a distraction: from Christmas onwards she had to take the little girl to catechism every day.

III

After genuflecting at the door, she walked up the centre aisle under the nave, opened the door of Madame Aubain's pew, sat down, and started looking about her.

The choir-stalls were all occupied, with the boys on the right and the girls on the left, while the *curé* stood by the lectern. In one of the stained-glass windows in the apse the Holy Ghost looked down on the Virgin; another window showed her kneeling before the Infant Jesus; and behind the tabernacle there was a wood-carving of Saint Michael slaying the dragon.

The priest began with a brief outline of sacred history. Listening to him, Félicité saw in imagination the Garden of Eden, the Flood, the Tower of Babel, cities burning, peoples dying, and idols being overthrown; and this dazzling vision left her with a great respect for the Almighty and profound fear of His wrath.

Then she wept as she listened to the story of the Passion. Why had they crucified Him, when He loved children, fed the multitudes, healed the blind, and had chosen out of humility to be born among the poor, on the litter of a stable? The sowing of the seed, the reaping of the harvest, the pressing of the grapes – all those familiar things of which the

Gospels speak had their place in her life. God had sanctified them in passing, so that she loved the lambs more tenderly for love of the Lamb of God, and the doves for the sake of the Holy Ghost.

She found it difficult, however, to imagine what the Holy Ghost looked like, for it was not just a bird but a fire as well, and sometimes a breath. She wondered whether that was its light she had seen flitting about the edge of the marshes at night, whether that was its breath she had felt driving the clouds across the sky, whether that was its voice she had heard in the sweet music of the bells. And she sat in silent adoration, delighting in the coolness of the walls and the quiet of the church.

Of dogma she neither understood nor even tried to understand anything. The *curé* discoursed, the children repeated their lesson, and she finally dropped off to sleep, waking up suddenly at the sound of their sabots clattering across the flagstones as they left the church.

It was in this manner, simply by hearing it expounded, that she learned her catechism, for her religious education had been neglected in her youth. From then on she copied all Virginie's observances, fasting when she did and going to confession with her. On the feast of Corpus Christi the two of them made an altar of repose together.

The preparations for Virginie's first communion caused her great anxiety. She worried over her shoes, her rosary, her missal, and her gloves. And how she trembled as she helped Madame Aubain to dress the child!

All through the Mass her heart was in her mouth. One side of the choir was hidden from her by Monsieur Bourais, but directly opposite her she could see the flock of maidens, looking like a field of snow with their white crowns perched on top of their veils; and she recognised her little darling from a distance by her dainty neck and her rapt attitude. The bell tinkled. Every head bowed low, and there was a silence. Then, to the thunderous accompaniment of the organ, choir and congregation joined in singing the *Agnus Dei*. Next the boys' procession began, and after that the girls got up from their seats. Slowly, their hands joined in prayer, they went towards the brightly-lit altar, knelt on the first step, received the Host one by one, and went back to their places in the same order. When it was Virginie's turn, Félicité leaned forward to see her, and in one of those imaginative flights born of real affection, it seemed to her that she herself was in the child's place. Virginie's face became her own, Virginie's dress clothed her, Virginie's heart was beating in her breast; and as she closed her eyes and opened her mouth, she almost fainted away.

Early next morning she went to the sacristy and asked Monsieur le *Curé* to give her communion. She received the sacrament with all due reverence, but did not feel the same rapture as she had the day before.

Madame Aubain wanted her daughter to possess every accomplishment, and since Guyot could not teach her English or music, she decided to send her as a boarder to the Ursuline Convent at Honfleur.

Virginie raised no objection, but Félicité went about sighing at Madame's lack of feeling. Then she thought that perhaps her mistress was right: such matters, after all, lay outside her province.

Finally the day arrived when an old wagonette stopped at their door, and a nun got down from it who had come to fetch Mademoiselle. Félicité hoisted the luggage up on top, gave the driver some parting instructions, and put six pots of jam, a dozen pears, and a bunch of violets in the boot.

At the last moment Virginie burst into a fit of sobbing. She threw her arms round her mother, who kissed her on the forehead, saying: 'Come now, be brave, be brave!' The step was pulled up and the carriage drove away.

Then Madame Aubain broke down and that evening all her friends, Monsieur and Madame Lormeau, Madame Lechaptois, the Rochefeuille sisters, Monsieur de Houppeville, and Bourais, came in to console her.

To begin with she missed her daughter badly. But she had a letter from her three times a week, wrote back on the other days, walked round her garden, did a little reading, and thus contrived to fill the empty hours.

As for Félicité, she went into Virginie's room every morning from sheer force of habit and looked round it. It upset her not having to brush the child's hair any more, tie her bootlaces, or tuck her up in bed; and she missed seeing her sweet face all the time and holding her hand when they went out together. For want of something to do, she tried making lace, but her fingers were too clumsy and broke the threads. She could not settle to anything, lost her sleep, and, to use her own words, was 'eaten up inside'.

To 'occupy her mind', she asked if her nephew Victor might come and see her, and permission was granted.

He used to arrive after Mass on Sunday, his cheeks flushed, his chest bare, and smelling of the countryside through which he had come. She laid a place for him straight away, opposite hers, and they had lunch together. Eating as little as possible herself, in order to save the expense, she stuffed him so full of food that he fell asleep after the meal. When the first bell for vespers rang, she woke him up, brushed his trousers, tied his tie, and set off for church, leaning on his arm with all a mother's pride.

His parents always told him to get something out of her – a packet of brown sugar perhaps, some soap, or a little brandy, sometimes even money. He brought her his clothes to be mended, and she did the work gladly, thankful for anything that would force him to come again.

In August his father took him on a coasting trip. The children's holidays were just beginning, and it cheered her up to have them home again. But Paul was turning capricious and Virginie was getting too old to be addressed familiarly – a state of affairs which put a barrier of constraint between them.

Victor went to Morlaix, Dunkirk, and Brighton in turn, and brought her a present after each trip. The first time it was a box covered with shells, the second a coffee-cup, the third a big gingerbread man. He was growing quite handsome, with his trim figure, his little moustache, his frank open eyes, and the little leather cap that he wore on the back of his head like a pilot. He kept her amused by telling her stories full of nautical jargon.

One Monday – it was the fourteenth of July 1819, a date she never forgot – Victor told her that he had signed on for an ocean voyage, and that on the Wednesday night he would be taking the Honfleur packet to join his schooner, which was due to sail shortly from Le Havre. He might be away, he said, for two years.

The prospect of such a long absence made Félicité extremely unhappy, and she felt she must bid him godspeed once more. So on the Wednesday evening, when Madame's dinner was over, she put on her clogs and swiftly covered the ten miles between Pont-l'Évêque and Honfleur.

When she arrived at the Calvary she turned right instead of left, got lost in the shipyards, and had to retrace her steps. Some people she spoke to advised her to hurry. She went right round the harbour, which was full of boats, constantly tripping over hawsers. Then the ground fell away, rays of light criss-crossed in front of her, and for a moment she thought she was going mad, for she could see horses up in the sky.

On the quayside more horses were neighing, frightened by the sea. A garnet was hoisting them into the air and dropping them into one of the boats, which was already crowded with passengers elbowing their way between barrels of cider, baskets of cheese, and sacks of grain. Hens were cackling and the captain swearing, while a cabin-boy stood leaning on the cat's-head, completely indifferent to it all. Félicité, who had not recognised him, shouted: 'Victor!' and he raised his head. She rushed forward, but at that very moment the gangway was pulled ashore.

The packet moved out of the harbour with women singing as they hauled it along, its ribs creaking and heavy waves lashing its bows. The sail swung round, hiding everyone on board from view, and against the silvery, moonlit sea the boat appeared as a dark shape that grew ever fainter, until at last it vanished in the distance.

As Félicité was passing the Calvary, she felt a longing to commend to God's mercy all that she held most dear; and she stood there praying for a long time, her face bathed in tears, her eyes fixed upon the clouds. The town was asleep, except for the Customs officers walking up and down. Water was pouring ceaselessly through the holes in the sluice-gate, making as much noise as a torrent. The clocks struck two.

The convent parlour would not be open before daybreak, and Madame would be annoyed if she were late; so, although she would have liked to give a kiss to the other child, she set off for home. The maids at the inn were just waking up as she got to Pont-l'Évêque.

So the poor lad was going to be tossed by the waves for months on end! His previous voyages had caused her no alarm. People came back from England and Brittany; but America, the Colonies, the Islands, were all so far away, somewhere at the other end of the world.

From then on Félicité thought of nothing but her nephew. On sunny days she hoped he was not too thirsty, and when there was a storm she was afraid he would be struck by lightning. Listening to the wind howling in the chimney or blowing slates off the roof, she saw him being buffeted by the very same storm, perched on the top of a broken mast, with his whole body bent backwards under a sheet of foam; or again – and these were reminiscences of the illustrated geography book – he was being eaten by savages, captured by monkeys in a forest, or dying on a desert shore. But she never spoke of her worries.

Madame Aubain had worries of her own about her daughter. The good nuns said that she was an affectionate child, but very delicate. The slightest emotion upset her, and she had to give up playing the piano.

Her mother insisted on regular letters from the convent. One morning when the postman had not called, she lost patience and walked up and down the room, between her chair and the window. It was really extraordinary! Four days without any news!

Thinking her own example would comfort her, Félicité said:

'I've been six months, Madame, without news.'

'News of whom?'

The servant answered gently:

'Why – of my nephew.'

'Oh, your nephew!' and Madame Aubain started pacing up and down again, with a shrug of her shoulders that seemed to say: 'I wasn't thinking of him – and indeed, why should I? Who cares about a young, good-for-nothing cabin-boy? Whereas my daughter – why, just think!'

Although she had been brought up the hard way, Félicité was indignant with Madame, but she soon forgot. It struck her as perfectly natural to lose one's head where the little girl was concerned. For her, the two children were of equal importance; they were linked together in her heart by a single bond, and their destinies should be the same.

The chemist told her that Victor's ship had arrived at Havana: he had seen this piece of information in a newspaper.

Because of its association with cigars, she imagined Havana as a place where nobody did anything but smoke, and pictured Victor walking about among crowds of Negroes in a cloud of tobacco-smoke. Was it possible, she wondered, 'in case of need' to come back by land? And how far was it from Pont-l'Évêque? To find out she asked Monsieur Bourais.

He reached for his atlas, and launched forth into an explanation of latitudes and longitudes, smiling like the pedant he was at Félicité's bewilderment. Finally he pointed with his pencil at a minute black dot inside a ragged oval patch, saying:

'There it is.'

She bent over the map, but the network of coloured lines meant nothing to her and only tired her eyes. So when Bourais asked her to tell him what was puzzling her, she begged him to show her the house where Victor was living. He threw up his hands, sneezed, and roared with laughter, delighted to come across such simplicity. And Félicité – whose intelligence was so limited that she probably expected to see an actual portrait of her nephew – could not make out why he was laughing.

It was a fortnight later that Liébard came into the kitchen at market-time, as he usually did, and handed her a letter from her brother-in-law. As neither of them could read, she turned to her mistress for help.

Madame Aubain, who was counting the stitches in her knitting, put it down and unsealed the letter. She gave a start, and, looking hard at Félicité, said quietly:

'They have some bad news for you . . . Your nephew . . .'

He was dead. That was all the letter had to say.

Félicité dropped on to a chair, leaning her head against the wall and closing her eyelids, which suddenly turned pink. Then, with her head bowed, her hands dangling, and her eyes set, she kept repeating:

'Poor little lad! Poor little lad!'

Liébard looked at her and sighed. Madame Aubain was trembling slightly. She suggested that she should go and see her sister at Trouville, but Félicité shook her head to indicate that there was no need for that.

There was a silence. Old Liébard thought it advisable to go.

Then Félicité said:

'It doesn't matter a bit, not to them it doesn't.'

Her head fell forward again, and from time to time she unconsciously picked up the knitting needles lying on the work-table.

Some women went past carrying a tray full of dripping linen.

Catching sight of them through the window, she remembered her own washing; she had passed the lye through it the day before and today it needed rinsing. So she left the room.

Her board and tub were on the bank of the Toucques. She threw a pile of chemises down by the water's edge, rolled up her sleeves, and picked up her battledore. The lusty blows she gave with it could be heard in all the neighbouring gardens.

The fields were empty, the river rippling in the wind; at the bottom long weeds were waving to and fro, like the hair of corpses floating in the water. She held back her grief, and was very brave until the evening; but in her room she gave way to it completely, lying on her mattress with her face buried in the pillow and her fists pressed against her temples.

Long afterwards she learned the circumstances of Victor's death from the captain of his ship. He had gone down with yellow fever, and they had bled him too much at the hospital. Four doctors had held him at once. He had died straight away, and the chief doctor had said:

'Good! There goes another!'

His parents had always treated him cruelly. She preferred not to see them again, and they made no advances, either because they had forgotten about her or out of the callousness of the poor.

Meanwhile Virginie was growing weaker. Difficulty in breathing, fits of coughing, protracted bouts of fever, and mottled patches on the cheek-bones all indicated some deep-seated complaint. Monsieur Poupart had advised a stay in Provence. Madame Aubain decided to follow this suggestion, and, if it had not been for the weather at Pont-l'Évêque, she would have brought her daughter home at once.

She arranged with a jobmaster to drive her out to the convent every Tuesday. There was a terrace in the garden, overlooking the Seine, and there Virginie, leaning on her mother's arm, walked up and down over the fallen vine-leaves. Sometimes, while she was looking at the sails in the distance, or at the long stretch of horizon from the Château de Tancarville to the lighthouses of Le Havre, the sun would break through the clouds and make her blink. Afterwards they would rest in the arbour. Her mother had secured a little cask of excellent Malaga, and, laughing at the idea of getting tipsy, Virginie used to drink a thimbleful, but no more.

Her strength revived. Autumn slipped by, and Félicité assured Madame Aubain that there was nothing to fear. But one evening, coming back from some errand in the neighbourhood, she found Monsieur Poupart's gig standing at the door. He was in the hall, and Madame Aubain was tying on her bonnet.

'Give me my foot-warmer, purse, gloves. Quickly now!'

Virginie had pneumonia and was perhaps past recovery.

'Not yet!' said the doctor; and the two of them got into the carriage with snowflakes swirling around them. Night was falling and it was very cold.

Félicité rushed into the church to light a candle, and then ran after the gig. She caught up with it an hour later, jumped lightly up behind, and hung on to the fringe. But then a thought struck her: the courtyard had not been locked up, and burglars might get in. So she jumped down again.

At dawn the next day she went to the doctor's. He had come home and gone out again on his rounds. Then she waited at the inn, thinking that somebody who was a stranger to the district might call there with a letter. Finally, when it was twilight, she got into the coach for Lisieux.

The convent was at the bottom of a steep lane. When she was halfway down the hill, she heard a strange sound which she recognised as a death-bell tolling.

'It's for somebody else,' she thought, as she banged the door-knocker hard.

After a few minutes she heard the sound of shuffling feet, the door opened a little way, and a nun appeared.

The good sister said with an air of compunction that 'she had just passed away'. At that moment the bell of Saint-Léonard was tolled more vigorously than ever.

Félicité went up to the second floor. From the doorway of the room she could see Virginie lying on her back, her hands clasped together, her mouth open, her head tilted back under a black crucifix that leaned over her, her face whiter than the curtains that hung motionless on either side. Madame Aubain was clinging to the foot of the bed and sobbing desperately. The Mother Superior stood on the right. Three candle-sticks on the chest of drawers added touches of red to the scene, and fog was whitening the windows. Some nuns led Madame Aubain away.

For two nights Félicité never left the dead girl. She said the same prayers over and over again, sprinkled holy water on the sheets, then sat down again to watch. At the end of her first vigil, she noticed that the child's face had gone yellow, the lips were turning blue, the nose looked sharper, and the eyes were sunken. She kissed them several times, and would not have been particularly surprised if Virginie had opened them again: to minds like hers, the supernatural is a simple matter. She laid her out, wrapped her in a shroud, put her in her coffin, placed a wreath on her, and spread out her hair. It was fair and amazingly long for her age. Félicité cut off a big lock, half of which she slipped into her bosom, resolving never to part with it.

The body was brought back to Pont-l'Évêque at the request of Madame Aubain, who followed the hearse in a closed carriage.

After the Requiem Mass, it took another three-quarters of an hour to reach the cemetery. Paul walked in front, sobbing. Then came Monsieur Bourais, and after him the principal inhabitants of the town, the women all wearing long black veils, and Félicité. She was thinking about her nephew; and since she had been unable to pay him these last honours, she felt an added grief, just as if they were burying him with Virginie.

Madame Aubain's despair passed all bounds. First of all she rebelled against God, considering it unfair of Him to have taken her daughter from her – for she had never done any harm, and her conscience was quite clear. But was it? She ought to have taken Virginie to the south; other doctors would have saved her life. She blamed herself, wished she could have joined her daughter, and cried out in anguish in her dreams. One dream in particular obsessed her. Her husband, dressed like a sailor, came back from a long voyage, and told her amid tears that he had been ordered to take Virginie away – whereupon they put their heads together to discover somewhere to hide her.

One day she came in from the garden utterly distraught. A few minutes earlier – and she pointed to the spot – father and daughter had appeared to her, doing nothing, but simply looking at her.

For several months she stayed in her room in a kind of stupor. Félicité scolded her gently, telling her that she must take care of herself for her son's sake, and also in remembrance of 'her'.

'Her?' repeated Madame Aubain, as if she were waking from a sleep. 'Oh, yes, of course! You don't forget her, do you!' This was an allusion to the cemetery, where she herself was strictly forbidden to go.

Félicité went there every day. She would set out on the stroke of four, going past the houses, up the hill, and through the gate, until she came to Virginie's grave. There was a little column of pink marble with a tablet at its base, and a tiny garden enclosed by chains. The beds were hidden under a carpet of flowers. She watered their leaves and changed the sand, going down on her knees to fork the ground thoroughly. The result was that when Madame Aubain was able to come here, she experienced a feeling of relief, a kind of consolation.

Then the years slipped by, each one like the last, with nothing to vary the rhythm of the great festivals: Easter, the Assumption, All Saints' Day. Domestic events marked dates that later served as points of reference. Thus in 1825 a couple of glaziers whitewashed the hall; in 1827 a piece of the roof fell into the courtyard and nearly killed a man; and in the summer of 1828 it was Madame's turn to provide the bread for consecration. About this time Bourais went away in a mysterious fashion; and one by one the old acquaintances disappeared: Guyot, Liébard, Madame Lechaptois, Robelin, and Uncle Grémanville, who had been paralysed for a long time.

One night the driver of the mail-coach brought Pont-l'Évêque news of the July Revolution. A few days later a new sub-prefect was appointed. This was the Baron de Larsonnière, who had been a consul in America, and who brought with him, besides his wife, his sister-in-law and three young ladies who were almost grown up. They were to be seen on their lawn, dressed in loose-fitting smocks; and they had a Negro servant and a parrot. They paid a call on Madame Aubain, who made a point of returning it. As soon as Félicité saw them coming, she would run and tell her mistress. But only one thing could really awaken her interest, and that was her son's letters.

He seemed to be incapable of following any career and spent all his time in taverns. She paid his debts, but he contracted new ones, and the sighs Madame Aubain heaved as she knitted by the window reached Félicité at her spinning-wheel in the kitchen.

The two women used to walk up and down together beside the espalier, forever talking of Virginie and debating whether such and such a thing would have appealed to her, or what she would have said on such and such an occasion.

All her little belongings were in a cupboard in the children's bed-room. Madame Aubain went through them as seldom as possible. One summer day she resigned herself to doing so, and the moths were sent fluttering out of the cupboard.

Virginie's frocks hung in a row underneath a shelf containing three dolls, a few hoops, a set of toy furniture, and the wash-basin she had used. Besides the frocks, they took out her petticoats, her stockings and her handkerchiefs, and spread them out on the two beds before folding them up again. The sunlight streamed in on these pathetic objects, bringing out the stains and showing up the creases made by the child's movements. The air was warm, the sky was blue, a blackbird was singing, and everything seemed to be utterly at peace.

They found a little chestnut-coloured hat, made of plush with a long nap; but the moths had ruined it. Félicité asked if she might have it. The two women looked at each other and their eyes filled with tears. Then the mistress opened her arms, the maid threw herself into them, and they clasped each other in a warm embrace, satisfying their grief in a kiss which made them equal.

It was the first time that such a thing had happened, for Madame Aubain was not of a demonstrative nature. Félicité was as grateful as if she had received a great favour, and henceforth loved her mistress with dog-like devotion and religious veneration.

Her heart grew softer as time went by.

When she heard the drums of a regiment coming down the street she stood at the door with a jug of cider and offered the soldiers a drink. She looked after the people who went down with cholera. She watched over the Polish refugees, and one of them actually expressed a desire to marry her. But they fell out, for when she came back from the Angelus one morning, she found that he had got into her kitchen and was calmly eating an oil-and-vinegar salad.

After the Poles it was Père Colmiche, an old man who was said to have committed fearful atrocities in '93. He lived by the river in a ruined pigsty. The boys of the town used to peer at him through the cracks in the walls, and threw pebbles at him which landed on the litter where he lay, constantly shaken by fits of coughing. His hair was extremely long, his eyelids inflamed, and on one arm there was a swelling bigger than his head. Félicité brought him some linen, tried to clean out his filthy hovel, and even wondered if she could install him in the wash-house without annoying Madame. When the tumour had burst, she changed his dressings every day, brought him some cake now and then, and put him out in the sun on a truss of hay. The poor old fellow would thank her in a faint whisper, slavering and trembling all the while, fearful of losing her and stretching his hands out as soon as he saw her moving away.

He died, and she had a Mass said for the repose of his soul.

That same day a great piece of good fortune came her way. Just as she was serving dinner, Madame de Larsonnière's Negro appeared carrying the parrot in its cage, complete with perch, chain, and padlock. The Baroness had written a note informing Madame Aubain that her husband had been promoted to a Prefecture and they were leaving that evening; she begged her to accept the parrot as a keepsake and a token of her regard.

This bird had engrossed Félicité's thoughts for a long time, for it came from America, and that word reminded her of Victor. So she had asked the Negro all about it, and once she had even gone so far as to say:

'How pleased Madame would be if it were hers!'

The Negro had repeated this remark to his mistress, who, unable to take the parrot with her, was glad to get rid of it in this way.

IV

His name was Loulou. His body was green, the tips of his wings were pink, his poll blue, and his breast golden.

Unfortunately he had a tiresome mania for biting his perch, and also used to pull his feathers out, scatter his droppings everywhere, and upset his bath-water. He annoyed Madame Aubain, and so she gave him to Félicité for good.

Félicité started training him, and soon he could say: 'Nice boy! Your servant, sir! Hail, Mary!' He was put near the door, and several people who spoke to him said how strange it was that he did not answer to the name of Jacquot, as all parrots were called Jacquot. They likened him to a turkey or a block of wood, and every sneer cut Félicité to the quick.

How odd, she thought, that Loulou should be so stubborn, refusing to talk whenever anyone looked at him!

For all that, he liked having people around him, because on Sunday, while the Rochefeuille sisters, Monsieur Houppeville and some new friends – the apothecary Onfroy, Monsieur Varin, and Captain Mathieu – were having their game of cards, he would beat on the window-panes with his wings and make such a din that it was impossible to hear oneself speak.

Bourais's face obviously struck him as terribly funny, for as soon as he saw it he was seized with uncontrollable laughter. His shrieks rang round the courtyard, the echo repeated them, and the neighbours came to their windows and started laughing too. To avoid being seen by the bird, Monsieur Bourais used to creep along by the wall, hiding his face behind his hat, until he got to the river, and then come into the house from the garden. The looks he gave the parrot were far from tender.

Loulou had once been cuffed by the butcher's boy for poking his head into his basket; and since then he was always trying to give him a nip through his shirt. Fabu threatened to wring his neck, although he was not a cruel fellow, in spite of his tattooed arms and bushy whiskers. On the contrary, he rather liked the parrot, so much so indeed that in a spirit of jovial camaraderie he tried to teach him a few swear-words. Félicité, alarmed at this development, put the bird in the kitchen. His little chain was removed and he was allowed to wander all over the house.

Coming downstairs, he used to rest the curved part of his beak on each step and then raise first his right foot, then his left; and Félicité was afraid that this sort of gymnastic performance would make him giddy. He fell ill and could neither talk nor eat for there was a swelling under his tongue such as hens sometimes have. She cured him by pulling this pellicule out with her fingernails. One day Monsieur Paul was silly enough to blow the smoke of his cigar at him; another time Madame Lormeau started teasing him with the end of her parasol, and he caught hold of the ferrule with his beak. Finally he got lost.

Félicité had put him down on the grass in the fresh air, and left him there for a minute. When she came back, the parrot had gone. First of all she looked for him in the bushes, by the river and on the rooftops, paying no attention to her mistress's shouts of: 'Be careful, now! You must be mad!' Next she went over all the gardens in Pont-l'Évêque, stopping passers-by and asking them: 'You don't happen to have seen my parrot

by any chance?' Those who did not know him already were given a description of the bird. Suddenly she thought she could make out something green flying about behind the mills at the foot of the hill. But up on the hill there was nothing to be seen. A pedlar told her that he had come upon the parrot a short time before in Mère Simon's shop at Saint-Melaine. She ran all the way there, but no one knew what she was talking about. Finally she came back home, worn out, her shoes falling to pieces, and death in her heart. She was sitting beside Madame on the garden seat and telling her what she had been doing, when she felt something light drop on her shoulder. It was Loulou! What he had been up to, no one could discover: perhaps he had just gone for a little walk round the town.

Félicité was slow to recover from this fright, and indeed never really got over it.

As the result of a chill she had an attack of quinsy, and soon after that her ears were affected. Three years later she was deaf, and she spoke at the top of her voice, even in church. Although her sins could have been proclaimed over the length and breadth of the diocese without dishonour to her or offence to others, Monsieur le *Curé* thought it advisable to hear her confession in the sacristy.

Imaginary buzzings in the head added to her troubles. Often her mistress would say: 'Heavens, how stupid you are!' and she would reply: 'Yes, Madame', at the same time looking all around her for something.

The little circle of her ideas grew narrower and narrower, and the pealing of bells and the lowing of cattle went out of her life. Every living thing moved about in a ghostly silence. Only one sound reached her ears now, and that was the voice of the parrot.

As if to amuse her, he would reproduce the click-clack of the turn-spit, the shrill call of a man selling fish, and the noise of the saw at the joiner's across the way; and when the bell rang he would imitate Madame Aubain's 'Félicité! The door, the door!'

They held conversations with each other, he repeating *ad nauseam* the three phrases in his repertory, she replying with words which were just as disconnected but which came from the heart. In her isolation, Loulou was almost a son or a lover to her. He used to climb up her fingers, peck at her lips, and hang on to her shawl; and as she bent over him, wagging her head from side to side as nurses do, the great wings of her bonnet and the wings of the bird quivered in unison.

When clouds banked up in the sky and there was a rumbling of thunder, he would utter piercing cries, no doubt remembering the sudden downpours in his native forests. The sound of the rain falling roused him to frenzy. He would flap excitedly around, shoot up to the ceiling, knocking everything over, and fly out of the window to splash about in the garden. But he would soon come back to perch on one of the firedogs, hopping about to dry his feathers and showing tail and beak in turn.

One morning in the terrible winter of 1837, when she had put him in front of the fire because of the cold, she found him dead in the middle of his cage, hanging head-down with his claws caught in the bars. He had probably died of a stroke, but she thought he had been poisoned with parsley, and despite the absence of any proof, her suspicions fell on Fabu.

She wept so much that her mistress said to her: 'Why don't you have him stuffed?'

Félicité asked the chemist's advice, remembering that he had always been kind to the parrot. He wrote to Le Havre, and a man called Fellacher agreed to do the job. As parcels sometimes went astray on the mail-coach, she decided to take the parrot as far as Honfleur herself.

On either side of the road stretched an endless succession of apple trees, all stripped of their leaves, and there was ice in the ditches. Dogs were barking around the farms; and Félicité, with her hands tucked under her mantlet, her little black sabots and her basket, walked briskly along in the middle of the road.

She crossed the forest, passed Le Haut-Chêne, and got as far as Saint-Gatien.

Behind her, in a cloud of dust, and gathering speed as the horses galloped downhill, a mail-coach swept along like a whirlwind. When he saw this woman making no attempt to get out of the way, the driver poked his head out above the hood, and he and the postilion shouted at her. His four horses could not be held in and galloped faster, the two leaders touching her as they went by. With a jerk of the reins the driver threw them to one side, and then, in a fury, he raised his long whip and gave her such a lash, from head to waist, that she fell flat on her back.

The first thing she did on regaining consciousness was to open her basket. Fortunately nothing had happened to Loulou. She felt her right cheek burning, and when she touched it her hand turned red; it was bleeding.

She sat down on a heap of stones and dabbed her face with her handkerchief. Then she ate a crust of bread which she had taken the precaution of putting in her basket, and tried to forget her wound by looking at the bird.

As she reached the top of the hill at Ecquemauville, she saw the lights of Honfleur twinkling in the darkness like a host of stars, and the shadowy expanse of the sea beyond. Then a sudden feeling of faintness made her stop; and the misery of her childhood, the disappointment of her first love, the departure of her nephew, and the death of Virginie all came back to her at once like the waves of a rising tide, and, welling up in her throat, choked her.

When she got to the boat she insisted on speaking to the captain, and without telling him what was in her parcel, asked him to take good care of it.

Fellacher kept the parrot a long time. Every week he promised it for the next; after six months he announced that a box had been sent off, and nothing more was heard of it. It looked as though Loulou would never come back, and Félicité told herself: 'They've stolen him for sure!'

At last he arrived – looking quite magnificent, perched on a branch screwed into a mahogany base, one foot in the air, his head cocked to one side, and biting a nut which the taxidermist, out of a love of the grandiose, had gilded.

Félicité shut him up in her room.

This place, to which few people were ever admitted, contained such a quantity of religious bric-à-brac and miscellaneous oddments that it looked like a cross between a chapel and a bazaar.

A big wardrobe prevented the door from opening properly. Opposite the window that overlooked the garden was a little round one looking on to the courtyard. There was a table beside the bed, with a water-jug, a couple of combs, and a block of blue soap on a chipped plate. On the walls there were rosaries, medals, several pictures of the Virgin, and a holy-water stoup made out of a coconut. On the chest of drawers, which was draped with a cloth just like an altar, was the shell box Victor had given her, and also a watering-can and a ball, some copybooks, the illustrated geography book, and a pair of ankle-boots. And on the nail supporting the looking-glass, fastened by its ribbons, hung the little plush hat.

Félicité carried this form of veneration to such lengths that she even kept one of Monsieur's frock-coats. All the old rubbish Madame

Aubain had no more use for, she carried off to her room. That was how there came to be artificial flowers along the edge of the chest of drawers, and a portrait of the Comte d'Artois in the window-recess.

With the aid of a wall bracket, Loulou was installed on a chimney-breast that jutted out into the room. Every morning when she awoke, she saw him in the light of the dawn, and then she remembered the old days, and the smallest details of insignificant actions, not in sorrow but in absolute tranquillity.

Having no intercourse with anyone, she lived in the torpid state of a sleepwalker. The Corpus Christi processions roused her from this condition, for she would go round the neighbours collecting candlesticks and mats to decorate the altar of repose which they used to set up in the street.

In church she was forever gazing at the Holy Ghost, and one day she noticed that it had something of the parrot about it. This resemblance struck her as even more obvious in a colour print depicting the baptism of Our Lord. With its red wings and its emerald-green body, it was the very image of Loulou.

She bought the print and hung it in the place of the Comte d'Artois, so that she could include them both in a single glance. They were linked together in her mind, the parrot being sanctified by this connection with the Holy Ghost, which itself acquired new life and meaning in her eyes. God the Father could not have chosen a dove as a means of expressing Himself, since doves cannot talk, but rather one of Loulou's ancestors. And although Félicité used to say her prayers with her eyes on the picture, from time to time she would turn slightly towards the bird.

She wanted to join the Children of Mary, but Madame Aubain dissuaded her from doing so.

An important event now loomed up – Paul's wedding.

After starting as a lawyer's clerk, he had been in business, in the Customs, and in Inland Revenue, and had even begun trying to get into the Department of Woods and Forests, when, at the age of thirty-six, by some heaven-sent inspiration, he suddenly discovered his real vocation – in the Wills and Probate Department. There he proved so capable that one of the auditors had offered him his daughter in marriage and promised to use his influence on his behalf.

Paul, grown serious-minded, brought her to see his mother. She criticised the way things were done at Pont-l'Évêque, put on airs, and hurt Félicité's feelings. Madame Aubain was relieved to see her go.

The following week came news of Monsieur Bourais's death in an inn in Lower Brittany. Rumours that he had committed suicide were confirmed, and doubts arose as to his honesty. Madame Aubain went over her accounts and was soon conversant with the full catalogue of his misdeeds – embezzlement of interest, secret sales of timber, forged receipts, etc. Besides all this, he was the father of an illegitimate child, and had had 'relations with a person at Dozulé'.

These infamies upset Madame Aubain greatly. In March 1853 she was afflicted with a pain in the chest; her tongue seemed to be covered with a film; leeches failed to make her breathing any easier; and on the ninth evening of her illness she died. She had just reached the age of seventy-two.

She was thought to be younger because of her brown hair, worn in bandeaux round her pale, pock-marked face. There were few friends to mourn her, for she had a haughty manner which put people off. Yet Félicité wept for her as servants rarely weep for their masters. That Madame should die before her upset her ideas, seemed to be contrary to the order of things, monstrous and unthinkable.

Ten days later – the time it took to travel hotfoot from Besançon – the heirs arrived. The daughter-in-law ransacked every drawer, picked out some pieces of furniture and sold the rest; and then back they went to the Wills and Probate Department.

Madame's armchair, her pedestal table, her foot-warmer, and the eight chairs had all gone. Yellow squares in the centre of the wall-panels showed where the pictures had hung. They had carried off the two cots with their mattresses, and no trace remained in the cupboard of all Virginie's things. Félicité climbed the stairs to her room, numbed with sadness.

The next day there was a notice on the door, and the apothecary shouted in her ear that the house was up for sale.

She swayed on her feet, and was obliged to sit down.

What distressed her most of all was the idea of leaving her room, which was so suitable for poor Loulou. Fixing an anguished look on him as she appealed to the Holy Ghost, she contracted the idolatrous habit of kneeling in front of the parrot to say her prayers. Sometimes the sun, as it came through the little window, caught his glass eye, so that it shot out a great luminous ray which sent her into ecstasies.

She had a pension of three hundred and eighty francs a year which her mistress had left her. The garden kept her in vegetables. As for clothes, she had enough to last her till the end of her days, and she saved on lighting by going to bed as soon as darkness fell.

She went out as little as possible, to avoid the second-hand dealer's shop, where some of the old furniture was on display. Ever since her fit of giddiness, she had been dragging one leg; and as her strength was failing, Mère Simon, whose grocery business had come to grief, came in every morning to chop wood and pump water for her.

Her eyes grew weaker. The shutters were not opened any more. Years went by, and nobody rented the house and nobody bought it.

For fear of being evicted, Félicité never asked for any repairs to be done. The laths in the roof rotted, and all through one winter her bolster was wet. After Easter she began spitting blood.

When this happened Mère Simon called in a doctor. Félicité wanted to know what was the matter with her, but she was so deaf that only one word reached her: 'Pneumonia'. It was a word she knew, and she answered gently: 'Ah! like Madame', thinking it natural that she should follow in her mistress's footsteps.

The time to set up the altars of repose was drawing near.

The first altar was always at the foot of the hill, the second in front of the post office, the third about halfway up the street. There was some argument as to the siting of this one, and finally the women of the parish picked on Madame Aubain's courtyard.

The fever and the tightness of the chest grew worse. Félicité fretted over not doing anything for the altar. If only she could have put something on it! Then she thought of the parrot. The neighbours protested that it would not be seemly, but the *curé* gave his permission, and this made her so happy that she begged him to accept Loulou, the only thing of value she possessed, when she died.

From Tuesday to Saturday, the eve of Corpus Christi, she coughed more and more frequently. In the evening her face looked pinched and drawn, her lips stuck to her gums, and she started vomiting. At dawn the next day, feeling very low, she sent for a priest.

Three good women stood by her while she was given extreme unction. Then she said that she had to speak to Fabu.

He arrived in his Sunday best, very ill at ease in this funereal atmosphere.

'Forgive me,' she said, making an effort to stretch out her arm. 'I thought it was you who had killed him.'

What could she mean by such nonsense? To think that she had

suspected a man like him of murder! He got very indignant and was obviously going to make a scene.

'Can't you see', they said, 'that she isn't in her right mind any more?'

From time to time Félicité would start talking to shadows. The women went away. Mère Simon had her lunch.

A little later she picked Loulou up and held him out to Félicité, saying:

'Come now, say goodbye to him.'

Although the parrot was not a corpse, the worms were eating him up. One of his wings was broken, and the stuffing was coming out of his stomach. But she was blind by now, and she kissed him on the forehead and pressed him against her cheek. Mère Simon took him away from her to put him on the altar.

V

The scents of summer came up from the meadows; there was a buzzing of flies; the sun was glittering in the river and warming the slates of the roof. Mère Simon had come back into the room and was gently nodding off to sleep.

The noise of church bells woke her up; the congregation was coming out from vespers. Félicité's delirium abated. Thinking of the procession, she could see it as clearly as if she had been following it.

All the schoolchildren, the choristers, and the firemen were walking along the pavements, while advancing up the middle of the street came the church officer armed with his halberd, the beadle carrying a great cross, the schoolmaster keeping an eye on the boys, and the nun fussing over her little girls – three of the prettiest, looking like curly-headed angels, were throwing rose petals into the air. Then came the deacon, with both arms outstretched, conducting the band, and a couple of censer-bearers who turned round at every step to face the Holy Sacrament, which the *curé*, wearing his splendid chasuble, was carrying under a canopy of poppy-red velvet held aloft by four churchwardens. A crowd of people surged along behind, between the white cloths covering the walls of the houses, and eventually they got to the bottom of the hill.

A cold sweat moistened Félicité's temples. Mère Simon sponged it up with a cloth, telling herself that one day she would have to go the same way.

The hum of the crowd increased in volume, was very loud for a moment, then faded away.

A fusillade shook the window-panes. It was the postilions saluting the monstrance. Félicité rolled her eyes and said as loud as she could: 'Is he all right?' – worrying about the parrot.

She entered into her death-agony. Her breath, coming ever faster, with a rattling sound, made her sides heave. Bubbles of froth appeared at the corners of her mouth, and her whole body trembled.

Soon the booming of the ophicleides, the clear voices of the children, and the deep voices of the men could be heard near at hand. Now and then everything was quiet, and the tramping of feet, deadened by a carpet of flowers, sounded like a flock moving across pastureland.

The clergy appeared in the courtyard. Mère Simon climbed on to a chair to reach the little round window, from which she had a full view of the altar below.

It was hung with green garlands and adorned with a flounce in English needle-point lace. In the middle was a little frame containing some relics, there were two orange trees at the corners, and all the way along stood silver candlesticks and china vases holding sunflowers, lilies, peonies, foxgloves, and bunches of hydrangea. This pyramid of bright colours stretched from the first floor right down to the carpet which was spread out over the pavement. Some rare objects caught the eye: a silver-gilt sugar basin wreathed in violets, some pendants of Alençon gems gleaming on a bed of moss, and two Chinese screens with landscape decorations. Loulou, hidden under roses, showed nothing but his blue poll, which looked like a plaque of lapis lazuli.

The churchwardens, the choristers, and the children lined up along the three sides of the courtyard. The priest went slowly up the steps and placed his great shining gold sun on the lace altar cloth. Everyone knelt down. There was a deep silence. And the censers, swinging at full tilt, slid up and down their chains.

A blue cloud of incense was wafted up into Félicité's room. She opened her nostrils wide and breathed it in with a mystical, sensuous fervour. Then she closed her eyes. Her lips smiled. Her heartbeats grew slower and slower, each a little fainter and gentler, like a fountain running dry, an echo fading away. And as she breathed her last, she thought she could see, in the opening heavens, a gigantic parrot hovering above her head.

Jules Verne

The writings of Jules Verne (1828–1905) display a passionate scientific imagination which rarely fails to delight children and cinema-goers alike. Often ignored by academic critics, he is now recognised as one of the most symptomatic voices of his time. Verne was expected to become a lawyer, like his father, but he rebelled, writing for the theatre, in association with Dumas *fils*, before turning to prose fiction. He discovered his métier with the serialisation of *Cinq semaines en ballon* in 1863, his first great success. Verne's friendships with explorers and scientists inspired his vivid inventiveness to produce tales of *Voyages extraordinaires*, bursting with a passion for science, travel and the exotic. His most famous works, notably *Voyage au centre de la terre* (1864), *Vingt mille lieues sous les mers* (1870) and *Le Tour du monde en quatre-vingt jours* (1873), have achieved an enduring popularity.

In the Twenty-Ninth Century: The Day of an American Journalist in 2889

AU XXIXME SIÈCLE : LA JOURNÉE D'UN
JOURNALISTE AMÉRICAIN EN 2889

*This 'fantasy', as its original Editor called it, has had an unusual history –
for some reason it was first published in English! It originally appeared in an
American magazine,* The Forum, *in February, 1889. Later it was published, though with several alterations, in French. Its Editor, however, says
that in preparing it for re-publication he sometimes had to refer to what he
calls the 'primitive English text'.*

*'Fantasy' though it may be, it has more serious aspects; it is obviously a
satire on certain tendencies which Verne observed in contemporary life. The
future inventions he describes may be left to speak for themselves: he had
boundless faith in the potentialities of electricity, and a reference in another
of his books,* Carpathian Castle, *shows that he regarded what he called the
'telephote' – a method of transmitting visual images by wire – as the obvious
adjunct to the telephone.*

*According to the French critic Étienne Cluzel, a number of these inven-
tions were derived by Verne from another forecast,* Le Vingtième Siècle *by
Albert Robida. As the latter's ideas of the submarine of the future were obviously based on Verne's* Nautilus *in* 20,000 Leagues Under the Sea, *the two
authors may possibly have had an amicable agreement to exchange ideas.*

*The somewhat dramatic incident related on pages 251–2 was omitted in
the original English version, possibly because Verne feared that in contemporary Transatlantic eyes it might be considered 'shocking'!*

THE MEN OF THE TWENTY-NINTH CENTURY LIVE IN A perpetual fairyland, though they do not seem to realise it. Bored with wonders, they are cold towards everything that progress brings them every day. It all seems only natural.

If they compared it with the past, they would better appreciate what our civilisation is, and realise what a road it has traversed. What would then seem finer than our modern cities, with streets a hundred yards wide, with buildings a thousand feet high, always at an equable temperature, and the sky furrowed by thousands of aero-cars and aero-buses! Compared with these towns, whose population may include up to ten million inhabitants, what were those villages, those hamlets of a thousand years ago, that Paris, that London, that New York – muddy and badly ventilated townships, traversed by jolting contraptions, hauled along by horses – yes! by horses! it's unbelievable!

If they recalled the erratic working of the steamers and the railways, their many collisions, and their slowness, how greatly would travellers value the aero-trains, and especially these pneumatic tubes laid beneath the oceans, which convey them with a speed of a thousand miles an hour? And would they not enjoy the telephone and the telephote even better if they recollected that our fathers were reduced to that antediluvial apparatus which they called the 'telegraph'?

It's very strange. These surprising transformations are based on principles which were quite well known to our ancestors, although these, so to speak, made no use of them. Heat, steam, electricity are as old as mankind. Towards the end of the nineteenth century, did not the savants declare that the only difference between the physical and chemical forces consists of the special rates of vibration of the etheric particles?

As so enormous a stride had been made, that of recognising the mutual relationship of all these forces, it is incredible that it took so long to work out the rates of vibration that differentiate between them. It is especially surprising that the method of passing directly from one to another, and of producing one without the other, has only been discovered so recently.

So it was, however, that things happened, and it was only in 2790, about a hundred years ago, that the famous Oswald Nyer succeeded in doing so.

A real benefactor of humanity, that great man! His achievement, a work of genius, was the parent of all the others! A constellation of inventors was born out of it, culminating in our extraordinary James Jackson. It is to him that we owe the new accumulators, some of which condense the force of the solar rays, others the electricity stored in the heart of our globe, and yet again others, energy coming from any source whatever, whether it be the waterfalls, winds, or rivers. It is to him that we owe no less the transformer which, at a touch on a simple switch, draws on the force that lives in the accumulators and releases it as heat, light, electricity, or mechanical power after it has performed any task we need.

Yes, it was from the day on which these two appliances were thought out that progress really dates. They have given mankind almost an infinite power. Through mitigating the bleakness of winter by restoring to it the excessive heat of the summer, they have revolutionised agriculture. By providing motive power for the appliances used in aerial navigation, they have enabled commerce to make a splendid leap forward. It is to them that we owe the unceasing production of electricity without either batteries or machines, light without combustion or incandescence, and finally that inexhaustible source of energy which has increased industrial production a hundredfold.

Very well then! The whole of these wonders, we shall meet them in an incomparable office block – the office of the *Earth Herald*, recently inaugurated in the 16823rd Avenue.

If the founder of the *New York Herald*, Gordon Bennett, were to be born a second time today, what would he say when he saw this palace of marble and gold that belongs to his illustrious descendant, Francis Bennett? Thirty generations had followed one another, and the *New York Herald* had always stayed in that same Bennett family. Two hundred years before, when the government of the Union had been transferred from Washington to Centropolis, the newspaper had followed the government – if it were not that the government had followed the newspaper – and it had taken its new title, the *Earth Herald*.

And let nobody imagine that it had declined under the administration of Francis Bennett. No! On the contrary, its new director had given it an equalled vitality and driving-power by the inauguration of telephonic journalism.

Everybody knows that system, made possible by the incredible diffusion of the telephone. Every morning, instead of being printed as in antiquity, the *Earth Herald* is 'spoken'. It is by means of a brisk conversation with a reporter, a political figure, or a scientist, that the subscribers can learn whatever happens to interest them. As for those who buy an odd number for a few cents, they know that they can get acquainted with the day's issue through the countless phonographic cabinets.

This innovation of Francis Bennett restored new life to the old journal. In a few months its clientèle numbered eighty-five million subscribers, and the director's fortune rose to three hundred million dollars, and has since gone far beyond that. Thanks to this fortune, he was able to build his new office – a colossal edifice with four façades each two miles long, whose roof is sheltered beneath the glorious flag, with its seventy-five stars, of the Confederation.

Francis Bennett, king of journalists, would then have been king of the two Americas, if the Americans would ever accept any monarch whatever. Do you doubt this? But the plenipotentiaries of every nation and our very ministers throng around his door, peddling their advice, seeking his approval, imploring the support of his all-powerful organ. Count up the scientists whom he has encouraged, the artists whom he employs, the inventors whom he subsidises! A wearisome monarchy was his, work without respite, and certainly nobody of earlier times would ever have been able to carry out so unremitting a daily grind. Fortunately, however, the men of today have a more robust constitution, thanks to the progress of hygiene and of gymnastics, which from thirty-seven years has now increased to sixty-eight the average length of human life – thanks too to the aseptic foods, while we wait for the next discovery: that of nutritious air which will enable us to take nourishment . . . only by breathing.

And now, if you would like to know everything that constitutes the day of a director of the *Earth Herald*, take the trouble to follow him in his multifarious operations – this very day, this July 25th of the present year, 2889.

That morning Francis Bennett awoke in rather a bad temper. This was eight days since his wife had been in France and he was feeling a little lonely. Can it be credited? They had been married ten years, and this was the first time that Mrs Edith Bennett, that *professional beauty*, had been so long away. Two or three days usually sufficed for her frequent journeys to Europe and especially to Paris, where she went to buy her hats.

As soon as he awoke, Francis Bennett switched on his phonotelephote, whose wires led to the house he owned in the Champs-Élysées.

The telephone, completed by the telephote, is another of our time's conquests! Though the transmission of speech by the electric current was already very old, it was only since yesterday that vision could also be transmitted. A valuable discovery, and Francis Bennett was by no means the only one to bless its inventor when, in spite of the enormous distance between them, he saw his wife appear in the telephotic mirror.

A lovely vision! A little tired by last night's theatre or dance, Mrs Bennett was still in bed. Although where she was it was nearly noon, her charming head was buried in the lace of the pillow. But there she was stirring . . . her lips were moving . . . No doubt she was dreaming? . . . Yes! She was dreaming . . . A name slipped from her mouth. 'Francis . . . dear Francis! . . .'

His name, spoken by that sweet voice, gave a happier turn to Francis Bennett's mood. Not wanting to wake the pretty sleeper, he quickly jumped out of bed, and went into his mechanised dressing-room.

Two minutes later, without needing the help of a valet, the machine deposited him, washed, shaved, shod, dressed and buttoned from top to toe, on the threshold of his office. The day's work was going to begin.

It was into the room of the serialised novelists that Francis first entered.

Very big, that room, surmounted by a large translucent dome. In a corner, several telephonic instruments by which the hundred authors of the *Earth Herald* related a hundred chapters of a hundred romances to the enfevered public.

Catching sight of one of these serialists who was snatching five minutes' rest, Francis Bennett said:

'Very fine, my dear fellow, very fine, that last chapter of yours! That scene where the young village girl is discussing with her admirer some of the problems of transcendental philosophy shows very keen powers of observation! These country manners have never been more clearly depicted! Go on that way, my dear Archibald, and good luck to you. Ten thousand new subscribers since yesterday, thanks to you!

'Mr John Last,' he continued, turning towards another of his collaborators, 'I'm not so satisfied with you! It hasn't any life, your story! You're in too much of a hurry to get to the end! Well! and what about all that documentation? You've got to dissect, John Last, you've got to dissect! It isn't with a pen one writes nowadays, it's with a scalpel! Every action in real life is the resultant of a succession of fleeting thoughts, and they've got to be carefully set out to create a living being! And what's easier than to use electrical hypnotism, which redoubles its subject and separates his twofold personality! Watch yourself living, John Last, my dear fellow! Imitate your colleague whom I've just been congratulating! Get yourself hypnotised . . . What? . . . You're having it done, you say? . . . Not good enough yet, not good enough!'

Having given this little lesson, Francis Bennett continued his inspection and went on into the reporters' room. His fifteen hundred reporters, placed before an equal number of telephones, were passing on to subscribers the news which had come in during the night from the four quarters of the earth.

The organisation of this incomparable service has often been described. In addition to his telephone, each reporter has in front of him a series of commutators, which allow him to get into communication with this or that telephotic line. Thus the subscribers have not only the story but the sight of these events. When it is a question of 'miscellaneous facts', which are things of the past by the time they are described, their principal phases alone are transmitted; these are obtained by intensive photography.

Francis Bennett questioned one of the ten astronomical reporters – a service which was growing because of the recent discoveries in the stellar world.

'Well, Cash, what have you got?'

'Phototelegrams from Mercury, Venus and Mars, sir.'

'Interesting, that last one?'

'Yes! a revolution in the Central Empire, in support of the reactionary liberals against the republican conservatives.'

'Just like us, then! And Jupiter?'

'Nothing so far! We haven't been able to understand the signals the Jovians make. Perhaps ours haven't reached them? . . .'

'That's your job, and I hold you responsible, Mr Cash!' Francis Bennett replied; extremely dissatisfied, he went on to the scientific editorial room.

Bent over their computers, thirty savants were absorbed in equations of the ninety-fifth degree. Some indeed were revelling in the formulae of algebraical infinity and of twenty-four-dimensional space, like a child in the elementary class dealing with the four rules of arithmetic.

Francis Bennett fell among them rather like a bombshell.

'Well, gentlemen, what's this they tell me? No reply from Jupiter? . . . It's always the same! Look here, Corley, it seems to me it's been twenty years that you've been pegging away at that planet . . .'

'What do you expect, sir?' the savant replied. 'Our optical science still leaves something to be desired, and even with our telescopes two miles long . . .'

'You hear that, Peer?' broke in Francis Bennett, addressing himself to Corley's neighbour. 'Optical science leaves something to be desired! . . . That's your speciality, that is, my dear fellow! Put on your glasses, devil take it! Put on your glasses!'

Then, turning back to Corley:

'But, failing Jupiter, aren't you getting some result from the moon, at any rate?'

'Not yet, Mr Bennett.'

'Well, this time, you can't blame optical science! The moon is six hundred times nearer than Mars, and yet our correspondence service is in regular operation with Mars. It can't be telescopes we're needing . . .'

'No, it's the inhabitants,' Corley replied with the thin smile of a savant stuffed with X.

'You dare tell me that the moon is uninhabited?'

'On the face it turns towards us, at any rate, Mr Bennett. Who knows whether on the other side . . . ?'

'Well, there's a very simple method of finding out . . .'

'And that is? . . .'

'To turn the moon round!'

And that very day, the scientists of the Bennett factory started working out some mechanical means of turning our satellite right round.

On the whole Francis Bennett had reason to be satisfied. One of the *Earth Herald*'s astronomers had just determined the elements of the new planet Gandini. It is at a distance of 12,841,348,284,623 metres and 7 decimetres that this planet describes its orbit round the sun in 572 years, 194 days, 12 hours, 43 minutes, 9.8 seconds.

Francis Bennett was delighted with such precision.

'Good!' he exclaimed. 'Hurry up and tell the reportage service about it. You know what a passion the public has for these astronomical questions. I'm anxious for the news to appear in today's issue!'

Before leaving the reporters' room he took up another matter with a special group of interviewers, addressing the one who dealt with celebrities: 'You've interviewed President Wilcox?' he asked.

'Yes, Mr Bennett, and I'm publishing the information that he's certainly suffering from a dilation of the stomach, and that he's most conscientiously undergoing a course of tubular irrigations.'

'Splendid. And that business of Chapmann the assassin? . . . Have you interviewed the jurymen who are to sit at the Assizes?'

'Yes, and they all agree that he's guilty, so that the case won't even have to be submitted to them. The accused will be executed before he's sentenced.'

'Splendid! Splendid!'

The next room, a broad gallery about a quarter of a mile long, was devoted to publicity, and it well may be imagined what the publicity for such a journal as the *Earth Herald* had to be. It brought in a daily average of three million dollars. Very ingeniously, indeed, some of the publicity obtained took an absolutely novel form, the result of a patent bought at an outlay of three dollars from a poor devil who had since died of hunger. They are gigantic signs reflected on the clouds, so large that they can be seen all over a whole country. From that gallery a thousand projectors were unceasingly employed in sending to the clouds, on which they were reproduced in colour, these inordinate advertisements.

But that day when Francis Bennett entered the publicity room he found the technicians with their arms folded beside their idle projectors. He asked them about it . . . The only reply he got was that somebody pointed to the blue sky.

'Yes! . . . A fine day,' he muttered, 'so we can't get any aerial publicity! What's to be done about that? If there isn't any rain, we can produce it! But it isn't rain, it's clouds that we need!'

'Yes, some fine snow-white clouds!' replied the chief technician.

'Well, Mr Simon Mark, you'd better get in touch with the scientific editors, meteorological service. You can tell them from me that they can get busy on the problem of artificial clouds. We really can't be at the mercy of the fine weather.'

After finishing his inspection of the different sections of the paper, Francis Bennett went to his reception hall, where he found awaiting him the ambassadors and plenipotentiary ministers accredited to the American government: these gentlemen had come to ask advice from the all-powerful director. As he entered the room they were carrying on rather a lively discussion.

'Pardon me, Your Excellency,' the French Ambassador addressed the Ambassador from Russia. 'But I can't see anything that needs changing in the map of Europe. The north to the Slavs, agreed! But the south to the Latins! Our common frontier along the Rhine seems quite satisfactory. Understand me clearly, that our government will certainly resist any attempt which may be made against our Prefectures of Rome, Madrid, and Vienna!'

'Well said!' Francis Bennett intervened in the discussion. 'What, Mr Russian Ambassador, you're not satisfied with your great empire, which extends from the banks of the Rhine as far as the frontiers of China? An empire whose immense coast is bathed by the Arctic Ocean, the Atlantic, the Black Sea, the Bosphorus, and the Indian Ocean?

'And besides, what's the use of threats? Is war with our modern weapons possible? These asphyxiating shells which can be sent a distance of a hundred miles, these electric flashes, sixty miles long, which can annihilate a whole army corps at a single blow, these projectiles loaded with the microbes of plague, cholera and yellow fever, and which can destroy a whole nation in a few hours?'

'We realise that, Mr Bennett,' the Russian Ambassador replied. 'But are we free to do what we like? . . . Thrust back ourselves by the Chinese on our eastern frontier, we must, at all costs, attempt something towards the west . . .'

'Is that all it is, sir?' Francis Bennett replied in reassuring tones— 'Well! as the proliferation of the Chinese is getting to be a danger to the world, we'll bring pressure to bear on the Son of Heaven. He'll simply have to impose a maximum birth-rate on his subjects, not to be exceeded on pain of death! A child too many? . . . A father less! That will keep things balanced.

'And you, sir,' the director of the *Earth Herald* continued, addressing the English consul, 'what can I do to be of service to you?'

'A great deal, Mr Bennett,' that personage replied. 'It would be enough for your journal to open a campaign on our behalf . . .'

'And with what purpose?'

'Merely to protest against the annexation of Great Britain by the United States . . .'

'Merely that!' Francis Bennett exclaimed. He shrugged his shoulders. 'An annexation that's a hundred and fifty years old already! But won't you English gentry ever resign yourselves to the fact that by a just compensation of events here below, your country has become an American colony? That's pure madness! How could your government ever have believed that I should even open so anti-patriotic a campaign? . . .'

'Mr Bennett, you know that the Monroe Doctrine is all America for the Americans, and nothing more than America, and not . . .'

'But England is only one of our colonies, one of the finest. Don't count upon our ever consenting to give her up!'

'You refuse? . . .'

'I refuse, and if you insist, we shall make it a *casus belli*, based on nothing more than an interview with one of our reporters.'

'So that's the end.' The consul was overwhelmed. 'The United Kingdom, Canada, and New Britain belong to the Americans, India to the Russians, and Australia and New Zealand to themselves! Of all that once was England, what's left? . . . Nothing!'

'Nothing, sir?' retorted Francis Bennett. 'Well, what about Gibraltar?'

At that moment the clock struck twelve. The director of the *Earth Herald*, ending the audience with a gesture, left the hall, and sat down in a rolling armchair. In a few minutes he had reached his dining-room, half a mile away, at the far end of the office.

The table was laid, and he took his place at it. Within reach of his hand was placed a series of taps, and before him was the curved surface of a phonotelephote, on which appeared the dining-room of his home in Paris. Mr and Mrs Bennett had arranged to have lunch at the same time – nothing could be more pleasant than to be face to face in spite of the distance, to see one another and talk by means of the phonotelephotic apparatus.

But the room in Paris was still empty.

'Edith is late,' Francis Bennett said to himself. 'Oh, women's punctuality! Everything makes progress, except that.'

And after this too just reflection, he turned on one of the taps.

Like everybody else in easy circumstances nowadays, Francis Bennett, having abandoned domestic cooking, is one of the subscribers to the *Society for Supplying Food to the Home*, which distributes dishes of a thousand types through a network of pneumatic tubes. This system is expensive, no doubt, but the cooking is better, and it has the advantage that it has suppressed that hair-raising race, the cooks of both sexes.

So, not without some regret, Francis Bennett was lunching in solitude. He was finishing his coffee when Mrs Bennett, having got back home, appeared in the telephote screen.

'Where have you been, Edith dear?' Francis Bennett enquired.

'What?' Mrs Bennett replied. 'You've finished? . . . I must be late, then? . . . Where have I been? Of course, I've been with my *modiste* . . .

This year's hats are so bewitching! They're not hats at all . . . they're domes, they're cupolas! I rather lost count of time!'

'Rather, my dear? You lost it so much that here's my lunch finished.'

'Well, run along then, my dear . . . run along to your work,' Mrs Bennett replied. 'I've still got a visit to make, to my *modeleur-couturier.*'

And this *couturier* was no other than the famous Wormspire, the very man who so judiciously remarked, 'Woman is only a question of shape!'

Francis Bennett kissed Mrs Bennett's cheek on the telephote screen and went across to the window, where his aero-car was waiting.

'Where are we going, sir?' asked the aero-coachman.

'Let's see. I've got time . . .' Francis Bennett replied. 'Take me to my accumulator works at Niagara.'

The aero-car, an apparatus splendidly based on the principle of 'heavier than air', shot across space at a speed of about four hundred miles an hour. Below him were spread out the towns with their moving pavements which carry the wayfarers along the streets, and the country-side, covered, as though by an immense spider's web, by the network of electric wires.

Within half an hour, Francis Bennett had reached his works at Niagara, where, after using the force of the cataracts to produce energy, he sold or hired it out to the consumers. Then, his visit over, he returned, by way of Philadelphia, Boston, and New York, to Centropolis, where his aero-car put him down about five o'clock.

The waiting-room of the *Earth Herald* was crowded. A careful look-out was being kept for Francis Bennett to return for the daily audience he gave to his petitioners. They included the capital's acquisitive inventors, company promoters with enterprises to suggest – all splendid, to listen to them. Among these different proposals he had to make a choice, reject the bad ones, look into the doubtful ones, give a welcome to the good ones.

He soon got rid of those who had only got useless or impracticable schemes. One of them – didn't he claim to revive painting, an art which had fallen into such desuetude that Millet's *Angelus* had just been sold for fifteen francs – thanks to the progress of colour photography invented at the end of the twentieth century by the Japanese, whose name was on everybody's lips – Aruziswa-Riochi-Nichome-Sanjukam-boz-Kio-Baski-Kû? Another, hadn't he discovered the biogene bacillus which, after being introduced into the human organism, would make man immortal? This one, a chemist, hadn't he discovered a new substance *Nihilium*, of which a gram would cost only three million dollars? That one, a most daring physician, wasn't he claiming that he'd found a remedy for a cold in the head?

All these dreamers were at once shown out.

A few of the others received a better welcome, and foremost among them was a young man whose broad brow indicated a high degree of intelligence.

'Sir,' he began, 'though the number of elements used to be estimated at seventy-five, it has now been reduced to three, as no doubt you are aware?'

'Perfectly,' Francis Bennett replied.

'Well, sir, I'm on the point of reducing the three to one. If I don't run out of money I'll have succeeded in three weeks.'

'And then?'

'Then, sir, I shall really have discovered the absolute.'

'And the results of that discovery?'

'It will be to make the creation of all forms of matter easy – stone, wood, metal, fibrin . . .'

'Are you saying you're going to be able to construct a human being?'

'Completely . . . The only thing missing will be the soul!'

'Only that!' was the ironical reply of Francis Bennett, who however assigned the young fellow to the scientific editorial department of his journal.

A second inventor, using as a basis some old experiments that dated from the nineteenth century and had often been repeated since, had the idea of moving a whole city in a single block. He suggested, as a demonstration, the town of Saaf, situated fifteen miles from the sea; after conveying it on rails down to the shore, he would transform it into a seaside resort. That would add an enormous value to the ground already built on and to be built over.

Francis Bennett, attracted by this project, agreed to take a half-share in it.

'You know, sir,' said a third applicant, 'that, thanks to our solar and terrestrial accumulators and transformers, we've been able to equalise the seasons. I suggest doing even better. By converting into heat part of the energy we have at our disposal and transmitting the heat to the polar regions we can melt the ice . . .'

'Leave your plans with me,' Francis Bennett replied, 'and come back in a week.'

Finally, a fourth savant brought the news that one of the questions which had excited the whole world was about to be solved that very evening.

As is well known, a century ago a daring experiment made by Dr Nathaniel Faithburn had attracted public attention. A convinced supporter of the idea of human hibernation – the possibility of arresting the vital functions and then reawakening them after a certain time – he had decided to test the value of the method on himself. After, by a holograph will, describing the operations necessary to restore him to life a hundred years later to the day, he had exposed himself to a cold of 172° centigrade (278° Fahrenheit) below zero; thus reduced to a mummified state, he had been shut up in a tomb for the stated period.

Now it was exactly on that very day, 25 July 2889, that the period expired, and Francis Bennett had just received an offer to proceed in one of the rooms of the *Earth Herald* office with the resurrection so impatiently waited for. The public could then be kept in touch with it second by second.

The proposal was accepted, and as the operation was not to take place until ten that evening, Francis Bennett went to stretch himself out in an easy-chair in the audition-room. Then, pressing a button, he was put into communication with the Central Concert.

After so busy a day, what a charm he found in the works of our greatest masters, based, as everybody knows, on a series of delicious harmonico-algebraic formulae!

The room had been darkened, and, plunged into an ecstatic half-sleep, Francis Bennett could not even see himself. But a door opened suddenly.

'Who's there?' he asked, touching a commutator placed beneath his hand.

At once, by an electric effect produced on the ether, the air became luminous.

'Oh, it's you, Doctor?' he asked.

'Myself,' replied Dr Sam, who had come to pay his daily visit (annual subscription). 'How's it going?'

'Fine!'

'All the better . . . Let's see your tongue?'

He looked at it through a microscope.

'Good . . . And your pulse?'

He tested it with a pulsograph, similar to the instruments which record earthquakes.

'Splendid! . . . And your appetite?'

'Ugh!'

'Oh, your stomach! . . . It isn't going too well, your stomach! . . . It's getting old, your stomach is! . . . We'll certainly have to get you a new one!'

'We'll see!' Francis Bennett replied, 'and meantime, Doctor, you'll dine with me.'

During the meal, phonotelephotic communication had been set up with Paris. Mrs Bennett was at her table this time, and the dinner, livened up by Dr Sam's jokes, was delightful. Hardly was it over than:

'When do you expect to get back to Centropolis, dear Edith?' asked Francis Bennett.

'I'm going to start this moment.'

'By tube or aero-train?'

'By tube.'

'Then you'll be here?'

'At eleven fifty-nine this evening.'

'Paris time?'

'No, no! . . . Centropolis time.'

'Goodbye then, and above all don't miss the tube!'

These submarine tubes, by which one travels from Paris in two hundred and ninety-five minutes, are certainly much preferable to the aero-trains, which only manage six hundred miles an hour.

The doctor had gone, after promising to return to be present at the resurrection of his colleague Nathaniel Faithburn. Wishing to draw up his daily accounts, Francis Bennett went into his private office. An enormous operation, when it concerns an enterprise whose expenditure rises to eight hundred thousand dollars every day! Fortunately, the development of modern mechanisation has greatly facilitated this work. Helped by the piano-electric-computer, Francis Bennett soon completed his task.

It was time. Hardly had he struck the last key of the mechanical totalisator than his presence was asked for in the experimental room. He went off to it at once, and was welcomed by a large cortège of scientists, who had been joined by Dr Sam.

Nathaniel Faithburn's body is there, on the bier, placed on trestles in the centre of the room.

The telephote is switched on. The whole world will be able to follow the various phases of the operation.

The coffin is opened . . . Nathaniel Faithburn's body is taken out . . .

It is still like a mummy, yellow hard, dry. It sounds like wood . . . It is submitted to heat . . . electricity . . . No result . . . It's hypnotised . . . It's exposed to suggestion . . . Nothing can overcome that ultra-cataleptic state.

'Well, Dr Sam?' asks Francis Bennett.

The doctor leans over the body; he examines it very carefully . . . He introduces into it, by means of a hypodermic, a few drops of the famous Brown-Séquard elixir, which is once again in fashion . . . The mummy is more mummified than ever.

'Oh well,' Dr Sam replies, 'I think the hibernation has lasted too long . . .'

'Oh!'

'And Nathaniel Faithburn is dead.'

'Dead?'

'As dead as anybody could be!'

'And how long has he been dead?'

'How long? . . .' Dr Sam replies. 'But . . . a hundred years – that is to say, since he had the unhappy idea of freezing himself for pure love of science!'

'Then', Francis Bennett comments, 'that's a method which still needs to be perfected!'

'Perfected is the word,' replies Dr Sam, while the scientific commission on hibernation carries away its funereal bundle.

Followed by Dr Sam, Francis Bennett regained his room, and as he seemed very tired after so very full a day, the doctor advised him to take a bath before going to bed.

'You're quite right, Doctor . . . That will refresh me . . .'

'It will, Mr Bennett, and if you like I'll order one on my way out . . .'

'There's no need for that, Doctor. There's always a bath all ready in the office, and I needn't even have the trouble of going out of my room to take it. Look, simply by touching this button, that bath will start moving, and you'll see it come along all by itself with the water at a temperature of sixty-five degrees!'

Francis Bennett had just touched the button. A rumbling sound began, got louder, increased . . . Then one of the doors opened, and the bath appeared, gliding along on its rails . . .

Heavens! While Dr Sam veils his face, little screams of frightened modesty arise from the bath . . .

Brought to the office by the transatlantic tube half an hour before, Mrs Bennett was inside it.

Next day, 26 July 2889, the director of the *Earth Herald* recommenced his tour of twelve miles across his office. That evening, when his total-isator had been brought into action, it was at two hundred and fifty thousand dollars that it calculated the profits of that day – fifty thousand more than the day before.

A fine job, that of a journalist at the end of the twenty-ninth century!

Villiers de l'Isle-Adam

Born into an impoverished, somewhat eccentric, aristocratic family, Jean-Marie-Mathias-Philippe-Auguste, Comte de Villiers de l'Isle-Adam (1838–89), earned his living by his pen and produced novels and short stories which ruthlessly derided the materialism of his age. He lived a vagabond existence and his novels, notably *Tribulat Bonhomet* (1887), reflect a loathing of the bourgeoisie. However, he was deeply influenced by the fashionable beliefs of his day, particularly occultism and spiritualism, and his taste for the uncanny is apparent in his *Contes cruels* (1883) and *Nouveaux contes cruels* (1888), from which this story is drawn. Villiers enjoys a gift for laconic irony which can disarm even the most battle-hardened of sceptical readers, and nowhere is this more apparent than in these fantastic tales inspired by Poe.

The Desire to be a Man

FOR MONSIEUR CATULLE MENDÈS

. . . Nature might stand up
And say to all the world: 'This was a man!'

SHAKESPEARE, Julius Caesar

T HE STOCK EXCHANGE CLOCK STRUCK MIDNIGHT, UNDER A
starry sky. At that time the citizens were still subject to military
law, and, in accordance with the curfew regulations, the waiters of
those establishments which were still lit up were hurriedly closing their
doors.

Inside the boulevard cafés the gas butterflies of the chandeliers fluttered quickly away, one by one, into the darkness. Outside could be
heard the noise of the chairs being arranged in quartets on the marble-
topped tables; it was the psychological moment when every café pro-
prietor thinks fit to show the last customers, with an arm ending in
a napkin, the Caudine Forks of the back door.

That Sunday the sad October wind was whistling through the
streets. A few yellow leaves, dusty and rustling, were blown along by
the squalls, touching the stones and skimming the asphalt, and then,
like bats, disappeared into the shadows, arousing the idea of commonplace days lived through once and for all. The theatres of the Boulevard
du Crime where, during the evening, all the Medicis, Salviatis and
Montefeltres had been stabbing one another with the utmost fervour,
stood silent, their mute portals guarded by their caryatids. Carriages
and pedestrians became fewer from one moment to the next; here and
there, the sceptical lanterns of rag-pickers gleamed already, phosphorescent glows given off by the rubbish-heaps over which they were
wandering.

Under a street-lamp level with the Rue Hauteville, at the corner of a fairly luxurious-looking café, a tall passer-by had come to a stop, as if automatically hesitating to cross the roadway separating him from the Boulevard Bonne-Nouvelle. He had a saturnine face, a smooth chin, a somnambulist's walk, long greying hair under a Louis Treize hat, black gloves holding an ivory-headed stick, and an old greatcoat in royal blue, trimmed with dubious astrakhan.

Was this tardy stroller on his way home? Had the mere chance of a walk late at night brought him to that street corner? It would have been difficult to decide from his appearance. However, the fact remains that, suddenly noticing on his right one of those mirrors – as tall and narrow as himself – which sometimes stand like public looking-glasses outside leading cafés, he halted abruptly, planted himself opposite his reflection, and deliberately looked himself up and down, from his boots to his hat. Then, all of a sudden, raising his hat with an old-world gesture, he greeted himself with a certain courtesy.

His head, thus unexpectedly bared, then revealed him as none other than the famous tragedian Esprit Chaudval, born Lepeinteur and known as Monanteuil, the scion of a worthy family of Saint-Malo pilots, and whom the mysteries of Providence had induced to become a leading man in the provinces, a star abroad, and the often fortunate rival of Frédérick Lemaître.

While he was considering himself with this sort of stupor, the waiters in the nearby café were helping their last customers into their overcoats and fetching their hats, others were noisily emptying the contents of the nickel money boxes and piling the day's takings on a tray. This haste and bustle was due to the ominous presence of two policemen who had suddenly appeared at the door and were standing there with folded arms, harrying the laggardly landlord with their cold gaze.

Soon the shutters were bolted into their iron frames, apart from the one over the mirror, which by a strange oversight was forgotten in the general hurry.

Then silence descended on the boulevard. Only Chaudval, heedless of everybody's departure, had remained in his ecstatic posture on the corner of the Rue Hauteville, on the pavement in front of the forgotten mirror.

This pale, moonlit looking-glass seemed to give the actor the feeling he would have had bathing in a pond. Chaudval shivered.

Alas, the fact is that in that cruel, dark crystal, the actor had just seen himself growing old.

He noticed that his hair, which only yesterday had still been grizzly, was turning silver; he was finished! It was goodbye to curtains and crowns, goodbye to the roses of Thalia and the laurels of Melpomene. It was time to take leave for ever, with handshakes and tears, of the Ellevious and the Laruettes, of the grand liveries and the soft curves of the Dugazons and the *ingénues*!

It was time to get down in a hurry from the chariot of Thespis and watch it drive away with his colleagues; to see the baubles and streamers which, that morning, had fluttered from the wheels in the sunshine, the playthings of the joyous wind of Hope, disappear in the twilight round a distant bend in the road.

Chaudval, suddenly conscious of his fifty years (he was a good fellow), heaved a sigh. A mist passed in front of his eyes; a sort of wintry fever took hold of him and a hallucination dilated his pupils.

The haggard fixity with which he was gazing into the providential mirror ended up by giving his eyes that ability to enlarge objects and endow them with importance which physiologists have observed in individuals under the stress of intense emotion.

The long mirror was accordingly deformed under the gaze of his eyes, which were filled with dim, murky ideas. Childhood memories of beaches and silvery waves danced about in his brain. And the mirror, doubtless because of the stars deepening its surface, reminded him at first of the sleeping waters of a gulf. Then, billowing out even more, thanks to the old man's sighs, the mirror took on the appearance of the sea and the night, those two old friends of lonely hearts.

He revelled for some time in his vision, but then the street-lamp which was reddening the cold drizzle behind him, above his head, struck him, reflected as it was in the depths of the dreadful mirror, as like the glow of a blood-red lighthouse, luring the doomed vessel of his future to shipwreck.

He shook off his hallucination and drew himself up to his full height, with a nervous burst of bitter, cynical laughter which startled the two policemen under the trees. Luckily for the actor, the latter, taking him for some drunkard or jilted lover, continued their official stroll without paying any attention to the wretched Chaudval.

'Very well, let us give up!' he said simply in an undertone, like the condemned man who, suddenly roused from sleep, says to the executioner: 'I am at your service.'

The old actor then launched into a dazed monologue.

'I acted prudently the other evening', he went on, 'when I asked my good comrade Mademoiselle Pinson (who shares the Minister's confidence and even his bed) to obtain for me, between two ardent confessions, that post as lighthouse-keeper which my ancestors occupied on the Atlantic coast. Ah! Now I understand the weird effect the reflection of this street-lamp in this mirror had on me! It was that idea at the back of my mind. Pinson will send me my letter of appointment, that's certain. And then I shall retire into my lighthouse like a rat into a cheese. I shall guide the ships in the distance, across the sea. A lighthouse always gives the impression of a stage-set. I am alone in the world: without a doubt it is the perfect refuge for my old age.'

All of a sudden Chaudval interrupted his reverie.

'Good Lord!' he said, feeling inside his greatcoat. 'But . . . that letter the postman delivered just as I was coming out must be the reply . . . I was going into this café to read it, and I forgot all about it! I'm losing my grip, and no mistake! . . . Good, here it is!'

Chaudval had just taken out of his pocket a large envelope from which, as soon as he broke the seal, a ministerial letter fell to the ground. He feverishly picked it up and read it at a single glance, in the red glow of the street-lamp.

'My lighthouse! My letter of appointment!' he exclaimed. 'Saved, thank God!' he added, as if out of force of habit and in a falsetto voice so sudden and so different from his own that he looked around, thinking that somebody else had spoken.

'Come, now,' he said, 'calm down . . . and *be a Man*!'

But at these words Esprit Chaudval, born Lepeinteur and known as Monanteuil, stopped as if changed into a statue of salt; this remark seemed to have petrified him.

'Eh?' he went on after a pause. 'What did I tell myself just then? To be a Man? . . . After all, why not?'

He folded his arms reflectively.

'For nearly half a century now I have been *acting* and *playing* other men's passions without ever feeling them – for at bottom I have never felt anything. So I am like those other men just for fun! So I am nothing but a shadow! Passions, feelings, *real* actions – that is what makes a genuine Man. Consequently, since my age forces me to rejoin Mankind, I must find myself some passions or *real* feelings – seeing that that is the *sine qua non* without which nobody can call himself a Man.

'There's a piece of good reasoning for you; it's positively bursting with common sense. So now to choose the passion most in keeping with my resuscitated nature.'

He meditated, then went on sadly:

'Love? . . . too late . . . Glory? . . . I have tasted it . . . Ambition? . . . let us leave that nonsense to the politicians!'

All of a sudden he gave a cry.

'I have it!' he said. 'Remorse! *There's* a passion that suits my dramatic temperament.'

He looked at himself in the mirror, assuming an expression which was drawn and convulsed as if by some supernatural horror.

'That's it!' he concluded. 'Nero! Macbeth! Orestes! Hamlet! Erostratus! The ghosts! Oh, yes, I want to see some real ghosts too! Like all those lucky fellows who could not take a single step without meeting a ghost.'

He struck his forehead.

'But how? . . . I'm as innocent as a lamb unwilling to be born.'

And after another pause he went on:

'But that doesn't matter! Where there's a will there's a way! I'm entitled to become what I ought to be, whatever the cost. I'm entitled to be a Man. Do I have to commit crimes in order to feel remorse? All right, so be it: what does it matter, provided it is in a good cause? Yes indeed, so be it!'

At this point he began to improvise a dialogue.

'I shall perpetrate some dreadful crimes . . . When? . . . Straight away. I cannot wait until tomorrow . . . What crimes? . . . A single one! But a grandiose crime, of extraordinary cruelty, calculated to rouse all the Furies from the Underworld! . . . And what crime is that? . . . Why, the most impressive of all! I have it! A fire! I just have time to start a fire, pack my bags, come back, duly hidden behind the window of a cab, to enjoy my victory in the midst of the horrified crowd, collect the curses of the dying – and catch the train for the north-west with enough remorse put by to last me the rest of my days. Then I shall go and hide in my brightly-lit eyrie on the shores of the Ocean – where the police will never find me, for the simple reason that my crime is *disinterested*. And there I shall die alone.'

Here Chaudval drew himself up and improvised this positively classical line:

'Saved from suspicion by the grandeur of the crime.'

The great artist looked around to make sure he was alone, picked up a stone, and concluded:

'Well, that's settled. And from now on *you* won't reflect anybody else.'

And he threw the stone at the mirror which shattered into a thousand shining pieces.

Having performed this duty, Chaudval made off in a hurry – as if satisfied with this first energetic feat – and rushed towards the boulevards, where, a few minutes later, he hailed a cab, jumped into it, and disappeared.

Two hours later, the flames of a huge fire, coming from some big warehouses stocked with petroleum, oil, and matches, were reflected in every window-pane in the Faubourg du Temple. Soon squads of firemen, rolling and pushing their pumps, came running up from all sides, the mournful wail of their horns rousing the inhabitants of that populous district from their sleep. Countless hurried steps rang out on the pavement: the Place du Château-d'Eau and the adjoining streets were crowded with people. Already human chains were being hurriedly organised. Within less than a quarter of an hour a cordon of troops had been formed round the fire. In the blooded light of the torches, policemen were holding the people back.

The carriages, trapped in the crowds, had come to a standstill. Everybody was shouting. Distant screams could be made out amidst the dreadful crackling of the flames. The victims of the fire, caught in the inferno, were howling, and the roofs of the houses falling in on them. About a hundred families, those of the workers employed in the burning buildings, were left penniless and homeless.

In the distance, a solitary cab, loaded with two bulky trunks, was standing behind the crowd at the Château-d'Eau. And in that cab sat Esprit Chaudval, born Lepeinteur and known as Monanteuil, drawing aside the blind from time to time and contemplating his handiwork.

'Oh!' he whispered to himself. 'How loathsome I feel in the eyes of God and men! Yes, that's the work of a criminal, sure enough!'

The kindly old actor's face lit up.

'O wretched man!' he muttered. 'What sleepless nights I'm going to enjoy among the ghosts of my victims! I can feel burgeoning within me the soul of Nero, burning Rome out of artistic fervour, of Erostratus, burning the temple of Ephesus out of a desire for glory, of Rostopchin, burning Moscow out of patriotism, of Alexander, burning Persepolis out of love for his immortal Thaïs! . . . I for my part burn out of duty, having no other means of *existence*. I burn because I owe it to myself. I burn to fulfil an obligation. What a Man I'm going to be! How I'm going

to live! Yes, at last I'm going to find out what it's like to be tortured by remorse. What wonderful nights of delicious horror I'm going to spend! Ah, I breathe again! I'm born again! I exist! When I think that I was an actor! Now, as I'm nothing in the coarse eyes of Mankind but a gallows-bird, let us fly like the wind! Let us hide in our lighthouse, to enjoy our remorse there in peace.'

In the evening, two days later, Chaudval, reaching his destination safely, took possession of his lonely old lighthouse on the north coast: a ruined building with an antiquated beacon which ministerial compassion had rekindled for his sake.

The light was of scarcely any use: it was just an excrescence, a sinecure, a dwelling with a lamp on top, which nobody needed except Chaudval.

So the worthy tragedian, having moved his bed into the lighthouse, together with stocks of food and a tall mirror in which to study his facial expressions, promptly shut himself up there, secure from all human suspicion.

Around him moaned the sea, in which the ancient abyss of the heavens bathed the light of its stars. He watched the waves attacking his tower under the shifts of the winds, much as the Stylite must have gazed at the sands being hurled against his column by the shimiel.

In the distance he followed with unthinking eyes the smoke of steamships or the sails of fishing-boats.

As he went up and down the stone staircase, the dreamer kept forgetting his fire.

On the evening of the third day, sitting in his room, sixty feet above the waves, he was rereading a Paris newspaper which told the story of the catastrophe which had taken place two days before.

An unknown malefactor had thrown some matches into the petroleum cellars. A colossal fire, which had kept the firemen and the people of the surrounding districts up all night, had broken out in the Faubourg du Temple.

Nearly a hundred victims had died; unfortunate families had been plunged into the direst poverty.

The whole place was in mourning and still smoking.

The name of the person who had committed this heinous crime was unknown, and so above all was the criminal's motive.

When he read this, Chaudval jumped for joy and, feverishly rubbing his hands, exclaimed:

'What a triumph! What a wonderful scoundrel I am! How I'm going to be haunted! How many ghosts I'm going to see! I knew that I should become a Man! Oh, I admit that the means I used was drastic, but it had to be, it had to be!'

Reading the Paris newspaper again, Chaudval noticed that a special performance was being given in aid of those who had suffered from the fire, and murmured:

'Well, well! I ought to have put my talent at the service of my victims. It would have been my farewell performance. I would have declaimed Orestes, I would have been marvellously true to life . . .'

Thereupon Chaudval began living in his lighthouse.

And the evenings and the nights fell, and followed one after another.

Something happened which astounded the actor. Something horrifying!

Contrary to his hopes and expectations, his conscience failed to torment him. Not a single ghost appeared. He felt nothing, *absolutely nothing*!

He could not believe the Silence. He could not get over it.

Sometimes, looking at himself in the mirror, he noticed that his debonair expression had not changed. Then he would hurl himself in a fury on his signals, altering them in the radiant hope of sinking some far-off ship, so as to rouse, quicken, stimulate his rebellious remorse, and awaken the longed-for ghosts.

It was all to no purpose.

His attempted crimes came to nothing. His efforts were in vain. He felt nothing. He did not see a single threatening phantom. He found it impossible to sleep any more, he was so stifled by shame and despair. The result was that when, one night, he suffered a stroke in his luminous eyrie, he had a death-agony in which – amid the noise of the ocean, with the sea-winds buffeting his tower lost in infinity – he cried out:

'Ghosts! . . . For the love of God! . . . Let me see one ghost at least! . . . *I've earned it!*'

But the God he was invoking did not grant him this favour – and the old actor died, still expressing, in his vain rhetoric, his ardent longing to see some ghosts . . . *without realising that he himself was what he was looking for*.

Alphonse Daudet

Alphonse Daudet (1840–97) is often associated with the Naturalism of
Émile Zola, but his writing displays a wry sense of humour, a subtle
intuition of the forms of human pain and an appeal to the popular imagination which defies such categorisation. Born in Nîmes, his work
often returns to the Midi, most notably in *Tartarin of Tarascon* (1872),
the confection containing his best-known character, the cowardly but
ambitious Provençal Tartarin, and in the semi-autobiographical novel
Le Petit Chose (1868). After his first published work, a collection of
poems entitled *Les Amoureuses* (1858), he turned to prose fiction, writing numerous tales and sketches and contributing to *Le Figaro*. He is
perhaps best remembered for his delicate, humorous evocations of
Provence in *Lettres de mon moulin* (1869), which first appeared in *Le
Figaro*. Saddened in his final years by the unhappiness of his son's marriage to Victor Hugo's granddaughter, he offered in *Rose et Ninette*
(1892) an early example of the literature of divorce. He died suddenly,
and the old mill of his *Lettres*, now transformed into a museum, stands
as a testament to him.

The Stars

IN THE DAYS WHEN I USED TO LOOK AFTER THE SHEEP ON THE Luberon, I would go entire weeks without seeing a living soul, all alone up on the pastures with my dog, Labri, and my flocks. Now and then, the hermit from Mont-de-l'Ure used to pass by looking for herbs, or sometimes I would see the black face of some charcoal-burner from Piedmont; but these were simple folk, made silent by solitude, having lost the inclination to speak, and knowing nothing of what was being talked about down below in the villages and towns. So, every fortnight, when I used to hear coming up the mountain path the sound of the bells of the mule from our farm bringing me my fortnightly provisions, and when I would see the cheerful face of the little farm lad or the russet cap of old Aunt Norade appearing over the brow of the hill, I was indeed the happiest of men. I used to get them to tell me the news of the valley, the baptisms, the marriages; but what interested me most of all was to hear all that they could tell me about my master's daughter, Stéphanette, the prettiest girl for more than ten leagues around. Without appearing to be taking too much interest, I would find out whether she had been going to many fairs or dances, or whether new suitors were calling on her; and to those who may ask what that had to do with me, a poor mountain shepherd, my answer is that I was twenty years old and Stéphanette was the most beautiful girl I had seen in all my life.

But one Sunday it happened that the fortnightly provisions were late arriving. During the morning I had kept saying to myself: 'It's because of High Mass'; then, about midday, there was a violent storm and I thought perhaps the mule had not been able to set out owing to the bad state of the roads. At last, about three o'clock, the sky having cleared and the mountain shining with water in the sun, I heard above the dripping of the leaves and the bubbling of the waters of the swollen streams, the sound of the mule-bells, as clear and gay as a full peal of church bells on an Easter day. But it was not the farm-boy, nor old Aunt Norade, who was leading the mule. It was . . . guess who? . . . my master's daughter Stéphanette in person, seated erect on the mule between the wicker panniers, her face pink and fresh from the mountain air and the storm.

The boy was sick, Aunt Norade on holiday with her children. Beautiful Stéphanette told me all this while getting off the mule, adding that she was late because she had lost her way; but to see her dressed in her best clothes, with her flowered ribbon, her laces, and her brilliantly glossy skirt, it seemed as if some dance had delayed her rather than the bushes through which she had had to find her way. Oh, what a daintily beautiful sight she was! I could not take my eyes off her. It is true I had never before seen her so close to. Sometimes, in winter, after the flocks had descended to the plain and I came into the farmhouse in the evening for supper, she would pass quickly through the room, hardly ever speaking to the servants, always beautifully dressed and a little proud . . . And now I had her there in front of me, just her and myself; was it not enough to turn my head?

When she had taken the provisions out of the panniers, Stéphanette began to look around her curiously. Lifting up her best skirt a little, to prevent it becoming soiled, she went into the sheepfold wishing to see the corner where I slept, the bedding of straw with its sheepskin, my great cloak hanging on the wall, my crook, my flintlock gun. It all gave her great amusement.

'So this is where you live, my poor shepherd? How bored you must be on your own all the time! What do you do? What d'you think about?'

I wanted to say: 'I think of you, mistress', and it would have been no lie; but I was so embarrassed I could hardly utter a word. I do believe she realised this and took a mischievous pleasure in increasing my embarrassment by saying:

'And does your sweetheart come up to see you sometimes, shepherd? I expect she must be the Fairy Estérelle who can only be seen on the mountain-tops . . .'

And as she said this, she herself might have been the Fairy Estérelle, her head tilted back as she laughed so prettily, and her haste to be gone making her seem all the more a visitor from fairyland.

'Goodbye, shepherd.'

'Farewell, mistress.'

And she was gone, taking with her the empty baskets.

When she disappeared down the steep path, it seemed to me that the pebbles rolling from under the mule's hoofs were falling one by one on to my heart. I listened to them for a long, long time; and until the day was ending I remained as in a sleep, not daring to move for fear my dream should fade. Towards evening, as the deep valleys far below began to turn blue, and the sheep were all bunched together bleating to get back into the fold, I heard somebody calling to me from down the slope, and I saw my young mistress, no longer laughing as she had been only a short time before, but all wet and shivering with fear and cold.

It seemed that at the bottom of the slope she had found the waters of the Sorgue swollen after the storm, and in trying to cross she had nearly drowned. What made things all the worse was that it was out of the question to think of returning to the farm at that late hour because my mistress would never have been able to find the short-cut down the mountain all by herself, and it was impossible for me to leave my flock. The thought of having to spend the night on the mountain caused her great distress, mostly because her family would become anxious about her. I tried to reassure her as well as I could:

'The nights are short in July, mistress. They will only have a bad moment or two.'

And I quickly lit a big fire to dry her feet and her dress, dripping wet from the water of the Sorgue. Then I put some milk and cheese before her, but the poor girl could think neither of warming herself nor of eating, and when I saw great tears filling her eyes, I felt like weeping myself.

Meantime, night had come swiftly. On the misty mountain-top facing the setting sun there remained only a rose-pink flush. I invited my young mistress into the sheepfold to rest there. After spreading out a fine new skin on top of some fresh straw, I wished her good night and sat down outside the door. God is my witness that in spite of the fire of love that was burning in my veins, no bad thought came to me, only a feeling of great pride that, in a corner of the sheepfold close to the sheep watching her curiously, my master's daughter – a ewe-lamb whiter, more precious than all of them – lay sleeping, trusting in my care. Never had the sky seemed to me so deep, never the stars so bright . . . Suddenly, the gate of the fold opened and the lovely Stéphanette stood there beside me. She was not able to sleep. The sheep kept rustling the straw as they moved, or bleated in their dreams. She preferred to come by the fire. So I threw my goatskin over her shoulders, I stirred up the fire, and we stayed seated side by side close to one another, without saying a word. If you have ever passed the night in the open under the stars, you will know that while we are sleeping a mysterious world awakens in the solitude and in the silence. Then the streams sing even more clearly, and on their pools dance little lights like flames. All the spirits of the mountains come and go as they will, and the air is filled with faint rustlings, imperceptible sounds, as if one were hearing the branches burgeoning and the grass growing. The day gives life to the world of humans and animals, but the night gives life to the world of things. And when one is not accustomed to this, it is frightening . . . So my young mistress kept shuddering with fear and holding herself close to me at every slightest sound. Once, a long, melancholy cry rose and fell again and again from the pool gleaming below us. At the same time, a beautiful shooting star passed overhead across the pool, and it was as if that sad cry and that beautiful light were each bearing the other with it.

'What is that?' Stéphanette whispered to me.

'A soul entering Paradise, mistress.' And I made the sign of the cross.

She crossed herself also, and remained a moment with her head raised, lost in her thoughts. Then she said:

'So it is true that all you shepherds are sorcerers?'

'Most certainly it isn't, mistress. But up here we live nearer to the stars and we know what happens among them better than the people of the plains.'

She still kept looking up at the sky, her chin resting on her hand, wrapped in the goatskin like a little shepherd from Paradise herself.

'What a lot there are! And how beautiful! I've never seen so many . . . Do you know their names, shepherd?'

'Of course, mistress . . . Look, right above us, is *Saint James's Way* (The Milky Way). From France it goes straight over to Spain. Saint James of Galicia set it there to show our wonderful Charlemagne the way when he was fighting the Saracens. Further on, you can see *The Chariot of Souls* (The Great Bear) with its four shining axles. The three stars at the front are *The Three Beasts*, and that very small one, close to the third, is *The Charioteer*. Do you see that shower of falling stars all around it? They are the souls the good Lord does not want with Him . . . And there, a little lower down, is *The Rake* or *The Three Kings* (Orion). We shepherds use them as our clock. Just by looking up at them, I can tell that it's now past midnight. A little lower still, to the south, you can see *John of Milan* (Sirius) burning like a torch. The shepherds tell a story about that star. One night, they say, *John of Milan* with *The Three Kings* and *The Chicken Coop* (The Pleiades) were invited to the wedding of a star who was a friend of theirs. *The Chicken Coop*, the most eager, set off first and took the upper road. There it is, up there, right at the top of the sky. *The Three Kings* took a lower road and caught up with him; but that lazy fellow, *John of Milan*, who had slept late, was left behind and was so annoyed he threw his staff after them to stop them. That is why *The Three Kings* are also called *John of Milan's Staff* . . . But the most beautiful of all the stars, mistress, is our own star, *The Shepherds' Star*, which lights us at dawn when we go out with our flocks, and in the evening also when we return with them. We sometimes call it *Maguelonne*, the beautiful Maguelonne, who runs after *Peter of Provence* (Saturn) and gets married to him, every seven years.'

'What! The stars get married, shepherd?'

'Oh, yes, mistress.'

And while I was trying to explain to her about these marriages, I felt something entirely beautiful resting lightly on my shoulder. With a sweet crumpling of her ribbons and laces and of the curls of her hair, she had laid her sleeping head on my arm. We stayed thus, without moving, until the stars paled, dimmed by the dawning day. And I looked and looked at her as she slept, vaguely disturbed deep down within me, yet miraculously protected by the night's clear holy light which has never given me any thoughts but beautiful ones. Around us, the stars continued their silent march, as orderly as a great flock of sheep; and, at times, it seemed to me that one of these stars, the loveliest and the brightest, having lost her way, had come to lie on my shoulder in order to sleep . . .

Émile Zola

Émile Zola (1840–1902) was the father of French literary Naturalism, a pseudo-scientific theory which developed the observational realism associated with Balzac and Flaubert. Son of an Italian father and French mother, Zola was born in Paris, educated in Aix-en-Provence, and returned to Paris in his late teens to work for the publishers Hachette. His first full-length novel *La Confession de Claude* was published in 1865, but he also continued to write plays, short stories and libretti, as well as art, drama and literary criticism for the press, until his death by carbon monoxide poisoning (due to a blocked chimney) in September 1902. His twenty-volume series *Les Rougons-Macquart*, subtitled a 'Natural and Social History of a Family under the Second Empire', illustrated his theory of the 'naturalistic' novel; and the money he earned from the scandalous success of the seventh novel, *L'Assommoir*, allowed him to buy an impressive house outside Paris at Médan. The myth of the 'group of Médan' (in reality a far from unified set) was forged in part by the publication of *Soirées de Médan* (1880), a collection of short stories about the horrors of the Franco-Prussian War which includes 'The Attack on the Mill' and also Maupassant's 'Boule-de-suif'. He is perhaps best remembered for his striking article 'J'accuse', an open letter to the president of the Republic, published in *L'Aurore* in 1898, which offered a courageous defence of the Jewish army officer, Alfred Dreyfus, who was falsely accused of spying on behalf of the Germans. Zola was subsequently forced to flee to London where he lived under the pseudonym Pascal (he had been rapturously received in the city after the publication of *Le Docteur Pascal* (1893), the triumphant completion of *Les Rougons-Macquart*). To risk his fame and fortune in the service of the principles of justice and truth speaks volumes for the courageous engagement and authentic sincerity of this prolific figure. His principled stand has been fundamental in defining the public role of the intellectual which has been such a conspicuous element in twentieth-century French cultural life.

The Attack on the Mill

I T WAS HIGH HOLIDAY AT FATHER MERLIER'S MILL ON THAT
pleasant summer afternoon. Three tables had been brought out into
the garden and placed end to end in the shadow of the great elm, and
now they were awaiting the arrival of the guests. It was known throughout the length and breadth of the land that that day was to witness the
betrothal of old Merlier's daughter, Françoise, to Dominique, a young
man who was said to be not over-fond of work, but whom never a
woman for three leagues of the country around could look at without
sparkling eyes, such a well-favoured young fellow was he.

That mill of Father Merlier's was truly a very pleasant spot. It was
situated right in the heart of Rocreuse, at the place where the main road
makes a sharp bend. The village has but a single street, bordered on
either side by a row of low, whitened cottages, but just there where the
road curves there are broad stretches of meadow land, and huge trees,
which follow the course of the Morelle, cover the low grounds of the
valley with a most delicious shade. All Lorraine has no more charming
bit of nature to show. To right and left dense forests, great monarchs of
the wood, centuries old, rise from the gentle slopes and fill the horizon,
with a sea of verdure, while away towards the south extends the plain, of
wondrous fertility and checkered almost to infinity with its small en-
closures, divided off from one another by their live hedges. But what
makes the crowning glory of Rocreuse is the coolness of this verdurous
nook, even in the hottest days of July and August. The Morelle comes
down from the woods of Gagny, and it would seem as if it gathered to
itself on the way all the delicious freshness of the foliage beneath which it
glides for many a league; it brings down with it the murmuring sounds,
the glacial, solemn shadows of the forest. And that is not the only source
of coolness; there are running waters of all kinds singing among the
copses; one cannot take a step without coming on a gushing spring, and
as one makes one's way along the narrow paths one seems to be treading

above subterranean lakes that seek the air and sunshine through the moss above and profit by every smallest crevice, at the roots of trees or among the chinks and crannies of the rocks, to burst forth in fountains of crystalline clearness. So numerous and so loud are the whispering voices of these streams that they silence the song of the bullfinches. It is as if one were in an enchanted park, with cascades falling on every side.

The meadows below are never athirst. The shadows beneath the gigantic chestnut trees are of inky blackness, and along the edges of the fields long rows of poplars stand like walls of rustling foliage. There is a double avenue of huge plane trees ascending across the fields towards the ancient castle of Gagny, now gone to rack and ruin. In this region, where drought is never known, vegetation of all kinds is wonderfully rank; it is like a flower-garden down there in the low ground between those two wooded hills, a natural garden, where the lawns are broad meadows and the giant trees represent colossal beds. When the noonday sun pours down his scorching rays the shadows lie blue upon the ground, the glowing vegetation slumbers in the heat, while every now and then a breath of icy coldness passes under the foliage.

Such was the spot where Father Merlier's mill enlivened with its cheerful clack Nature run riot. The building itself, constructed of wood and plaster, looked as if it might be coeval with our planet. Its foundations were in part washed by the Morelle, which here expands into a clear pool. A dam, a few feet in height, afforded sufficient head of water to drive the old wheel, which creaked and groaned as it revolved with the asthmatic wheezing of a faithful servant who has grown old in her place. Whenever Father Merlier was advised to change it, he would shake his head and say that like as not a young wheel would be lazier and not so well acquainted with its duties, and then would set to work and patch up the old one with anything that came to hand, old hogshead-staves, bits of rusty iron, zinc or lead. The old wheel only seemed the gayer for it, with its old profile, all plumed and feathered with tufts of moss and grass, and when the water poured over it in a silvery tide its gaunt black skeleton was decked out with a gorgeous display of pearls and diamonds.

That portion of the mill which was bathed by the Morelle had something of the look of a barbaric arch that had been dropped down there by chance. A good half of the structure was built on piles; the water came in under the floor, and there were deep holes, famous throughout the whole country for the eels and the huge crawfish that were to be caught

there. Below the fall the pool was as clear as a mirror, and when it was not clouded by foam from the wheel one could see troops of great fish swimming about in it with the slow, majestic movements of a squadron. There was a broken stairway leading down to the stream, near a stake to which a boat was fastened, and over the wheel was a gallery of wood. Such windows as there were were arranged without any attempt at order. The whole was a quaint conglomeration of nooks and corners, bits of wall, additions made here and there as afterthoughts, beams and roofs, that gave the mill the aspect of an old, dismantled citadel; but ivy and all sorts of creeping plants had grown luxuriantly and kindly covered up such crevices as were too unsightly, casting a mantle of green over the old dwelling. Young ladies who passed that way used to stop and sketch Father Merlier's mill in their albums.

The side of the house that faced the road was less irregular. A gateway in stone afforded access to the principal courtyard, on the right and left hand of which were sheds and stables. Beside a well stood an immense elm that threw its shade over half the court. At the further end, opposite the gate, stood the house, surmounted by a dovecote, the four windows of its first floor in a symmetrical line. The only vanity that Father Merlier ever allowed himself was to paint this façade every ten years. It had just been freshly whitened at the time of our story, and dazzled the eyes of all the village when the sun lighted it up in the middle of the day.

For twenty years had Father Merlier been mayor of Rocreuse. He was held in great consideration on account of his fortune; he was supposed to be worth something like eighty thousand francs, the result of patient saving. When he married Madeleine Guillard, who brought him the mill as her dowry, his entire capital lay in his two strong arms, but Madeleine had never repented of her choice, so manfully had he conducted their joint affairs. Now his wife was dead, and he was left a widower with his daughter Françoise. Doubtless he might have set himself down to take his rest and suffered the old mill-wheel to sleep among its moss, but he would have found idleness too irksome and the house would have seemed dead to him. He kept on working still for the pleasure of it. In those days Father Merlier was a tall old man, with a long, silent face, on which a laugh was never seen, but beneath which there lay, none the less, a large fund of good-humour. He had been elected mayor on account of his money, and also for the impressive air that he knew how to assume when it devolved on him to marry a couple.

Françoise Merlier had just completed her eighteenth year. She was small, and for that reason was not accounted one of the beauties of the country. Until she reached the age of fifteen she had been even homely; the good folks of Rocreuse could not see how it was that the daughter of Father and Mother Merlier, such a hale, vigorous couple, had such a hard time of it in getting her growth. When she was fifteen, however, though still remaining delicate, a change came over her and she took on the prettiest little face imaginable. She had black hair, black eyes, and was red as a rose withal; her mouth was always smiling, there were delicious dimples in her cheeks, and a crown of sunshine seemed to be ever resting on her fair, candid forehead. Although small as girls went in that region, she was far from being thin; she might not have been able to raise a sack of wheat to her shoulder, but she became quite plump as she grew older, and gave promise of becoming eventually as well-rounded and appetising as a partridge. Her father's habits of taciturnity had made her reflective while yet a young girl; if she always had a smile on her lips it was in order to give pleasure to others. Her natural disposition was serious.

As was no more than to be expected, she had every young man in the countryside at her heels as a suitor, more even for her money than for her attractiveness, and she had made a choice at last, a choice that had been the talk and scandal of the entire neighbourhood.

On the other side of the Morelle lived a strapping young fellow who went by the name of Dominique Penquer. He was not to the manner born; ten years previously he had come to Rocreuse from Belgium to receive the inheritance of an uncle who had owned a small property on the very borders of the forest of Gagny, just facing the mill and distant from it only a few musket-shots. His object in coming was to sell the property, so he said, and return to his own home again; but he must have found the land to his liking, for he made no move to go away. He was seen cultivating his bit of a field and gathering the few vegetables that afforded him an existence. He fished, he hunted; more than once he was near coming in contact with the law through the intervention of the keepers. This independent way of living, of which the peasants could not very clearly see the resources, had in the end given him a bad name. He was vaguely looked upon as nothing better than a poacher. At all events he was lazy, for he was frequently found sleeping in the grass at hours when he should have been at work. Then, too, the hut in which he lived, in the shade of the last trees of the forest, did not seem like the abode of an honest young man; the old women would not have been surprised at any time to hear that he was on friendly terms with the wolves in the ruins of Gagny. Still, the young girls would now and then venture to stand up for him, for he was altogether a splendid specimen of manhood, was this individual of doubtful antecedents, tall and straight as a young poplar, with a milk-white skin and ruddy hair and moustaches that seemed to be of gold when the sun shone on them. Now one fine morning it came to pass that Françoise told Father Merlier that she loved Dominique, and that never, never would she consent to mary any other young man.

It may be imagined what a knock-down blow it was that Father Merlier received that day! As was his wont, he said never a word; his countenance wore its usual reflective look, only the fun that used to bubble up from within no longer shone in his eyes. Françoise, too, was very serious, and for a week father and daughter scarcely spoke to each other. What troubled Father Merlier was to know how that rascal of a poacher had succeeded in bewitching his daughter. Dominique had never shown himself at the mill. The miller played the spy a little, and was rewarded by catching sight of the gallant, on the other side of the Morelle, lying among the grass and pretending to be asleep. Françoise could see him from her chamber window. The thing was clear enough; they had been making sheep's eyes at each other over the old mill-wheel, and so had fallen in love.

A week slipped by; Françoise became more and more serious. Father Merlier still continued to say nothing. Then, one evening, of his own accord, he brought Dominique to the house, without a word. Françoise was just setting the table. She made no demonstration of surprise; all she did was to add another plate, but her laugh had come back to her, and the little dimples appeared again upon her cheeks. Father Merlier had gone that morning to look for Dominique at his hut on the edge of the forest, and there the two men had had a conference, with closed doors and windows, that lasted three hours. No one ever knew what they said to each other; the only thing certain is that when Father Merlier left the hut he already treated Dominique as a son. Doubtless the old man had discovered that he whom he had gone to visit was a worthy young fellow, even though he did lie in the grass to gain the love of young girls.

All Rocreuse was up in arms. The women gathered at their doors and could not find words strong enough to characterise Father Merlier's folly in thus receiving a ne'er-do-well into his family. He let them talk. Perhaps he thought of his own marriage. Neither had he possessed a penny to his name at the time he married Madeleine and her mill, and yet that had not prevented him from being a good husband to her. Moreover, Dominique put an end to their tittle-tattle by setting to work in such strenuous fashion that all the countryside was amazed. It so happened just then that the boy of the mill drew an unlucky number and had to go for a soldier, and Dominique would not hear of their engaging another. He lifted sacks, drove the carts, wrestled with the old wheel when it took an obstinate fit and refused to turn, and all so pluckily and cheerfully that people came from far and near merely for the pleasure of seeing him. Father Merlier laughed his silent laugh. He was highly elated that he had read the youngster aright. There is nothing like love to hearten up young men.

In the midst of all that laborious toil Françoise and Dominique fairly worshipped each other. They had not much to say, but their tender smiles conveyed a world of meaning. Father Merlier had not said a word thus far on the subject of their marriage, and they had both respected his silence, waiting until the old man should see fit to give expression to his will. At last, one day towards the middle of July, he had had three tables laid in the courtyard, in the shade of the big elm, and had invited his friends of Rocreuse to come that afternoon and drink a glass of wine with him. When the courtyard was filled with people, and everyone there had a full glass in his hand, Father Merlier raised his own high above his head and said:

'I have the pleasure of announcing to you that Françoise and this lad will be married in a month from now, on Saint Louis' fête-day.'

Then there was a universal touching of glasses, attended by a tremendous uproar; everyone was laughing. But Father Merlier, raising his voice above the din, again spoke:

'Dominique, kiss your wife that is to be. It is no more than customary.'

And they kissed, very red in the face, both of them, while the company laughed louder still. It was a regular fête; they emptied a small cask. Then, when only the intimate friends of the house remained, conversation went on in a calmer strain. Night had fallen, a starlit night, and very clear. Dominique and Françoise sat on a bench, side by side, and said nothing. An old peasant spoke of the war that the Emperor had declared against Prussia. All the lads of the village were already gone off to the Army. Troops had passed through the place only the night before. There were going to be hard knocks.

'Bah!' said Father Merlier, with the selfishness of a man who is quite happy, 'Dominique is a foreigner; he won't have to go – and if the Prussians come this way, he will be here to defend his wife.'

The idea of the Prussians coming there seemed to the company an exceedingly good joke. The Army would give them one good conscientious thrashing, and the affair would be quickly ended.

'I have seen them before, I have seen them before,' the old peasant repeated, in a low voice.

There was silence for a little, then they all touched glasses once again. Françoise and Dominique had heard nothing; they had managed to clasp hands behind the bench in such a way as not to be seen by the others, and this condition of affairs seemed so beatific to them that they sat there mute, their gaze lost in the darkness of the night.

What a magnificent, balmy night! The village lay slumbering on either side of the white road as peacefully as a little child. The deep silence was undisturbed save by the occasional crow of a cock in some distant barnyard acting on a mistaken impression that dawn was at hand. Perfumed breaths of air, like long-drawn sighs, came down from the great woods that lay around and above, sweeping softly over the roofs, as if caressing them. The meadows, with their black intensity of shadow, took on a dim, mysterious majesty of their own, while all the springs, all the brooks and watercourses that gurgled in the darkness, might have been taken for the cool, rhythmical breathing of the sleeping country. Every now and then the old dozing mill-wheel seemed to be dreaming like a watchdog that barks uneasily in his slumber; it creaked, it talked to itself, rocked by the fall of the Morelle, whose current gave forth the deep, sustained music of an organ pipe. Never was there a more charming or happier nook, never did a deeper peace come down to cover it.

II

One month later, to a day, on the eve of the fête of Saint Louis, Rocreuse was in a state of alarm and dismay. The Prussians had beaten the Emperor, and were advancing on the village by forced marches. For a week past people passing along the road had brought tidings of the enemy: 'They are at Lormières, they are at Nouvelles'; and by dint of hearing so many stories of the rapidity of their advance, Rocreuse woke up every morning in the full expectation of seeing them swarming down out of Gagny wood. They did not come, however, and that only served to make the affright the greater. They would certainly fall upon the village in the night-time, and put every soul to the sword.

There had been an alarm the night before, a little before daybreak. The inhabitants had been aroused by a great noise of men tramping upon the road. The women were already throwing themselves upon their knees and making the sign of the cross, when someone, to whom it happily occurred to peep through a half-opened window, caught sight of red trousers. It was a French detachment. The captain had forthwith asked for the mayor, and, after a long conversation with Father Merlier, had remained at the mill.

The sun shone bright and clear that morning, giving promise of a warm day. There was a golden light floating over the woodland, while in the low grounds white mists were rising from the meadows. The pretty village, so neat and trim, awoke in the cool dawning, and the country, with its streams and its fountains, was as gracious as a freshly-plucked bouquet. But the beauty of the day brought gladness to the face of no one; the villagers had watched the captain, and seen him circle round and round the old mill, examine the adjacent houses, then pass to the other bank of the Morelle, and from thence scan the country with a field-glass; Father Merlier, who accompanied him, appeared to be giving explanations. After that the captain had posted some of his men behind walls, behind trees, or in hollows. The main body of the detachment had encamped in the courtyard of the mill. So there was going to be a fight, then? And when Father Merlier returned they questioned him. He spoke no word, but slowly and sorrowfully nodded his head. Yes, there was going to be a fight.

Françoise and Dominique were there in the courtyard, watching him. He finally took his pipe from his lips, and gave utterance to these few words:

'Ah! my poor children, I shall not be able to marry you today!'

Dominique, with lips tight set and an angry frown upon his forehead, raised himself on tiptoe from time to time and stood with eyes bent on Gagny wood, as if he would have been glad to see the Prussians appear and end the suspense they were in. Françoise, whose face was grave and very pale, was constantly passing back and forth, supplying the needs of the soldiers. They were preparing their soup in a corner of the courtyard, joking and chaffing one another while awaiting their meal.

The captain appeared to be highly pleased. He had visited the chambers and the great hall of the mill that looked out on the stream. Now, seated beside the well, he was conversing with Father Merlier.

'You have a regular fortress here,' he was saying. 'We shall have no trouble in holding it until evening. The bandits are late; they ought to be here by this time.'

The miller looked very grave. He saw his beloved mill going up in flame and smoke, but uttered no word of remonstrance or complaint, considering that it would be useless. He only opened his mouth to say:

'You ought to take steps to hide the boat; there is a hole behind the wheel fitted to hold it. Perhaps you may find it of use to you.'

The captain gave an order to one of his men. This captain was a tall, fine-looking man of about forty, with an agreeable expression of countenance. The sight of Dominique and Françoise seemed to afford him much pleasure; he watched them as if he had forgotten all about the approaching conflict. He followed Françoise with his eyes as she moved about the courtyard, and his manner showed clearly enough that he thought her charming. Then, turning to Dominique:

'You are not with the Army, I see, my boy?' he abruptly asked.

'I am a foreigner,' the young man replied.

The captain did not seem particularly pleased with the answer; he winked his eyes and smiled. Françoise was doubtless a more agreeable companion than a musket would have been. Dominique, noticing his smile, made haste to add:

'I am a foreigner, but I can lodge a rifle bullet in an apple at five hundred yards. See, there's my rifle behind you.'

'You may find use for it,' the captain drily answered.

Françoise had drawn near; she was trembling a little, and Dominique, regardless of the bystanders, took and held firmly clasped in his own the two hands that she held forth to him, as if committing herself to his protection. The captain smiled again, but said nothing more. He remained seated, his sword between his legs, his eyes fixed on space, apparently lost in dreamy reverie.

It was ten o'clock. The heat was already oppressive. A deep silence prevailed. The soldiers had sat down in the shade of the sheds in the courtyard and begun to eat their soup. Not a sound came from the village, where the inhabitants had all barricaded their houses, doors and windows. A dog, abandoned by his master, howled mournfully upon the road. From the woods and the nearby meadows, that lay fainting in the heat, came a long-drawn, whispering, soughing sound, produced by the union of what wandering breaths of air there were. A cuckoo called. Then the silence became deeper still.

And all at once, upon that lazy, sleepy air, a shot rang out. The captain rose quickly to his feet, the soldiers left their half-emptied plates. In a few seconds all were at their posts; the mill was occupied from top to bottom. And yet the captain, who had gone out through the gate, saw nothing; to right and left the road stretched away, desolate and blindingly white in the fierce sunshine. A second report was heard, and still nothing to be seen, not even so much as a shadow; but just as he was turning to re-enter he chanced to look over towards Gagny and there beheld a little puff of smoke floating away on the tranquil air, like thistledown. The deep peace of the forest was apparently unbroken.

'The rascals have occupied the wood,' the officer murmured. 'They know we are here.'

Then the firing went on, and became more and more continuous between the French soldiers posted about the mill and the Prussians concealed among the trees. The bullets whistled over the Morelle without doing any mischief on either side. The firing was irregular; every bush seemed to have its marksman, and nothing was to be seen save those bluish smoke-wreaths that hung for a moment on the wind before they vanished. It lasted thus for nearly two hours. The officer hummed a tune with a careless air. Françoise and Dominique, who had remained in the courtyard, raised themselves to look out over a low wall. They were more particularly interested in a little soldier who had his post on the bank of the Morelle, behind the hull of an old boat; he would lie face downwards on the ground, watch his chance, deliver his fire, then slip back into a ditch a few steps in his rear to reload, and his movements were so comical, he displayed such cunning and activity, that it was difficult for anyone watching him to refrain from smiling. He must have caught sight of a Prussian, for he rose quickly and brought his piece to the shoulder, but before he could discharge it he uttered a loud cry, whirled completely around in his tracks and fell backwards into the ditch, where for an instant his legs moved convulsively, just as the claws of a fowl do when it is beheaded. The little soldier had received a bullet directly through his heart. It was the first casualty of the day. Françoise instinctively seized Dominique's hand, and held it tight in a convulsive grasp.

'Come away from there,' said the captain. 'The bullets reach us here.'

As if to confirm his words a slight, sharp sound was heard up in the old elm, and the end of a branch came to the ground, turning over and over as it fell, but the two young people never stirred, riveted to the spot as they were by the interest of the spectacle. On the edge of the wood a Prussian had suddenly emerged from behind a tree, as an actor comes upon the stage from the wings, beating the air with his arms and falling over upon his back. And beyond that there was no movement; the two dead men appeared to be sleeping in the bright sunshine; there was not a soul to be seen in the fields on which the heat lay heavy. Even the sharp rattle of the musketry had ceased. Only the Morelle kept on whispering to itself with its low, musical murmur.

Father Merlier looked at the captain with an astonished air, as if to enquire whether that were the end of it.

'Here comes their attack,' the officer murmured. 'Look out for yourself! Don't stand there!'

The words were scarcely out of his mouth when a terrible discharge of musketry ensued. The great elm was riddled, its leaves came eddying down as thick as snowflakes. Fortunately the Prussians had aimed too high. Dominique dragged, almost carried, Françoise from the spot, while Father Merlier followed them, shouting:

'Get into the small cellar; the walls are thicker there.'

But they paid no attention to him; they made their way to the main hall, where ten or a dozen soldiers were silently waiting, watching events outside through the chinks of the closed shutters. The captain was left alone in the courtyard, where he sheltered himself behind the low wall, while the furious fire was maintained uninterruptedly. The soldiers whom he had posted outside only yielded their ground inch by inch; they came crawling in, however, one after another, as the enemy dislodged them from their positions. Their instructions were to gain all the time they could, taking care not to show themselves, in order that the Prussians might remain in ignorance of the force they had opposed to them. Another hour passed, and as a sergeant came in, reporting that there were now only two or three men left outside, the officer took his watch from his pocket, murmuring:

'Half past two. Come, we must hold out for four hours yet.'

He caused the great gate of the courtyard to be tightly secured, and everything was made ready for an energetic defence. The Prussians were on the other side of the Morelle, consequently there was no reason to fear an assault at the moment. There was a bridge indeed, a mile and a quarter away, but they were probably unaware of its existence, and it was hardly to be supposed that they would attempt to cross the stream by fording. The officer, therefore, simply caused the road to be watched; the attack, when it came, was to be looked for from the direction of the fields.

The firing had ceased again. The mill appeared to lie there in the sunlight, void of all life. Not a shutter was open, not a sound came from within. Gradually, however, the Prussians began to show themselves at the edge of Gagny wood. Heads were protruded here and there; they seemed to be mustering up their courage. Several of the soldiers within the mill brought up their pieces to aim, but the captain shouted:

'No, no; not yet; wait. Let them come nearer.'

They displayed a great deal of prudence in their advance, looking at the mill with a distrustful air; they seemed hardly to know what to make of the old structure, so lifeless and gloomy, with its curtain of ivy. Still they kept on advancing. When there were fifty of them or so in the open, directly opposite, the officer uttered one word:

'Now!'

A crashing, tearing discharge burst from the position, succeeded by an irregular, dropping fire. Françoise, trembling violently, involuntarily raised her hands to her ears. Dominique, from his position behind the soldiers, peered out upon the field, and when the smoke drifted away a little, counted three Prussians extended on their backs in the middle of the meadow. The others had sought shelter among the willows and the poplars. And then commenced the siege.

For more than an hour the mill was riddled with bullets; they beat and rattled on its old walls like hail. The noise they made was plainly audible as they struck the stonework, were flattened, and fell back into the water; they buried themselves in the woodwork with a dull thud. Occasionally a creaking sound would announce that the wheel had been hit. Within the building the soldiers husbanded their ammunition, firing only when they could see something to aim at. The captain kept consulting his watch every few minutes, and as a ball split one of the shutters in halves and then lodged in the ceiling:

'Four o'clock,' he murmured. 'We shall never be able to hold the position.'

The old mill, in truth, was gradually going to pieces beneath that terrific fire. A shutter that had been perforated again and again, until it looked like a piece of lace, fell off its hinges into the water, and had to be replaced by a mattress. Every moment, almost, Father Merlier exposed himself to the fire in order to take account of the damage sustained by his poor wheel, every wound of which was like a bullet in his own heart. Its period of usefulness was ended this time for certain; he would never be able to patch it up again.

Dominique had besought Françoise to retire to a place of safety, but she was determined to remain with him; she had taken a seat behind a great oaken clothes-press, which afforded her protection. A bullet struck the press, however, the sides of which gave out a dull hollow sound, whereupon Dominique stationed himself in front of Françoise. He had as yet taken no part in the firing, although he had his rifle in his hand; the soldiers occupied the whole breadth of the windows, so that he could not get near them. At every discharge the floor trembled.

'Look out! look out!' the captain suddenly shouted.

He had just descried a dark mass emerging from the wood. As soon as they gained the open they set up a telling platoon fire. It struck the mill like a tornado. Another shutter parted company, and the bullets came whistling through the yawning aperture. Two soldiers rolled upon the floor; one lay where he fell and never moved a limb; his comrades pushed him up against the wall because he was in their way. The other writhed and twisted, beseeching someone to end his agony, but no one had ears for the poor wretch; the bullets were still pouring in, and everyone was looking out for himself and searching for a loophole whence he might answer the enemy's fire. A third soldier was wounded; that one said not a word, but with staring, haggard eyes sank down beneath a table. Françoise, horror-stricken by the dreadful spectacle of the dead and dying men, mechanically pushed away her chair and seated herself on the floor, against the wall; it seemed to her that she would be smaller there and less exposed. In the meantime, men had gone and secured all the mattresses in the house; the opening of the window was partially closed again. The hall was filled with debris of every description, broken weapons, dislocated furniture.

'Five o'clock,' said the captain. 'Stand fast, boys. They are going to make an attempt to pass the stream.'

Just then Françoise gave a shriek. A bullet had struck the floor, and, rebounding, grazed her forehead on the ricochet. A few drops of blood appeared. Dominique looked at her, then went to the window and fired his first shot, and from that time kept on firing uninterruptedly. He kept on loading and discharging his piece mechanically, paying no attention to what was passing at his side, only pausing from time to time to cast a look at Françoise. He did not fire hurriedly or at random, moreover, but took deliberate aim. As the captain had predicted, the Prussians were skirting the belt of poplars and attempting the passage of the Morelle, but each time that one of them showed himself he fell with one of Dominique's bullets in his brain. The captain, who was watching the performance, was amazed; he complimented the young man, telling him that he would like to have many more marksmen of his skill. Dominique did not hear a word he said. A bullet struck him in the shoulder, another raised a contusion on his arm. And still he kept on firing.

There were two more deaths. The mattresses were torn to shreds and no longer availed to stop the windows. The last volley that was poured in seemed as if it would carry away the mill bodily, so fierce it was. The position was no longer tenable. Still, the officer kept repeating:

'Stand fast. Another half-hour yet.'

He was counting the minutes, one by one, now. He had promised his commanders that he would hold the enemy there until nightfall, and he would not budge a hair's-breadth before the moment that he had fixed on for his withdrawal. He maintained his pleasant air of good-humour, smiling at Françoise by way of reassuring her. He had picked up the musket of one of the dead soldiers and was firing away with the rest.

There were but four soldiers left in the room. The Prussians were showing themselves *en masse* on the other side of the Morelle, and it was evident that they might now pass the stream at any moment. A few moments more elapsed; the captain was as determined as ever, and would not give the order to retreat, when a sergeant came running into the room, saying:

'They are on the road; they are going to take us in the rear.'

The Prussians must have discovered the bridge. The captain drew out his watch again.

'Five minutes more,' he said. 'They won't be here within five minutes.'

Then, exactly at six o'clock, he at last withdrew his men through a little postern that opened on a narrow lane, whence they threw themselves into the ditch, and in that way reached the forest of Sauval. The captain took leave of Father Merlier with much politeness, apologising profusely for the trouble he had caused. He even added:

'Try to keep them occupied for a while. We shall return.'

While this was occurring Dominique had remained alone in the hall.

He was still firing away, hearing nothing, conscious of nothing; his sole thought was to defend Françoise. The soldiers were all gone, and he had not the remotest idea of the fact; he aimed and brought down his man at every shot. All at once there was a great tumult. The Prussians had entered the courtyard from the rear. He fired his last shot, and they fell upon him with his weapon still smoking in his hand.

It required four men to hold him; the rest of them swarmed about him, vociferating like madmen in their horrible dialect. Françoise rushed forward to intercede with her prayers. They were on the point of killing him on the spot, but an officer came in and made them turn the prisoner over to him. After exchanging a few words in German with his men he turned to Dominique and said to him, in very good French:

'You will be shot in two hours from now.'

III

It was the standing regulation, laid down by the German staff, that every Frenchman, not belonging to the regular army, taken with arms in his hands should be shot. Even the *compagnies franches* were not recognised as belligerents. It was the intention of the Germans, in making such terrible examples of the peasants who attempted to defend their firesides, to prevent a rising *en masse*, which they greatly dreaded.

The officer, a tall, square man of about fifty years old, subjected Dominique to a brief examination. Although he spoke French fluently, he was unmistakably Prussian in the stiffness of his manner.

'You are a native of this country?'

'No, I am a Belgian.'

'Why did you take up arms? These are matters with which you have no concern.'

Dominique made no reply. At this moment the officer caught sight of Françoise where she stood listening, very pale; her slight wound had marked her white forehead with a streak of red. He looked from one to the other of the young people and appeared to understand the situation; he merely added:

'You do not deny having fired on my men?'

'I fired as long as I was able to do so,' Dominique quietly replied.

The admission was scarcely necessary, for he was black with powder, wet with sweat, and the blood from the wound in his shoulder had trickled down and stained his clothing.

'Very well,' the officer repeated. 'You will be shot two hours hence.'

Françoise uttered no cry. She clasped her hands and raised them above her head in a gesture of mute despair. Her action was not lost upon the officer. Two soldiers had led Dominique away to an adjacent room, where their orders were to guard him and not lose sight of him. The girl had sunk upon a chair; her strength had failed her, her legs refused to support her; she was denied the relief of tears, it seemed as if her emotion was strangling her. The officer continued to examine her attentively, and finally addressed her:

'Is this young man your brother?' he enquired.

She shook her head in negation. He was as rigid and unbending as ever, without the suspicion of a smile on his face. Then, after an interval of silence, he spoke again:

'Has he been living in the neighbourhood long?'

She answered yes, by another motion of the head.

'Then he must be well acquainted with the woods about here?'

This time she made a verbal answer. 'Yes, sir,' she said, looking at him with some astonishment.

He said nothing more, but turned on his heel, requesting that the mayor of the village should be brought before him. But Françoise had risen from her chair, a faint tinge of colour on her cheeks, believing that she had caught the significance of his questions, and with renewed hope she ran off to look for her father.

As soon as the firing had ceased Father Merlier had hurriedly descended by the wooden gallery to have a look at his wheel. He adored his daughter and had a strong feeling of affection for Dominique, his son-in-law who was to be; but his wheel also occupied a large space in his heart. Now that the two little ones, as he called them, had come safe and sound out of the fray, he thought of his other love, which must have suffered sorely, poor thing, and bending over the great wooden skeleton he was scrutinising its wounds with a heartbroken air. Five of the buckets were reduced to splinters, the central framework was honey-combed. He was thrusting his fingers into the cavities that the bullets had made to see how deep they were and reflecting how he was ever to repair all that damage. When Françoise found him he was already plugging up the crevices with moss and such debris as he could lay hands on.

'They are asking for you, father,' said she.

And at last she wept as she told him what she had just heard. Father Merlier shook his head. It was not customary to shoot people like that. He would have to look into the matter. And he re-entered the mill with his usual placid, silent air. When the officer made his demand for supplies for his men, he answered that the people of Rocreuse were not accustomed to be ridden roughshod, and that nothing would be obtained from them through violence; he was willing to assume all the responsibility, but only on condition that he was allowed to act independently. The officer at first appeared to take umbrage at this easy way of viewing matters, but finally gave way before the old man's brief and distinct representations. As the latter was leaving the room the other recalled him to ask:

'Those woods there, opposite, what do you call them?'

'The woods of Sauval.'

'And how far do they extend?'

The miller looked him straight in the face. 'I do not know,' he replied.

And he withdrew. An hour later the subvention in money and provisions that the officer had demanded was in the courtyard of the mill. Night was coming on; Françoise followed every movement of the soldiers with an anxious eye. She never once left the vicinity of the room in which Dominique was imprisoned. About seven o'clock she had a harrowing emotion; she saw the officer enter the prisoner's apartment, and for a quarter of an hour heard their voices raised in violent discussion. The officer came to the door for a moment and gave an order in German which she did not understand, but when twelve men came and formed in the courtyard with shouldered muskets, she was seized with a fit of trembling and felt as if she should die. It was all over, then; the execution was about to take place. The twelve men remained there ten minutes; Dominique's voice kept rising higher and higher in a tone of vehement denial. Finally the officer came out, closing the door behind him with a vicious bang and saying:

'Very well; think it over. I give you until tomorrow morning.'

And he ordered the twelve men to break ranks by a motion of his hand. Françoise was stupefied. Father Merlier, who had continued to puff away at his pipe while watching the platoon with a simple, curious air, came and took her by the arm with fatherly gentleness. He led her to her chamber.

'Don't fret,' he said to her; 'try to get some sleep. Tomorrow it will be light and we shall see more clearly.'

He locked the door behind him as he left the room. It was a fixed principle with him that women are good for nothing, and that they spoil

everything whenever they meddle in important matters. Françoise did
not lie down, however; she remained a long time seated on her bed, listening to the various noises in the house. The German soldiers quartered in the courtyard were singing and laughing; they must have kept
up their eating and drinking until eleven o'clock, for the riot never
ceased for an instant. Heavy footsteps resounded from time to time
through the mill itself, doubtless the tramp of the guards as they were
relieved. What had most interest for her was the sounds that she could
catch in the room that lay directly under her own; several times she
threw herself prone upon the floor and applied her ear to the boards.
That room was the one in which they had locked up Dominique. He
must have been pacing the apartment, for she could hear for a long time
his regular, cadenced tread passing from the wall to the window and
back again; then there was a deep silence; doubtless he had seated himself. The other sounds ceased too; everything was still. When it seemed
to her that the house was sunk in slumber she raised her window as
noiselessly as possible and leaned out.

Without, the night was serene and balmy. The slender crescent of the
moon, which was just setting behind Sauval wood, cast a dim radiance over the landscape. The lengthening shadows of the great trees
stretched far athwart the fields in bands of blackness, while in such spots
as were unobscured the grass appeared of a tender green, soft as velvet.
But Françoise did not stop to consider the mysterious charm of night.
She was scrutinising the country and looking to see where the Germans
had posted their sentinels. She could clearly distinguish their dark
forms outlined along the course of the Morelle. There was only one stationed opposite the mill, on the far bank of the stream, by a willow
whose branches dipped in the water. Françoise had an excellent view of
him; he was a tall young man, standing quite motionless with his face
upturned towards the sky, with the meditative air of a shepherd.

When she had completed her careful inspection of localities she
returned and took her former seat upon the bed. She remained there an
hour, absorbed in deep thought. Then she listened again; there was not
a breath to be heard in the house. She went again to the window and
took another look outside, but one of the moon's horns was still hanging
above the edge of the forest, and this circumstance doubtless appeared
to her unpropitious, for she resumed her waiting. At last the moment
seemed to have arrived; the night was now quite dark; she could no
longer discern the sentinel opposite her, the landscape lay before her

black as a sea of ink. She listened intently for a moment, then formed her resolve. Close beside her window was an iron ladder made of bars set in the wall, which ascended from the mill-wheel to the granary at the top of the building, and had formerly served the miller as a means of inspecting certain portions of the gearing, but a change having been made in the machinery the ladder had long since become lost to sight beneath the thick ivy that covered all that side of the mill.

Françoise bravely climbed over the balustrade of the little balcony in front of her window, grasped one of the iron bars and found herself suspended in space. She commenced the descent; her skirts were a great hindrance to her. Suddenly a stone became loosened from the wall and fell into the Morelle with a loud splash. She stopped, benumbed with fear, but reflection quickly told her that the waterfall, with its continuous roar, was sufficient to deaden any noise that she could make, and then she descended more boldly, putting aside the ivy with her foot, testing each round of her ladder. When she was on a level with the room that had been converted into a prison for her lover she stopped. An unforeseen difficulty came near depriving her of all her courage: the window of the room beneath was not situated directly under the window of her bedroom; there was a wide space between it and the ladder, and when she extended her hand it only encountered the naked wall.

Would she have to go back the way she came and leave her project unaccomplished? Her arms were growing very tired; the murmuring of the Morelle, far down below, was beginning to make her dizzy. Then she broke off bits of plaster from the wall and threw them against Dominique's window. He did not hear; perhaps he was asleep. Again she crumbled fragments from the wall, until the skin was peeled from her fingers. Her strength was exhausted; she felt that she was about to fall back into the stream when at last Dominique softly raised his sash.

'It is I,' she murmured. 'Take me quick; I am about to fall.' Leaning from the window he grasped her and drew her into the room, where she had a paroxysm of weeping, stifling her sobs in order that she might not be heard. Then, by a supreme effort of the will she overcame her emotion.

'Are you guarded?' she asked in a low voice.

Dominique, not yet recovered from his stupefaction at seeing her there, answered by simply pointing towards his door. There was a sound of snoring audible on the outside; it was evident that the sentinel had been overpowered by sleep and had thrown himself upon the floor close against the door in such a way that it could not be opened without arousing him.

'You must fly,' she continued earnestly. 'I came here to bid you fly and say farewell.'

But he seemed not to hear her. He kept repeating:

'What, is it you, is it you? Oh, what a fright you gave me! You might have killed yourself.' He took her hands, he kissed them again and again. 'How I love you, Françoise! You are as courageous as you are good. The only thing I feared was that I might die without seeing you again; but you are here, and now they may shoot me when they will. Let me but have a quarter of an hour with you and I am ready.'

He had gradually drawn her to him; her head was resting on his shoulder. The peril that was so near at hand brought them closer to each other, and they forgot everything in that long embrace.

'Ah, Françoise!' Dominique went on in low, caressing tones, 'today is the fête of Saint Louis, our wedding day, that we have been awaiting for so long. Nothing has been able to keep us apart, for we are both here, faithful to our appointment, are we not? It is now our wedding morning.'

'Yes, yes,' she repeated after him, 'our wedding morning.'

They shuddered as they exchanged a kiss. But suddenly she tore herself from his arms; the terrible reality arose before her eyes.

'You must fly, you must fly,' she murmured breathlessly. 'There is not a moment to lose.' And as he stretched out his arms in the darkness to draw her to him again, she went on in tender, beseeching tones: 'Oh! listen to me, I entreat you. If you die, I shall die. In an hour it will be daylight. Go, go at once; I command you to go.'

Then she rapidly explained her plan to him. The iron ladder extended downwards to the wheel; once he had got so far he could climb down by means of the buckets and get into the boat, which was hidden in a recess. Then it would be an easy matter for him to reach the other bank of the stream and make his escape.

'But are there no sentinels?' said he.

'Only one, directly opposite here, at the foot of the first willow.'

'And if he sees me, if he gives the alarm?'

Françoise shuddered. She placed in his hand a knife that she had brought down with her. They were silent.

'And your father – and you?' Dominique continued. 'But no, it is not to be thought of; I must not fly. When I am no longer here those soldiers are capable of murdering you. You do not know them. They offered to spare my life if I would guide them into Sauval forest. When they discover that I have escaped, their fury will be such that they will be ready for every atrocity.'

The girl did not stop to argue the question. To all the considerations that he adduced to her one simple answer was: 'Fly. For the love of me, fly. If you love me, Dominique, do not linger here a single moment longer.'

She promised that she would return to her bedroom; no one should know that she had helped him. She concluded by folding him in her arms and smothering him with kisses in an extravagant outburst of passion. He was vanquished. He only put one more question to her:

'Will you swear to me that your father knows what you are doing, and that he counsels my flight?'

'It was my father who sent me to you,' Françoise unhesitatingly replied.

She told a falsehood. At that moment she had but one great, overmastering longing, to know that he was in safety, to escape from the horrible thought that the morning's sun was to be the signal for his death. When he should be far away, then calamity and evil might burst upon her head; whatever fate might be in store for her would seem endurable, so that only his life might be spared. Before and above all other considerations, the selfishness of her love demanded that he should be saved.

'It is well,' said Dominique; 'I will do as you desire.'

No further word was spoken. Dominique went to the window to raise it again. But suddenly there was a noise that chilled them with affright. The door was shaken violently; they thought that someone was about to open it; it was evidently a party going the rounds who had heard their voices. They stood by the window, closely locked in each other's arms, awaiting the event with anguish unspeakable. Again there came the rattling at the door, but it did not open. Each of them drew a deep sigh of relief; they saw how it was. The soldier lying across the threshold had turned over in his sleep. Silence was restored indeed, and presently the snoring began again.

Dominique insisted that Françoise should return to her room first of all. He took her in his arms, he bade her a silent farewell, then helped her to grasp the ladder, and himself climbed out on it in turn. He refused to descend a single step, however, until he knew that she was in her chamber. When she was safe in her room she let fall, in a voice scarce louder than a whisper, the words:

'*Au revoir.* I love you!'

She kneeled at the window, resting her elbows on the sill, straining her eyes to follow Dominique. The night was still very dark. She looked for the sentinel, but could see nothing of him; the willow alone was dimly visible, a pale spot upon the surrounding blackness. For a moment she heard the rustling of the ivy as Dominique descended, then the wheel creaked, and there was a faint splash which told that the young man had found the boat. This was confirmed when, a minute later, she descried the shadowy outline of the skiff on the grey bosom of the Morelle. Then a horrible feeling of dread seemed to clutch her by the throat. Every moment she thought she heard the sentry give the alarm; every faintest sound among the dusky shadows seemed to her overwrought imagination to be the hurrying tread of soldiers, the clash of steel, the click of musket-locks. The seconds slipped by, however, the landscape still preserved its solemn peace. Dominique must have landed safely on the other bank. Françoise no longer had eyes for anything. The silence was oppressive. And she heard the sound of trampling feet, a hoarse cry, the dull thud of a heavy body falling. This was followed by another silence, even deeper than that which had gone before. Then, as if conscious that Death had passed that way, she became very cold in the presence of the impenetrable night.

IV

At early daybreak the repose of the mill was disturbed by the clamour of angry voices. Father Merlier had gone and unlocked Françoise's door. She descended to the courtyard, pale and very calm, but when there, could not repress a shudder upon being brought face to face with the body of a Prussian soldier that lay on the ground beside the well, stretched out upon a cloak.

Around the corpse soldiers were shouting and gesticulating angrily. Several of them shook their fists threateningly in the direction of the village. The officer had just sent a summons to Father Merlier to appear before him in his capacity as mayor of the commune.

'Here is one of our men,' he said, in a voice that was almost unintelligible from anger, 'who was found murdered on the bank of the stream. The murderer must be found, so that we may make a salutary example of him, and I shall expect you to co-operate with us in finding him.'

'Whatever you desire,' the miller replied, with his customary impassiveness. 'Only it will be no easy matter.'

The officer stooped down and drew aside the skirt of the cloak which concealed the dead man's face, disclosing as he did so a frightful wound. The sentinel had been struck in the throat and the weapon had not been withdrawn from the wound. It was a common kitchen knife, with a black handle.

'Look at that knife,' the officer said to Father Merlier. 'Perhaps it will assist us in our investigation.'

The old man had started violently, but recovered himself at once; not a muscle of his face moved as he replied:

'Everyone about here has knives like that. Like enough your man was tired of fighting and did the business himself. Such things have happened before now.'

'Be silent!' the officer shouted in a fury. 'I don't know what it is that keeps me from setting fire to the four corners of your village.'

His anger fortunately kept him from noticing the great change that had come over Françoise's countenance. Her feelings had compelled her to sit down upon the stone bench beside the well. Do what she would, she could not remove her eyes from the body that lay stretched upon the ground, almost at her feet. He had been a tall, handsome young man in life, very like Dominique in appearance, with blue eyes and yellow hair. The resemblance went to her heart. She thought that perhaps the dead man had left behind him in his German home some sweetheart who would weep for his loss. And she recognised her knife in the dead man's throat. She had killed him.

The officer, meantime, was talking of visiting Rocreuse with some terrible punishment, when two or three soldiers came running in. The guard had just that moment ascertained the fact of Dominique's escape. The agitation caused by the tidings was extreme. The officer went to inspect the locality, looked out through the still open window, saw at once how the event had happened, and returned in a state of exasperation.

Father Merlier appeared greatly vexed by Dominique's flight. 'The idiot!' he murmured; 'he has upset everything.'

Françoise heard him, and was in an agony of suffering. Her father, moreover, had no suspicion of her complicity. He shook his head, saying to her in an undertone:

'We are in a nice box now!'

'It was that scoundrel! it was that scoundrel!' cried the officer. 'He has got away to the woods; but he must be found, or the village shall stand the consequences.' And addressing himself to the miller: 'Come, you must know where he is hiding?'

Father Merlier laughed in his silent way, and pointed to the wide stretch of wooded hills.

'How can you expect to find a man in that wilderness?' he asked.

'Oh! there are plenty of hiding-places that you are acquainted with. I am going to give you ten men; you shall act as guide to them.'

'I am perfectly willing. But it will take a week to beat up all the woods of the neighbourhood.'

The old man's serenity enraged the officer; he saw, indeed, what a ridiculous proceeding such a hunt would be. It was at that moment that he caught sight of Françoise where she sat, pale and trembling, on her bench. His attention was aroused by the girl's anxious attitude. He was silent for a moment, glancing suspiciously from father to daughter and back again.

'Is not that man', he at last coarsely asked the old man, 'your daughter's lover?'

Father Merlier's face became ashy pale, and he appeared for a moment as if about to throw himself on the officer and throttle him. He straightened himself up and made no reply. Françoise had hid her face in her hands.

'Yes, that is how it is,' the Prussian continued; 'you or your daughter have helped him to escape. You are his accomplices. For the last time, will you surrender him?'

The miller did not answer. He had turned away and was looking at the distant landscape with an air of indifference, just as if the officer were talking to some other person. That put the finishing touch on the latter's wrath.

'Very well, then!' he declared, 'you shall be shot in his stead.'

And again he ordered out the firing party. Father Merlier was as imperturbable as ever. He scarcely did so much as shrug his shoulders; the whole drama appeared to him to be in very doubtful taste. He probably believed that they would not take a man's life in that unceremonious manner. When the platoon was on the ground he gravely said:

'So, then, you are in earnest? Very well, I am willing it should be so. If you feel you must have a victim, it may as well be I as another.'

But Françoise arose, greatly troubled, stammering:

'Have mercy, sir: do not harm my father. Kill me instead of him. It was I who helped Dominique to escape; I am the only guilty one.'

'Hold your tongue, my girl,' Father Merlier exclaimed. 'Why do you tell such a falsehood? She passed the night locked in her room, sir: I assure you that she does not speak the truth.'

'I *am* speaking the truth,' the girl eagerly replied. 'I got down by the window; I incited Dominique to fly. It is the truth, the whole truth.'

The old man's face was very white. He could read in her eyes that she was not lying, and her story terrified him. Ah, those children! those children! how they spoiled everything, with their hearts and their feelings! Then he said angrily:

'She is crazy; do not listen to her. It is a lot of trash she is telling you. Come, let us get through this business.'

She persisted in her protestations; she kneeled, she raised her clasped hands in supplication. The officer stood tranquilly by and watched the harrowing scene.

'*Mon Dieu!*' he said at last, 'I take your father because the other has escaped me. Bring me back the other man, and your father shall have his liberty.'

She looked at him for a moment with eyes dilated by the horror which his proposal inspired in her.

'It is dreadful,' she murmured. 'Where can I look for Dominique now? He is gone; I know nothing beyond that.'

'Well, make your choice between them; him or your father.'

'Oh, my God! how can I choose? Even if I knew where to find Dominique I could not choose. You are breaking my heart. I would rather die at once. Yes, it would be more quickly ended thus. Kill me, I beseech you, kill me—'

The officer finally became weary of this scene of despair and tears. He cried:

'Enough of this! I wish to treat you kindly; I will give you two hours. If your lover is not here within two hours, your father shall pay the penalty that he has incurred.'

And he ordered Father Merlier away to the room that had served as a prison for Dominique. The old man asked for tobacco, and began to smoke. There was no trace of emotion to be descried on his impassive face. Only when he was alone he wept two big tears that coursed slowly down his cheeks. His poor, dear child, what a fearful trial she was enduring!

Françoise remained in the courtyard. Prussian soldiers passed back and forth, laughing. Some of them addressed her with coarse pleasantries which she did not understand. Her gaze was bent upon the door through which her father had disappeared, and with a slow movement she raised her hand to her forehead, as if to keep it from bursting. The officer turned sharply on his heel, and said to her:

'You have two hours. Try to make good use of them.'

She had two hours. The words kept buzzing, buzzing in her ears. Then she went forth mechanically from the courtyard; she walked straight ahead with no definite end. Where was she to go? what was she to do? She did not even endeavour to arrive at any decision, for she felt how utterly useless were her efforts. And yet she would have liked to see Dominique; they could have come to some understanding together, perhaps they might have hit on some plan to extricate them from their difficulties. And so, amid the confusion of her whirling thoughts, she took her way downwards to the bank of the Morelle, which she crossed below the dam by means of some stepping-stones which were there. Proceeding onwards, still involuntarily, she came to the first willow, at the corner of the meadow, and stooping down, beheld a sight that made her grow deathly pale – a pool of blood. It was the spot. And she followed the track that Dominique had left in the tall grass; it was evident that he had run, for the footsteps that crossed the meadow in a diagonal line were separated from one another by wide intervals. Then, beyond that point, she lost the trace, but thought she had discovered it again in an adjoining field. It led her onwards to the border of the forest, where the trail came abruptly to an end.

Though conscious of the futility of the proceeding, Françoise penetrated into the wood. It was a comfort for her to be alone. She sat down for a moment, then, reflecting that time was passing, rose again to her feet. How long was it since she left the mill? Five minutes, or a half-hour? She had lost all idea of time. Perhaps Dominique had sought concealment in a clearing that she knew of, where they had gone together one afternoon and eaten hazel-nuts. She directed her step towards the clearing; she searched it thoroughly. A blackbird flew out, whistling his sweet and melancholy note; that was all. Then she thought that he might have taken refuge in a hollow among the rocks where he went sometimes with his gun, but the spot was untenanted. What use was there in looking for him? She would never find him, and little by little the desire to discover the hiding-place became a passionate longing. She proceeded at a more rapid pace. The idea suddenly took possession of her that he had climbed into a tree, and thenceforth she went along with eyes raised aloft and called him by name every fifteen or twenty steps, so that he might know she was near him. The cuckoos answered her; a breath of air that rustled the leaves made her think that he was there and was coming down to her. Once she even imagined that she saw him; she stopped with a sense of suffocation, with a desire to run away. What was she to say to him? Had she come there to take him back with her and have him shot? Oh! no, she would not mention those things; she would not tell him that he must fly, that he must not remain in the neighbourhood. Then she thought of her father awaiting her return, and the reflection caused her most bitter anguish. She sank upon the turf, weeping hot tears, crying aloud:

'My God! My God! why am I here?'

It was a mad thing for her to have come. And as if seized with sudden panic, she ran hither and thither. She sought to make her way out of the forest. Three times she lost her way, and had begun to think she was never to see the mill again, when she came out into a meadow, directly opposite Rocreuse. As soon as she caught sight of the village she stopped. Was she going to return alone?

She was standing there when she heard a voice calling her by name, softly:

'Françoise! Françoise!'

And she beheld Dominique raising his head above the edge of a ditch. Just God! she had found him.

Could it be, then, that Heaven willed his death? She suppressed a cry that rose to her lips, and slipped into the ditch beside him.

'You were looking for me?' he asked.

'Yes,' she replied bewilderedly, scarcely knowing what she was saying.

'Ah! What has happened?'

She stammered, with eyes downcast: 'Why, nothing; I was anxious, I wanted to see you.'

Thereupon, his fears alleviated, he went on to tell her how it was that he had remained in the vicinity. He was alarmed for them. Those rascally Prussians were not above wreaking their vengeance on women and old men. All had ended well, however, and he added, laughing:

'The wedding will be put off for a week, that's all.'

He became serious, however, upon noticing that her dejection did not pass away.

'But what is the matter? You are concealing something from me.'

'No, I give you my word I am not. I am tired; I ran all the way here.'

He kissed her, saying it was imprudent for them both to talk there any longer, and was about to climb out of the ditch in order to return to the forest. She stopped him; she was trembling violently.

'Listen, Dominique; perhaps it will be as well for you to stay here, after all. There is no one looking for you; you have nothing to fear.'

'Françoise, you are concealing something from me,' he said again.

Again she protested that she was concealing nothing. She only liked to know that he was near her. And there were other reasons still that she gave in stammering accents. Her manner was so strange that no consideration could now have induced him to go away. He believed, moreover, that the French would return presently. Troops had been seen over towards Sauval.

'Ah! let them make haste; let them come as quickly as possible,' she murmured fervently.

At that moment the clock of the church at Rocreuse struck eleven; the strokes reached them, clear and distinct. She arose in terror; it was two hours since she had left the mill.

'Listen,' she said, with feverish rapidity, 'should we need you, I will go up to my room and wave my handkerchief from the window.'

And she started off homewards at a run, while Dominique, greatly disturbed in mind, stretched himself at length beside the ditch to watch the mill. Just as she was about to enter the village Françoise encountered an old beggarman, Father Bontemps, who knew everyone and everything in that part of the country. He saluted her; he had just seen the miller, he said, surrounded by a crowd of Prussians; then, making numerous signs of the cross and mumbling some inarticulate words, he went his way.

'The two hours are up,' the officer said when Françoise made her appearance.

Father Merlier was there, seated on the bench beside the well. He was smoking still. The young girl again proffered her supplication, kneeling before the officer and weeping. Her wish was to gain time. The hope that she might yet behold the return of the French had been gaining strength in her bosom, and amid her tears and sobs she thought she could distinguish in the distance the cadenced tramp of an advancing army. Oh! if they would but come and deliver them all from their fearful trouble!

'Hear me, sir: grant us an hour, just one little hour. Surely you will not refuse to grant us an hour!'

But the officer was inflexible. He even ordered two men to lay hold of her and take her away, in order that they might proceed undisturbed with the execution of the old man. Then a dreadful conflict took place in

Françoise's heart. She could not allow her father to be murdered in that manner; no, no, she would die in company with Dominique rather; and she was just darting away in the direction of her room in order to signal to her fiancé, when Dominique himself entered the courtyard.

The officer and his soldiers gave a great shout of triumph, but he, as if there had been no soul there but Françoise, walked straight up to her: he was perfectly calm, and his face wore a slight expression of sternness.

'You did wrong,' he said. 'Why did you not bring me back with you? Had it not been for Father Bontemps I should have known nothing of all this. Well, I am here, at all events.'

V

It was three o'clock. The heavens were piled high with great black clouds, the tail-end of a storm that had been raging somewhere in the vicinity. Beneath the coppery sky and ragged scud the valley of Rocreuse, so bright and smiling in the sunlight, became a grim chasm, full of sinister shadows. The Prussian officer had done nothing with Dominique beyond placing him in confinement, giving no indication of his ultimate purpose in regard to him. Françoise, since noon, had been suffering unendurable agony; notwithstanding her father's entreaties, she would not leave the courtyard. She was waiting for the French troops to appear, but the hours slipped by, night was approaching, and she suffered all the more since it appeared as if the time thus gained would have no effect on the final result.

About three o'clock, however, the Prussians began to make their preparations for departure. The officer had gone to Dominique's room and remained closeted with him for some minutes, as he had done the day before. Françoise knew that the young man's life was hanging in the balance; she clasped her hands and sent up fervent prayers. Beside her sat Father Merlier, rigid and silent, declining, like the true peasant he was, to attempt any interference with accomplished facts.

'Oh! my God! my God!' Françoise exclaimed, 'they are going to kill him!'

The miller drew her to him, and took her on his lap as if she had been a little child. At this juncture the officer came from the room, followed by two men conducting Dominique between them.

'Never, never!' the latter exclaimed. 'I am ready to die.'

'You had better think the matter over,' the officer replied. 'I shall have no trouble in finding someone else to render us the service which you refuse. I am generous with you; I offer you your life. It is simply a matter of guiding us across the forest to Montredon; there must be paths.'

Dominique made no answer.

'Then you persist in your obstinacy?'

'Shoot me, and let's have done with it,' he replied.

Françoise, in the distance, entreated her lover with clasped hands; she was forgetful of all considerations save one – she would have had him commit a treason. But Father Merlier seized her hands, that the Prussians might not see the wild gestures of a woman whose mind was disordered by her distress.

'He is right,' he murmured, 'it is best for him to die.'

The firing party was in readiness. The officer still had hopes of bringing Dominique over, and was waiting to see him exhibit some signs of weakness. Deep silence prevailed. Heavy peals of thunder were heard in the distance, the fields and woods lay lifeless beneath the sweltering heat. And it was in the midst of this oppressive silence that suddenly the cry arose:

'The French! the French!'

It was a fact; they were coming. The line of red trousers could be seen advancing along the Sauval road, at the edge of the forest. In the mill the confusion was extreme; the Prussian soldiers ran to and fro, giving vent to guttural cries. Not a shot had been fired as yet.

'The French! the French!' cried Françoise, clapping her hands for joy. She was like a woman possessed. She had escaped from her father's embrace and was laughing boisterously, her arms raised high in the air. They had come at last, then, and had come in time, since Dominique was still there, alive!

A crash of musketry that rang in her ears like a thunderclap caused her suddenly to turn her head. The officer had muttered, 'We will finish this business first,' and with his own hands pushing Dominique up against the wall of a shed, had given the command to the squad to fire. When Françoise turned, Dominique was lying on the ground, pierced by a dozen bullets.

She did not shed a tear; she stood there like one suddenly rendered senseless. Her eyes were fixed and staring, and she went and seated herself beneath the shed, a few steps from the lifeless body. She looked at it wistfully; now and then she would make a movement with her hands in an aimless, childish way. The Prussians had seized Father Merlier as a hostage.

It was a pretty fight. The officer, perceiving that he could not retreat without being cut to pieces, rapidly made the best disposition possible of his men; it was as well to sell their lives dearly. The Prussians were now the defenders of the mill, and the French were the attacking party. The musketry fire began with unparalleled fury; for half an hour there was no lull in the storm. Then a deep report was heard, and a bullet carried away a main branch of the old elm. The French had artillery; a battery, in position just beyond the ditch where Dominique had concealed himself, commanded the main street of Rocreuse. The conflict could not last long after that.

Ah! the poor old mill! The cannon-balls raked it from wall to wall. Half the roof was carried away; two of the walls fell in. But it was on the side towards the Morelle that the damage was most lamentable. The ivy, torn from the tottering walls, hung in tatters, débris of every description floated away upon the bosom of the stream, and through a great breach Françoise's chamber was visible, with its little bed, the snow-white curtains of which were carefully drawn. Two bullets struck the old wheel in quick succession, and it gave one parting groan; the buckets were carried away downstream, the frame was crushed into a shapeless mass. It was the soul of the stout old mill parting from the body.

Then the French came forward to carry the place by storm. There was a mad hand-to-hand conflict with the bayonet. Under the dull sky the pretty valley became a huge slaughter-pen; the broad meadows looked on in horror, with their great isolated trees and their rows of poplars, dotting them with shade, while to right and left the forest was like the walls of a tilting ground enclosing the combatants, and in Nature's universal panic the gentle murmur of the springs and water-courses sounded like sobs and wails.

Françoise had not stirred from the shed where she remained hanging over Dominique's body. Father Merlier had met his death from a stray bullet. Then the French captain, the Prussians being exterminated and the mill on fire, entered the courtyard at the head of his men. It was the first success that he had gained since the breaking out of the war, so, all inflamed with enthusiasm, drawing himself up to the full height of his lofty stature, he laughed pleasantly, as a handsome cavalier like him might laugh. Then, perceiving poor idiotic Françoise where she crouched between the corpses of her father and her betrothed, among the smoking ruins of the mill, he saluted her gallantly with his sword, and shouted:

'Victory! Victory!'

Anatole France

Anatole France (1844–1924) was born Jacques-Anatole-François Thibault, the son of a Paris bookseller. He wrote widely and was awarded the Nobel Prize for Literature in 1921. His fiction, including novels, short stories and poetry, is eclipsed by his voluminous literary criticism, notably *La Vie littéraire* (1888–92) and *Le Génie latin* (1913) which, with their accounts of authors including Vigny, Baudelaire, Balzac and Zola, bear witness to the cultural movements of his age. His most impressive writing – particularly his volumes of short stories *Balthasar* (1889), *L'Étui de nave* (1892), from which 'The Procurator of Judaea' has been taken, and *Le Puits de Sainte-Claire* (1895) – embodies a witty scepticism and a taste for satirical allegory. His finest novel, though, is *Les Dieux ont soif* (1912), which analyses the fanatical and corrupt excesses of the revolutionary spirit. An ardent Dreyfusard, he derides French politics in his *Histoire contemporaine* (1897–1901), and offers a critical view of human progress in *L'Île des pingouins* (1908) and of religious faith in *La Révolte des anges* (1914). He was elected to the Académie Française in 1896.

The Procurator of Judaea

L AELIUS LAMIA, BORN IN ITALY OF ILLUSTRIOUS PARENTS, had not yet discarded the *toga praetexta* when he set out for the schools of Athens to study philosophy. Subsequently he took up his residence at Rome, and in his house on the Esquiline, amid a circle of youthful wastrels, abandoned himself to licentious courses. But being accused of engaging in criminal relations with Lepida, the wife of Sulpicius Quirinus, a man of consular rank, and being found guilty, he was exiled by Tiberius Caesar. At that time he was just entering his twenty-fourth year. During the eighteen years that his exile lasted he traversed Syria, Palestine, Cappadocia, and Armenia, and made prolonged visits to Antioch, Caesarea, and Jerusalem. When, after the death of Tiberius, Caius was raised to the purple, Lamia obtained permission to return to Rome. He even regained a portion of his possessions. Adversity had taught him wisdom.

He avoided all intercourse with the wives and daughters of Roman citizens, made no efforts towards obtaining office, held aloof from public honours, and lived a secluded life in his house on the Esquiline. Occupying himself with the task of recording all the remarkable things he had seen during his distant travels, he turned, as he said, the vicissitudes of his years of expiation into a diversion for his hours of rest. In the midst of these calm employments, alternating with assiduous study of the works of Epicurus, he recognised with a mixture of surprise and vexation that age was stealing upon him. In his sixty-second year, being afflicted with an illness which proved in no slight degree troublesome, he decided to have recourse to the waters at Baiae. The coast at that point, once frequented by the halcyon, was at this date the resort of the wealthy Roman, greedy of pleasure. For a week Lamia lived alone, without a friend in the brilliant crowd. Then one day, after dinner, an inclination to which he yielded urged him to ascend the incline, which, covered with vines that resembled bacchantes, looked out upon the waves.

Having reached the summit he seated himself by the side of a path beneath a terebinth, and let his glances wander over the lovely landscape. To his left, livid and bare, the Phlegraean plain stretched out towards the ruins of Cumae. On his right, Cape Misenum plunged its abrupt spur beneath the Tyrrhenian sea. Beneath his feet luxurious Baiae, following the graceful outline of the coast, displayed its gardens, its villas thronged with statues, its porticoes, its marble terraces along the shores of the blue ocean where the dolphins sported. Before him, on the other side of the bay, on the Campanian coast, gilded by the already sinking sun, gleamed the temples which far away rose above the laurels of Posilippo, whilst on the extreme horizon Vesuvius looked forth smiling.

Lamia drew from a fold of his toga a scroll containing the *Treatise upon Nature*, extended himself upon the ground, and began to read. But the warning cries of a slave necessitated his rising to allow of the passage of a litter which was being carried along the narrow pathway through the vineyards. The litter being uncurtained permitted Lamia to see stretched upon the cushions as it was borne nearer to him the figure of an elderly man of immense bulk, who, supporting his head on his hand, gazed out with a gloomy and disdainful expression. His nose, which was aquiline, and his chin, which was prominent, seemed desirous of meeting across his lips, and his jaws were powerful.

From the first moment Lamia was convinced that the face was familiar to him. He hesitated a moment before the name came to him. Then suddenly hastening towards the litter with a display of surprise and delight—

'Pontius Pilate!' he cried. 'The gods be praised who have permitted me to see you once again!'

The old man gave a signal to the slaves to stop, and cast a keen glance upon the stranger who had addressed him.

'Pontius, my dear host,' resumed the latter, 'have twenty years so far whitened my hair and hollowed my cheeks that you no longer recognise your friend Aelius Lamia?'

At this name Pontius Pilate dismounted from the litter as actively as the weight of his years and the heaviness of his gait permitted him, and embraced Aelius Lamia again and again.

'Gods! what a treat it is to me to see you once more! But, alas! you call up memories of those long-vanished days when I was Procurator of Judaea in the province of Syria. Why, it must be thirty years ago that I first met you. It was at Caesarea, whither you came to drag out your weary term of exile. I was fortunate enough to alleviate it a little, and out of friendship, Lamia, you followed me to that depressing place Jerusalem, where the Jews filled me with bitterness and disgust. You remained for more than ten years my guest and my companion, and in converse about Rome and things Roman we both of us managed to find consolation – you for your misfortunes, and I for my burdens of state.'

Lamia embraced him afresh.

'You forget two things, Pontius; you are overlooking the facts that you used your influence on my behalf with Herod Antipas, and that your purse was freely open to me.'

'Let us not talk of that,' replied Pontius, 'since after your return to Rome you sent me by one of your freedmen a sum of money which repaid me with usury.'

'Pontius, I could never consider myself out of your debt by the mere payment of money. But tell me, have the gods fulfilled your desires? Are you in the enjoyment of all the happiness you deserve? Tell me about your family, your fortunes, your health.'

'I have withdrawn to Sicily, where I possess estates, and where I cultivate wheat for the market. My eldest daughter, my best-beloved Pontia, who has been left a widow, lives with me, and directs my household. The gods be praised, I have preserved my mental vigour; my memory is not in the least degree enfeebled. But old age always brings in its train a long procession of griefs and infirmities. I am cruelly tormented with gout. And at this very moment you find me on my way to the Phlegraean plain in search of a remedy for my sufferings. From that burning soil, whence at night flames burst forth, proceed acrid exhalations of sulphur, which, so they say, ease the pains and restore suppleness to the stiffened joints. At least, the physicians assure me that it is so.'

'May you find it so in your case, Pontius. But, despite the gout and its burning torments, you scarcely look as old as myself, although in reality you must be my senior by ten years. Unmistakably you have retained a greater degree of vigour than I ever possessed, and I am overjoyed to find you looking so hale. Why, dear friend, did you retire from the public service before the customary age? Why, on resigning your governorship in Judaea, did you withdraw to a voluntary exile on your Sicilian estates? Give me an account of your doings from the moment that I ceased to be a witness of them. You were preparing to suppress a Samaritan rising when I set out for Cappadocia, where I hoped to draw some profit from the breeding of horses and mules. I have not seen you since then. How did that expedition succeed? Pray tell me. Everything interests me that concerns you in any way.'

Pontius Pilate sadly shook his head.

'My natural disposition,' he said, 'as well as a sense of duty, impelled me to fulfil my public responsibilities, not merely with diligence, but even with ardour. But I was pursued by unrelenting hatred. Intrigues and calumnies cut short my career in its prime, and the fruit it should have looked to bear has withered away. You ask me about the Samaritan insurrection. Let us sit down on this hillock. I shall be able to give you an answer in few words. Those occurrences are as vividly present to me as if they had happened yesterday.

'A man of the people, of persuasive speech – there are many such to be met with in Syria – induced the Samaritans to gather together in arms on Mount Gerizim (which in that country is looked upon as a holy place) under the promise that he would disclose to their sight the sacred vessels which in the ancient days of Evander and our father, Aeneas, had been hidden away by an eponymous hero, or rather a tribal deity, named Moses. Upon this assurance the Samaritans rose in rebellion; but having been warned in time to forestall them, I dispatched detachments of infantry to occupy the mountain, and stationed cavalry to keep the approaches to it under observation.

'These measures of prudence were urgent. The rebels were already laying siege to the town of Tyrathaba, situated at the foot of Mount Gerizim. I easily dispersed them, and stifled the as yet scarcely organised revolt. Then, in order to give a forcible example with as few victims as possible, I handed over to execution the leaders of the rebellion. But you are aware, Lamia, in what strait dependence I was kept by the proconsul Vitellius, who governed Syria not in, but against the interests of Rome, and looked upon the provinces of the Empire as territories which could be farmed out to tetrarchs. The headmen among the Samaritans, in their resentment against me, came and fell at his feet lamenting. To listen to them, nothing had been further from their thoughts than to disobey Caesar. It was I who had provoked the rising, and it was purely in order to withstand my violence that they had gathered together round Tyrathaba. Vitellius listened to their complaints, and handing over the affairs of Judaea to his friend Marcellus, commanded me to go and justify my proceedings before the Emperor himself. With a heart overflowing with grief and resentment I took ship. Just as I approached the shores of Italy, Tiberius, worn out with age and the cares of empire, died suddenly on the selfsame Cape Misenum, whose peak we see from this very spot magnified in the mists of evening. I demanded justice of Caius, his successor, whose perception was naturally acute, and who was acquainted with Syrian affairs. But marvel with me, Lamia, at the maliciousness of fortune, resolved on my discomfiture. Caius then had in his suite at Rome the Jew Agrippa, his companion, the friend of his childhood, whom he cherished as his own eyes. Now Agrippa favoured Vitellius, inasmuch as Vitellius was the enemy of Antipas, whom Agrippa pursued with his hatred. The Emperor adopted the prejudices of his beloved Asiatic and refused even to listen to me. There was nothing for me to do but bow beneath the stroke of unmerited misfortune. With tears for my meat and gall for my portion, I withdrew to my estates in Sicily, where I should have died of grief if my sweet Pontia had not come to console her father. I have cultivated wheat, and succeeded in producing the fullest ears in the whole province. But now my life is ended; the future will judge between Vitellius and me.'

'Pontius,' replied Lamia, 'I am persuaded that you acted towards the Samaritans according to the rectitude of your character, and solely in the interests of Rome. But were you not perchance on that occasion a trifle too much influenced by that impetuous courage which has always swayed you? You will remember that in Judaea it often happened that I who, younger than you, should naturally have been more impetuous than you, was obliged to urge you to clemency and suavity.'

'Suavity towards the Jews!' cried Pontius Pilate. 'Although you have lived amongst them, it seems clear that you ill understand those enemies of the human race. Haughty and at the same time base, combining an invincible obstinacy with a despicably mean spirit, they weary alike your love and your hatred. My character, Lamia, was formed upon the maxims of the divine Augustus. When I was appointed Procurator of Judaea, the world was already penetrated with the majestic ideal of the *Pax Romana*. No longer, as in the days of our internecine strife, were we witnesses to the sack of a province for the aggrandisement of a proconsul. I knew where my duty lay. I was careful that my actions should be governed by prudence and moderation. The gods are my witnesses that I was resolved upon mildness, and upon mildness only. Yet what did my benevolent intentions avail me? You were at my side, Lamia, when, at the outset of my career as ruler, the first rebellion came to a head. Is there any need for me to recall the details to you? The garrison had been transferred from Caesarea to take up its winter quarters at Jerusalem. Upon the ensigns of the legionaries appeared the present-ment of Caesar. The inhabitants of Jerusalem, who did not recognise the indwelling divinity of the Emperor, were scandalised at this, as though, when obedience is compulsory, it were not less abject to obey a god than a man. The priests of their nation appeared before my tribunal implor-ing me with supercilious humility to have the ensigns removed from within the holy city. Out of reverence for the divine nature of Caesar and the majesty of the empire, I refused to comply. Then the rabble made common cause with the priests, and all around the praetorium portent-ous cries of supplication arose. I ordered the soldiers to stack their spears in front of the tower of Antonia, and to proceed, armed only with sticks like lictors, to disperse the insolent crowd. But, heedless of blows, the Jews continued their entreaties, and the more obstinate amongst them threw themselves on the ground and, exposing their throats to the rods, deliberately courted death. You were a witness of my humiliation on that occasion, Lamia. By the order of Vitellius I was forced to send the insignia back to Caesarea. That disgrace I had certainly not merited. Before the immortal gods I swear that never once during my term of office did I flout justice and the laws. But I am grown old. My enemies and detractors are dead. I shall die unavenged. Who will now retrieve my character?'

He moaned and lapsed into silence. Lamia replied:

'That man is prudent who neither hopes nor fears anything from the uncertain events of the future. Does it matter in the least what estimate men may form of us hereafter? We ourselves are after all our own wit-nesses, and our own judges. You must rely, Pontius Pilate, on the testi-mony you yourself bear to your own rectitude. Be content with your own personal respect and that of your friends. For the rest, we know that mildness by itself will not suffice for the work of government. There is but little room in the actions of public men for that indulgence of human frailty which the philosophers recommend.'

'We'll say no more at present,' said Pontius. 'The sulphureous fumes which rise from the Phlegraean plain are more powerful when the ground which exhales them is still warm beneath the sun's rays. I must hasten on. Adieu! But now that I have rediscovered a friend, I should wish to take advantage of my good fortune. Do me the favour, Aelius Lamia, to give me your company at supper at my house tomorrow. My house stands on the seashore, at the extreme end of the town in the direction of Misenum. You will easily recognise it by the porch, which bears a painting representing Orpheus surrounded by tigers and lions, whom he is charming with the strains from his lyre.

'Till tomorrow, Lamia,' he repeated, as he climbed once more into his litter. 'Tomorrow we will talk about Judaea.'

The following day at the supper hour Lamia presented himself at the house of Pontius Pilate. Two couches only were in readiness for occupants. Creditably but simply equipped, the table held a silver service in which were set out beccaficos in honey, thrushes, oysters from the Lucrine lake, and lampreys from Sicily. As they proceeded with their repast, Pontius and Lamia interchanged enquiries with one another about their ailments, the symptoms of which they described at considerable length, mutually emulous of communicating the various remedies which had been recommended to them. Then, congratulating themselves on being thrown together once more at Baiae, they vied with one another in praise of the beauty of that enchanting coast and the mildness of the climate they enjoyed. Lamia was enthusiastic about the charms of the courtesans who frequented the seashore laden with golden ornaments and trailing draperies of barbaric broidery. But the aged Procurator deplored the ostentation with which by means of trumpery jewels and filmy garments foreigners and even enemies of the empire beguiled the Romans of their gold. After a time they turned to the subject of the great engineering feats that had been accomplished in the country; the prodigious bridge constructed by Caius between Puteoli and Baiae, and the canals which Augustus excavated to convey the waters of the ocean to Lake Avernus and the Lucrine lake.

'I also,' said Pontius, with a sigh, 'I also wished to set afoot public works of great utility. When, for my sins, I was appointed Governor of Judaea, I conceived the idea of furnishing Jerusalem with an abundant supply of pure water by means of an aqueduct. The elevation of the levels, the proportionate capacity of the various parts, the gradient for the brazen reservoirs to which the distribution pipes were to be fixed – I had gone into every detail, and decided everything for myself with the assistance of mechanical experts. I had drawn up regulations for the superintendents so as to prevent individuals from making unauthorised depredations. The architects and the workmen had their instructions. I gave orders for the commencement of operations. But far from viewing with satisfaction the construction of that conduit, which was intended to carry to their town upon its massive arches not only water but health, the inhabitants of Jerusalem gave vent to lamentable outcries. They gathered tumultuously together, exclaiming against the sacrilege and impiousness, and, hurling themselves upon the workmen, scattered the very foundation-stones. Can you picture to yourself, Lamia, a filthier set of barbarians? Nevertheless, Vitellius decided in their favour, and I received orders to put a stop to the work.'

'It is a knotty point', said Lamia, 'how far one is justified in devising things for the commonweal against the will of the populace.'

Pontius Pilate continued as though he had not heard this interruption.

'Refuse an aqueduct! What madness! But whatever is of Roman origin is distasteful to the Jews. In their eyes we are an unclean race, and our very presence appears a profanation to them. You will remember that they would never venture to enter the praetorium for fear of defiling themselves, and that I was consequently obliged to discharge my magisterial functions in an open-air tribunal on that marble pavement your feet so often trod.

'They fear us and they despise us. Yet is not Rome the mother and warden of all those peoples who nestle smiling upon her venerable bosom? With her eagles in the van, peace and liberty have been carried to the very confines of the universe. Those whom we have subdued we look on as our friends, and we leave those conquered races, nay, we secure to them the permanence of their customs and their laws. Did Syria, aforetime rent asunder by its rabble of petty kings, ever even begin to taste of peace and prosperity until it submitted to the armies of Pompey? And when Rome might have reaped a golden harvest as the price of her goodwill, did she lay hands on the hoards that swell the treasuries of barbaric temples? Did she despoil the shrine of Cybele at Pessinus, or the Morimene and Cilician sanctuaries of Jupiter, or the temple of the Jewish god at Jerusalem? Antioch, Palmyra and Apamea, secure despite their wealth, and no longer in dread of the wandering Arab of the desert, have erected temples to the genius of Rome and the divine Caesar. The Jews alone hate and withstand us. They withhold their tribute till it is wrested from them, and obstinately rebel against military service.'

'The Jews', replied Lamia, 'are profoundly attached to their ancient customs. They suspected you, unreasonably I admit, of a desire to abolish their laws and change their usages. Do not resent it, Pontius, if I say

that you did not always act in such a way as to disperse their unfortunate illusion. It gratified you, despite your habitual self-restraint, to play upon their fears, and, more than once, have I seen you betray in their presence the contempt with which their beliefs and religious ceremonies inspired you. You irritated them particularly by giving instructions for the sacerdotal garments and ornaments of their high priest to be kept in ward by your legionaries in the Antonine tower. One must admit that though they have never risen like us to an appreciation of things divine, the Jews celebrate rites which their very antiquity renders venerable.'

Pontius Pilate shrugged his shoulders.

'They have very little exact knowledge of the nature of the gods,' he said. 'They worship Jupiter, yet they abstain from naming him or erecting a statue of him. They do not even adore him under the semblance of a rude stone, as certain of the Asiatic peoples are wont to do. They know nothing of Apollo, of Neptune, of Mars, nor of Pluto, nor of any goddess. At the same time, I am convinced that in days gone by they worshipped Venus. For even to this day their women bring doves to the altar as victims; and you know as well as I that the dealers who trade beneath the arcades of their temple supply those birds in couples for sacrifice. I have even been told that on one occasion some madman proceeded to overturn the stalls bearing these offerings, and their owners with them. The priests raised an outcry about it, and looked on it as a case of sacrilege. I am of opinion that their custom of sacrificing turtle-doves was instituted in honour of Venus. Why are you laughing, Lamia?'

'I was laughing', said Lamia, 'at an amusing idea which, I hardly know how, just occurred to me. I was thinking that perchance some day the Jupiter of the Jews might come to Rome and vent his fury upon you. Why should he not? Asia and Africa have already enriched us with a considerable number of gods. We have seen temples in honour of Isis and the dog-faced Anubis erected in Rome. In the public squares, and even on the racecourses, you may run across the Bona Dea of the Syrians mounted on an ass. And did you never hear how, in the reign of Tiberius, a young patrician passed himself off as the horned Jupiter of the Egyptians, Jupiter Ammon, and in this disguise procured the favours of an illustrious lady who was too virtuous to deny anything to a god? Beware, Pontius, lest the invisible Jupiter of the Jews disembark some day on the quay at Ostia!'

At the idea of a god coming out of Judaea, a fleeting smile played over the severe countenance of the Procurator. Then he replied gravely:

'How would the Jews manage to impose their sacred law on outside peoples when they are in a perpetual state of tumult amongst themselves as to the interpretation of that law? You have seen them yourself, Lamia, in the public squares, split up into twenty rival parties, with staves in their hands, abusing each other and clutching one another by the beard. You have seen them on the steps of the temple, tearing their filthy garments as a symbol of lamentation, with some wretched creature in a frenzy of prophetic exaltation in their midst. They have never realised that it is possible to discuss peacefully and with an even mind those matters concerning the divine which yet are hidden from the profane and wrapped in uncertainty. For the nature of the immortal gods remains hidden from us, and we cannot arrive at a knowledge of it. Though I am of the opinion, none the less, that it is a prudent thing to believe in the providence of the gods. But the Jews are devoid of philosophy, and cannot tolerate any diversity of opinions. On the contrary, they judge worthy of the extreme penalty all those who on divine subjects profess opinions opposed to their law. And as, since the genius of Rome has towered over them, capital sentences pronounced by their own tribunals can only be carried out with the sanction of the proconsul or the Procurator, they harry the Roman magistrate at any hour to procure his signature to their baleful decrees, they besiege the praetorium with their cries of 'Death!' A hundred times, at least, have I know them, mustered, rich and poor together, all united under their priests, make a furious onslaught on my ivory chair, seizing me by the skirts of my robe, by the thongs of my sandals, and all to demand of me – nay, to exact from me – the death sentence on some unfortunate whose guilt I failed to perceive, and as to whom I could only pronounce that he was as mad as his accusers. A hundred times, do I say! Not a hundred, but every day and all day. Yet it was my duty to execute their law as if it were ours, since I was appointed by Rome not for the destruction, but for the upholding of their customs, and over them I had the power of the rod and the axe. At the outset of my term of office I endeavoured to persuade them to hear reason; I attempted to snatch their miserable victims from death. But this show of mildness only irritated them the more; they demanded their prey, fighting around me like a horde of vultures with wing and beak. Their priests reported to Caesar that I was violating their law, and their appeals, supported by Vitellius, drew down upon me a severe reprimand. How many times did I long, as the Greeks used to say, to dispatch accusers and accused in one convoy to the crows!

'Do not imagine, Lamia, that I nourish the rancour of the discomfited, the wrath of the superannuated, against a people which in my person has prevailed against both Rome and tranquillity. But I foresee the extremity to which sooner or later they will reduce us. Since we cannot govern them, we shall be driven to destroy them. Never doubt it. Always in a state of insubordination, brewing rebellion in their inflammatory minds, they will one day burst forth upon us with a fury beside which the wrath of the Numidians and the mutterings of the Parthians are mere child's play. They are secretly nourishing preposterous hopes, and madly premeditating our ruin. How can it be otherwise, when, on the strength of an oracle, they are living in expectation of the coming of a prince of their own blood whose kingdom shall extend over the whole earth? There are no half-measures with such a people. They must be exterminated. Jerusalem must be laid waste to the very foundation. Perchance, old as I am, it may be granted me to behold the day when her walls shall fall and the flames shall envelop her houses, when her inhabitants shall pass under the edge of the sword, when salt shall be strewn on the place where once the temple stood. And in that day I shall at length be justified.'

Lamia exerted himself to lead the conversation back to a less acrimonious note.

'Pontius,' he said, 'it is not difficult for me to understand both your long-standing resentment and your sinister forebodings. Truly, what you have experienced of the character of the Jews is nothing to their advantage. But I lived in Jerusalem as an interested onlooker, and mingled freely with the people, and I succeeded in detecting certain obscure virtues in these rude folk which were altogether hidden from you. I have met Jews who were all mildness, whose simple manners and faithfulness of heart recalled to me what our poets have related concerning the Spartan lawgiver. And you yourself, Pontius, have seen perish beneath the cudgels of your legionaries simple-minded men, who have died for a cause they believed to be just without revealing their names. Such men do not deserve our contempt. I am saying this because it is desirable in all things to preserve moderation and an even mind. But I own that I never experienced any lively sympathy for the Jews. The Jewesses, on the contrary, I found extremely pleasing. I was young then, and the Syrian women stirred all my senses to response. Their ruddy lips, their liquid eyes that shone in the shade, their sleepy gaze pierced me to the very marrow. Painted and stained, smelling of

nard and myrrh, steeped in odours, their physical attractions are both
rare and delightful.'

Pontius listened impatiently to these praises.

'I was not the kind of man to fall into the snares of the Jewish
women,' he said; 'and since you have opened the subject yourself,
Lamia, I was never able to approve of your laxity. If I did not express
with sufficient emphasis formerly how culpable I held you for having
intrigued at Rome with the wife of a man of consular rank, it was
because you were then enduring heavy penance for your misdoings.
Marriage from the patrician point of view is a sacred tie; it is one of the
institutions which are the support of Rome. As to foreign women and
slaves, such relations as one may enter into with them would be of little
account were it not that they habituate the body to a humiliating effem-
inacy. Let me tell you that you have been too liberal in your offerings to
the Venus of the Market-place; and what, above all, I blame in you is that
you have not married in compliance with the law and given children to
the Republic, as every good citizen is bound to do.'

But the man who had suffered exile under Tiberius was no longer
listening to the venerable magistrate. Having tossed off his cup of Fal-
ernian, he was smiling at some image visible to his eye alone.

After a moment's silence he resumed in a very deep voice, which rose
in pitch by little and little:

'With what languorous grace they dance, those Syrian women! I
knew a Jewess at Jerusalem who used to dance in a poky little room, on a
threadbare carpet, by the light of one smoky little lamp, waving her
arms as she clanged her cymbals. Her loins arched, her head thrown
back, and, as it were, dragged down by the weight of her heavy red hair,
her eyes swimming with voluptuousness, eager, languishing, compli-
ant, she would have made Cleopatra herself grow pale with envy. I was
in love with her barbaric dances, her voice – a little raucous and yet so
sweet – her atmosphere of incense, the semi-somnolescent state in
which she seemed to live. I followed her everywhere. I mixed with the
vile rabble of soldiers, conjurors, and extortioners with which she was
surrounded. One day, however, she disappeared, and I saw her no more.
Long did I seek her in disreputable alleys and taverns. It was more difficult to learn to do without her than to lose the taste for Greek wine.
Some months after I lost sight of her, I learned by chance that she had
attached herself to a small company of men and women who were fol-
lowers of a young Galilean thaumaturgist. His name was Jesus; he came

from Nazareth, and he was crucified for some crime, I don't quite know what. Pontius, do you remember anything about the man?'

Pontius Pilate contracted his brows, and his hand rose to his forehead in the attitude of one who probes the deeps of memory. Then after a silence of some seconds:

'Jesus?' he murmured, 'Jesus – of Nazareth? I cannot call him to mind.'

Guy de Maupassant

No selection of French short stories would be complete without an example of the craft (and craftiness) to be found in the writing of Guy de Maupassant (1850–93). He was introduced into literary circles by Flaubert, an old family friend, and there he met Zola. His six novels are often associated with Zola's Naturalism, but it is in short fiction that his mordant and pithy style is most effective. Many of his early stories appeared in periodicals under pseudonyms, but 'Boule-de-suif', his contribution to the collective volume *Les Soirées de Médan*, brought him overnight fame. He enjoyed ten prodigiously successful years, leading a life of great self-indulgence, and he was noted in the high circles in which he moved for his sexual and sporting prowess – he once saved Swinburne from drowning. However, he contracted syphilis and in the final years of his life suffered fits of depression. By 1891 he could no longer write and, like his brother, he died insane, having been interned in an asylum after he attempted suicide in 1892. This mixture of anxiety and exuberance characterises his writing which is by turns vicious, witty and sad.

Miss Harriet

THERE WERE SEVEN OF US IN A FOUR-IN-HAND, FOUR WOMEN and three men, one of whom was on the box-seat beside the coachman. We were following at a footpace the broad highway which serpentines along the coast.

Setting out from Étretat at break of day in order to visit the ruins of Tancarville, we were still asleep, chilled by the fresh air of the morning. The women especially, who were but little accustomed to these early excursions, let their eyelids fall and rise every moment, nodding their heads or yawning, quite insensible to the glory of the dawn.

It was autumn. On both sides of the road the bare fields stretched out, yellowed by the corn and wheat stubble which covered the soil like a bristling growth of beard. The spongy earth seemed to smoke. Larks were singing high up in the air, while other birds piped in the bushes.

At length the sun rose in front of us, a bright red on the plane of the horizon, and as it ascended, growing clearer from minute to minute, the country seemed to awake, to smile, to shake and stretch itself, like a young girl who is leaving her bed in her white, airy chemise. The Count d'Etraille, who was seated on the box, cried:

'Look! Look! A hare!' And he pointed towards the left, indicating a piece of hedge. The leveret threaded its way along, almost concealed by the field, only its large ears visible. Then it swerved across a deep rut, stopped, again pursued its easy course, changed its direction, stopped anew, disturbed, spying out every danger and undecided as to the route it should take. Suddenly it began to run with great bounds from its hind-legs, disappearing finally in a large patch of beetroot. All the men woke up to watch the course of the beast.

René Lemanoir then exclaimed: 'We are not at all gallant this morning,' and, looking at his neighbour, the little Baroness of Stérennes, who was struggling with drowsiness, he said to her in a subdued voice: 'You

are thinking of your husband, Baroness. Reassure yourself; he will not
return before Saturday, so you have still four days.'

She responded to him with a sleepy smile.

'How rude you are.' Then, shaking off her torpor, she added: 'Now
let somebody say something that will make us all laugh. You, Monsieur
Chenal, who have the reputation of possessing a larger fortune than the
Duke of Richelieu, tell us a love-story in which you have been mixed up,
anything you like.'

Lécon Chenal, an old painter who had once been very handsome,
very strong, who was very proud of his physique and very amiable, took
his long white beard in his hand and smiled; then after a few moments'
reflection he became suddenly grave.

'Ladies, it will not be an amusing tale, for I am going to relate to you
the most lamentable love-affair of my life, and I sincerely hope that none
of my friends has ever passed through a similar experience.'

I

'At that time I was twenty-five years old and was making daubs along the
coast of Normandy. I call "making daubs" that wandering about with a
bag on one's back from mountain to mountain under the pretext of studying and of sketching nature. I know nothing more enjoyable than
that happy-go-lucky wandering life in which you are perfectly free, without shackles of any kind, without care, without preoccupation, without
thought even of tomorrow. You go in any direction you please without any
guide save your fancy, without any counsellor save your eyes. You pull up
because a running brook seduces you or because you are attracted in front
of an inn by the smell of potatoes frying. Sometimes it is the perfume of
clematis which decides you in your choice, or the naïve glance of the servant at an inn. Do not despise me for my affection for these rustics. These
girls have soul as well as feeling, not to mention firm cheeks and fresh lips,
while their hearty and willing kisses have the flavour of wild fruit. Love
always has its price, come whence it may. A heart that beats when you
make your appearance, an eye that weeps when you go away, these are
things so rare, so sweet, so precious, that they must never be despised.

'I have had rendezvous in ditches in which cattle repose and in barns
among the straw still steaming from the heat of the day. I have recollections of canvas spread on rude and creaky benches and of hearty, fresh,
free kisses, more delicate, free from affectation and sincere than the
subtle attractions of charming and distinguished women.

'But what you love most amid all these varied adventures are the country, the woods, the risings of the sun, the twilight, the light of the moon. For the painter these are honeymoon trips with nature. You are alone with her in that long and tranquil rendezvous. You go to bed in the fields amid marguerites and wild poppies and, with eyes wide open, you watch the going down of the sun and descry in the distance the little village with its pointed clock tower which sounds the hour of midnight.

'You sit down by the side of a spring which gushes out from the foot of an oak, amid a covering of fragile herbs, growing and redolent of life. You go down on your knees, bend forward and drink the cold and pellucid water, wetting your moustache and nose; you drink it with a physical pleasure, as though you were kissing the spring, lip to lip. Sometimes, when you encounter a deep hole along the course of these tiny brooks, you plunge into it, quite naked, and on your skin, from head to foot, like an icy and delicious caress, you feel the lovely and gentle quivering of the current.

'You are gay on the hills, melancholy on the verges of pools, exalted when the sun is crowned in an ocean of blood-red shadows and when it casts on the rivers its red reflection. And at night under the moon, as it passes the vault of heaven, you think of things, singular things, which would never have occurred to your mind under the brilliant light of day.

'So in wandering through the same country we are in this year I came to the little village of Bénouville, on the Falaise, between Yport and Étretat. I came from Fécamp, following the coast, a high coast, perpendicular as a wall, with projecting and rugged rocks falling sheer down into the sea. I had walked since the morning on the close-clipped grass as smooth and as yielding as a carpet. Singing lustily, I walked with long strides, looking sometimes at the slow and lazy flight of a gull, with its short white wings, sailing in the blue heavens, sometimes at the green sea or at the brown sails of a fishing bark. In short, I had passed a happy day, a day of listlessness and of liberty.

'I was shown a little farmhouse where travellers were put up, a kind of inn, kept by a peasant, which stood in the centre of a Norman court, surrounded by a double row of beeches.

'Quitting the Falaise, I reached the hamlet, which was hemmed in by trees, and I presented myself at the house of Mother Lecacheur.

'She was an old, wrinkled and austere rustic, who always seemed to yield to the pleasure of new customs with a kind of contempt.

'It was the month of May: the spreading apple trees covered the court with a whirling shower of blossoms which rained unceasingly both upon people and upon the grass.

'I said: "Well, Madame Lecacheur, have you a room for me?"

'Astonished to find that I knew her name, she answered:

' "That depends; everything is let, but, all the same, there will be no harm in looking."

'In five minutes we were in perfect accord, and I deposited my bag upon the bare floor of a rustic room furnished with a bed, two chairs, a table and a washstand. The room opened into the large and smoky kitchen, where the lodgers took their meals with the people of the farm and with the farmer himself, who was a widower.

'I washed my hands, after which I went out. The old woman was fricasséeing a chicken for dinner in a large fireplace in which hung the stewpot, black with smoke.

' "You have travellers then at the present time?" I said to her.

'She answered in an offended tone of voice:

' "I have a lady, an English lady, who has attained to years of maturity. She is occupying my other room."

'By means of an extra five sous a day I obtained the privilege of dining out in the court when the weather was fine.

'My cover was then placed in front of the door, and I started to gnaw with hunger the lean members of the Normandy chicken, to drink the clear cider and to munch the hunk of white bread which, though four days old, was excellent.

'Suddenly the wooden barrier which opened on to the highway was opened, and a strange person directed her steps towards the house. She was very slender, very tall, enveloped in a Scotch shawl with red borders. You would have believed that she had no arms, if you had not seen a long hand appear just above the hips holding a white tourist umbrella. The face of a mummy, surrounded with sausage rolls of plaited grey hair, which bounded at every step she took, made me think, I know not why, of a sour herring adorned with curling papers. Lowering her eyes, she passed quickly in front of me and entered the house.

'This singular apparition made me curious. She undoubtedly was my neighbour, the aged English lady of whom our hostess had spoken.

'I did not see her again that day. The next day, when I had begun to paint at the end of that beautiful valley which, you know, extends as far as Étretat, lifting my eyes suddenly, I perceived something singularly attired standing on the crest of the declivity; it looked like a pole decked

out with flags. It was she. On seeing me she suddenly disappeared. I re-entered the house at midday for lunch and took my seat at the common table so as to make the acquaintance of this old and original creature. But she did not respond to my polite advances, was insensible even to my little attentions. I poured water out for her with great alacrity; I passed her the dishes with great eagerness. A slight, almost impercept-ible movement of the head and an English word, murmured so low that I did not understand it, were her only acknowledgements.

'I ceased occupying myself with her, although she had disturbed my thoughts. At the end of three days I knew as much about her as did Madame Lecacheur herself.

'She was called Miss Harriet. Seeking out a secluded village in which to pass the summer, she had been attracted to Bénouville some six months before and did not seem disposed to quit it. She never spoke at table, ate rapidly, reading all the while a small book treating of some Protestant propaganda. She gave a copy of it to everybody. The *curé* himself had received no less than four copies at the hands of an urchin to whom she had paid two sous' commission. She said sometimes to our hostess abruptly, without preparing her in the least for the declaration:

' "I love the Saviour more than all; I worship him in all creation; I adore him in all nature; I carry him always in my heart."

'And she would immediately present the old woman with one of her brochures which were destined to convert the universe.

'In the village she was not liked. In fact, the schoolmaster had de-clared that she was an atheist and that a sort of reproach attached to her. The *curé*, who had been consulted by Madame Lecacheur, responded:

' "She is a heretic, but God does not wish the death of the sinner, and I believe her to be a person of pure morals."

'These words "atheist", "heretic", words which no one can precisely define, threw doubts into some minds. It was asserted, however, that this Englishwoman was rich and that she had passed her life in travelling through every country in the world, because her family had thrown her off. Why had her family thrown her off? Because of her natural impiety?

'She was, in fact, one of those people of exalted principles, one of those opinionated puritans of whom England produces so many, one of those good and insupportable old women who haunt the tables d'hôte of every hotel in Europe, who spoil Italy, poison Switzerland, render the charming cities of the Mediterranean uninhabitable, carry everywhere their fantastic manias, their petrified vestal manners, their indescribable toilets and a certain odour of India rubber, which makes one believe that at night they slip themselves into a case of that material. When I meet one of these people in a hotel I act like birds which see a manikin in a field.

'This woman, however, appeared so singular that she did not displease me.

'Madame Lecacheur, hostile by instinct to everything that was not rustic, felt in her narrow soul a kind of hatred for the ecstatic extravagances of the old girl. She had found a phrase by which to describe her, I know not how, but a phrase assuredly contemptuous, which had sprung to her lips, invented, probably, by some confused and mysterious travail of soul. She said: "That woman is a demoniac." This phrase, as uttered by that austere and sentimental creature, seemed to me irresistibly comic. I myself never called her now anything else but "the demoniac", feeling a singular pleasure in pronouncing this word on seeing her.

'I would ask Mother Lecacheur: "Well, what is our demoniac about today?" To which my rustic friend would respond with an air of having been scandalised:

' "What do you think, sir? She has picked up a toad which has had its leg battered and carried it to her room and has put it in her washstand and dressed it up like a man. If that is not profanation I should like to know what is!"

'On another occasion, when walking along the Falaise, she had bought a large fish which had just been caught, simply to throw it back into the sea again. The sailor from whom she had bought it, though paid handsomely, was greatly provoked at this act – more exasperated, indeed, than if she had put her hand into his pocket and taken his money. For a whole month he could not speak of the circumstance without getting into a fury and denouncing it as an outrage. Oh yes! She was indeed a demoniac, this Miss Harriet, and Mother Lecacheur must have had an inspiration of genius in thus christening her.

'The stable-boy, who was called Sapeur because he had served in Africa in his youth, entertained other aversions. He said with a roguish air: "She is an old hag who has lived her days." If the poor woman had but known!

'Little kind-hearted Céleste did not wait upon her willingly, but I was never able to understand why. Probably her only reason was that she was a stranger, of another race, of a different tongue and of another religion. She was in good truth a demoniac!

'She passed her time wandering about the country, adoring and searching for God in nature. I found her one evening on her knees in a cluster of bushes. Having discovered something red through the leaves, I brushed aside the branches, and Miss Harriet at once rose to her feet, confused at having been found thus, looking at me with eyes as terrible as those of a wildcat surprised in open day.

'Sometimes when I was working among the rocks I would suddenly descry her on the banks of the Falaise, standing like a semaphore signal. She gazed passionately at the vast sea glittering in the sunlight and the boundless sky empurpled with fire. Sometimes I would distinguish her at the bottom of an alley, walking quickly with her elastic English step, and I would go towards her, attracted by I know not what, simply to see her illuminated visage, her dried-up features, which seemed to glow with an ineffable, inward and profound happiness.

'Often I would encounter her in the corner of a field, sitting on the grass under the shadow of an apple tree with her little Bible lying open on her knee, while she looked meditatively into the distance.

'I could no longer tear myself away from that quiet country neighbourhood, bound to it as I was by a thousand links of love for its soft and sweeping landscapes. At this farm I was out of the world, far removed from everything, but in close proximity to the soil – the good, healthy, beautiful green soil. And, I must avow it, there was something besides curiosity which retained me at the residence of Mother Lecacheur. I wished to become acquainted a little with this strange Miss Harriet and to learn what passes in the solitary souls of those wandering old English dames.'

II

'We became acquainted in a rather singular manner. I had just finished a study which appeared to me to display genius and power, as it must have, since it was sold for ten thousand francs fifteen years later. It was as simple, however, as that two and two make four, and had nothing to do with academic rules. The whole of the right side of my canvas represented a rock, an enormous rock covered with sea wrack, brown, yellow and red, across which the sun poured like a stream of oil. The light, without which one could see the stars concealed in the background, fell upon the stone and gilded it as if with fire. That was all. A first stupid attempt at dealing with light, with burning rays, with the sublime.

'On the left was the sea, not the blue sea, the slate-coloured sea, but a sea of jade, as greenish, milky and thick as the overcast sky.

'I was so pleased with my work that I danced from sheer delight as I carried it back to the inn. I wished that the whole world could have seen it at one and the same moment. I can remember that I showed it to a cow which was browsing by the wayside, exclaiming at the same time: "Look at that, my old beauty; you will not often see its like again."

'When I had reached the front of the house I immediately called out to Mother Lecacheur, shouting with all my might:

' "*Ohé! Ohé!* My mistress, come here and look at this."

'The rustic advanced and looked at my work with stupid eyes which distinguished nothing and did not even recognise whether the picture was the representation of an ox or a house.

'Miss Harriet came into the house and passed behind me just at the moment when, holding out my canvas at arm's length, I was exhibiting it to the female innkeeper. The "demoniac" could not help but see it, for I took care to exhibit the thing in such a way that it could not escape her notice. She stopped abruptly and stood motionless, stupefied. It was her rock which was depicted, the one which she usually climbed to dream away her time, undisturbed.

'She uttered a British "Oh", which was at once so accentuated and so flattering that I turned round to her, smiling, and said:

' "This is my latest work, mademoiselle."

'She murmured ecstatically, comically and tenderly:

' "Oh, monsieur, you must understand what it is to have a palpitation."

'I coloured up, of course, and was more excited by that compliment than if it had come from a queen. I was seduced, conquered, vanquished. I could have embraced her – upon my honour.

'I took my seat at the table beside her, as I had always done. For the first time she spoke, drawling out in a loud voice:

' "Oh! I love nature so much."

'I offered her some bread, some water, some wine. She now accepted these with the vacant smile of a mummy. I began to converse with her about the scenery.

'After the meal we rose from the table together and walked leisurely across the court; then, attracted by the fiery glow which the setting sun cast over the surface of the sea, I opened the outside gate which faced in the direction of the Falaise, and we walked on side by side, as satisfied as any two persons could be who have just learned to understand and penetrate each other's motives and feelings.

'It was a misty, relaxing evening, one of those enjoyable evenings which impart happiness to mind and body alike. All is joy; all is charm. The luscious and balmy air, loaded with the perfumes of herbs, with the perfumes of grass wrack, with the odour of the wild flowers, caresses the soul with a penetrating sweetness. We were going to the brink of the abyss which overlooked the vast sea and rolled past us at a distance of less than a hundred metres.

'We drank with open mouth and expanded chest that fresh breeze from the ocean which glides slowly over the skin, salted as it is by long contact with the waves.

'Wrapped up in her square shawl, inspired by the balmy air and with teeth firmly set, the Englishwoman gazed fixedly at the great sun ball as it descended towards the sea. Soon its rim touched the waters, just behind a ship which had appeared on the horizon, until by degrees it was swallowed up by the ocean. We watched it plunge, diminish and finally disappear.

'Miss Harriet contemplated with passionate regard the last glimmer of the flaming orb of day.

'She muttered: "Oh! Love – I love—" I saw a tear start in her eye. She continued: "I wish I were a little bird so that I could rise up into the firmament."

'She remained standing as I had often before seen her, perched on the river-bank, her face as red as her flaming shawl. I should have liked to sketch her in my album. It would have been an ecstatic caricature. I turned my face away from her so as to be able to laugh.

'I then spoke to her of painting, as I would have done to a fellow-artist, using the technical terms common among the devotees of the profession. She listened attentively to me, eagerly seeking to divine the sense of the obscure words, so as to penetrate my thoughts. From time to time she would exclaim: "Oh! I understand; I understand. This is very interesting." We returned home.

'The next day on seeing me she approached me eagerly, holding out her hand, and we became firm friends immediately.

'She was a brave creature with an elastic sort of a soul which became enthusiastic at a bound. She lacked equilibrium, like all women who are spinsters at the age of fifty. She seemed to be pickled in vinegary innocence, though her heart still retained something of youth and of girlish effervescence. She loved both nature and animals with a fervent ardour, a love like old wine, mellow through age, with a sensual love that she had never bestowed on men.

'One thing is certain: a mare roaming in a meadow with a foal at its side, a bird's nest full of young ones squeaking, with their open mouths and enormous heads, made her quiver with the most violent emotion.

'Poor solitary beings! Sad wanderers from table d'hôte to table d'hôte, poor beings, ridiculous and lamentable, I love you ever since I became acquainted with Miss Harriet!

'I soon discovered that she had something she would like to tell me but dared not, and I was amused at her timidity. When I started out in the morning with my box on my back she would accompany me as far as the end of the village, silent, but evidently struggling inwardly to find words with which to begin a conversation. Then she would leave me abruptly and, with jaunty step, walk away quickly.

'One day, however, she plucked up courage:

' "I would like to see how you paint pictures. Will you show me? I have been very curious."

'And she coloured up as though she had given utterance to words extremely audacious.

'I conducted her to the bottom of the Petit-Val, where I had commenced a large picture.

'She remained standing near me, following all my gestures with concentrated attention. Then suddenly, fearing, perhaps, that she was disturbing me, she said to me: "Thank you," and walked away.

'But in a short time she became more familiar and accompanied me every day, her countenance exhibiting visible pleasure. She carried her folding stool under her arm, would not consent to my carrying it, and she sat always by my side. She would remain there for hours, immovable and mute, following with her eye the point of my brush in its every movement. When I would obtain by a large splotch of colour spread on with a knife a striking and unexpected effect she would, in spite of herself, give vent to a half-suppressed "Oh!" of astonishment, of joy, of admiration. She had the most tender respect for my canvases, an almost religious respect for that human reproduction of a part of nature's work divine. My studies appeared to her to be pictures of sanctity, and sometimes she spoke to me of God with the idea of converting me.

'Oh! He was a queer good-natured being, this God of hers. He was a sort of village philosopher without any great resources and without great power, for she always figured him to herself as a being quivering over injustices committed under his eyes and helpless to prevent them.

'She was, however, on excellent terms with him, affecting even to be the confidante of his secrets and of his whims. She said:

' "God wills," or, "God does not will," just like a sergeant announcing to a recruit: "The colonel has commanded."

'At the bottom of her heart she deplored my ignorance of the intention of the Eternal, which she strove, nay, felt herself compelled, to impart to me.

'Almost every day I found in my pockets, in my hat when I lifted it from the ground, in my box of colours, in my polished shoes standing in the mornings in front of my door those little pious brochures which she, no doubt, received directly from Paradise.

'I treated her as one would an old friend, with unaffected cordiality. But I soon perceived that she had changed somewhat in her manner, but for a while I paid little attention to it.

'When I walked about, whether to the bottom of the valley or through some country lanes, I would see her suddenly appear, as though she were returning from a rapid walk. She would then sit down abruptly, out of breath, as though she had been running or overcome by some profound emotion. Her face would be red, that English red which is denied to the people of all other countries; then without any reason she would grow pale, become the colour of the ground and seem ready to faint away. Gradually, however, I would see her regain her ordinary colour, whereupon she would begin to speak.

'Then without warning she would break off in the middle of a sentence, spring up from her seat and march off so rapidly and so strongly that it would sometimes put me to my wits' end to try and discover whether I had done or said anything to displease or offend her.

'I finally came to the conclusion that this arose from her early habits and training, somewhat modified, no doubt, in honour of me, since the first days of our acquaintanceship.

'When she returned to the farm after walking for hours on the wind-beaten coast her long curled hair would be shaken out and hanging loose, as though it had broken away from its bearings. It was seldom that this gave her any concern, though sometimes she looked as though she had been dining *sans cérémonie*, her locks having become dishevelled by the breezes.

'She would then go up to her room in order to adjust what I called her glass lamps. When I would say to her with familiar gallantry which, however, always offended her:

' "You are as beautiful as a planet today, Miss Harriet," a little blood would immediately mount into her cheeks, the blood of a young maiden, the blood of sweet fifteen.

'Then she would become abruptly savage and cease coming to watch me paint. But I always thought:

' "This is only a fit of temper she is passing through."

'But it did not always pass away. When I spoke to her sometimes she would answer me, either with an air of affected indifference or in sullen anger, and she became by turns rude, impatient and nervous. For a time I never saw her except at meals, and we spoke but little. I concluded at length that I must have offended her in something, and accordingly I said to her one evening:

' "Miss Harriet, why is it that you do not act towards me as formerly? What have I done to displease you? You are causing me much pain!"

'She responded in an angry tone, in a manner altogether *sui generis*:

' "I am always the same with you as formerly. It is not true, not true," and she ran upstairs and shut herself in her room.

'At times she would look upon me with strange eyes. Since that time I have often said to myself that those condemned to death must look thus when informed that their last day has come. In her eye there lurked a species of folly, a folly at once mysterious and violent – even more, a fever, an exasperated desire, impatient, at once incapable of being realised and unrealisable!

'Nay, it seemed to me that there was also going on within her a combat in which her heart struggled against an unknown force that she wished to overcome – perhaps, even, something else. But what could I know? What could I know?'

III

'This was indeed a singular revelation.

'For some time I had started to work as soon as daylight appeared on a picture, the subject of which was as follows.

'A deep ravine, steep banks dominated by two declivities, lined with brambles and long rows of trees, hidden, drowned in milky vapour, clad in that misty robe which sometimes floats over valleys at break of day. At the extreme end of that thick and transparent fog you see coming, or rather already come, a human couple, a stripling and a maiden embraced, interlaced, she with head leaning on him, he inclined towards her, and lip to lip.

'A ray of the sun glistening through the branches has traversed the fog of dawn and illuminated it with a rosy reflection just behind the rustic lovers, whose vague shadows are reflected on it in clear silver. It was well done; yes indeed, well done.

'I was working on the declivity which led to the Val d'Étretat. This particular morning I had, by chance, the sort of floating vapour which was necessary for my purpose. Suddenly an object appeared in front of me, a kind of phantom; it was Miss Harriet. On seeing me she took to flight. But I called after her, saying: "Come here; come here, mademoiselle, I have a nice little picture for you."

'She came forward, though with seeming reluctance. I handed her my sketch. She said nothing but stood for a long time motionless, looking at it. Suddenly she burst into tears. She wept spasmodically, like men who have been struggling hard against shedding tears but who can do so no longer and abandon themselves to grief, though unwillingly. I got up, trembling, moved myself by the sight of a sorrow I did not comprehend, and I took her by the hand with a gesture of brusque affection, a true French impulse which impels one quicker than one thinks.

'She let her hands rest in mine for a few seconds, and I felt them quiver, as if her whole nervous system was twisting and turning. Then she withdrew her hands abruptly or, rather, tore them out of mine.

'I recognised that shiver as soon as I had felt it; I was deceived in nothing. Ah! The love shudder of a woman, whether she is fifteen or fifty years of age, whether she is one of the people or one of the *monde*, goes so straight to my heart that I never had any difficulty in understanding it!

'Her whole frail being trembled, vibrated, yielded. I knew it. She walked away before I had time to say a word, leaving me as surprised as if I had witnessed a miracle and as troubled as if I had committed a crime.

'I did not go in to breakfast. I took a walk on the banks of the Falaise, feeling that I could just as soon weep as laugh, looking on the adventure as both comic and deplorable and my position as ridiculous, compelled to believe that I had lost my head.

'I asked myself what I ought to do. I debated whether I ought not to take my leave of the place, and almost immediately my resolution was formed.

'Somewhat sad and perplexed, I wandered about until dinner-time and entered the farmhouse just when the soup had been served up.

'I sat down at the table, as usual. Miss Harriet was there, munching away solemnly without speaking to anyone, without even lifting her eyes. She wore, however, her usual expression, both of countenance and manner.

'I waited patiently till the meal had been finished. Then, turning towards the landlady, I said: "Madame Lecacheur, it will not be long now before I shall have to take my leave of you."

'The good woman, at once surprised and troubled, replied in a quivering voice: "My dear sir, what is it I have just heard you say? Are you going to leave us after I have become so much accustomed to you?"

'I looked at Miss Harriet from the corner of my eye. Her countenance did not change in the least but the underservant came towards me with eyes wide open. She was a fat girl of about eighteen years of age, rosy, fresh, strong as a horse, yet possessing a rare attribute in one in her position – she was very neat and clean. I had kissed her at odd times in out-of-the-way corners in the manner of a mountain guide, nothing more.

'The dinner being over, I went to smoke my pipe under the apple trees, walking up and down at my ease from one end of the court to the other. All the reflections which I had made during the day, the strange discovery of the morning, that grotesque and passionate attachment for me, the recollections which that revelation had suddenly called up, recollections at once charming and perplexing, perhaps, also, that look which the servant had cast on me at the announcement of my departure – all these things, mixed up and combined, put me now in an excited bodily state with the tickling sensation of kisses on my lips, and in my veins something which urged me on to commit some folly.

'Night having come on, casting its dark shadows under the trees, I descried Céleste, who had gone to shut the hen-coops at the other end of the enclosure. I darted towards her, running so noiselessly that she heard nothing, and as she got up from closing the small traps by which the chickens went in and out, I clasped her in my arms and rained on her coarse, fat face a shower of kisses. She made a struggle, laughing all the same, as she was accustomed to do in such circumstances. What made me suddenly loose my grip of her? Why did I at once experience a shock? What was it that I heard behind me?

'It was Miss Harriet who had come upon us, who had seen us and who stood in front of us, as motionless as a spectre. Then she disappeared in the darkness.

'I was ashamed, embarrassed, more annoyed at having been surprised by her than if she had caught me committing some criminal act.

'I slept badly that night; I was worried and haunted by sad thoughts. I seemed to hear loud weeping, but in this I was no doubt deceived. Moreover, I thought several times that I heard someone walking up and down in the house and that someone opened my door from the outside.

'Towards morning I was overcome by fatigue, and sleep seized on me. I got up late and did not go downstairs until breakfast-time, being still in a bewildered state, not knowing what kind of face to put on.

'No one had seen Miss Harriet. We waited for her at table, but she did not appear. At length Mother Lecacheur went to her room. The Englishwoman had gone out. She must have set out at break of day, as she was wont to do, in order to see the sunrise.

'Nobody seemed astonished at this, and we began to eat in silence.

'The weather was hot, very hot, one of those still, sultry days when not a leaf stirs. The table had been placed out-of-doors under an apple tree, and from time to time Sapeur had gone to the cellar to draw a jug of cider, everybody was so thirsty. Céleste brought the dishes from the kitchen, a ragout of mutton with potatoes, a cold rabbit and a salad. Afterwards she placed before us a dish of strawberries, the first of the season.

'As I wanted to wash and freshen these, I begged the servant to go and bring a pitcher of cold water.

'In about five minutes she returned, declaring that the well was dry. She had lowered the pitcher to the full extent of the cord and had touched the bottom, but on drawing the pitcher up again it was empty. Mother Lecacheur, anxious to examine the thing for herself, went and looked down the hole. She returned announcing that one could see clearly something in the well, something altogether unusual. But this, no doubt, was bundles of straw which, out of spite, had been cast down it by a neighbour.

'I wished also to look down the well, hoping to clear up the mystery, and perched myself close to its brink. I perceived indistinctly a white object. What could it be? I then conceived the idea of lowering a lantern at the end of a cord. When I did so the yellow flame danced on the layers of stone and gradually became clearer. All four of us were leaning over the opening, Sapeur and Céleste having now joined us. The lantern rested on a black-and-white, indistinct mass, singular, incomprehensible. Sapeur exclaimed:

' "It is a horse. I see the hoofs. It must have escaped from the meadow during the night and fallen in headlong."

'But suddenly a cold shiver attacked my spine; I first recognised a foot, then a clothed limb; the body was entire, but the other limb had disappeared under the water.

'I groaned and trembled so violently that the light of the lamp danced hither and thither over the object, discovering a slipper.

"It is a woman! Who – who – can it be? It is Miss Harriet."

'Sapeur alone did not manifest horror. He had witnessed many such scenes in Africa.

'Mother Lecacheur and Céleste began to scream and to shriek and ran away.

'But it was necessary to recover the corpse of the dead. I attached the boy securely by the loins to the end of the pulley rope; then I lowered him slowly and watched him disappear in the darkness. In the one hand he had a lantern and held on to the rope with the other. Soon I recognised his voice, which seemed to come from the centre of the earth, crying:

' "Stop."

'I then saw him fish something out of the water. It was the other limb. He bound the two feet together and shouted anew:

' "Haul up."

'I started to wind him up, but I felt my arms strain, my muscles twitch, and was in terror lest I should let the boy fall to the bottom. When his head appeared over the brink I asked:

' "What is it?" as though I only expected that he would tell me what he had discovered at the bottom.

'We both got on to the stone slab at the edge of the well and, face to face, hoisted the body.

'Mother Lecacheur and Céleste watched us from a distance, concealed behind the wall of the house. When they saw issuing from the well the black slippers and white stockings of the drowned person they disappeared.

'Sapeur seized the ankles of the poor, chaste woman, and we drew it up, inclined, as it was, in the most immodest posture. The head was in a shocking state, bruised and black, and the long grey hair, hanging down, was tangled and disordered.

' "In the name of all that is holy, how lean she is!" exclaimed Sapeur in a contemptuous tone.

'We carried her into the room, and as the women did not put in an appearance, I, with the assistance of the lad, dressed the corpse for burial.

'I washed her disfigured face. By the touch of my hand an eye was slightly opened: it seemed to scan me with that pale stare, with that cold, that terrible look which corpses have, a look which seems to come from the beyond. I plaited up, as well as I could, her dishevelled hair, and I adjusted on her forehead a novel and singularly formed lock. Then I took off her dripping-wet garments, baring, not without a feeling of shame, as though I had been guilty of some profanation, her shoulders and her chest and her long arms, slim as the twigs of branches.

'I next went to fetch some flowers, corn poppies, bluebottles, marguerites and fresh and perfumed herbs, with which to strew her funeral couch.

'Being the only person near her, it was necessary for me to perform the usual ceremonies. In a letter found in her pocket, written at the last moment, she asked that her body be buried in the village in which she had passed the last days of her life. A frightful thought then oppressed my heart. Was it not on my account that she wished to be laid at rest in this place?

'Towards the evening all the female gossips of the locality came to view the remains of the deceased, but I would not allow a single person to enter; I wanted to be alone, and I watched by the corpse the whole night.

'By the flickering light of the candles I looked at the body of this miserable woman, wholly unknown, who had died so lamentably and so far away from home. Had she left no friends, no relatives behind her? What had her infancy been? What had been her life? When had she come thither all alone, a wanderer, like a dog driven from home? What secrets of suffering and of despair were sealed up in that disagreeable body, in that spent and withered body, that impenetrable hiding-place of a mystery which had driven her far away from affection and from love?

'How many unhappy beings there are! I felt that upon that human creature weighed the eternal injustice of implacable nature! Life was over with her without her ever having experienced, perhaps, that which sustains the most miserable of us all – to wit, the hope of being once loved! Otherwise why should she thus have concealed herself, have fled from the face of others? Why did she love everything so tenderly and so passionately, everything living that was not a man?

'I recognised also that she believed in a God and that she hoped for compensation from him for the miseries she had endured. She had now begun to decompose and to become, in turn, a plant. She who had blossomed in the sun was now to be eaten up by the cattle, carried away in herbs and in the flesh of beasts, again to become human flesh. But that which is called the soul had been extinguished at the bottom of the dark well. She suffered no longer. She had changed her life for that of others yet to be born.

'Hours passed away in this silent and sinister communion with the dead. A pale light at length announced the dawn of a new day, and a bright ray glistened on the bed, shedding a dash of fire on the bedclothes and on her hands. This was the hour she had so much loved, when the waking birds began to sing in the trees.

'I opened the window to its fullest extent; I drew back the curtains so that the whole heavens might look in upon us. Then, bending towards the glassy corpse, I took in my hands the mutilated head and slowly, without terror or disgust, imprinted a long, long kiss upon those lips which had never before received the salute of love.'

Léon Chenal remained silent. The women wept. We heard on the box-seat Count d'Etraille blow his nose from time to time. The coachman alone had gone to sleep. The horses, which felt no longer the sting of the whip, had slackened their pace and dragged softly along. And the four-in-hand, hardly moving at all, became suddenly torpid, as if laden with sorrow.

Edmond Haraucourt

Though Edmond Haraucourt (1856–1941) lived long into the twentieth century, he was primarily a poet of the aftermath of Parnassianism,
a movement which aimed to overcome the excesses of Romanticism in
favour of a more scientific and disciplined approach to verse. In addition
to the collections of poetry *L'Âme nue* (1885) and *L'Espoir du monde*
(1890), he also wrote a *mystère* entitled *La Passion* (1890).

The Work of a Lifetime

NO ONE EVER THOUGHT OF DENYING THE MILLIONAIRE Goldenstock's enlightened taste in art: not only was he admitted to be, like so many others, a passionate collector and a connoisseur of discernment, but he had in addition that sort of innate, intuitive science, superior to all acquired knowledge, which amounts to an instinctive appreciation of the beautiful. He had the same nose for a masterpiece that a hound has for the fox, and his quarry were men of undiscovered talent. To gain access to his gallery was the first step to fame; so it came about that he acquired the most remarkable works of the younger generation at a low price. But none dreamed of complaining because they had sold him their best canvas for next to nothing; for it was more than a stroke of luck to sell Goldenstock anything – it meant your fortune was made; the approbation of this man who would only take what was excellent and who never made a mistake, had a better market value than a whole collection of medals, and rated an artist like stock on the Exchange; his choice was a criterion of infallible success, and the dealers in London, Berlin, New York, Chicago, Paris, and Vienna kept an eye on Goldenstock's elect, with the intention of adopting them in their turn.

He was, moreover, generous at times, and when he wished to get possession of a work, was ready to give a good price, and a very good one if necessary; he even paid out the money gladly. What is more, he had nothing to do with dealers, as he never sold what he purchased, but kept everything; every picture that entered his gallery remained there. His ambition was to organise a museum of twentieth-century art in his house, to assemble there all the glory of an epoch, and to leave behind him this monument of his eclecticism and his wealth. He would say 'my works' in speaking of his collection, and you never could tell if the words were a mark of modesty or of vanity on his lips.

He appeared less proud of the accumulation of his enormous

fortune, but it is permissible to assume that this attitude was in no way sincere and that, if he loved art as a luxury, he worshipped nothing but gold as a source of power.

He had made millions in the tinned foods business, and his brand was the most reputed in the world; from the Sahara to the two Poles, his name was read on his tins, and in these days of frenzied exploration, of caravans, missions, and colonies, he could well boast that he fed the universe. He did boast of it, as a matter of fact, with a big, sonorous laugh that made him seem good-natured, though he was in no way a good-natured man.

He was said to be underhand, but he did his best to appear, on the contrary, brutally outspoken. Hard, clear-headed, curt in business, pitiless, he negotiated, gave his signature, received and made payments, and apart from painting, cared for nothing nor for anyone. Because of his conserves and his museum, he was nicknamed the Conservator. He had, in appearance at any rate, the stolid placidity of that office. He admitted only three things in this world – his own interests, his picture-gallery, and the law, that is his own rights.

Nobody knew if he had ever been shaken by any emotion, either pity or grief, or even joy. He received instalments of happiness or bereavement without blenching, and entered them on his current account. In the same way, he showed no compassion for the sufferings of others, no forbearance for weakness.

His only son died at the age of ten.

'It can't be helped. It's in the course of nature.'

One of his most devoted agents, the help and companion of his early struggles, a true friend, was unwise enough, in a moment of aberration and great need, to take a sum of money from the cash-box, meaning to refund it at the end of the month. Goldenstock had him arrested, sentenced, and ruined his family.

'It can't be helped. It's the law.'

His young wife, who was said to be unhappy, and was twenty years younger than he was, left him, got a divorce, and married again.

'It can't be helped. Women are like that.'

She married a painter who was already famous and whom she had met at Goldenstock's.

'It can't be helped. Such is fame.'

In this circumstance, however, people admired the Conservator's behaviour, and asked each other in amazement if they ought not to admit that he had a noble spirit. He did indeed show uncommon stoicism, and proved without doubt that he ranked Art above everything, even personal enmity.

Men on the Exchange were astounded at his forbearance, for they knew he was tenacious in his hatred, and more than once he had proved it; they knew Goldenstock always succeeded in getting revenge for any wrong done him or intended, and that he even took his revenge with ostentation, terribly, so as to discourage his aggressors.

'It can't be helped. It's the struggle for life.'

But he took no revenge for his wife's desertion. Perhaps he did not care. People supposed it was so, or at any rate that Goldenstock intended it to appear so. Instead of disparaging the artist, he affected to retain all his admiration for him.

'It can't be helped. It's the man.'

Forgetting the rival and remembering only the painter, he continued to collect the young master's work, in spite of the increased expense involved in buying it through dealers.

Then time passed, time which brings oblivion in its wake.

The wife died, and the businessman used this event to become reconciled to the artist: an excellent arrangement that gave him the noble part to play, and at the same time suppressed the necessity of dealers between the producer and buyer! Goldenstock gained doubly by it.

It was a solemn reconciliation, an absolution of the past, the renunciation of passions in the presence of the majesty of death. They shook hands loyally in the presence of witnesses. The scene was not without dignity and simplicity; the artist was touched . . . He had loved his wife dearly, and, in the hour of grief, her first husband seemed only a living memory of her: he found consolation for his own bereavement in the friendship of this other widower, and in his loneliness he sought refuge with him. At first his liking for Goldenstock was inspired by love for his wife, then by gratitude, and last of all by habit.

Yet these two men seemed to have nothing in common save the memory of the dead woman.

Clément Gonthaud had a noble character, full of enthusiasm and idealism, incapable of mercenary or sordid motives, silent and probably shy. Being a poet as well as a painter, his mastery of the brush and the subtlety of his eye were enhanced by the intensity of his feelings. This revealed itself in his pictures, gave them life; more than in his skilful composition and his admirable palette, the beauty of his works lay in the indefinable emotion they expressed; in addition to what the eye could see, there was in them something that could not be seen, but only felt, as if the painter had mingled love and sadness in his impasto.

This poetry became more intense in the pictures he composed after his wife's death, and all envious rivals came to do him homage. Gonthaud was truly the undisputed master: in the work of his bereavement he synthesised the restless spirit of the age, all the *morbidezza* of the twentieth century, and his panegyrists could say in all justice that 'such a pure monument of beauty would hold its place in the history of Art'.

Goldenstock had got possession of this genius.

Except for a single picture, sold in America during their rupture, and a second-rate painting acquired in earlier days by the State, the financier possessed all his work: he had consecrated a special room to Gonthaud in his gallery, known in the two hemispheres as the 'Salle Gonthaud'.

'I want all your work, my friend,' he would say to the painter, 'the work of your lifetime! I think I have given sufficient proof of my admiration for your genius, haven't I? You will recompense me, I hope, by reserving all your pictures for me. We will never bargain, you have only to name your price, Gonthaud, and you shall have it, provided you let me have everything.'

Goldenstock knew he was running no great risk in talking thus, and that Gonthaud was not the man to trade upon it. Nevertheless, being prudent by nature, he added: 'And is it not a wonderful advantage for a great artist to have his life's work collected so as to form a unity, expressing the whole of his personality? You belong to this country, to which I intend to bequeath this treasure on my death.'

Yet there remained an empty place in full evidence in the Salle Gonthaud, above the great sixteenth-century chimney-piece.

In the early days of his marriage, the painter had sold in America the only picture he had produced during those happy months – rather than a portrait of his young wife, the *Transfiguration* was a love-song, a hymn of joy, and the title alone sufficed to indicate the state of mind that inspired both artist and model. Buller-Smith, the Iron King of Chicago, had purchased this masterpiece for the sum of six or eight thousand dollars: doubtless he would continue to refuse to relinquish it; but Goldenstock did not lose hope. He offered twenty thousand, thirty thousand dollars, without success. Gonthaud wanted to give his friend a remarkable canvas he had just completed to fill the empty place, but the merchant refused this present.

'No, no, my dear Gonthaud! It is your fault the place is empty, if you will pardon my saying so; it must remain empty. If you please, we shall call this empty place – the reproach.'

Gonthaud bent his head; the millionaire laid his hand on his shoulder and resumed:

'You quite understand, don't you, that I am grateful for your offer, but that I cannot accept this present? It would look as if you were paying me, and we should be quits, shouldn't we? No, no. However great may be the value of your works, such payment would not suffice, my friend.'

He introduced so much bitterness into the tone of those insulting words, that Gonthaud was offended, and raising his head he stared at the man who was addressing him: Goldenstock's eyes were clouded and his lips pinched. But he quickly regained his self-possession, and added with his big, friendly laugh:

'Don't let us despair, my dear Gonthaud, and let us be patient. I'll get this masterpiece back from America! It will come back, I mean it to. Since it has travelled across the water, it must travel back again. I'll pay any price, by Jove!'

He spoke the truth. Two years later, the empty place was filled: the Iron King had yielded to the offers of the King of Conserves.

'There! You've cost me a million, my dear Gonthaud. Your lawful wedlock has been an expensive item for me, hasn't it? But no matter; I am giving the price, and I have the means . . . Come, now . . . Don't knit your noble brow. What I said was not intended to hurt you. Let's admit that for once I've been wanting in delicacy and generosity. Each of us in his turn. It can't be helped! It's in our blood. I spoke in a moment of anger; I won't do it again, and I give my word that in the future you will hear only one other allusion from me, the last . . . Don't question me; I have my little secret; I am keeping it . . . yes, keeping it.'

Then, wishing to efface the impression made by these enigmatic words, he continued in ingratiating tones:

'You have no idea how much pleasure it gives me to have got possession of Buller-Smith's picture at last! All your work! I've all Gonthaud's work now, his life's work!'

He rubbed his hands together and his face flushed.

'I've done a thing no other man has ever done! Oh, if Rubens, Rembrandt, and Velázquez had had the good fortune to meet a Goldenstock!

At bottom, you know, my dear friend, I am proud of what I have done. I have linked my fame to yours, you famous man! My name will live with yours in immortal glory, and poets will celebrate the story of the great painter and the wealthy merchant.'

For another three years Gonthaud let Goldenstock have all his canvases and was paid generously. But soon the artist began to produce very little: his strength was failing him at last. His soul had consumed his body, and the life he had put into his paintings had gradually abandoned him.

He was ill for two years more, idle and depressed, spending his time in watering-places, in the mountains, Egypt, Provence; he went from place to place, emaciated, round-shouldered, thin-necked, wrapped in a shawl, and with his hollow eyes he gazed lingeringly on the beauty of the world.

Goldenstock had generously placed a cheque-book at his disposal, so that he should want for nothing.

But, before he died, Gonthaud longed above all things to see his work once more. The merchant was waiting for him at the station, and took him to his house that he might be nursed more carefully, and die among his pictures, surrounded by himself. His ingenious kindness even went to the length of having the dying man's bed put in the Salle Gonthaud, opposite the *Transfiguration*, which had been taken down from the wall so that a fire might be lighted in the tall Renaissance chimney.

At the end of a week the doctor announced that his patient could not live more than twenty-four hours.

Goldenstock sent everyone away. With his own hands he helped Gonthaud to rise.

Together they went round the spacious room: Gonthaud leaned on his benefactor's arm. They stood for a long time in front of the *Transfiguration*: the image of the dead woman's face smiled on her painter from the other world and called him to her. The millionaire shook his head. The sick man went back to his couch.

'I can see', he said, 'it is good . . . On the point of death one can judge things from afar, without vanity or prejudice. I am sure now that it is good. I am leaving something behind me. I can die now.'

With his withered hand he clutched Goldenstock's wrist, and murmured: 'Thank you.'

But the other protested:

'Don't, for Heaven's sake, thank me! I don't want to be thanked! You've no reason to thank me! What Goldenstock does, he does for his own ends. It can't be helped! It's for my own pleasure.'

Standing in the middle of the room, he glanced round the walls.

'All Clément Gonthaud's work! The work of a lifetime!'

He was laughing.

He helped the painter into bed, and with his powerful hand he thrust another log of oak on to the fire.

'You see, I'm taking care of you, my dear Gonthaud.'

The artist, already struggling for breath, answered: 'You are kind and good—'

The Conserve King burst out laughing. Then the poor man of genius, lying flat, stretched himself feebly; on the pillow his face looked yellow above the white sheets which he held against his shoulders with his two clasped hands; only the tips of his fingers were visible.

He said, 'I shall never get up again.'

Goldenstock sat down near the head of the bed.

'No, great man, you will never get up again! Never again will you paint a masterpiece, never again will you steal a man's wife, and never again will you indulge in the luxury of humiliating those who are stronger than you! No, great man! . . . Don't answer; you would tire yourself . . .'

Again he burst into peals of violent laughter, filling the empty room. Then he rose.

Gonthaud was disturbed, trying to understand. His feet could be seen moving at the bottom of the bed. Goldenstock went towards the fireplace, and crouched down to poke the fire.

'I promised never again to refer to that unhappy incident, save once only: I think the time has come, don't you?'

Gonthaud did not stir. Goldenstock returned to his bedside.

'You remember, Gonthaud, that I have a secret to tell you. I promised to, and I keep my promises . . . You seem very disturbed and you can hardly breathe. Calm yourself. I will wait a moment: confound it all, you've still at least an hour to live.'

He kept a watchful eye on the dying man. After a silence, he resumed.

'There . . . you're feeling better now, aren't you? . . . You were a man of genius, but a man of dreams too, you see, and so you did not realise the power of gold. You will understand it now, but rather too late in the day . . . I possess all your work, all the immortal work of Clément Gonthaud, don't I? Yes, I know, there is one valueless picture I have not got, a second-rate canvas acquired by the State, and the future would treat you unjustly if it judged you by that. Yes, indeed, my poor friend, if that was all you left behind you, you would cut a sorry figure in posterity!'

Goldenstock laughed longer than before, then paused to take breath and said: 'Now, listen, Gonthaud, I'm going to burn all the others.'

The dying man lay staring straight in front of him, motionless and haggard, almost lifeless already. The oak log in the Renaissance fire-place was flaming high. Goldenstock drew a gold penknife from his pocket.

'You took my wife from me: you got what you wanted. I am taking your work from you! . . . What do you say to that, my fine fellow? All your work. Pshaw! A few flames, a little smoke, a nasty smell, and that is all you will leave behind you: the servants will open the windows to air the room, and you will vanish from the world in a draught of fresh air.'

Clément Gonthaud did not stir.

Goldenstock drew nearer, fearing that he was dead and unable to hear him.

The dying man was still breathing. Goldenstock bent down and spoke right in his face.

'Do not imagine I am boasting. A thing is no sooner said than done with me, as everyone knows on the market. I shall do as I have said, and this very evening, my boy. I've bought them! My works of art are my own, to do as I like with. I've bought them! . . . What will people say? They'll say that Goldenstock takes revenge, and it will be a useful les-son: it will not be sheer loss to me. And what a first-rate advertisement, my dear fellow!'

He left the bed and went towards the easel.

'It can't be helped! I've the right to do it.'

Gonthaud turned his head very slowly, and saw the man standing in front of his masterpiece, brandishing his penknife with its fine, glisten-ing blade; he saw the steel pierce a corner of the canvas and slide noisily right round the frame.

The millionaire shook the soft, flat thing, flapping like a wet apron, in his face.

'Cost me a million!' he cried, 'a million thrown into the fire! But a first-rate advertisement!'

He threw the thing into the fire. The painter's face, white as a statue, was petrified, his eyes were dim.

Goldenstock went to the bedside, bent down to listen: he fancied he could feel an imperceptible breath struggling at the great painter's lips. Perhaps his eyes could still see?

Quickly he cut another canvas, all the canvases, and threw them on the fire. The work lasted a long time.

But before he had done, Clément Gonthaud was dead.

Marcel Schwob

Marcel Schwob (1867–1905), born of an old family of Jewish intellectuals, has been the source of recent critical interest. Works such as *Le Roi au masque d'or* (1892) and *Vies imaginaires* (1896) have a conspicuously modern interest in those questions of sexuality, myth and time which are so vital to the twentieth-century mindset. An erudite essayist and critic, who wrote on George Meredith and Robert Louis Stevenson, amongst others, in his texts Schwob shows an impressively broad range of intellectual concerns, including mystical and idealist philosophy, Latin, Greek, Anglo-Saxon and medieval French literature, and slang. His interest in English fiction led him to translate *Moll Flanders* into French.

The Veiled Man

OF THE COMBINATION OF CIRCUMSTANCES THAT HAVE BEEN my undoing I can say nothing; certain accidents of human life are as artistically contrived by chance or by the laws of nature as by the most demoniacal invention: one cries out in wonder before them as before a painting by an impressionist who has captured a singular and momentary truth. But if my head should fall, I trust that this narrative will survive me and that in the history of human lives it might be a true oddity, as it were a lurid opening on to the unknown.

When I entered that terrible carriage, two persons were occupying it. One facing away from me, enveloped in a travelling-rug, was fast asleep. His covering was flecked with spots on a yellowish ground, like a leopard-skin. Many such are sold in travel-goods departments: but I can say at once that, touching it later, I realised that this was really the skin of a wild animal. Likewise the sleeper's bonnet, when I observed it with the especially acute power of vision that came to me, seemed to me to be of an infinitely fine white felt. The other traveller, who had a pleasant face, appeared just into his thirties. Beyond that he had the insignificant appearance of a man who readily sleeps on railway trains.

The sleeper did not show his ticket, nor did he turn his face while I was installing myself opposite him. And once I was seated on the bench I ceased to observe my fellow-travellers so as to reflect upon the various matters that preoccupied me.

The movement of the train did not interrupt my thoughts, but it directed their current in a curious fashion. The song of the axle and the wheels, the grip of the wheels on the rails, the crossings of the points with the juddering that periodically shakes badly-suspended carriages transformed itself into a mental refrain. It was a species of vague thought that broke in regular intervals upon my other ideas. After a quarter of an hour the reiteration bordered on the obsessive. By a violent effort of will I rid myself of it; but the vague mental refrain took on the form of a musical notation which I anticipated. Each jolt was not a note, but it was the echo in unison of a note conceived in advance, at once feared and desired; to such an extent that these eternally similar shocks ran the most extended gamut of notes corresponding, in truth, in its superimposed octaves beyond the compass of any instrument, to the layers of suppositions that are often piled up by the mind in travail.

In the end, to break the spell, I took up a newspaper. But, once I had read them, entire lines detached themselves from the columns and, with a sort of plaintive and uniform sound, reintroduced themselves to my view at intervals I anticipated but could not modify. I leaned back against the seat, experiencing a singular sensation of disquiet and of emptiness in my head.

It was then that I observed the first phenomenon that plunged me into the realms of the uncanny. The traveller on the far side of the carriage, having raised his bench and adjusted his pillow, stretched out and closed his eyes. Almost at the same moment the sleeper facing me silently rose and drew about the globe of the lamp the little spring-loaded blue shade. In this operation I should have been able to see his face – *and I did not see it*. I caught a glimpse of a confused blur, the colour of a human face, but of which I could not distinguish the least feature. The action had been accomplished with a silent rapidity that stupefied me. I had not had the time to take in the sight of the sleeper standing erect when, already, I saw only the white crown of his bonnet above the speckled cover. It was a trifling matter, but it disturbed me. How had the sleeper so quickly been able to grasp that the other had closed his eyes? He had turned his face in my direction and I had not seen it; the rapidity and the mysterious quality of his motion were inexpressible.

A blue obscurity now hung between the upholstered benches, now and then barely broken by the veil of yellow light projected from without by an oil-lamp.

The circle of thoughts that haunted me closed in as the train's pulsations increased in the darkness. The uneasy quality of the motion had fixed it; and, slowly modified in time to the monotonous singsong of the rails, stories of murderers on trains welled up out of the gloom. A cruel fear contracted my heart, all the more cruel since it was vague, and incertitude augments terror. Visible, palpable, I sensed the image of Jud starting up – a thin face with cavernous eyes, prominent cheek-bones and a filthy goatee-beard – the face of Jud the murderer, who killed at night in first-class carriages and who, after his escape, had never been recaptured. The darkness aided me in painting with the features of Jud the confused blur I had seen in the lamplight, to imagine beneath the speckled covers a man crouched, ready to spring.

I was violently tempted to hurl myself to the far end of the carriage, to shake the sleeping traveller, to cry aloud to him my peril. A sense of propriety held me back. Could I explain my disquiet? How could I respond to that well-intentioned man's astonished glance? He was sleeping comfortably, well wrapped up, his head on the pillow, his gloved hands crossed on his chest: by what right was I to awaken him because another traveller had shaded the lamp? Was there not already a symptom of madness in my mind, which persisted in linking the man's action with the consciousness he must have had of the other's sleep? Were these two not different events, belonging to different series, linked by a simple coincidence? But at this point my fear stood pat and became insistent; so much so that, in the train's rhythmical silence, I sensed my temples throbbing; a tumult in my blood, which contrasted painfully with my outward calm, set things swirling round me, and events vague and still to come, but with the conjectured precision of things that are about to happen, marched through my brain in endless procession.

And suddenly a profound calm established itself within me. I felt the tension of my muscles relax in a complete abandon. The swirling of my thoughts was stilled. I experienced the inward slackening that precedes sleep and swooning and, with eyes open, I was in fact swooning. Yes: with eyes open and endowed with an infinite power of which they availed themselves without effort. And this relaxation was so complete that I was incapable of governing my senses, or of taking a decision, or even of representing to myself any thought of action of my own devising. Those superhuman eyes were of themselves directed upon the mysterious-faced man and, whilst seeing through obstacles, at the same time saw them. Thus I *knew* that I was looking through a leopard-skin, and through a flesh-coloured silken mask, a *crépon* covering a swarthy face. And my eyes immediately met with other eyes, eyes that shone with an insupportable blackness: I saw a man dressed in yellow, with buttons seemingly of silver, enveloped in a brown overcoat; I knew he was covered in a leopard-skin, but I saw him. I also heard (for my hearing had just taken on an extreme acuity) his breathing, urgent and panting, like that of a man making a considerable effort. But it must have been an inward effort, for the man was moving neither arms nor legs: it was indeed such – for his will annihilated my own.

One last resistance manifested itself in my being. I was aware of a struggle in which, in reality, I played no part, a struggle carried on by that deep-seated egoism of which one is never aware and which governs one's self. Then ideas came drifting into my mind – ideas that were not mine, that I had not created, in which I recognised nothing in common with my substance, perfidious and attractive as the black waters over which one leans.

One of these was murder. But I no longer conceived it as an act filled with dread, accomplished by Jud, as the issue of a nameless terror. With a certain glimmer of curiosity and an infinite prostration of everything that had ever been my will, I experienced it as possible.

Then the veiled man rose and, regarding me fixedly through his flesh-coloured veil, went with gliding steps towards the sleeping traveller. With one hand he seized him by the nape of the neck, firmly; and at the same time he stuffed a silken pad into his mouth. I felt no distress, nor had I any desire to cry out. But I was there, and dull-eyed I watched. The man drew a narrow, sharp-pointed Turkestan knife, the hollow-ground blade of which had a central channel, and he cut the traveller's throat as one would bleed a sheep. The blood spurted up to the luggage-rack. Drawing it sharply towards him, he had thrust in his knife at the right side. The throat gaped open. He uncovered the lamp and I saw the red gash. Then he emptied the man's pockets and dabbled his hands in the bloody pool. Next he came towards me and, without revulsion, I endured his smearing my inert fingers and my face, of which not a wrinkle twitched.

The veiled man rolled up his travelling-rug and threw on his over-coat; whilst I remained next to the *murdered* traveller. The terrible word made no impression upon me – until suddenly I found myself desolate of support, without the will to make up for the lack of my own, empty of ideas, befuddled. And coming to myself by degrees, gummy-eyed, phlegmy-mouthed, my neck stiff, as if held in a leaden grip, I found I was alone, in the early grey dawn, with a corpse that tossed about like a bundle. The train was threading its way through an intensely mono-tonous stretch of open country dotted with clumps of trees – and when, after a long-drawn-out whistle that echoed on the clear morning air, it stopped, I blundered stupidly to the carriage door, my face striped with clotted blood.

Marcel Proust

It may seem ironic for a collection of short stories to include an example of the work of Marcel Proust (1871–1922), a writer whose reputation rests on his 3,000-page novel, *A la recherche du temps perdu* (1913–27). This epic combines the odyssey of the narrator's own life with the secret history of Belle Époque society and a subtle account of moments of grand historical crisis such as the Dreyfus Affair. Its ending, in which the narrator explains why he has chosen to write his own life story, is an example of the way in which modernist literature not only designates the outside world but also looks inwards at its own writing procedures. Though the first volume was published in 1913, it was only by locking himself away in a cork-lined room during World War I that the sickly Proust could shut himself off from society and find the right tone and sensibility to perfect his vast enterprise. However, his work is not limited to his *magnum opus*, and includes *Les Plaisirs et les jours* (1896), a collection of short stories and poems, prefaced by Anatole France. Often caricatured as a dandyish dilettante, Proust was also neurotic, a condition complicated by his efforts to conceal his homosexual tendencies.

A Young Girl's Confession

The cravings of the senses drag us hither and thither, but when the hour is spent, what do you bring back with you? Remorse of conscience and dissipation of the spirit. You go out in joy and in sadness you return, and the pleasures of the evening sadden the morning. Thus the joys of the senses first flatter us, but in the end they wound and kill.

Imitation of Jesus Christ, *Book I, c. xviii*

Through the forgetfulness we seek from counterfeit delights,
Amidst our frenzies comes, more virginal and sweet,
The melancholy scent of lilacs.

HENRI DE REGNIER

AT LAST DELIVERANCE IS ALMOST HERE. OF COURSE I WAS clumsy. I didn't know how to shoot; I almost missed myself. Of course it would have been better to have died at once, but after all, they were not able to extract the bullet and then heart complications set in.

It cannot be much longer now. And yet – eight days more! It can last another eight days! during which I shall be able to do nothing but reconstruct the horrible chain of events. If I were not so weak, if I had sufficient strength of will to get up, to leave here, I would go to Les Oublis to die, in the park where all my summers were spent until I was fifteen. No other place is so full of my mother, so completely has her presence and even more her absence, impregnated it with her being. For to one who loves, is not absence the most effective, the most tenacious, the most indestructible, the most faithful of presences?

My mother would take me to Les Oublis towards the end of April, would leave again after two days, spend two more days there in the middle of May, then, in the last week of June would come to take me away. These visits, so short, were the sweetest and the most cruel thing to me. During these two days she would be lavish of her tenderness which habitually, in order to strengthen me and mitigate my excessive susceptibility, she would avariciously withhold. On the two evenings she spent at Les Oublis, she would come to kiss me good night after I was in bed, an old custom which she had abandoned because it caused me too much pleasure and too much pain, because due to my calling her back to say good night again and again I could never go to sleep, not daring finally to call her any more, but feeling more than ever the passionate need, always inventing new excuses, my burning pillow to be turned, my icy feet which her hands alone could warm. Such sweet moments gained an added sweetness from my feeling that during them my mother was her true self and that her habitual reserve must cost her dearly. The day she left, day of despair, when I would cling to her skirts until she got on the train, imploring her to take me with her to Paris, I readily discerned the truth through her dissimulation, sensed her sadness through her gay and irritated reproaches at my 'stupid, ridiculous' sadness which she wanted to teach me to dominate but which she shared. I still feel the emotion of a certain day of departure (the identical emotion, intact, unaltered in its painful return today) on which I made the sweet discovery of her tenderness, so similar and so superior to my own. Like all discoveries, I had already sensed, divined it, but it seemed so often in practice to be contradicted! My happiest recollections are of those times when she would be called back to Les Oublis when I was ill. Not only was it an extra visit on which I had not counted but, above all, during that time she was all overflowing gentleness and tenderness, undisguised and unrestrained. Even at that time, before they had acquired an added poignancy from the thought that one day they would no longer be there for me, that gentleness and tenderness meant so much to me that the charm of convalescence was always unbearably sad: the day was approaching when I should be sufficiently well again for my mother to leave me, and until then not sufficiently ill to keep her any longer from returning to her former severity and unmitigated justice.

One day my uncles with whom I stayed at Les Oublis had kept from me the news that my mother was coming that day, fearing that in the joyful anguish of that expectation, I should neglect a young cousin who had come to visit me for a few hours. That deception was perhaps the first of the circumstances which, independent of my own volition, were the accomplices of all those evil tendencies which, like other children of my age, and no more than they, I bore within me. This young cousin, a boy of fifteen – I was then fourteen – was already very depraved, and told me things which instantly made me shudder with remorse and voluptuousness. Listening to him, letting his hands fondle mine, I tasted a joy poisoned at its very source; soon I found strength enough to leave him, and fled through the park feeling an insane need of my mother whom I knew, alas! to be in Paris, calling to her, in spite of myself, along all the *allées*. Suddenly, as I was running past a vine-covered arbour, I saw her sitting on a bench, smiling and holding out her arms to me. She threw back her veil to kiss me and I flung myself against her cheeks, bursting into tears. I cried for a long time, telling her all those ugly things which it took the ignorance of my youth to be able to confess, and to which, without understanding them, my mother listened divinely, minimising their importance with a goodness that lightened the weight of my conscience. That weight grew lighter, grew lighter; my crushed and humiliated soul rose more and more buoyant and strong, overflowed – I was all soul. A divine fragrance emanated from my mother and from my recovered innocence. Soon I was conscious of another odour in my nostrils just as fresh and pure. It came from a lilac bush, one of whose branches, hidden by my mother's parasol, was already in flower and unseen was filling the air with its perfume. High in the trees birds were singing with all their strength. Higher still, between the green tops, the sky was so deep a blue that it seemed merely the entrance to a sky where one could climb for ever. I kissed my mother. Never have I recaptured the sweetness of that kiss. She left again the following day, and that departure was more cruel than all those that had preceded it. It seemed to me now, having once sinned, that together with happiness, strength and the necessary succour were abandoning me.

All these separations taught me, in spite of myself, what the coming of the irrevocable one would be, although at the time I had never really considered the possibility of surviving my mother. I had determined to kill myself the instant following her death. Later, absence taught me other and still more bitter lessons, that one grows accustomed to absence, that the greatest diminution of oneself, the most humiliating suffering is to feel that one no longer suffers. These lessons, moreover, were later to be contradicted. I keep thinking now especially of that little garden where I used to breakfast with my mother, and where there were innumerable pansies. They always seemed to me a little sad, grave as emblems, but soft and velvety, often mauve, sometimes violet, almost black with graceful and mysterious yellow images, some altogether white and of a fragile innocence. I gather them all in memory now, those pansies, their sadness has been increased from having been understood, their velvet softness has forever disappeared.

II

How is it possible that the pure water of these memories, gushing forth again, could flow through my impure soul of today without being defiled? What special virtue has the matinal fragrance of lilacs that is able to pass through such fetid vapours without mingling with them and without losing any of its strength? Alas! although within me, it is yet so far from me – it is outside myself – that my fourteen-year-old soul wakes again. I know well that it is my soul no longer, and that it is no longer within my power to make it mine again. In those days, however, I did not think that I should one day regret its loss. It was but pure, I was to make it strong and capable in the future of the highest tasks. Often at Les Oublis, after being with my mother beside waters full of the play of sunlight and fishes during the hottest part of the day – or mornings and evenings, walking with her through the fields, I would dream with confidence of that future which was never fair enough to satisfy her love or my desire to please her, nor the forces, if not of will at least of imagination and of feeling, which stirred in me, tumultuously calling upon the destiny wherein they would be realised, knocking repeatedly against the wall of my heart as though to burst it open and to rush forth into life. If in those days I jumped up and down with all my might, kissed my mother a thousand times, running far ahead of her like a little dog, or lagged behind to pick cornflowers and poppies and brought them to her, shouting, it was not so much for the joy the walk and the gathering of flowers afforded me, as to give vent to my happiness in feeling so much life within me ready to gush forth and spread out infinitely towards perspectives even vaster and more enchanting than the farthermost horizon of forest and sky which I longed to reach at a single bound. O poppies, cornflowers and clover, if I bore you off in such a frenzy, all aquiver and with blazing eyes, if you made me laugh and made me cry, it was because in the bunches that I made of you, all those hopes of mine were tied up too. Hopes which, like you, have dried and withered but which, without ever having flowered like you, have all returned to dust.

What grieved my mother was my lack of will. I did everything on the impulse of the moment. As long as the impulse came from mind or heart

my life, while not perfect, was not altogether bad. The realisation of all my fine projects for work, for calm and reflection preoccupied my mother and myself above everything else, because we felt, she more clearly, I vaguely but intensely, that it would be nothing more than the image, projected into life, of that will created by myself within myself which my mother had conceived and nurtured. But always I would put it off until tomorrow. I would give myself time, miserable sometimes to see it passing, but after all, for me there was still so much ahead! I was a little frightened, nevertheless, and felt vaguely that this habit of getting along without using my will weighed on me more and more with the years, sadly suspecting that things would not change suddenly, that I could scarcely count on a miracle which would cost me nothing to change my life and create a will for me. To wish to possess a will was not enough. What I had to do was precisely what I could not do without a will: to will to have one.

III

And concupiscence' furious wind
Set your flesh clacking like an old flag.

BAUDELAIRE

During my sixteenth year I went through a period of nervous depression which affected my health. To divert me my parents had me make my début. Young men began to call on me. One of them was depraved and evil. His manners were, at once, gentle and impudent. He was the one with whom I fell in love. My parents discovered it but, fearing to hurt me, they avoided taking any precipitous steps. Spending all the time I was not with him thinking about him, I finally sank so low as to resemble him as nearly as that was possible. He initiated me to depravity almost without my realising it, then accustomed me to encourage the evil thoughts that awoke in me and which I had not the will to oppose, the only power capable of forcing them back into the infernal darkness from whence they came. When love died, habit had taken its place, and there was no lack of immoral young men to exploit it. The accomplices of my sins, they made themselves apologists to my conscience as well. At first I was filled with the most atrocious remorse. I made confessions which were not understood. My companions dissuaded me from being more explicit with my father. They convinced me, little by little, that all girls did the same things and that parents only pretended not to know it.

My imagination soon likened the lies I was forced to tell to silences that must be kept on some ineluctable necessity. At that time my way of living was already bad; still I dreamed, thought, felt.

Seeking to divert my mind from my evil desires and to drive them away, I began to go more and more into society. Its withering pleasures accustomed me to living perpetually in company, and I lost, with my taste for solitude, the secret of those joys which, until now, nature and art had given me. Never had I gone to concerts as often as during those years. Never, entirely preoccupied as I was with the desire of being admired in some fashionable box, did I feel the music less profoundly. I listened and heard nothing. If by chance I did hear, I could no longer see all that music is able to unveil. Even my walks were stricken with sterility. Things which formerly had been enough to make me happy for the entire day – a touch of sunlight yellowing the grass, the perfume that the leaves discharged with the last drops of rain – such things had lost, as I had too, their sweetness and their gaiety. The woods, the sky, the waters, seemed to turn away from me, and when, alone with them face to face, I would anxiously question them, they no longer murmured their vague replies which had formerly enraptured me. The heavenly hosts, whose presence the voices of waters, leaves and sky proclaim, deign only to visit those whose hearts, through living within themselves, are purified.

It was then, in searching for an inverse remedy, and because I had not the courage to will the true remedy which was so near and, alas, so far from me – deep within myself – that I allowed myself to be drawn again towards those sinful pleasures, hoping thus to rekindle the flame which society had extinguished. It was in vain. Dominated by the pleasure of pleasing, I put off from day to day the final decision, the choice, the truly free act, the option of solitude. I did not renounce one of these two vices for the other. I combined them. What am I saying? Each vice being bent on destroying all the obstacles of thought and feeling which could have stopped the other, seemed also to call the other forth. I would go into society to calm myself after sinning and then, no sooner calm, would sin again. It was at this terrible moment after I had lost my innocence and before the advent of today's remorse, at the very moment of my life when I was the most worthless, that everyone esteemed me most. I had been considered an affected, silly little girl; now, on the contrary, the ashes of my imagination, suited to the taste of society, were its delight. Just when I was committing the worst crime against my mother, everyone thought me, because of my tenderly respectful manner towards her, a model daughter. After the suicide of my mind everyone admired my intelligence, was enchanted by my wit. My dried-up imagination, my arid sensibility satisfied the thirst of those most avid of an intellectual life, their thirst being as artificial and lying as the source at which they thought to quench it. No one, however, ever suspected the secret crime that was my life, and to everyone I seemed an ideal young girl. How many parents told my mother at that time, if my social position had been less brilliant, if they could have dared to think of me, they would have wished no other wife for their sons. In spite of my obliterated conscience, these undeserved praises caused me desperate shame which, however, never reached the surface, and I had fallen so low that I had the indecency to jest about them with the accomplices of my crimes.

IV

To anyone who has lost that which can never . . . never be recovered!

BAUDELAIRE

In the winter of my twentieth year my mother's health, which had never been robust, grew very much worse. I learned that she had heart disease, and while not serious, it was essential that she should be spared all anxiety. One of my uncles told me that my mother was anxious to see me married. I was faced with a definite and imperious duty. I would be able to prove to my mother how much I loved her. I accepted the first offer of marriage which she transmitted to me and which I approved, thus letting necessity, in lieu of will, force me to change my way of living. Because of his remarkable intelligence, his gentleness and energy, my fiancé was just the young man to have the happiest influence over me. Furthermore, he had resolved to live with us. I would not be separated from my mother, which would have been the most cruel of sorrows.

Now I had the courage to tell my confessor all my sins. I asked him if I should make the same confession to my fiancé. He had the compassion to advise against it but made me swear never to yield to temptation again, and gave me absolution. Belated flowers, born of joy in a heart which I had thought forever sterile, bore fruit. The grace of God, the grace of youth – through whose vitality so many wounds heal themselves – had cured me.

If, as Saint Augustine has said, it is more difficult to recover chastity than to have been chaste, I knew that difficult virtue then. No one suspected that I was worth infinitely more than before, and every day my mother kissed my forehead that she had never ceased to believe pure, not knowing that it was regenerated. More than that, I was unjustly reproached, at this time, for my absent manner, my silence and my melancholy in society. It did not annoy me: the secret that existed between myself and my appeased conscience afforded me sufficient rapture. The convalescence of my soul – which now smiled at me with a countenance like my mother's, looking at me with tender reproach through drying tears – was infinitely languorous and sweet. Yes, my soul was being born again. I did not understand myself how I could have persecuted it, made it suffer, almost killed it. And I thanked God fervently for having saved it in time.

It was the harmony between that profound, pure joy and the fresh serenity of the sky that I was drinking in on the very evening when *all was accomplished*. The absence of my fiancé who had gone to visit his sister for two days, the presence at dinner of the young man who was principally to blame for my past sins, cast not the slightest sadness over that limpid May evening. There was not a cloud in the sky which was the perfect image of my heart. Moreover, my mother, as though there existed between her and my soul – although she knew nothing of my sins – a mysterious solidarity, had almost recovered. 'You must be careful of her for another two weeks,' the doctor had said, 'and after that there will be no possible danger of a relapse.' Those words alone were to me the promise of a future of such rapturous happiness, they made me weep for joy.

My mother, that evening, wore a gown rather more formal than usual, and for the first time since my father's death, although that had occurred ten years ago, had added a touch of lavender to her customary black. She was all confusion to be thus dressed as in her younger days, and sad and happy to have done violence to her sorrow and her mourning in order to give me pleasure and to celebrate my joy. I offered her a pink carnation which she at first refused, and then, because it came from me, pinned on with a hand a little reluctant and ashamed. Just as we were going in to dinner, standing near the window, I drew towards me her face now delicately smoothed of all traces of her past sufferings, and kissed her passionately. I was wrong when I said that I had never felt again the sweetness of that kiss at Les Oublis. The kiss of this evening was as sweet as any other. Or rather it was the same kiss which, evoked by the attraction of a similar moment, had glided softly out of the depth of the past to alight between my mother's cheeks, still a little pale, and my lips.

We drank to my coming marriage. I never drank anything but water because of the overstimulating effect that wine had on my nerves. My uncle insisted that on such an occasion as this I could make an exception. I can see his jovial face as he pronounced those stupid words . . . My God! My God! I have confessed everything so calmly until now, must I stop here? I can no longer see! Yes . . . my uncle said that I could, very well, on such an occasion as this, make an exception. He looked at me laughing as he said it. I drank quickly without glancing at my mother for fear she would stop me. She said gently: 'One should never make a place for evil, no matter how small.' But the champagne was so cool that I drank two more glasses. My head grew heavy, I felt a need to rest and, at the same time, to expend my nervous energy. We rose from the table; Jacques came up to me and said, looking at me steadily, 'Won't you come with me; I want to show you some poems I've written.'

His beautiful eyes shone softly in his healthy face as his hand slowly stroked his moustache. I understood that I was lost and I was without power to resist. Trembling all over, I said, 'Yes, I should be glad to.'

It was when I uttered those words, or perhaps, even before, when I drank my second glass of champagne, that I committed the really responsible act, the abominable act. After that I did no more than let myself go. We had closed and locked the two doors, and he, his breath on my cheeks, seized me in his arms, exploring my body with his hands. Then, while more and more pleasure took possession of me, I felt at the same time, stirring in the depth of my heart, an infinite sadness and desolation; it seemed to me that I was causing my mother's soul, the soul of my guardian angel, the soul of God to weep. I have never been able to read without shuddering with horror stories of those beasts who torture animals, their own wives, their own children; I now confusedly felt that in every sensual and sinful act there is just as much ferocity on the part of the body in the throes of pleasure, and that in us so many good intentions, so many pure angels are martyred, and weep.

Soon my uncles would have finished their game of cards and would be coming back. We would be there before them, I would never yield again, it was the last time . . . Then, above the mantelpiece, I saw myself in the mirror. None of the vague anguish of my soul was written on my face, but everything about it, from my shining eyes to my blazing cheeks, proclaimed a sensual, stupid, brutal joy. I thought then of the horror of anyone who, having observed me a little while ago kissing my mother with such melancholy tenderness, should see me thus transformed into a beast. But soon in the mirror Jacques' mouth, avid under his moustache, appeared against my cheek. Shaken to the depths of my being, I leaned my head closer to his, when I saw, yes, I tell it just as it happened, listen to me since I am able to tell you, on the balcony outside the window, I saw my mother looking at me aghast. I do not know whether she cried out. I heard nothing, but she fell backwards and lay there with her head caught between two bars of the railing . . .

It is now the last time I tell you this: I have told you before, I almost missed myself, and yet I had aimed carefully but I fired badly. However, they could not extract the bullet and heart complications set in. Only, I may stay like this another week, and during all that time I shall be unable to stop trying to grasp the beginnings . . . never stop *seeing* the end. I should rather my mother had seen me commit still other crimes, and even that one too, than that she should have seen that look of joy on my face in the mirror. No, she could not have seen it . . . It was a coincidence . . . she had had a stroke of apoplexy a moment before seeing me . . . she did not see it . . . That could not be! God who knew all would not have wished it.

Colette

Sidonie-Gabrielle Colette (1873–1954) is now regarded as one of the outstanding French women writers of our time, but her reputation has varied widely between that of a hack writer of mass-produced fiction and her subsequent evolution into a feminist icon. Born in Burgundy to an invalid ex-army captain and a resourceful mother (later celebrated in *La Maison de Claudine* (1922) and *Sido* (1929)), she was married off to Henri Gauthier-Villars, the popular novelist otherwise known as Willy. He pressed her into ghostwriting for him and this literary slavery, combined with Willy's infidelities, led to the breakup of their marriage in 1906. Colette then led a bohemian lifestyle, appearing on the Parisian stage and forming a scandalous liaison with the Marquise de Morny. This freedom allowed her to establish her own originality, expressed in the freshness and somewhat scandalous sensuality of the Claudine series and in the creation of the specifically feminine perspective which is apparent in *La Vagabonde* (1910). Her second marriage, to Baron Henry de Jouvenel, produced her daughter 'Bel-Gazou' and renowned novels such as *Chéri* (1920) and *Le Blé en herbe* (1923). In 1935 she married a younger man, Maurice de Goudeket. She spent the war years in Paris, fearing for the safety of her Jewish husband and yet managing to write novels such as *Gigi*, which later gained fame as a film. Her novels portray men as desirable yet weak and immature, an insight which has led to her recognition as a feminist to rival Simone de Beauvoir.

Green Sealing-Wax

ROUND ABOUT FIFTEEN, I WAS AT THE HEIGHT OF A MANIA for 'desk-furniture'. In this I was only imitating my father whose mania for it lasted in full force all his life. At the age when every kind of vice gets its claws into adolescence, like the hundred little hooks of a burr sticking into one's hair, a girl of fifteen runs plenty of risks. My glorious freedom exposed me to all of them and I believed it to be unbounded, unaware that Sido's maternal instinct, which disdained any form of spying, worked by flashes of intuition and leapt telepathically to the danger point.

When I had just turned fifteen, Sido gave me a dazzling proof of her second sight. She guessed that a man above suspicion had designs on my little pointed face, the plaits that whipped against my calves and my well-made body. Having entrusted me to this man's family during the holidays, she received a warning as clear and shattering as the gift of sudden faith and she cursed herself for having sent me away to strangers. Promptly, she put on her little bonnet that tied under the chin, got into the clanking, jolting train – they were beginning to send antique coaches along a brand-new line – and found me in a garden, playing with two other little girls, under the eyes of a taciturn man, leaning on his elbow like the meditative Demon on the ledge of Notre-Dame.

Such a spectacle of peaceful family life could not deceive Sido. She noticed, moreover, that I looked prettier than I did at home. That is how girls blossom in the warmth of a man's desire, whether they are fifteen or thirty. There was no question of scolding me and Sido took me away with her without the irreproachably respectable man's having dared to ask her reason for her arrival or for our departure. In the train, she fell asleep before my eyes, worn out like someone who had won a battle. I remember that lunch-time went by and I complained of being hungry. Instead of flushing, looking at her watch, promising me my favourite delicacies – wholemeal bread, cream cheese and pink onions – all she did was to shrug her shoulders. Little did she care about my hunger pangs, she had saved the most precious thing of all.

I had done nothing wrong, nor had I abetted this man, except by my torpor. But torpor is a far graver peril for a girl of fifteen than all the usual excited giggling and blushing and clumsy attempts at flirtation. Only a few men can induce that torpor from which girls awake to find themselves lost. That, so to speak, surgical intervention of Sido's cleared up all the confusion inside me and I had one of those relapses into childishness in which adolescence revels when it is simultaneously ashamed of itself and intoxicated by its own ego.

My father, a born writer, left few pages behind him. At the actual moment of writing, he dissipated his desire in material arrangements, setting out all the objects a writer needs and a number of superfluous ones as well. Because of him, I am not proof against this mania myself. As a result of having admired and coveted the perfect equipment of a writer's work-table, I am still exacting about the tools on my desk. Since adolescence does nothing by halves, I stole from my father's work-table, first a little mahogany set square that smelt like a cigar-box, then a white metal ruler. Not to mention the scolding, I received full in my face the glare of a small, blazing grey eye, the eye of a rival, so fierce that I did not risk it a third time. I confined myself to prowling, hungrily, with my mind full of evil thoughts, round all these treasures of stationery. A pad of virgin blotting-paper; an ebony ruler; one, two, four, six pencils, sharpened with a penknife and all of different colours; pens with medium nibs and fine nibs, pens with enormously broad nibs, drawing pens no thicker than a blackbird's quill; sealing-wax, red, green and violet; a hand blotter, a bottle of liquid glue, not to mention slabs of transparent amber-coloured stuff known as 'mouth-glue'; the minute remains of a Spahi's cloak reduced to the dimensions of a pen-wiper with scalloped edges; a big ink-pot flanked by a small ink-pot, both in bronze, and a lacquer bowl filled with a golden powder to dry the wet page; another bowl containing sealing-wafers of all colours (I used to eat the white ones); to right and left of the table, reams of paper, cream-laid, ruled, water-marked, and, of course, that little stamping machine that bit into the white sheet, and, with one snap of its jaws, adorned it with an embossed name: *J. -J. Colette*. There was also a glass of water for washing paintbrushes, a box of water-colours, an address book, the bottles of red, black and violet ink, the mahogany set square, a pocket-

case of mathematical instruments, the tobacco-jar, a pipe, the spirit-lamp for melting the sealing-wax.

A property owner tries to extend his domain; my father therefore tried to acclimatise adventitious subjects on his vast table. At one time there appeared on it a machine that could cut through a pile of a hundred sheets, and some frames filled with a white jelly on which you laid a written page face downwards and then, from this looking-glass original, pulled off blurred, sticky, anaemic copies. But my father soon wearied of such gadgets and the huge table returned to its serenity, to its classical style that was never disturbed by inspiration with its disorderly litter of crossed-out pages, cigarette-ends and 'roughs' screwed up into paper balls. I have forgotten, Heaven forgive me, the paperknife section, three or four boxwood ones, one of imitation silver, and the last of yellowed ivory, cracked from end to end.

From the age of ten I had never stopped coveting those material goods, invented for the glory and convenience of a mental power, which come under the general heading of 'desk-furniture'. Children only delight in things they can hide. For a long time I secured possession of one wing, the left one, of the great four-doored double bookcase (it was eventually sold by order of the court). The doors of the upper part were glass-fronted, those of the lower, solid and made of beautiful figured mahogany. When you opened the lower left-hand door at a right angle, the flap touched the side of the chest of drawers, and, as the bookcase took up nearly the whole of one panelled wall, I would immure myself in a quadrangular nook formed by the side of the chest of drawers, the wall, the left section of the bookcase and its wide-open door. Sitting on a little footstool, I could gaze at the three mahogany shelves in front of me, on which were displayed the objects of my worship, ranging from cream-laid paper to a little cup of the golden powder. 'She's a chip off the old block,' Sido would say teasingly to my father. It was ironical that, equipped with every conceivable tool for writing, my father rarely committed himself to putting pen to paper, whereas Sido – sitting at any old table, pushing aside an invading cat, a basket of plums, a pile of linen, or else just putting a dictionary on her lap by way of a desk – Sido really did write. A hundred enchanting letters prove that she did. To continue a letter or finish it off, she would tear a page out of her household account book or write on the back of a bill.

She therefore despised our useless altars. But she did not discourage me from lavishing care on my desk and adorning it to amuse myself. She even showed anxiety when I explained that my little house was becoming too small for me . . . 'Too small. Yes, much too small,' said the grey eyes. 'Fifteen . . . Where is Pussy-Darling going, bursting out of her nook like a hermit-crab driven out of its borrowed shell by its own growth? Already, I've snatched her from the clutches of that man. Already, I've had to forbid her to go dancing on the "Ring" on Low Sunday. Already, she's escaping and I shan't be able to follow her. Already, she wants a long dress and, if I give her one, the blindest will notice that she's a young girl. And if I refuse, everyone will look below the too-short skirt and stare at her woman's legs. Fifteen . . . How can I stop her from being fifteen, then sixteen, then seventeen years old?'

Sometimes, during that period, she would come and lean over the mahogany half-door that isolated me from the world. 'What are you doing?' She could see perfectly well what I was doing but she could not understand it. I refused her the answer given her so generously by everything else she observed, the bee, the caterpillar, the hydrangea, the ice-plant. But at least she could see I was there, sheltered from danger. She indulged my mania. The lovely pieces of shiny coloured wrapping paper were given me to bind my books and I made the gold string into book-markers. I had the first penholder sheathed in a glazed turquoise-coloured substance, with a moiré pattern on it, that appeared in Reumont's, the stationers.

One day my mother brought me a little stick of sealing-wax and I recognised the stub of green wax, the prize jewel of my father's desk. No doubt I considered the gift too overwhelming, for I gave no sign of ecstatic joy. I clutched the sealing-wax in my hand, and, as it grew warm, it gave out a slightly oriental fragrance of incense.

'It's very old sealing-wax,' Sido told me, 'and, as you can see, it's powdered with gold. Your father already had it when we were married; he'd been given it by his mother and his mother assured him that it was a stick of wax that had been used by Napoleon the First. But you've got to remember that my mother-in-law lied every time she opened her mouth, so . . .'

'Is he giving it to me or have you taken it?'

Sido became impatient; she always turned irritable when she thought she was going to be forced to lie and was trying to avoid lying.

'When *will* you stop twisting a lock of hair around the end of your nose?' she cried. 'You're doing your best to have a red nose with a blob at the tip like a cherry! That sealing-wax? Let's say your father's lending it to you and leave it at that. Of course, if you don't want . . .'

My wild clutch of possession made Sido laugh again, and she said, with pretended lightness:

'If he wanted it, he'd ask you to give it back, of course!'

But he did not ask me to give it back. For a few months, gold-flecked green sealing-wax perfumed my narrow empire bounded by four mahogany walls, then my pleasure gradually diminished as do all pleasures to which no one disputes our right. Besides, my devotion to stationery temporarily waned in favour of a craze to be glamorous. I asserted my right to wear a 'bustle', that is to say, I enlarged my small, round behind with a horsehair cushion which, of course, made my skirts much shorter at the back than in front. In our village, the frenzy of adolescence turned girls between thirteen and fifteen into madwomen who stole horsehair, cotton and wool, stuffed rags in a bag, and tied on the hideous contraption known as a 'false bottom' on dark staircases, out of their mothers' sight. I also longed for a thick, frizzy fringe, leather belts so tight I could hardly breathe, high boned collars, violet scent on my handkerchief . . .

From that phase, I relapsed once more into childhood, for a feminine creature has to make several attempts before it finally hatches out. I revelled in being a Plain Jane, with my hair in pigtails and straight wisps straggling over my cheeks. I gladly renounced all my finery in favour of my old school pinafores with their pockets stuffed with nuts and string and chocolate. Paths edged with brambles, clumps of bulrushes, liquorice 'shoelaces', cats – in short, everything I still love to this day – became dear to me again. There are no words to hymn such times in one's life, no clear memories to illuminate them; looking back on them, I can only compare them to the depths of blissful sleep. The smell of haymaking sometimes brings them back to me, perhaps because, suddenly tired, as growing creatures are, I would drop for an hour into a dreamless sleep among the new-mown hay.

It was at this point there occurred the episode known for long afterwards as 'the Hervouët will affair'. Old Monsieur Hervouët died and no will could be found. The provinces have always been rich in fantastic figures. Somewhere, under old tiled roofs, yellow with lichen, in icy drawing-rooms and dining-rooms dedicated to eternal shade, on waxed floors strewn with death-traps of knitted rugs, in kitchen-garden paths between the hard-headed cabbages and the curly parsley, queer characters are always to be found. A little town or a village prides itself on possessing a mystery. My own village acknowledged placidly, even respectfully, the rights of young Gatreau to rave unmolested. This admirable example of a romantic madman, a wooden cigar between his lips, was always wildly tossing his streaming black curls and staring fixedly at young girls with his long, Arab eyes. A voluntary recluse used to nod good morning through a window-pane and passers would say of her admiringly:

'That makes twenty-two years since Madame Sibile left her room! My mother used to see her there, just as you see her now. And, you know, there's nothing the matter with her. In one way, it's a fine life!'

But Sido used to hurry her quick step and pull me along when we passed level with the aquarium that housed the lady who had not gone out for twenty-two years. Behind her clear glass pane the prisoner would be smiling. She always wore a linen cap; sometimes her little yellow hand held a cup. A sure instinct for what is horrible and prohibited made Sido turn away from that ground-floor window and that bobbing head. But the sadism of childhood made me ask her endless questions:

'How old do you think she is, Madame Sibile? At night does she sleep by the window in her armchair? Do they undress her? Do they wash her? And how does she go to the lavatory?'

Sido would start as if she had been stung.

'Be quiet. I forbid you to think about those things.'

Monsieur Hervouët had never passed for one of those eccentrics to whom a market town extends its slightly derisive protection. For sixty years he had been well-off and ill-dressed, first a 'big catch' to marry, then a big catch married. Left a widower, he had remarried. His second wife was a former postmistress, thin and full of fire.

When she struck her breastbone, exclaiming '*That's* where I can feel it burning!' her Spanish eyes seemed to make the person she was talking to responsible for this unquenchable ardour. 'I am not easily frightened,' my father used to say; 'but Heaven preserve me from being left alone with Mademoiselle Matheix!'

After his second marriage, Monsieur Hervouët no longer appeared in public. As he never left his home, no one knew exactly when he developed the gastric trouble that was to carry him off. He was a man dressed, in all weathers, in black, including a cap with ear-flaps. Smothered in fleecy white hair and a beard like cotton wool, he looked like an apple tree attacked by woolly aphis. High walls and a gateway that was nearly always closed protected his second season of conjugal bliss. In summer a single rose tree clothed three sides of his one-storeyed house and the thick fringe of wisteria on the crest of the wall provided food for the first bees. But we had never heard anyone say that Monsieur Hervouët was fond of flowers and, if we now and then caught sight of his black figure pacing to and fro under the pendants of the wisteria and the showering roses, he struck us as being neither responsible for nor interested in all this wealth of blossom.

When Mademoiselle Matheix became Madame Hervouët, the ex-postmistress lost none of her resemblance to a black-and-yellow wasp. With her sallow skin, her squeezed-in waist, her fine, inscrutable eyes and her mass of dark hair, touched with white and restrained in a knot on the nape of her neck, she showed no surprise at being promoted to middle-class luxury. She appeared to be fond of gardening. Sido, the impartial, thought it only fair to show some interest in her; she lent her books, and in exchange accepted cuttings and also roots of tree-violets whose flowers were almost black and whose stem grew naked out of the ground like the trunk of a tiny palm tree. To me, Madame Hervouët-Matheix was an anything but sympathetic figure. I was vaguely scandalised that when making some assertions of irreproachable banality, she did so in a tone of passionate and plaintive supplication.

'What do you expect?' said my mother. 'She's an old maid.'

'But, Mamma, she's married!'

'Do you really imagine', retorted Sido acidly, 'people stop being old maids for a little thing like that?'

One day, my father, returning from the daily 'round of the town' by which this man who had lost one leg kept himself fit, said to my mother:

'A piece of news! The Hervouët relatives are attacking the widow.'

'*No!*'

'And going all out for her, too! People are saying the grounds of the accusation are extremely serious.'

'A new Lafarge case?'

'You're demanding a lot,' said my father.

I thrust my sharp little mug between my two parents.

'What's that, the Lafarge case?'

'A horrible business between husband and wife. There's never been a period without one. A famous poisoning case.'

'Ah!' I exclaimed excitedly. 'What a piece of luck!'

Sido gave me a look that utterly renounced me.

'There you are,' she muttered. 'That's what they're all like at that age . . . A girl ought never to be fifteen.'

'Sido, are you listening to me or not?' broke in my father. 'The relatives, put up to it by a niece of Hervouët's, are claiming that Hervouët didn't die intestate and that his wife has destroyed the will.'

'In that case', observed Sido, 'you could bring an action against all widowers and all widows of intestates.'

'No,' retorted my father, 'men who have children don't need to make a will. The flames of Hervouët's lady can only have scorched Hervouët from the waist up since . . .'

'Colette,' my mother said to him severely, indicating me with a look.

'Well,' my father went on. 'So there she is in a nice pickle. Hervouët's niece says she saw the will, yes, saw it with her very own eyes. She can even describe it. A big envelope, five seals of green wax with gold flecks in it . . .'

'Fancy that!' I said innocently.

'. . . and on the front of it, the instructions: "To be opened after my death in the presence of my solicitor, Monsieur Hourblin or his successor."'

'And suppose the niece is lying?' I ventured to ask.

'And suppose Hervouët changed his mind and destroyed his will?' suggested Sido. 'He was perfectly free to do so, I presume?'

'There you go, the two of you! Already siding with the bull against the bullfighter!' cried my father.

'Exactly,' said my mother. 'Bullfighters are usually men with fat buttocks and that's enough to put me against them!'

'Let's get back to the point,' said my father. 'Hervouët's niece has a husband, a decidedly sinister gentleman by name of Pellepuits.'

I soon got tired of listening. On the evidence of such words as 'The relatives are attacking the widow!' I had hoped for bloodshed and foul play and all I heard was bits of gibberish such as 'disposable portion of estate', 'holograph will', 'charge against X'.

All the same my curiosity was reawakened when Monsieur Hervouët's widow paid us a call. Her little mantle of imitation Chantilly lace worn over hock-bottle shoulders, her black mittens from which protruded unusually thick, almost opaque nails, the luxuriance of her black-and-white hair, a big black taffeta pocket suspended from her belt that dangled over the skirt of her mourning, her 'houri eyes', as she called them; all these details, that I seemed to be seeing for the first time, took on a new, sinister significance.

Sido received the widow graciously, took her into the garden and offered her a thimbleful of Frontignan and a wedge of home-made cake. The June afternoon buzzed over the garden, russet caterpillars dropped about us from the walnut tree, not a cloud floated in the sky. My mother's pretty voice and Madame Hervouët's imploring one exchanged tranquil remarks; as usual, they talked about nothing but salpiglossis, gladiolus and the misdemeanours of servants. Then the visitor rose to go and my mother escorted her. 'If you don't mind,' said Madame Hervouët, 'I'll come over in a day or two and borrow some books; I'm so lonely.'

'Would you like to take them now?' suggested Sido.

'No, no, there's no hurry. Besides, I've noted down the titles of some adventure stories. Goodbye for the time being, and thank you.'

As she said this, Madame Hervouët, instead of taking the path that led to the house, took the one that circled the lawn and walked twice round the plot of grass.

'Good gracious, whatever am I doing? Do forgive me.'

She allowed herself a modest laugh and eventually reached the hall where she groped too high and to the left of the two sides of the folding door for a latch she had twenty times found on the right. My mother opened the front door for her and, out of politeness, stood for a moment at the top of the steps. We watched Madame Hervouët go off, keeping at first very close to the house, then crossing the road very hurriedly, picking up her skirts as if she were fording a river.

My mother shut the door again and saw that I had followed her.

'She is lost,' she said.

'Who? Madame Hervouët? Why do you say that? How d'you mean, lost?'

Sido shrugged her shoulders.

'I've no idea. It's just my impression. Keep that to yourself.'

I kept silence faithfully. This was all the easier as, continuing my series of metamorphoses like a grub, I had entered a new phase – the 'enlightened bibliophile' – and I forgot Madame Hervouët in a grand turnout of my stationery shop. A few days later, I was installing Jules Verne between *Les Fleurs Animées* and a relief atlas when Madame Hervouët appeared on the scene without the bell having warned me. For we left the front door open nearly all day so that our dog Domino could go in and out.

'How nice of a big girl like you to tidy up the bookshelves,' exclaimed the visitor. 'What books are you going to lend me today?'

When Madame Hervouët raised her voice, I clenched my teeth and screwed up my eyes very small.

'Jules Verne,' she read, in a plaintive voice. 'You can't read him twice. Once you know the secret, it's finished.'

'There's Balzac up there, on the big shelves,' I said, pointing to them.

'He's very heavy going,' said Madame Hervouët.

Balzac, heavy going? Balzac, my cradle, my enchanted forest, my voyage of discovery? Amazed, I looked up at the tall black woman, a head taller than myself. She was toying with a cut rose and staring into space. Her features expressed nothing which could be remotely connected with opinions on literature. She became aware I was gazing at her and pretended to be interested in my writer's equipment.

'It's charming. What a splendid collection!'

Her mouth had grown older in the last week. She remained stooping over my relics, handling this one and that. Then she straightened herself up with a start.

'But isn't your dear mother anywhere about? I'd like to see her.'

Only too glad to move, to get away from this 'lost' lady, I rushed wildly out into the garden, calling 'Mamma!' as if I were shouting 'Fire!'

'She took a few books away with her,' Sido told me when we were alone. 'But I could positively swear she didn't even glance at their titles.'

The rest of the 'Hervouët affair' is linked, in my memory, with a vague general commotion, a kind of romantic blur. My clearest recollection of it comes to me through Sido, thanks to the extraordinary 'presence' I still have of the sound of her voice. Her stories, her conversations with my father, the intolerant way she had of arguing and refuting, those are the things that riveted a sordid provincial drama in my mind.

One day, shortly after Madame Hervouët's last visit, the entire district was exclaiming 'The will's been found!' and describing the big envelope with five seals that the widow had just deposited in Monsieur Hourblin's study. At once uneasy and triumphant, the Pellepuits-Hervouët couple and another lot, the Hervouët-Guillamats, appeared, along with the widow, at the lawyer's office. There, Madame Hervouët, all by herself, faced up to the solid, pitiless group, to what Sido called those 'gaping, legacy-hunting sharks'. 'It seems', my mother said, telling the story, 'that she smelt of brandy.' At this point, my mother's voice is superseded by the hunchback's voice of Julia Vincent, a woman who went out ironing by the day and came to us once a week. For I don't know how many consecutive Fridays, I pressed Julia till I wrung out of her all she knew. The precise sound of that nasal voice, squeezed between the throat, the hump and the hollow, deformed chest, was a delight to me.

'The man as was most afeared was the lawyer. To begin with he's not a tall man, not half so tall as that woman. She, all dressed in black she was, and her veil falling down in front right to her feet. Then the lawyer picked up the envelope, big as that it was' (Julia unfolded one of my father's vast handkerchiefs) 'and he passed it just as it was to the nephews so they could recognise the seals.'

'But you weren't there, Julia, were you?'

'No, it was Monsieur Hourblin's junior clerk who was watching through the keyhole. One of the nephews said a word or two. Then Madame Hervouët stared at him like a duchess. The lawyer coughed, a-hem, a-hem, he broke the seals and he read it out.'

In my recollection, it is sometimes Sido talking, sometimes some scandalmonger eager to gossip about the Hervouët affair. Sometimes it seems too that some illustrator, such as Bertall or Tony Johannot, has actually etched a picture for me of the tall, thin woman who never withdrew her Spanish eyes from the group of heirs-at-law and kept licking her lip to taste the *marc* brandy she had gulped down to give herself courage.

So Monsieur Hourblin read out the will. But, after the first lines, the document began to shake in his hands and he broke off, with an apology, to wipe his glasses. He resumed his reading and went right through to the end. Although the testator declared himself to be 'sound in body and mind', the will was nothing but a tissue of absurdities, among others, the acknowledgement of a debt of two million francs contracted to Louise-Léonie-Alberte Matheix, beloved spouse of Clovis-Edme Hervouët.

The reading finished in silence and not one voice was raised from the block of silent heirs.

'It seems', said Sido, 'that, after the reading, the silence was such you could hear the wasps buzzing in the vine-arbour outside the window. The Pellepuits and the various Guillamats did nothing but stare at Madame Hervouët, without stirring a finger. Why aren't cupidity and avarice possessed of second sight? It was a female Guillamat, less stupid than the others, who said afterwards that, before anyone had spoken, Madame Hervouët began to make peculiar movements with her neck, like a hen that's swallowed a hairy caterpillar.'

The story of the last scene of that meeting spread like wildfire through the streets, through people's homes, through the cafés, through the fairgrounds. Monsieur Hourblin had been the first to speak above the vibrating hum of the wasps.

'On my soul and conscience, I find myself obliged to declare that the handwriting of the will does not correspond . . .'

A loud yelping interrupted him. Before him, before the heirs, there was no longer any Widow Hervouët, but a sombre Fury whirling round and stamping her feet, a kind of black dervish, lacerating herself, muttering and shrieking. To her admissions of forgery, the crazy woman added others, so rich in the names of vegetable poisons, such as buckthorn and hemlock, that the lawyer, in consternation, exclaimed naïvely:

'Stop, my poor good lady, you're telling us far more than anyone has asked you to!'

A lunatic asylum engulfed the madwoman and, if the Hervouët affair persisted in some memories, at least, there was no 'Hervouët case' at the assizes.

'Why, Mamma?' I asked.

'Mad people aren't tried. Or else they'd have to have judges who were mad too. That wouldn't be a bad idea, when you come to think of it . . .'

To pursue her train of thought better, she dropped the task with which her hands were busy; graceful hands that she took no care of. Perhaps, that particular day, she was shelling haricot beans. Or else, with her little finger stuck in the air, she was coating my father's crutch with black varnish . . .

'Yes, judges who would be able to assess the element of calculation in madness, who could sift out the hidden grain of lucidity, of deliberate fraud.'

The moralist who was raining these unexpected conclusions on a fifteen-year-old head was encased in a gardener's blue apron, far too big for her, that made her look quite plump. Her grey gaze, terribly direct, fixed me now through her spectacles, now over the top of them. But in spite of the apron, the rolled-up sleeves, the sabots and the haricot beans, she never looked humble or common.

'What I do blame Madame Hervouët for', Sido went on, 'is her megalomania. *Folie de grandeur* is the source of any number of crimes. Nothing exasperates me more than the imbecile who imagines he's capable of planning and executing a crime without being punished for it. Don't you agree it's Madame Hervouët's stupidity that makes her case so sickening? Poisoning poor old Hervouët with extremely bitter herbal concoctions, right, that wasn't difficult. Inept murderer, stupid victim, it's tit for tat. But to try and imitate a handwriting without having the slightest gift for forgery, to trust to a special, rare kind of sealing-wax, what petty ruses, great heavens, what fatuous conceit!'

'But why did she confess?'

'Ah,' said Sido reflectively. 'That's because a confession is almost inevitable. A confession is like . . . let's see . . . yes . . . it's like a stranger you carry inside you . . .'

'Like a child?'

'No, not a child. With a child, you know the exact date it's going to leave you. Whereas a confession bursts out quite suddenly, just when you weren't expecting it, it tastes its liberty, it stretches its limbs. It shouts, it cuts capers. She accompanied hers with a dance, that poor murderess who thought herself so clever.'

It shouts, it cuts capers . . . Just like that, then and there, my own secret burst out into Sido's ear: on the very day of Madame Hervouët's last visit I had noticed the disappearance of the little stick of green sealing-wax powdered with gold.

Jean-Paul Sartre

Through much of the mid-twentieth century, that particularly French public role of the intellectual celebrity was filled by the writer and thinker Jean-Paul Sartre (1905–80). He studied philosophy at the École Normale Supérieure (failing the prestigious *agrégation* in 1928 only to come top the following year) and was profoundly affected by his experiences of war (as a conscript, prisoner, and friend of the Resistance). Sartre used literature of many kinds to explore the difficult relationship between the Existential ideas of personal choice and freedom and the role of determinism expounded by the Marxists. It was in Paris that he met Simone de Beauvoir, subsequently famed for her pioneering feminist study, *Le Deuxième sexe* (1949). The couple resisted the concepts of marriage, children and family life, and never set up home together, preferring to live separately in cheap hotels during the 1930s and 1940s. His chief early literary work was the novel, *La Nausée* (1939), which explores the absurdity of the world through its solitary anti-hero Roquentin. His best-known philosophical work, *L'Être et le néant*, which studies the nature of consciousness, appeared in 1943; and in the post-war years he continued writing politically engaged drama such as *Les Mains sales* (1947) as well as philosophy and fiction. His cultural heroes included Gustave Flaubert whom he consecrated in his last great work, *L'Idiot de la famille* (1971–2). He died on 15 April 1980 and his funeral at Montmartre was attended by a huge procession, a testament both to the man and to the culture he felt so compelled to criticise.

The Wall

THEY PUSHED US INTO A LARGE WHITE ROOM AND MY EYES began to blink because the light hurt them. Then I saw a table and four fellows seated at the table, civilians, looking at some papers. The other prisoners were herded together at one end and we were obliged to cross the entire room to join them. There were several I knew, and others who must have been foreigners. The two in front of me were blond with round heads. They looked alike. I imagine they were French. The smaller one kept pulling at his trousers, out of nervousness.

This lasted about three hours. I was dog-tired and my head was empty. But the room was well-heated, which struck me as rather agreeable; we had not stopped shivering for twenty-four hours. The guards led the prisoners in one after the other in front of the table. Then the four fellows asked them their names and what they did. Most of the time that was all – or perhaps from time to time they would ask such questions as: 'Did you help sabotage the munitions?' or, 'Where were you on the morning of the ninth and what were you doing?' They didn't even listen to the replies, or at least they didn't seem to. They just remained silent for a moment and looked straight ahead, then they began to write. They asked Tom if it was true he had served in the International Brigade. Tom couldn't say he hadn't because of the papers they had found in his jacket. They didn't ask Juan anything, but after he told them his name, they wrote for a long while.

'It's my brother José who's the anarchist,' Juan said. 'You know perfectly well he's not here now. I don't belong to any party. I never did take part in politics.' They didn't answer.

Then Juan said, 'I didn't do anything. And I'm not going to pay for what the others did.'

His lips were trembling. A guard told him to stop talking and led him away. It was my turn.

'Your name is Pablo Ibbieta?'

I said yes.

The fellow looked at his papers and said, 'Where is Ramon Gris?'

'I don't know.'

'You hid him in your house from the sixth to the nineteenth.'

'I did not.'

They continued to write for a moment and the guards led me away. In the hall, Tom and Juan were waiting between two guards. We started walking. Tom asked one of the guards, 'What's the idea?' 'How do you mean?' the guard asked. 'Was that just the preliminary questioning, or was that the trial?' 'That was the trial,' the guard said. 'So now what? What are they going to do with us?' The guard answered drily, 'The verdict will be told you in your cell.'

In reality, our cell was one of the cellars of the hospital. It was terribly cold there because it was very draughty. We had been shivering all night long and it had hardly been any better during the day. I had spent the preceding five days in a cellar in the archbishop's palace, a sort of dungeon that must have dated back to the Middle Ages. There were lots of prisoners and not much room, so they housed them just anywhere. But I was not homesick for my dungeon. I hadn't been cold there, but I had been alone, and that gets to be irritating. In the cellar I had company. Juan didn't say a word; he was afraid, and besides, he was too young to have anything to say. But Tom was a good talker and knew Spanish well.

In the cellar there were a bench and four straw mattresses. When they led us back we sat down and waited in silence. After a while Tom said, 'Our goose is cooked.'

'I think so too,' I said. 'But I don't believe they'll do anything to the kid.'

Tom said, 'They haven't got anything on him. He's the brother of a fellow who's fighting, and that's all.'

I looked at Juan. He didn't seem to have heard.

Tom continued, 'You know what they do in Saragossa? They lay the guys across the road and then they drive over them with trucks. It was a Moroccan deserter who told us that. They say it's just to save ammunition.'

I said, 'Well, it doesn't save gasoline.'

I was irritated with Tom; he shouldn't have said that.

He went on, 'There are officers walking up and down the roads with their hands in their pockets, smoking, and they see that it's done right. Do you think they'd put 'em out of their misery? Like hell they do.

They just let 'em holler. Sometimes as long as an hour. The Moroccan said the first time he almost puked.'

'I don't believe they do that here,' I said, 'unless they really are short of ammunition.'

The daylight came in through four air vents and a round opening that had been cut in the ceiling, to the left, and which opened directly on to the sky. It was through this hole, which was ordinarily closed by means of a trapdoor, that they unloaded coal into the cellar. Directly under the hole, there was a big pile of coal dust; it had been intended for heating the hospital, but at the beginning of the war they had evacuated the patients and the coal had stayed there unused; it even got rained on from time to time, when they forgot to close the trapdoor.

Tom started to shiver. 'God damn it,' he said, 'I'm shivering. There, it is starting again.'

He rose and began to do gymnastic exercises. At each movement, his shirt opened and showed his white, hairy chest. He lay down on his back, lifted his legs in the air and began to do the scissors movement. I watched his big buttocks tremble. Tom was tough, but he had too much fat on him. I kept thinking that soon bullets and bayonet points would sink into that mass of tender flesh as though it were a pat of butter.

I wasn't exactly cold, but I couldn't feel my shoulders or my arms. From time to time, I had the impression that something was missing and I began to look around for my jacket. Then I would suddenly remember they hadn't given me a jacket. It was rather awkward. They had taken our clothes to give them to their own soldiers and had left us only our shirts and these cotton trousers the hospital patients wore in mid-summer. After a moment, Tom got up and sat down beside me, breath-less.

'Did you get warmed up?'

'Damn it, no. But I'm all out of breath.'

Around eight o'clock in the evening, a Major came in with two Falangists.

'What are the names of those three over there?' he asked the guard.

'Steinbock, Ibbieta and Mirbal,' said the guard.

The Major put on his glasses and examined his list.

'Steinbock – Steinbock . . . Here it is. You are condemned to death. You'll be shot tomorrow morning.'

He looked at his list again.

'The other two, also,' he said.

'That's not possible,' said Juan. 'Not me.'

The Major looked at him with surprise. 'What's your name?'

'Juan Mirbal.'

'Well, your name is here', said the Major, 'and you're condemned to death.'

'I didn't do anything,' said Juan.

The Major shrugged his shoulders and turned towards Tom and me. 'You are both Basque?'

'No, nobody's Basque.'

He appeared exasperated.

'I was told there were three Basques. I'm not going to waste my time running after them. I suppose you don't want a priest?'

We didn't even answer.

Then he said, 'A Belgian doctor will be around in a little while. He has permission to stay with you all night.'

He gave a military salute and left.

'What did I tell you?' Tom said. 'We're in for something swell.'

'Yes,' I said. 'It's a damned shame for the kid.'

I said that to be fair, but I really didn't like the kid. His face was too refined and it was disfigured by fear and suffering, which had twisted all his features. Three days ago, he was just a kid with a kind of affected manner some people like. But now he looked like an ageing fairy, and I thought to myself he would never be young again, even if they let him go. It wouldn't have been a bad thing to show him a little pity, but pity makes me sick, and besides, I couldn't stand him. He hadn't said anything more, but he had turned grey. His face and hands were grey. He sat down again and stared, round-eyed, at the ground. Tom was good-hearted and tried to take him by the arm, but the kid drew himself away violently and made an ugly face. 'Leave him alone,' I said quietly. 'Can't you see he's going to start to bawl?' Tom obeyed regretfully. He would have liked to console the kid; that would have kept him occupied and he wouldn't have been tempted to think about himself. But it got on my nerves. I had never thought about death, for the reason that the question had never come up. But now it had come up, and there was nothing else to do but think about it.

Tom started talking. 'Say, did you ever bump anybody off?' he asked me. I didn't answer. He started to explain to me that he had bumped off six fellows since August. He hadn't yet realised what we were in for, and I saw clearly he didn't *want* to realise it. I myself hadn't quite taken it in.

I wondered if it hurt very much. I thought about the bullets; I imagined their fiery hail going through my body. All that was beside the real question; but I was calm, we had all night in which to realise it. After a while Tom stopped talking and I looked at him out of the corner of my eye. I saw that he, too, had turned grey and that he looked pretty miserable. I said to myself, 'It's starting.' It was almost dark, a dull light filtered through the air vents across the coal pile and made a big spot under the sky. Through the hole in the ceiling I could already see a star. The night was going to be clear and cold.

The door opened and two guards entered. They were followed by a blond man in a tan uniform. He greeted us.

'I'm the doctor,' he said. 'I've been authorised to give you any assistance you may require in these painful circumstances.'

He had an agreeable, cultivated voice.

I said to him, 'What are you going to do here?'

'Whatever you want me to do. I shall do everything in my power to lighten these few hours.'

'Why did you come to us? There are lots of others: the hospital's full of them.'

'I was sent here,' he answered vaguely. 'You'd probably like to smoke, wouldn't you?' he added suddenly. 'I've got some cigarettes and even some cigars.'

He passed around some English cigarettes and some *puros*, but we refused them. I looked him straight in the eye and he appeared uncomfortable.

'You didn't come here out of compassion,' I said to him. 'In fact, I know who you are. I saw you with some Fascists in the barracks yard the day I was arrested.'

I was about to continue, when all at once something happened to me which surprised me: the presence of this doctor had suddenly ceased to interest me. Usually, when I've got hold of a man I don't let go. But somehow the desire to speak had left me. I shrugged my shoulders and turned away. A little later, I looked up and saw he was watching me with an air of curiosity. The guards had sat down on one of the mattresses. Pedro, the tall thin one, was twiddling his thumbs, while the other one shook his head occasionally to keep from falling asleep.

'Do you want some light?' Pedro suddenly asked the doctor. The other fellow nodded, 'Yes.' I think he was not over-intelligent, but doubtless he was not malicious. As I looked at his big, cold, blue eyes, it seemed to me the worst thing about him was his lack of imagination. Pedro went out and came back with an oil-lamp which he set on the corner of the bench. It gave a poor light, but it was better than nothing; the night before we had been left in the dark. For a long while I stared at the circle of light the lamp threw on the ceiling. I was fascinated. Then, suddenly, I came to, the light circle paled, and I felt as if I were being crushed under an enormous weight. It wasn't the thought of death, and it wasn't fear; it was something anonymous. My cheeks were burning hot and my head ached.

I roused myself and looked at my two companions. Tom had his head in his hands and only the fat, white nape of his neck was visible. Juan was by far the worst off; his mouth was wide open and his nostrils were trembling. The doctor came over to him and touched him on the shoulder, as though to comfort him; but his eyes remained cold. Then I saw the Belgian slide his hand furtively down Juan's arm to his wrist. Indifferent, Juan let himself be handled. Then, as though absent-mindedly, the Belgian laid three fingers over his wrist; at the same time, he drew away somewhat and managed to turn his back to me. But I leaned over backwards and saw him take out his watch and look at it a moment before relinquishing the boy's wrist. After a moment, he let the inert hand fall and went and leaned against the wall. Then, as if he had suddenly remembered something very important that had to be noted down immediately, he took a notebook from his pocket and wrote a few lines in it. 'The son of a bitch,' I thought angrily. 'He better not come and feel my pulse; I'll give him a punch in his dirty jaw.'

He didn't come near me, but I felt he was looking at me. I raised my head and looked back at him. In an impersonal voice, he said, 'Don't you think it's frightfully cold here?'

He looked purple with cold.

'I'm not cold,' I answered him.

He kept looking at me with a hard expression. Suddenly I understood, and I lifted my hands to my face. I was covered with sweat. Here, in this cellar, in midwinter, right in a draught, I was sweating. I ran my fingers through my hair, which was stiff with sweat; at the same time, I realised my shirt was damp and sticking to my skin. I had been streaming with perspiration for an hour, at least, and had felt nothing. But this fact hadn't escaped that Belgian swine. He had seen the drops rolling down my face and had said to himself that it showed an almost pathological terror; and he himself had felt normal and proud of it because he was cold. I wanted to get up and and punch his face in, but I had hardly started to make a move before my shame and anger had disappeared. I dropped back on to the bench with indifference.

I was content to rub my neck with my handkerchief because now I felt the sweat dripping from my hair on to the nape of my neck and that was disagreeable. I soon gave up rubbing myself, however, for it didn't do any good; my handkerchief was already wringing wet and I was still sweating. My buttocks, too, were sweating, and my damp trousers stuck to the bench.

Suddenly, Juan said, 'You're a doctor, aren't you?'

'Yes,' said the Belgian.

'Do people suffer – very long?'

'Oh! When . . . ? No, no,' said the Belgian, in a paternal voice, 'it's quickly over.'

His manner was as reassuring as if he had been answering a paying patient.

'But I . . . Somebody told me – they often have to fire two volleys.'

'Sometimes', said the Belgian, raising his head, 'it just happens that the first volley doesn't hit any of the vital organs.'

'So then they have to reload their guns and aim all over again?' Juan thought for a moment, then added hoarsely, 'But that takes time!'

He was terribly afraid of suffering. He couldn't think about anything else, but that went with his age. As for me, I hardly thought about it any more and it certainly was not fear of suffering that made me perspire.

I rose and walked towards the pile of coal dust. Tom gave a start and looked at me with a look of hate. I irritated him because my shoes squeaked. I wondered if my face was as putty-coloured as his. Then I noticed that he, too, was sweating. The sky was magnificent; no light at all came into our dark corner and I had only to lift my head to see the Big Bear. But it didn't look the way it had looked before. Two days ago, from my cell in the archbishop's palace, I could see a big patch of sky and each time of day brought back a different memory. In the morning, when the sky was a deep blue, and light, I thought of beaches along the Atlantic; at noon, I could see the sun, and I remembered a bar in Seville where I used to drink Manzanilla and eat anchovies and olives; in the afternoon, I was in the shade, and I thought of the deep shadow which covers half of the arena while the other half gleams in the sunlight: it really gave me a pang to see the whole earth reflected in the sky like that. Now, however, no matter how much I looked up in the air, the sky no longer recalled anything. I liked it better that way. I came back and sat down next to Tom. There was a long silence.

Then Tom began to talk in a low voice. He had to keep talking, otherwise he lost his way in his own thoughts. I believe he was talking to me, but he didn't look at me. No doubt he was afraid to look at me, because I was grey and sweating. We were both alike and worse than mirrors for each other. He looked at the Belgian, the only one who was alive.

'Say, do you understand? I don't.'

Then I, too, began to talk in a low voice. I was watching the Belgian.

'Understand what? What's the matter?'

'Something's going to happen to us that I don't understand.'

There was a strange odour about Tom. It seemed to me that I was more sensitive to odours than ordinarily. With a sneer, I said, 'You'll understand, later.'

'That's not so sure,' he said stubbornly. 'I'm willing to be courageous, but at least I ought to know . . . Listen, they're going to take us out into the courtyard. All right. The fellows will be standing in line in front of us. How many of them will there be?'

'Oh, I don't know. Five, or eight. Not more.'

'That's enough. Let's say there'll be eight of them. Somebody will shout "Shoulder arms!" and I'll see all eight rifles aimed at me. I'm sure I'm going to feel like going through the wall. I'll push against the wall as hard as I can with my back, and the wall won't give in. The way it is in a nightmare . . . I can imagine all that. Ah, if you only knew how well I can imagine it!'

'Skip it!' I said. 'I can imagine it too.'

'It must hurt like the devil. You know they aim at your eyes and mouth so as to disfigure you,' he added maliciously. 'I can feel the wounds already. For the last hour I've been having pains in my head and neck. Not real pains – it's worse still. They're the pains I'll feel tomorrow morning. And after that, then what?'

I understood perfectly well what he meant, but I didn't want to seem to understand. As for the pains, I, too, felt them all through my body, like a lot of little gashes. I couldn't get used to them, but I was like him, I didn't think they were very important.

'After that', I said roughly, 'you'll be eating daisies.'

He started talking to himself, not taking his eyes off the Belgian, who didn't seem to be listening to him. I knew what he had come for, and that what we were thinking didn't interest him. He had come to look at our bodies, our bodies which were dying alive.

'It's like in a nightmare,' said Tom. 'You want to think of something, you keep having the impression you've got it, that you're going to understand, and then it slips away from you, it eludes you and it's gone again. I say to myself, afterwards, there won't be anything. But I don't really understand what that means. There are moments when I almost do – and then it's gone again. I start to think of the pains, the bullets, the noise of the shooting. I am a materialist, I swear it; and I'm not going crazy, either. But there's something wrong. I see my own corpse. That's not hard, but it's *I* who see it, with *my* eyes. I'll have to get to the point where I think – where I think I won't see anything more. I won't hear anything more, and the world will go on for the others. We're not made to think that way, Pablo. Believe me, I've already stayed awake all night waiting for something. But this is not the same thing. This will grab us from behind, Pablo, and we won't be ready for it.'

'Shut up,' I said. 'Do you want me to call a father confessor?'

He didn't answer. I had already noticed that he had a tendency to prophesy and call me 'Pablo' in a kind of pale voice. I didn't like that very much, but it seems all the Irish are like that. I had a vague impression that he smelt of urine. Actually, I didn't like Tom very much, and I didn't see why, just because we were going to die together, I should like him any better. There are certain fellows with whom it would be different – with Ramon Gris, for instance. But between Tom and Juan, I felt alone. In fact, I liked it better that way. With Ramon I might have grown soft. But I felt terribly hard at that moment, and I wanted to stay hard.

Tom kept on muttering, in a kind of absent-minded way. He was certainly talking to keep from thinking. Naturally, I agreed with him, and I could have said everything he was saying. It's not *natural* to die. And since I was going to die, nothing seemed natural any more: neither the coal pile, nor the bench, nor Pedro's dirty old face. Only it was disagreeable for me to think the same things Tom thought. And I knew perfectly well that all night long, within five minutes of each other, we would keep on thinking things at the same time, sweating or shivering at the same time. I looked at him sideways and, for the first time, he seemed strange to me. He had death written on his face. My pride was wounded. For twenty-four hours I had lived side by side with Tom, I had listened to him, I had talked to him, and I knew we had nothing in common. And now we were as alike as twin brothers, simply because we were going to die together. Tom took my hand without looking at me.

'Pablo, I wonder . . . I wonder if it's true that we just cease to exist.'

I drew my hand away.

'Look between your feet, you dirty dog.'

There was a puddle between his feet and water was dripping from his trousers.

'What's the matter?' he said, frightened.

'You're wetting your pants,' I said to him.

'It's not true,' he said furiously. 'I can't be . . . I don't feel anything.'

The Belgian had come closer to him. With an air of false concern, he asked, 'Aren't you feeling well?'

Tom didn't answer. The Belgian looked at the puddle without comment.

'I don't know what that is,' Tom said savagely, 'but I'm not afraid. I swear to you, I'm not afraid.'

The Belgian made no answer. Tom rose and went to the corner. He came back, buttoning his fly, and sat down, without a word. The Belgian was taking notes.

We were watching the doctor. Juan was watching him too. All three of us were watching him because he was alive. He had the gestures of a living person, the interests of a living person; he was shivering in this cellar the way living people shiver; he had an obedient, well-fed body. We, on the other hand, didn't feel our bodies any more – not the same way, in any case. I felt like touching my trousers, but I didn't dare to. I looked at the Belgian, well-planted on his two legs, master of his muscles – and able to plan for tomorrow. We were like three shadows deprived of blood; we were watching him and sucking his life like vampires.

Finally he came over to Juan. Was he going to lay his hand on the nape of Juan's neck for some professional reason, or had he obeyed a charitable impulse? If he had acted out of charity, it was the one and only time during the whole night. He fondled Juan's head and the nape of his neck. The kid let him do it, without taking his eyes off him. Then, suddenly, he took hold of the doctor's hand and looked at it in a funny way. He held the Belgian's hand between his own two hands and there was nothing pleasing about them, those two grey paws squeezing that fat red hand. I sensed what was going to happen and Tom must have sensed it, too. But all the Belgian saw was emotion, and he smiled paternally. After a moment, the kid lifted the big red paw to his mouth and started to bite it. The Belgian drew back quickly and stumbled towards the wall. For a second, he looked at us with horror. He must have suddenly understood that we were not men like himself. I began to laugh, and one of the guards started up. The other had fallen asleep with his eyes wide open, showing only the whites.

I felt tired and over-excited at the same time. I didn't want to think any more about what was going to happen at dawn – about death. It didn't make sense, and I never got beyond just words, or emptiness. But whenever I tried to think about something else I saw the barrels of rifles aimed at me. I must have lived through my execution twenty times in succession; one time I thought it was the real thing; I must have dozed off for a moment. They were dragging me towards the wall and I was resisting; I was imploring their pardon. I woke with a start and looked at the Belgian. I was afraid I had cried out in my sleep. But he was smoothing his moustache; he hadn't noticed anything. If I had wanted to, I believe I could have slept for a while. I had been awake for the last forty-eight hours, and I was worn out. But I didn't want to lose two hours of life. They would have had to come and wake me at dawn. I would have followed them, drunk with sleep, and I would have gone off without so much as 'Gosh!' I didn't want it that way, I didn't want to die like an animal. I wanted to understand. Besides, I was afraid of having nightmares. I got up and began to walk up and down and, so as to think about something else, I began to think about my past life. Memories crowded in on me, helter-skelter. Some were good and some were bad – at least that was how I had thought of them *before*. There were faces and happenings. I saw the face of a little *novillero* who had got himself gored during the *Feria*, in Valencia. I saw the face of one of my uncles, of Ramon Gris. I remembered all kinds of things that had happened: how I had been on strike for three months in 1926, and had almost died of hunger. I recalled a night I had spent on a bench in Granada; I hadn't eaten for three days, I was nearly wild, I didn't want to throw in the sponge. I had to smile. With what eagerness I had run after happiness, and women, and liberty! And to what end? I had wanted to liberate Spain, I admired Py Margall, I had belonged to the anarchist movement, I had spoken at public meetings. I took everything as seriously as if I had been immortal.

At that time I had the impression that I had my whole life before me, and I thought to myself, 'It's all a god-damned lie.' Now it wasn't worth anything because it was finished. I wondered how I had ever been able to go out and have a good time with girls. I wouldn't have lifted my little finger if I had ever imagined that I would die like this. I saw my life before me, finished, closed, like a bag, and yet what was inside was not finished. For a moment I tried to appraise it. I would have liked to say to myself, 'It's been a good life.' But it couldn't be appraised, it was only an outline. I had spent my time writing cheques on eternity, and had understood nothing. Now, I didn't miss anything. There were a lot of things I might have missed: the taste of Manzanilla, for instance, or the swims I used to take in summer in a little creek near Cadiz. But death had taken the charm out of everything.

Suddenly the Belgian had a wonderful idea.

'My friends,' he said to us, 'if you want me to – and providing the military authorities give their consent – I could undertake to deliver a word or some token from you to your loved ones . . .'

Tom growled, 'I haven't got anybody.'

I didn't answer. Tom waited for a moment, then he looked at me with curiosity. 'Aren't you going to send any message to Concha?'

'No.'

I hated that sort of sentimental conspiracy. Of course, it was my fault, since I had mentioned Concha the night before, and I should have kept my mouth shut. I had been with her for a year. Even as late as last night, I would have cut my arm off with a hatchet just to see her again for five minutes. That was why I had mentioned her. I couldn't help it. Now I didn't care any more about seeing her. I hadn't anything more to say to her. I didn't even want to hold her in my arms. I loathed my body because it had turned grey and was sweating – and I wasn't even sure that I didn't loathe hers too. Concha would cry when she heard about my death; for months she would have no more interest in life. But still it was I who was going to die. I thought of her beautiful, loving eyes. When she looked at me something went from her to me. But I thought to myself that it was all over; if she looked at me *now* her gaze would not leave her eyes, it would not reach out to me. I was alone.

Tom too was alone, but not the same way. He was seated astride his chair and had begun to look at the bench with a sort of smile, with surprise, even. He reached out his hand and touched the wood cautiously, as though he were afraid of breaking something, then he drew his hand back hurriedly, and shivered. I wouldn't have amused myself touching that bench, if I had been Tom, that was just some more Irish play-acting. But somehow it seemed to me too that the different objects had something funny about them. They seemed to have grown paler, less massive than before. I had only to look at the bench, the lamp or the pile of coal dust to feel I was going to die. Naturally, I couldn't think clearly about my death, but I saw it everywhere, even on the different objects, the way they had withdrawn and kept their distance, tactfully, like people talking at the bedside of a dying person. It was *his own death* Tom had just touched on the bench.

In the state I was in, if they had come and told me I could go home quietly, that my life would be saved, it would have left me cold. A few hours, or a few years of waiting are all the same, when you've lost the illusion of being eternal. Nothing mattered to me any more. In a way, I was calm. But it was a horrible kind of calm – because of my body. My body – I saw with its eyes and I heard with its ears, but it was no longer I. It sweated and trembled independently, and I didn't recognise it any longer. I was obliged to touch it and look at it to know what was happening to it, just as if it had been someone else's body. At times I still felt it, I felt a slipping, a sort of headlong plunging, as in a falling aeroplane, or else I heard my heart beating. But this didn't give me confidence. In fact, everything that came from my body had something damned dubious about it. Most of the time it was silent, it stayed put and I didn't feel anything other than a sort of heaviness, a loathsome presence against me. I had the impression of being bound to an enormous vermin.

The Belgian took out his watch and looked at it.

'It's half past three,' he said.

The son of a bitch! He must have done it on purpose. Tom jumped up. We hadn't yet realised the time was passing. The night surrounded us like a formless, dark mass; I didn't even remember it had started.

Juan started to shout. Wringing his hands, he implored, 'I don't want to die! I don't want to die!'

He ran the whole length of the cellar with his arms in the air, then he dropped down on to one of the mattresses, sobbing. Tom looked at him with dismal eyes and didn't even try to console him any more. The fact was, it was no use; the kid made more noise than we did, but he was less affected, really. He was like a sick person who defends himself against his malady with a high fever. When there's not even any fever left, it's much more serious.

He was crying. I could tell he felt sorry for himself; he was thinking about death. For one second, one single second, I too felt like crying,

crying out of pity for myself. But just the contrary happened. I took one look at the kid, saw his thin, sobbing shoulders, and I felt I was inhuman. I couldn't feel pity either for these others or for myself. I said to myself, 'I want to die decently.'

Tom had got up and was standing just under the round opening looking out for the first signs of daylight. I was determined, I wanted to die decently, and I only thought about that. But underneath, ever since the doctor had told us the time, I felt time slipping, flowing by, one drop at a time.

It was still dark when I heard Tom's voice.

'Do you hear them?'

'Yes.'

People were walking in the courtyard.

'What the hell are they doing? After all, they can't shoot in the dark.'

After a moment, we didn't hear anything more. I said to Tom, 'There's the daylight.'

Pedro got up yawning, and came and blew out the lamp. He turned to the man beside him. 'It's hellish cold.'

The cellar had grown grey. We could hear shots at a distance.

'It's about to start,' I said to Tom. 'That must be in the back courtyard.'

Tom asked the doctor to give him a cigarette. I didn't want any; I didn't want either cigarettes or alcohol. From that moment on, the shooting didn't stop.

'Can you take it in?' Tom said.

He started to add something, then he stopped and began to watch the door. The door opened and a lieutenant came in with four soldiers. Tom dropped his cigarette.

'Steinbock?'

Tom didn't answer. Pedro pointed him out.

'Juan Mirbal?'

'He's the one on the mattress.'

'Stand up,' said the Lieutenant.

Juan didn't move. Two soldiers took hold of him by the armpits and stood him up on his feet. But as soon as they let go of him he fell down.

The soldiers hesitated a moment.

'He's not the first one to get sick,' said the Lieutenant. 'You'll have to carry him, the two of you. We'll arrange things when we get there.' He turned to Tom. 'All right, come along.'

Tom left between two soldiers. Two other soldiers followed, carrying the kid by his arms and legs. He was not unconscious; his eyes were wide open and tears were rolling down his cheeks. When I started to go out, the Lieutenant stopped me.

'Are you Ibbieta?'

'Yes.'

'You wait here. They'll come and get you later on.'

They left. The Belgian and the two gaolers left too, and I was alone. I didn't understand what had happened to me, but I would have liked it better if they had ended it all right away. I heard the volleys at almost regular intervals; at each one, I shuddered. I felt like howling and tearing my hair. But instead, I gritted my teeth and pushed my hands deep into my pockets, because I wanted to stay decent.

An hour later, they came to fetch me and took me up to the first floor in a little room which smelt of cigar-smoke and was so hot it seemed to me suffocating. Here there were two officers sitting in comfortable chairs, smoking, with papers spread out on their knees.

'Your name is Ibbieta?'

'Yes.'

'Where is Ramon Gris?'

'I don't know.'

The man who questioned me was small and stocky. He had hard eyes behind his glasses.

'Come nearer,' he said to me.

I went nearer. He rose and took me by the arms, looking at me in a way calculated to make me go through the floor. At the same time he pinched my arms with all his might. He didn't mean to hurt me; it was quite a game; he wanted to dominate me. He also seemed to think it was necessary to blow his fetid breath right into my face. We stood like that for a moment, only I felt more like laughing than anything else. It takes a lot more than that to intimidate a man who's about to die: it didn't work. He pushed me away violently and sat down again.

'It's your life or his,' he said. 'You'll be allowed to go free if you tell us where he is.'

After all, these two bedizened fellows with their riding-crops and boots were just men who were going to die one day. A little later than I, perhaps, but not a great deal. And there they were, looking for names among their papers, running after other men in order to put them in prison or do away with them entirely. They had their opinions on the

future of Spain and on other subjects. Their petty activities seemed to
me to be offensive and ludicrous. I could no longer put myself in their
place. I had the impression they were crazy.

The little fat fellow kept looking at me, tapping his boots with his
riding-crop. All his gestures were calculated to make him appear like a
spirited, ferocious animal.

'Well? Do you understand?'

'I don't know where Gris is,' I said. 'I thought he was in Madrid.'

The other officer lifted his pale hand indolently. This indolence was
also calculated. I saw through all their little tricks, and I was dumbfounded that men should still exist who took pleasure in that kind of
thing.

'You have fifteen minutes to think it over,' he said slowly. 'Take him
to the linen-room, and bring him back here in fifteen minutes. If he con-
tinues to refuse, he'll be executed at once.'

They knew what they were doing. I had spent the night waiting. After
that, they had made me wait another hour in the cellar, while they
shot Tom and Juan, and now they locked me in the linen-room. They
must have arranged the whole thing the night before. They figured
that sooner or later people's nerves wear out and they hoped to get me
that way.

They made a big mistake. In the linen-room I sat down on a ladder
because I felt very weak, and I began to think things over. Not their
proposition, however. Naturally I knew where Gris was. He was hiding
in his cousins' house, about two miles outside of the city. I knew, too,
that I would not reveal his hiding-place, unless they tortured me (but
they didn't seem to be considering that). All that was definitely settled
and didn't interest me in the least. Only I would have liked to understand the reasons for my own conduct. I would rather die than betray
Gris. Why? I no longer liked Ramon Gris. My friendship for him had
died shortly before dawn along with my love for Concha, along with my
own desire to live. Of course I still admired him – he was hard. But it
was not for that reason that I was willing to die in his place; his life was
no more valuable than mine. No life was of any value. A man was going
to be stood up against a wall and fired at till he dropped dead. It didn't
make any difference whether it was I or Gris or somebody else. I knew
perfectly well he was more useful to the Spanish cause than I was, but I
didn't give a god-damn about Spain or anarchy, either; nothing had any
importance now. And yet, there I was. I could save my skin by betraying

Gris and I refused to do it. It seemed more ludicrous to me than anything else; it was stubbornness.

I thought to myself, 'Am I hard-headed?' And I was seized with a strange sort of cheerfulness.

They came to fetch me and took me back to the two officers. A rat darted out under our feet and that amused me. I turned to one of the Falangists and said to him, 'Did you see that rat?'

He made no reply. He was gloomy, and took himself very seriously. As for me, I felt like laughing, but I restrained myself because I was afraid that if I started, I wouldn't be able to stop. The Falangist wore moustaches. I kept after him, 'You ought to cut off those moustaches, you fool.'

I was amused by the fact that he let hair grow all over his face while he was still alive. He gave me a kind of half-hearted kick, and I shut up.

'Well,' said the fat officer, 'have you thought things over?'

I looked at them with curiosity, like insects of a very rare species.

'I know where he is,' I said. 'He's hiding in the cemetery. Either in one of the vaults, or in the gravediggers' shack.'

I said that just to make fools of them. I wanted to see them get up and fasten their belts and bustle about giving orders.

They jumped to their feet.

'Fine. Moles, go and ask Lieutenant Lopez for fifteen men. And as for you,' the little fat fellow said to me, 'if you've told the truth, I don't go back on my word. But you'll pay for this, if you're pulling our leg.'

They left noisily and I waited in peace, still guarded by the Falangists. From time to time I smiled at the thought of the face they were going to make. I felt dull and malicious. I could see them lifting up the gravestones, or opening the doors of the vaults one by one. I saw the whole situation as though I were another person: the prisoner determined to play the hero, the solemn Falangists with their moustaches and the men in uniform running around among the graves. It was irresistibly funny.

After half an hour, the little fat fellow came back alone. I thought he had come to give the order to execute me. The others must have stayed in the cemetery.

The officer looked at me. He didn't look at all foolish.

'Take him out in the big courtyard with the others,' he said. 'When military operations are over, a regular tribunal will decide his case.'

I thought I must have misunderstood.

'So they're not – they're not going to shoot me?' I asked.

'Not now, in any case. Afterwards, that doesn't concern me.'

I still didn't understand.

'But why?' I said to him.

He shrugged his shoulders without replying, and the soldiers led me away. In the big courtyard there were a hundred or so prisoners, women, children and a few old men. I started to walk around the grass plot in the middle. I felt absolutely idiotic. At noon we were fed in the dining-hall. Two or three fellows spoke to me. I must have known them, but I didn't answer. I didn't even know where I was.

Towards evening, about ten new prisoners were pushed into the courtyard. I recognised Garcia, the baker.

He said to me, 'Lucky dog! I didn't expect to find you alive.'

'They condemned me to death,' I said, 'and then they changed their minds. I don't know why.'

'I was arrested at two o'clock,' Garcia said.

'What for?'

Garcia took no part in politics.

'I don't know,' he said. 'They arrest everybody who doesn't think the way they do.'

He lowered his voice.

'They got Gris.'

I began to tremble.

'When?'

'This morning. He acted like a damned fool. He left his cousins' house Tuesday because of a disagreement. There were any number of fellows who would have hidden him, but he didn't want to be indebted to anybody any more. He said, "I would have hidden at Ibbieta's, but since they've got him, I'll go and hide in the cemetery."'

'In the cemetery?'

'Yes. It was the god-damnedest thing. Naturally they passed by there this morning; that had to happen. They found him in the gravediggers' shack. They opened fire at him and they finished him off.'

'In the cemetery!'

Everything went around in circles, and when I came to I was sitting on the ground. I laughed so hard the tears came to my eyes.

Albert Camus

Albert Camus (1913–60), philosopher and writer, was born into the working-class European milieu of Algeria. Though he was to escape to a life of success and notoriety in Paris, he never forgot his colonial past and it permeates his work. *L'Étranger* (1942), in which the narrator Meursault recalls murdering an Arab on a beach and his subsequent condemnation in the courtroom, strongly evokes the atmosphere of North Africa. Camus moved away from an attitude of stoical individual resilience, typified by the Sisyphus-figure, to a concern for collective attitudes which is explored in *La Peste* (1947) and later *L'Homme révolté* (1951). The former is a remarkable fictional account of life in a plague-infested city, but it can also be read as a description of life under oppression or, more profoundly, as an allegory of the human condition. Camus's later career was overshadowed by his ambivalent feelings during the Algerian War and his ideological differences with Jean-Paul Sartre, which emerged when Sartre gave his *L'Homme révolté* an unfavourable review. Camus was awarded the Nobel Prize for Literature following the publication of his collection of short stories *L'Exil et le royaume* in 1957. He died in a car crash in 1962. The manuscript of *Le Premier Homme*, a strongly autobiographical novel set in Algiers, which was found in the car at the time, was finally published in 1994.

The Guest

THE SCHOOLMASTER WAS WATCHING THE TWO MEN CLIMB towards him. One was on horseback, the other on foot. They had not yet tackled the abrupt rise leading to the schoolhouse built on the hillside. They were toiling onwards, making slow progress in the snow, among the stones, on the vast expanse of the high, deserted plateau. From time to time the horse stumbled. Without hearing anything yet, he could see the breath issuing from the horse's nostrils. One of the men, at least, knew the region. They were following the trail although it had disappeared days ago under a layer of dirty white snow. The schoolmaster calculated that it would take them half an hour to get on to the hill. It was cold; he went back into the school to get a sweater.

He crossed the empty, frigid classroom. On the blackboard the four rivers of France, drawn with four different-coloured chalks, had been flowing towards their estuaries for the past three days. Snow had suddenly fallen in mid-October after eight months of drought without the transition of rain, and the twenty pupils, more or less, who lived in the villages scattered over the plateau had stopped coming. With fair weather they would return. Daru now heated only the single room that was his lodging, adjoining the classroom and giving also on to the plateau to the east. Like the class windows, his window looked to the south too. On that side the school was a few kilometres from the point where the plateau began to slope towards the south. In clear weather could be seen the purple mass of the mountain range where the gap opened on to the desert.

Somewhat warmed, Daru returned to the window from which he had first seen the two men. They were no longer visible. Hence they must have tackled the rise. The sky was not so dark, for the snow had stopped falling during the night. The morning had opened with a dirty light which had scarcely become brighter as the ceiling of clouds lifted. At two in the afternoon it seemed as if the day were merely beginning.

But still this was better than those three days when the thick snow was falling amidst unbroken darkness with little gusts of wind that rattled the double door of the classroom. Then Daru had spent long hours in his room, leaving it only to go to the shed and feed the chickens or get some coal. Fortunately the delivery truck from Tadjid, the nearest village to the north, had brought his supplies two days before the blizzard. It would return in forty-eight hours.

Besides, he had enough to resist a siege, for the little room was cluttered with bags of wheat that the administration left as a stock to distribute to those of his pupils whose families had suffered from the drought. Actually they had all been victims because they were all poor. Every day Daru would distribute a ration to the children. They had missed it, he knew, during these bad days. Possibly one of the fathers or big brothers would come this afternoon and he could supply them with grain. It was just a matter of carrying them over to the next harvest. Now shiploads of wheat were arriving from France and the worst was over. But it would be hard to forget that poverty, that army of ragged ghosts wandering in the sunlight, the plateaux burnt to a cinder month after month, the earth shrivelled up little by little, literally scorched, every stone bursting into dust under one's foot. The sheep had died then by thousands and even a few men, here and there, sometimes without anyone's knowing.

In contrast with such poverty, he who lived almost like a monk in his remote schoolhouse, none the less satisfied with the little he had and with the rough life, had felt like a lord with his whitewashed walls, his narrow couch, his unpainted shelves, his well, and his weekly provision of water and food. And suddenly this snow, without warning, without the foretaste of rain. This is the way the region was, cruel to live in, even without men – who didn't help matters either. But Daru had been born here. Everywhere else, he felt exiled.

He stepped out on to the terrace in front of the schoolhouse. The two men were now halfway up the slope. He recognised the horseman as Balducci, the old gendarme he had known for a long time. Balducci was holding on the end of a rope an Arab who was walking behind him with hands bound and head lowered. The gendarme waved a greeting to which Daru did not reply, lost as he was in contemplation of the Arab dressed in a faded blue jellaba, his feet in sandals but covered with socks of heavy raw wool, his head surmounted by a narrow, short *chèche*. They were approaching. Balducci was holding back his horse in order not to hurt the Arab, and the group was advancing slowly.

Within earshot, Balducci shouted: 'One hour to do the three kilometres from El Ameur!' Daru did not answer. Short and square in his thick sweater, he watched them climb. Not once had the Arab raised his head. 'Hallo,' said Daru when they got up on to the terrace. 'Come in and warm up.' Balducci painfully got down from his horse without letting go the rope. From under his bristling moustache he smiled at the schoolmaster. His little dark eyes, deep-set under a tanned forehead, and his mouth surrounded with wrinkles made him look attentive and studious. Daru took the bridle, led the horse to the shed, and came back to the two men, who were now waiting for him in the school. He led them into his room. 'I am going to heat up the classroom,' he said. 'We'll be more comfortable there.' When he entered the room again, Balducci was on the couch. He had undone the rope tying him to the Arab, who had squatted near the stove. His hands still bound, the *chèche* pushed back on his head, he was looking towards the window. At first Daru noticed only his huge lips, fat, smooth, almost Negroid; yet his nose was straight, his eyes were dark and full of fever. The *chèche* revealed an obstinate forehead and, under the weathered skin now rather discoloured by the cold, the whole face had a restless and rebellious look that struck Daru when the Arab, turning his face towards him, looked him straight in the eyes. 'Go into the other room,' said the schoolmaster, 'and I'll make you some mint tea.' 'Thanks,' Balducci said. 'What a chore! How I long for retirement.' And addressing his prisoner in Arabic: 'Come on, you.' The Arab got up and, slowly, holding his bound wrists in front of him, went into the classroom.

With the tea, Daru brought a chair. But Balducci was already enthroned on the nearest pupil's desk and the Arab had squatted against the teacher's platform facing the stove, which stood between the desk and the window. When he held out the glass of tea to the prisoner, Daru hesitated at the sight of his bound hands. 'He might perhaps be untied.' 'Sure,' said Balducci. 'That was for the trip.' He started to get to his feet. But Daru, setting the glass on the floor, had knelt beside the Arab. Without saying anything, the Arab watched him with his feverish eyes. Once his hands were free, he rubbed his swollen wrists against each other, took the glass of tea, and sucked up the burning liquid in swift little sips.

'Good,' said Daru. 'And where are you headed?'

Balducci withdrew his moustache from the tea. 'Here, son.'

'Odd pupils! And you're spending the night?'

'No. I'm going back to El Ameur. And you will deliver this fellow to Tinguit. He is expected at police headquarters.'

Balducci was looking at Daru with a friendly little smile.

'What's this story?' asked the schoolmaster. 'Are you pulling my leg?'

'No, son. Those are the orders.'

'The orders? I'm not . . .' Daru hesitated, not wanting to hurt the old Corsican. 'I mean, that's not my job.'

'What! What's the meaning of that? In wartime people do all kinds of jobs.'

'Then I'll wait for the declaration of war!'

Balducci nodded.

'OK. But the orders exist and they concern you too. Things are brewing, it appears. There is talk of a forthcoming revolt. We are mobilised, in a way.'

Daru still had his obstinate look.

'Listen, son,' Balducci said. 'I like you and you must understand. There's only a dozen of us at El Ameur to patrol throughout the whole territory of a small department and I must get back in a hurry. I was told to hand this guy over to you and return without delay. He couldn't be kept there. His village was beginning to stir; they wanted to take him back. You must take him to Tinguit tomorrow before the day is over. Twenty kilometres shouldn't faze a husky fellow like you. After that, all will be over. You'll come back to your pupils and your comfortable life.'

Behind the wall the horse could be heard snorting and pawing the earth. Daru was looking out of the window. Decidedly, the weather was clearing and the light was increasing over the snowy plateau. When all the snow was melted, the sun would take over again and once more would burn the fields of stone. For days, still, the unchanging sky would shed its dry light on the solitary expanse where nothing had any connection with man.

'After all,' he said, turning around towards Balducci, 'what did he do?' And, before the gendarme had opened his mouth, he asked: 'Does he speak French?'

'No, not a word. We had been looking for him for a month, but they were hiding him. He killed his cousin.'

'Is he against us?'

'I don't think so. But you can never be sure.'

'Why did he kill?'

'A family squabble, I think. One owed the other grain, it seems. It's not at all clear. In short, he killed his cousin with a billhook. You know, like a sheep, *kreezk*!'

Balducci made the gesture of drawing a blade across his throat and the Arab, his attention attracted, watched him with a sort of anxiety. Daru felt a sudden wrath against the man, against all men with their rotten spite, their tireless hates, their blood-lust.

But the kettle was singing on the stove. He served Balducci more tea, hesitated, then served the Arab again, who, a second time, drank avidly. His raised arms made the jellaba fall open and the schoolmaster saw his thin, muscular chest.

'Thanks, kid,' Balducci said. 'And now, I'm off.'

He got up and went towards the Arab, taking a small rope from his pocket.

'What are you doing?' Daru asked drily.

Balducci, disconcerted, showed him the rope.

'Don't bother.'

The old gendarme hesitated. 'It's up to you. Of course, you are armed?'

'I have my shotgun.'

'Where?'

'In the trunk.'

'You ought to have it near your bed.'

'Why? I have nothing to fear.'

'You're crazy, son. If there's an uprising, no one is safe, we're all in the same boat.'

'I'll defend myself. I'll have time to see them coming.'

Balducci began to laugh, then suddenly the moustache covered the white teeth.

'You'll have time? OK. That's just what I was saying. You have always been a little cracked. That's why I like you; my son was like that.'

At the same time he took out his revolver and put it on the desk.

'Keep it; I don't need two weapons from here to El Ameur.'

The revolver shone against the black paint of the table. When the gendarme turned towards him, the schoolmaster caught the smell of leather and horseflesh.

'Listen, Balducci,' Daru said suddenly, 'every bit of this disgusts me, and first of all your fellow here. But I won't hand him over. Fight, yes, if I have to. But not that.'

The old gendarme stood in front of him and looked at him severely.

'You're being a fool,' he said slowly. 'I don't like it either. You don't get used to putting a rope on a man even after years of it, and you're even ashamed – yes, ashamed. But you can't let them have their way.'

'I won't hand him over,' Daru said again.

'It's an order, son, and I repeat it.'

'That's right. Repeat to them what I've said to you: I won't hand him over.'

Balducci made a visible effort to reflect. He looked at the Arab and at Daru. At last he decided.

'No, I won't tell them anything. If you want to drop us, go ahead; I'll not denounce you. I have an order to deliver the prisoner and I'm doing so. And now you'll just sign this paper for me.'

'There's no need. I'll not deny that you left him with me.'

'Don't be mean with me. I know you'll tell the truth. You're from hereabouts and you are a man. But you must sign, that's the rule.'

Daru opened his drawer, took out a little square bottle of purple ink, the red wooden penholder with the 'sergeant-major' pen he used for making models of penmanship, and signed. The gendarme carefully folded the paper and put it into his wallet. Then he moved towards the door.

'I'll see you off,' Daru said.

'No,' said Balducci. 'There's no use being polite. You insulted me.'

He looked at the Arab, motionless in the same spot, sniffed peevishly, and turned away towards the door. 'Goodbye, son,' he said. The door shut behind him. Balducci appeared suddenly outside the window and then disappeared. His footsteps were muffled by the snow. The horse stirred on the other side of the wall and several chickens fluttered in fright. A moment later Balducci reappeared outside the window leading the horse by the bridle. He walked towards the little rise without turning around and disappeared from sight with the horse following him. A big stone could be heard bouncing down. Daru walked back towards the prisoner, who, without stirring, never took his eyes off him. 'Wait,' the schoolmaster said in Arabic and went towards the bedroom. As he was going through the door, he had a second thought, went to the desk, took the revolver, and stuck it in his pocket. Then, without looking back, he went into his room.

For some time he lay on his couch watching the sky gradually close over, listening to the silence. It was this silence that had seemed painful to him during the first days here, after the war. He had requested a post in the little town at the base of the foothills separating the upper plateaux from the desert. There, rocky walls, green and black to the north, pink and lavender to the south, marked the frontier of eternal summer. He had been named to a post farther north, on the plateau itself. In the beginning, the solitude and the silence had been hard for him on these wastelands peopled only by stones. Occasionally, furrows suggested cultivation, but they had been dug to uncover a certain kind of stone good for building. The only ploughing here was to harvest rocks. Elsewhere a thin layer of soil accumulated in the hollows would be scraped out to enrich paltry village gardens. This is the way it was: bare rock covered three-quarters of the region. Towns sprang up, flourished, then disappeared; men came by, loved one another or fought bitterly, then died. No one in this desert, neither he nor his guest, mattered. And yet, outside this desert neither of them, Daru knew, could have really lived.

When he got up, no noise came from the classroom. He was amazed at the unmixed joy he derived from the mere thought that the Arab might have fled and that he would be alone with no decision to make. But the prisoner was there. He had merely stretched out between the stove and the desk. With eyes open, he was staring at the ceiling. In that position, his thick lips were particularly noticeable, giving him a pouting look. 'Come,' said Daru. The Arab got up and followed him. In the bedroom, the schoolmaster pointed to a chair near the table under the window. The Arab sat down without taking his eyes off Daru.

'Are you hungry?'

'Yes,' the prisoner said.

Daru set the table for two. He took flour and oil, shaped a cake in a frying-pan, and lighted the little stove that functioned on bottled gas. While the cake was cooking, he went out to the shed to get cheese, eggs, dates, and condensed milk. When the cake was done he set it on the window-sill to cool, heated some condensed milk diluted with water, and beat up the eggs into an omelette. In one of his motions he knocked against the revolver stuck in his right pocket. He set the bowl down, went into the classroom, and put the revolver in his desk drawer. When he came back to the room, night was falling. He put on the light and served the Arab. 'Eat,' he said. The Arab took a piece of the cake, lifted it eagerly to his mouth, and stopped short.

'And you?' he asked.

'After you. I'll eat too.'

The thick lips opened slightly. The Arab hesitated, then bit into the cake determinedly.

The meal over, the Arab looked at the schoolmaster. 'Are you the judge?'

'No, I'm simply keeping you until tomorrow.'

'Why do you eat with me?'

'I'm hungry.'

The Arab fell silent. Daru got up and went out. He brought back a folding bed from the shed, set it up between the table and the stove, perpendicular to his own bed. From a large suitcase which, upright in a corner, served as a shelf for papers, he took two blankets and arranged them on the camp bed. Then he stopped, felt useless, and sat down on his bed. There was nothing more to do or to get ready. He had to look at this man. He looked at him, therefore, trying to imagine his face bursting with rage. He couldn't do so. He could see nothing but the dark yet shining eyes and the animal mouth.

'Why did you kill him?' he asked in a voice whose hostile tone surprised him.

The Arab looked away.

'He ran away. I ran after him.'

He raised his eyes to Daru again and they were full of a sort of woeful interrogation. 'Now what will they do to me?'

'Are you afraid?'

He stiffened, turning his eyes away.

'Are you sorry?'

The Arab stared at him open-mouthed. Obviously he did not understand. Daru's annoyance was growing. At the same time he felt awkward and self-conscious with his big body wedged between the two beds.

'Lie down there,' he said impatiently. 'That's your bed.'

The Arab didn't move. He called to Daru:

'Tell me!'

The schoolmaster looked at him.

'Is the gendarme coming back tomorrow?'

'I don't know.'

'Are you coming with us?'

'I don't know. Why?'

The prisoner got up and stretched out on top of the blankets, his feet towards the window. The light from the electric bulb shone straight into his eyes and he closed them at once.

'Why?' Daru repeated, standing beside the bed.

The Arab opened his eyes under the blinding light and looked at him, trying not to blink.

'Come with us,' he said.

In the middle of the night, Daru was still not asleep. He had gone to bed after undressing completely; he generally slept naked. But when he suddenly realised that he had nothing on, he hesitated. He felt vulnerable and the temptation came to him to put his clothes back on. Then he shrugged his shoulders; after all, he wasn't a child and, if need be, he could break his adversary in two. From his bed he could observe him, lying on his back, still motionless with his eyes closed under the harsh light. When Daru turned out the light, the darkness seemed to coagulate all of a sudden. Little by little, the night came back to life in the window where the starless sky was stirring gently. The schoolmaster soon made out the body lying at his feet. The Arab still did not move, but his eyes seemed open. A faint wind was prowling around the schoolhouse. Perhaps it would drive away the clouds and the sun would reappear.

During the night the wind increased. The hens fluttered a little and then were silent. The Arab turned over on his side with his back to Daru, who thought he heard him moan. Then he listened for his guest's breathing, become heavier and more regular. He listened to that breath so close to him and mused without being able to go to sleep. In this room where he had been sleeping alone for a year, this presence bothered him. But it bothered him also by imposing on him a sort of brotherhood he knew well but refused to accept in the present circumstances. Men who share the same rooms, soldiers or prisoners, develop a strange alliance as if, having cast off their armour with their clothing, they fraternised every evening, over and above their differences, in the ancient community of dream and fatigue. But Daru shook himself; he didn't like such musings, and it was essential to sleep.

A little later, however, when the Arab stirred slightly, the schoolmaster was still not asleep. When the prisoner made a second move, he stiffened, on the alert. The Arab was lifting himself slowly on his arms with almost the motion of a sleepwalker. Seated upright in bed, he waited motionless without turning his head towards Daru, as if he were listening attentively. Daru did not stir; it had just occurred to him that the revolver was still in the drawer of his desk. It was better to act at once. Yet he continued to observe the prisoner, who, with the same slithery motion, put his feet on the ground, waited again, then began to stand up slowly. Daru was about to call out to him when the Arab began to walk, in a quite natural but extraordinarily silent way. He was heading towards the door at the end of the room that opened into the shed. He lifted the latch with precaution and went out, pushing the door behind him but without shutting it. Daru had not stirred. 'He is running away,' he merely thought. 'Good riddance!' Yet he listened attentively. The hens were not fluttering; the guest must be on the plateau. A faint sound of water reached him, and he didn't know what it was until the Arab again stood framed in the doorway, closed the door carefully, and came back to bed without a sound. Then Daru turned his back on him and fell asleep. Still later he seemed, from the depths of his sleep, to hear furtive steps around the schoolhouse. 'I'm dreaming! I'm dreaming!' he repeated to himself. And he went on sleeping.

When he awoke, the sky was clear; the loose window let in a cold, pure air. The Arab was asleep, hunched up under the blankets now, his mouth open, utterly relaxed. But when Daru shook him, he started dreadfully, staring at Daru with wild eyes as if he had never seen him and such a frightened expression that the schoolmaster stepped back. 'Don't be afraid. It's me. You must eat.' The Arab nodded his head and said yes. Calm had returned to his face, but his expression was vacant and listless.

The coffee was ready. They drank it seated together on the folding bed as they munched their pieces of the cake. Then Daru led the Arab under the shed and showed him the tap where he washed. He went back into the room, folded the blankets and the bed, made his own bed and put the room in order. Then he went through the classroom and out on to the terrace. The sun was already rising in the blue sky; a soft, bright light was bathing the deserted plateau. On the ridge the snow was melting in spots. The stones were about to reappear. Crouched on the edge of the plateau, the schoolmaster looked at the deserted expanse. He thought of Balducci. He had hurt him, for he had sent him off in a way as if he didn't want to be associated with him. He could still hear the gendarme's farewell and, without knowing why, he felt strangely empty and vulnerable. At that moment, from the other side of the schoolhouse, the prisoner coughed. Daru listened to him almost despite himself and then, furious, threw a pebble that whistled through the air before sinking into the snow. That man's stupid crime revolted him, but to hand him over was contrary to honour. Merely thinking of it made him smart with humiliation. And he cursed at one and the same time his own people who had sent him this Arab and the Arab too who had dared to kill and not managed to get away. Daru got up, walked in a circle on the terrace, waited motionless, and then went back into the schoolhouse.

The Arab, leaning over the cement floor of the shed, was washing his teeth with two fingers. Daru looked at him and said: 'Come.' He went back into the room ahead of the prisoner. He slipped a hunting-jacket on over his sweater and put on walking-shoes. Standing, he waited until the Arab had put on his *chèche* and sandals. They went into the classroom and the schoolmaster pointed to the exit, saying: 'Go ahead.' The fellow didn't budge. 'I'm coming,' said Daru. The Arab went out. Daru went back into the room and made a package of pieces of rusk, dates, and sugar. In the classroom, before going out, he hesitated a second in front of his desk, then crossed the threshold and locked the door. 'That's the way,' he said. He started towards the east, followed by the prisoner. But, a short distance from the schoolhouse, he thought he heard a slight sound behind them. He retraced his steps and examined the surroundings of the house; there was no one there. The Arab watched him without seeming to understand. 'Come on,' said Daru.

They walked for an hour and rested beside a sharp peak of limestone. The snow was melting faster and faster and the sun was drinking up the puddles at once, rapidly cleaning the plateau, which gradually dried and vibrated like the air itself. When they resumed walking, the ground rang under their feet. From time to time a bird rent the space in front of them with a joyful cry. Daru breathed in deeply the fresh morning light. He felt a sort of rapture before the vast familiar expanse, now almost entirely yellow under its dome of blue sky. They walked an hour more, descending towards the south. They reached a level height made up of crumbly rocks. From there on, the plateau sloped down, eastwards, towards a low plain where there were a few spindly trees and, to the south, towards outcroppings of rock that gave the landscape a chaotic look.

Daru surveyed the two directions. There was nothing but the sky on the horizon. Not a man could be seen. He turned towards the Arab, who was looking at him blankly. Daru held out the package to him. 'Take it,' he said. 'There are dates, bread, and sugar. You can hold out for two days. Here are a thousand francs too.' The Arab took the package and the money but kept his full hands at chest level as if he didn't know what to do with what was being given him. 'Now look,' the schoolmaster said as he pointed in the direction of the east, 'there's the way to Tinguit. You have a two-hour walk. At Tinguit you'll find the administration and the police. They are expecting you.' The Arab looked towards the east, still holding the package and the money against his chest. Daru took his elbow and turned him rather roughly towards the south. At the foot of the height on which they stood could be seen a faint path. 'That's the trail across the plateau. In a day's walk from here you'll find pasture-lands and the first nomads. They'll take you in and shelter you accord-ing to their law.' The Arab had now turned towards Daru and a sort of panic was visible in his expression. 'Listen,' he said. Daru shook his head: 'No, be quiet. Now I'm leaving you.' He turned his back on him, took two long steps in the direction of the school, looked hesitantly at the motionless Arab, and started off again. For a few minutes he heard nothing but his own step resounding on the cold ground and did not turn his head. A moment later, however, he turned around. The Arab was still there on the edge of the hill, his arms hanging now, and he was looking at the schoolmaster. Daru felt something rise in his throat. But he swore with impatience, waved vaguely, and started off again. He had already gone some distance when he again stopped and looked. There was no longer anyone on the hill.

Daru hesitated. The sun was now rather high in the sky and was beginning to beat down on his head. The schoolmaster retraced his steps, at first somewhat uncertainly, then with decision. When he reached the little hill, he was bathed in sweat. He climbed it as fast as he could and stopped, out of breath, at the top. The rock-fields to the south stood out sharply against the blue sky, but on the plain to the east a steamy heat was already rising. And in that slight haze, Daru, with heavy heart, made out the Arab walking slowly on the road to prison.

A little later, standing before the window of the classroom, the schoolmaster was watching the clear light bathing the whole surface of the plateau, but he hardly saw it. Behind him on the blackboard, among the winding French rivers, sprawled the clumsily chalked-up words he had just read: 'You handed over our brother. You will pay for this.' Daru looked at the sky, the plateau, and, beyond, the invisible lands stretching all the way to the sea. In this vast landscape he had loved so much, he was alone.

Acknowledgements

Every effort has been made to contact copyright holders; in the event of an inadvertent omission or error, the editorial department should be notified at The Folio Society, 44 Eagle Street, London WC1R 4FS.

The Folio Society wishes to thank the following writers, publishers and literary representatives for their permission to use copyright material:

'Cosi Sancta: A Little Ill for a Great Good' by Voltaire, translated by Richard Aldington © The Estate of Richard Aldington.

'The Self-Made Cuckold, or the Unexpected Reconciliation' taken from *The Misfortunes of Virtue and Other Early Tales* by the Marquis de Sade, edited and translated by David Coward. Reprinted by permission of Oxford University Press.

'Dead Man's Combe' by Charles Nodier taken from *French Short Stories*, selected and translated by K. Rebillon Lambley. Reprinted by permission of Oxford University Press.

'The Adventures of Seven Stars on Earth' by Alexandre Dumas taken from *The Phantom White Hare and Other Tales*, translated by Douglas Munro. Reprinted by permission of Oxford University Press.

'Medical Advice' by Charles de Bernard taken from *French Short Stories*, selected and translated by K. Rebillon Lambley. Reprinted by permission of Oxford University Press.

'The Greatest Love of Don Juan' by Jules Barbey D'Aurevilly, translated by E. Boyd, taken from *French Short Stories of the 19th and 20th Centuries* edited by Ernest Rhys (Everyman, 1933). Reprinted by permission of David Campbell Publishers Ltd.

'A Simple Heart' taken from *Three Tales* by Gustave Flaubert, translated by Robert Baldick (Penguin Classics, 1961) copyright © Robert Baldick, 1961. Reprinted by permission of Penguin Books Ltd.

'The Desire to be a Man' from *Cruel Tales* by Villiers de l'Isle-Adam, translated by Robert Baldick. Reprinted by permission of Oxford University Press.

'The Stars' from *Letters from my Windmill* by Alphonse Daudet, translated by Frederick Davies (Penguin Classics, 1978) copyright © Frederick Davies, 1978. Reprinted by permission of Penguin Books Ltd.

'The Work of a Life' by Edmond Haraucourt taken from *French Short Stories*, selected and translated by K. Rebillon Lambley. Reprinted by permission of Oxford University Press.

'The Veiled Man' by Marcel Schwob taken from *The King in the Golden Mask*, translated by Ian White. Reprinted by permission of Carcanet Press Ltd.

'A Young Girl's Confession' by Marcel Proust taken from *Pleasures and Regrets*, translated by Louise Varese (Crown Publishers, 1948). Reprinted by permission of Peter Owen Ltd, London.

'Green Sealing-Wax' by Colette taken from *The Rainy Moon and Other Stories*, translated by Antonia White (Martin Secker & Warburg, 1958). Copyright Antonia White. Reprinted by permission of Curtis Brown Group Ltd, London.

'The Wall' by Jean-Paul Sartre, originally published under the title 'Le Mur', © Editions Gallimard, Paris, 1939. Translation by Maria Jolas taken from *The Bedside Book of Famous French Short Stories* edited by Belle Brecker and Robert N. Linscott, copyright © 1945 and renewed 1973 by Random House, Inc. Reprinted by permission of Random House, Inc. and New Directions Publishing Corporation.

'The Guest' by Albert Camus, translated by Justin O'Brien, taken from *Exile and the Kingdom*. Copyright © 1957, 1958 by Alfred A. Knopf, Inc. Reprinted by permission of Alfred A. Knopf, Inc. and Hamish Hamilton Ltd.